LINE ᴏꜰ DESCENT

M. K. Jones

A CASE FOR
MAZE INVESTIGATIONS –
THE GENEALOGY DETECTIVES

WORDCATCHER publishing

LINE OF DESCENT
Maze Investigations – The Genealogy Detectives

British Library Cataloguing in Publication Data.
A catalogue record for this book is available from the British
Library.

Published by Wordcatcher Publishing, Cardiff, UK.
www.wordcatcher.com
Facebook.com/WordcatcherPublishing

Paperback ISBN: 9781912056590
Ebook ISBN: 9781912056897

First Edition: October 2017
Category: Supernatural Crime & Mystery

Prologue

The Manor House,
Llanyrafon, South Wales
December, 1735

Outside, the night was bitterly cold. The boy knew this because he could see frost glinting on the grass and on the breath of the short man below. But he couldn't feel it, couldn't feel any sensation. He sighed. He waved goodbye. He would wave hello again when the man came back later. All unseen.

Turning away from the window, his attention was attracted to the click of the door latch quietly opening, and quickly closing. Someone had followed the man out. The boy tensed, went back to the window, and peered down. He relaxed when he saw the girl. Nothing to worry about there. He watched her follow the man along the path towards the riverbank. He could see such a long way now.

Another click of the door. More footsteps. Another man. The tall one. The one who watched and waited. Talked to himself when he thought nobody was listening. This was worrying. Why was *he* following?

The boy clenched the edge of the bedcover nearest to the window, unable to move. This man was trouble. Why was he out early? Why was he walking so carefully, making sure his footsteps made no sound?

"Look back," he called urgently to the girl. "Please, look back." But she kept walking, catching up to the short man in front of her. Helpless, the boy watched her call out to the short man at the river's edge. The man stopped, looked around, saw the girl, and shouted at her to go back.

"I told thee, girl, we shall speak later this day. Do not trouble me now; I have business to attend to. You know my mind."

"Yes, father," she replied, hands clasped, eyes

appealing. "And I am glad. But I am still fearful. He was angered by your words."

"I shall speak with him again later. He will do as I bid. The manor will be yours and your husband's. That is my decision, it will all be written, and he shall abide by it."

The girl blushed. The short man held out his hand and she took it. Neither of them could see that the tall man had closed in on them, hidden behind a bush, hearing their words, bending down to pick up a rock.

With a great roar, he rushed at the pair, ramming into them, dividing them, using all his height and weight to push the short man into the river.

The girl screamed, rushed to the bank, leaned over to grasp the flailing, wet, slippery hand. The short man could not swim and the river was swollen with winter flood water. She pulled as hard as she could, but the river was too strong. His fingers slipped from her grasp and the man disappeared under the rushing crests.

She turned, wailing, aware of the presence above her, just as the full force of the jagged rock hit her in the face. Something popped. She put her hand up to her eye, to find a gaping socket. The rock crashed down repeatedly on her wrists and fingers, her elbows and shoulders; then on her knees and ankles. She couldn't resist. The shock was too great. She could no longer feel pain, although she could hear the cracking of smashed bones. Then he stopped.

"My manor," he whispered, and kicked her into rushing river.

* * *

The girl felt her body floating. There was no pain, no cold. Something on the edge of her awareness told her there should be, but never mind. Death was approaching. She was on her back. She felt crashes and bumps as her body bounced off the boulders of the riverbed. She felt regret, but also a sense of lightness and immense joy. God was close now.

Then, a rough hand grabbed her shoulder and pulled

2

her to the shore. She tried to protest, but she had no voice. A blurred head came into view. As she tried to focus through her remaining eye, a wave of pain coursed like a shockwave through her body. She thought she was screaming, but she was so deep in the pain that she couldn't be sure.

"I can stop this." The voice was neither comforting, nor threatening. "Do you want me to stop this?"

The girl moved her head in what she hoped was a nod. A trace of something hot brushed across her forehead. The pain receded and her vision cleared a little. She thought she saw a woman. The woman's head leaned in close. "Your father is dead. I cannot help that. You are almost dead. I can stop that."

Now the girl trembled with fear. This must be the Devil himself in the form of a woman. Because Death could not otherwise be stopped.

The voice continued softly, "The man who did this to you and your father will take over your home and goods. He will dispossess your mother and your sisters. He has already killed your brother."

The girl's eye registered amazement.

"Yes, indeed I tell you nothing but the truth. Your brother did not die by chance."

Her little Twm. Eight years old.

"His head was held under the water. By the same man who reported his loss and found his body."

A cold hand stroked her forehead. "You are fading. Death will be with you soon. But I can stop it. If you let me. You can avenge yourself, if that be your wish."

There was something repulsive about her touch. But now the feeling inside her was anger. No, more than anger. Hatred. Rage. Revenge.

She would join the Devil. For Twm.

The woman understood.

The girl felt calm. Light began to enter her vision. So bright, so blinding. Then, nothing.

1

Maggie Gilbert stamped her feet for the umpteenth time and watched the white mist from her mouth disintegrate into the air. This was a Christmas Eve ritual that she could have done without, particularly since the temperature had, she felt sure, acquired several minus points since she had joined the turkey-collection queue. Queuing for the Christmas turkey outside the butcher's shop that her mother had frequented for fifty years, scarf tied up to her mouth, hat pulled down over her ears.

Christmas – their second in the old house at Garth Hill, the house she had bought without knowing that it had been built by her great-grandfather. The house whose story had changed her life beyond recognition in the past year.

Even muffled up, she had been recognised by a couple of people, had responded to their eager nods, and signed an autograph or two. That had made everyone else crane around to look at her with quizzical expressions. Not *that* famous, then. Maze Investigations had a popular weekly radio slot dedicated to discussing the solving of family mysteries for amateur genealogy researchers. As the front for Maze, Maggie had gained some local celebrity. Maggie, Zelah, and Nick – the genealogy dream team – according to Zelah. Maggie enjoyed this job more than anything else she had ever done before.

She stamped her feet again on the snow and glanced around for her daughter, Alice, as the queue shuffled forward. Alice was sitting on the low wall talking to a couple of boys that Maggie recognised from school. Maggie's small wave produced a quick eye-roll and a turned back. I would have done the same if my mother had seen me talking to boys when I was eleven, she thought.

Although, I'd probably have got a sarcastic earful when I got home.

Another shuffle ahead caused her to turn back in line with the queue. Almost there.

A shout came from across the car park. It wasn't for her, but it drew her attention to the building across the road. She could see Llanyrafon Manor clearly, despite the snow that had begun to fall again. It had always intrigued Maggie. She had waited for her school bus outside its high wall for seven years, always wondering what went on inside that evocative, sixteenth century gentleman's house and farm next to the river with its water wheel.

It had been abandoned for longer than she had been alive. She knew that a local trader had lived there for a while, but eventually the upkeep and repair had become unmanageable and he had abandoned it in the early sixties. Since then it had stood empty, slowly decaying. The trader had given it to the local council, as a piece of history, a gift to the community. *Probably glad to be rid of the burden*, Maggie thought, although she had read that his children had a wonderful time growing up in its grounds.

For a while it had opened as a museum of local farming life. But, without a budget for repairs and few visitors, it slid into a steady decline that reversed the upkeep it had enjoyed as a residence for several hundred years. Maggie had visited only once as a girl. She'd finally plucked up the courage one day on her way home after school. Another building that had drawn her in.

She had been shocked to find it damp, dark, and smelly. The flagstones were eighteenth century, the fireplace original seventeenth century. It was all stone and no comfort. Maggie had wandered around the four large downstairs rooms, but had been unable to go upstairs because the staircase had become dangerous. All the time she walked round, she could hear the creaking and groaning of the floorboards upstairs.

She questioned the curator as they stood in what had once been the parlour.

"There's no one up there, dear. You can't walk around up there nowadays. Most of the floors are in a state of collapse. We won't be able to stay open much longer."

"What will happen to it?" Maggie asked with concern. "It won't be knocked down, will it?"

"No, dear. Too important for that. I expect they'll just make it safe, then close it up. Anyway, getting dark now. Time to finish up." She leaned towards Maggie, her voice a whisper, "I don't like to be here when it gets dark."

"Why not?" asked Maggie.

"Well, things. You know."

"No, I don't. What *things*?"

"Over there, behind that door, that little room with the unfinished stairs. Funny noises, sometimes. And a light. Red it is. Shines through the door." The woman burst out laughing. "Just pulling your leg, dear! Come on, you need to go now, so I can lock up."

Young Maggie returned a stiff smile.

The woman walked away, with another throwaway line that made Maggie shudder, the exact words now unremembered. She only recalled that it left her staring at the door to the little room. The door was original – heavy and wooden with large, rusty nails. The floorboards upstairs creaked again and the door rattled. Maggie turned and ran.

She had never visited the manor again.

Now it was transformed into a delightful community facility. Local people, after a lot of hard lobbying, had finally received a grant and fundraised enough to turn the property back to its original state. One half of the lower floor retained its original features and had been decorated and furnished in the style of the pre-Industrial Revolution manor house. The other half was now a popular tea room. Upstairs the floors, walls, beams, and fireplaces had been restored so the rooms could be used by local groups for meetings and events.

Maggie had taken Jack, her son, and Alice to visit

6

events and fairs last summer. But she could never quite shake off the childhood memory of the dank, crumbling structure and the creaking footsteps. And there was that something else the woman had said that now caused her to feel a knot of fear in her stomach, about the little room with the unfinished staircase. But what was it?

For a second she thought she saw a red light glowing in one of the windows. "Get a grip," she muttered. The queue shuffled forward, it was her turn.

* * *

After Christmas lunch, they settled in Maggie's living room in front of the fire. Zelah was snoring gently on the settee, a cup of coffee balanced precariously on her lap. Nick stood up to take it away and Maggie smirked at him. Jack and Alice were in the kitchen, in the recently completed conservatory extension, battling out a new game on their laptops.

The snow had settled sufficiently for Zelah and Nick to drive to Maggie's house late on Christmas Eve. They had both stayed the night and joined in the Gilbert Christmas morning ritual of present opening, then potato and vegetable peeling, followed by a walk before lunch.

In November Maggie had been relieved when her sister Fiona had announced that she and her family were going away for Christmas. Relations between the sisters had thawed since the summer and following Maggie's announcement that she would be joining Maze Investigations instead of starting the corporate job. Fiona had said things that stopped the sisters speaking to each other for months.

"She'll come round, don't worry," Nick had said. "Give her time. She's just not like you. She doesn't take risks."

"I'm not sure if I want her to come round," Maggie had bitten back.

"Lovely day, thanks Maggie. So glad you invited us," Nick said, watching orange peel shrivel up on the blazing logs, throwing out a bittersweet citrus scent.

When Maggie had discovered that both of her Maze Investigations colleagues had spent several previous Christmases alone, she decided to have a "proper Gilbert day" and they had both quickly accepted.

They had all agreed to keep away from business for the holiday, but Maggie could see Nick's eyebrows going into questioning mode, which was the prelude to a potentially awkward question. She waited. The question was not what she expected.

"Did you get your turkey from Llanyrafon?"

"Yes. It's a family tradition. Why?"

"The butcher's family used to live at the manor."

"Yes, I know. The community group has done a great job of doing it up. Have you been in?"

"No," said Nick.

"They're having a New Year fayre next week. Fancy coming with me?"

"No." Spoken with such gloom and finality that Maggie shot him a look of surprise.

"Problem there, Nick?"

She could tell when he looked directly at her that this was significant. Nick rarely looked anyone in the eye. She saw him breathe deeply, choosing his words.

"Yes."

"Elaborate?"

"Not now. Later. Perhaps."

"Zelah would tell you to get it out," Maggie replied, glancing at her snoring friend and colleague, "as you know."

"Quite right," came a slurred mutter from the sofa.

"You're awake."

"I wasn't asleep. Just resting my eyes. And my stomach. And get that smirk off your face."

Maggie turned to Nick. "Up to you, Nick. Whatever, it's your story. When you're ready."

"Same goes for you," Zelah added. "Whatever it is that's been on your mind for the past couple of weeks."

8

"How do you do it?" Maggie asked.

"Talent. And more understanding than either of you give me credit for. People tell you a lot when they're trying to hide something."

"OK," Maggie said with a resigned tone, "but after Christmas, not today. Or tomorrow. When we get back to work in the New Year. OK?"

Zelah and Nick nodded. Maggie thought she saw a look of relief on Nick's face. It would give him thinking time. And her. Zelah was right, there was something important to talk about.

"Four o'clock and it's getting dark. Which means that it's time for Cluedo and a film before supper." She called out to Jack and Alice who came running. They were both ready for the board game challenge and what came after.

"I love Christmas," Alice, the turkey sandwich fanatic, whispered to her mother as she helped her get ready.

2

Cwmbran, South Wales
December 2016

Thick snow lay on the ground for the final days of the holiday week. Maggie had seen a TV news report about an enterprising person who had set up a ski lift on a hill near Abergavenny and was renting out skis, sticks, and boots. She put it to Jack and Alice and didn't get to the end of the sentence before they were on their way to their rooms to dig out their snow boots and skiing gear.

An hour later they were on the 'slope'. It was New Year's Eve and crowds packed the hill. There were skiers, tobogganers, enthusiastic spectators, and a crowd of youngsters who just wanted to throw themselves and each other into the snow drifts around the edges of the field whilst loudly shrieking and laughing. A man had set up a table selling hot glühwein. He was playing jolly Tyrolean music out of a boom box. You could almost imagine you were in Austria, if you ignored the lack of Alps.

After a couple of runs, Maggie decided enough was enough. She wasn't the fittest and her knees were wobbling. She took back her skis and started on the warming wine, her Christmas-themed, fingerless gloves – a present from Jack – wrapped around the polystyrene cup, when the wine seller spoke to her.

"Aren't you the woman off the radio, who does the family history stuff?"

She was getting used to this now, and gave him the warm smile she had cultivated to replace the nervous, quizzical look that had overwhelmed her when the recognition first started. "Yes, I am. Are you interested in your family's history?" Immediately asking this question gave them something to talk about, instead of being quizzed about what it was like to be on the radio.

"Oh, yes. Done mine. But I like listening to your spot. You tell a good story. And I liked you on that TV piece before Christmas. You're older than you sound, mind, I thought when I saw you in the flesh, so to speak. No offence intended. But you were good on TV. Funny." He smiled at her and she decided to smile back. *No offence taken. Much*, she thought. They discussed family history research for ten minutes while she watched Jack and Alice tearing down the slope, occasionally gesturing approval with a thumbs-up.

"Well, I have to grab those kids and go now. It was lovely to meet you, and thanks for sharing your story."

"Can you use it on the radio?" he asked, eager at the prospect.

There had been nothing unusual or unexpected in what he had told her, but… you never knew.

"As soon as I get home, I'll write up some notes, and I'll see what I can do. But no promises, OK?"

He nodded, content with the mere possibility. Then stared off into the distance over her shoulder. "I'm not the only one who's recognised you today. That bloke over

10

there has been staring at us since you came over here."

Maggie turned to look. He was at the edge of the field, alone. A thickset man with a round face was all she could see between the cold-weather clothing and the furry hat with ear flaps. He was intense, unsmiling. Quite out of place amidst the fun going on around him.

"You sure he's looking at me? Perhaps he's from the Inland Revenue, making sure you're going to pay tax on your hot drink profits – unlike some we could mention," she laughed.

He smiled wryly back at her. "Hmm... didn't think of that. Have to make sure I set myself up as an offshore corporation next time it snows in Abergavenny. But no, it's definitely you he's watching. Look, he's seen us. He's heading off sharpish now."

Maggie saw the man, head down, walking fast enough to make the earflaps bounce, towards the exit.

"A shy fan, probably. Or a stalker. Yuk." She shrugged and, for a moment, felt a tightening of concern. She could never think of a stalker without thinking of Eira Probert.

"Right." She signalled to Jack and Alice, who had just reached the bottom of the hill again. They saw her and skied over to the stall.

"Time to go. Jack, if you want to get ready for that party, you've only got a couple of hours." Jack had been invited to his first ever teenage New Year's Eve party at a friend's house. At first Maggie had said no, but after talking to the parents, much to Jack's disgust and embarrassment, she had relented.

Alice smirked at him. "Sure it's enough time to make yourself beautiful for Rhiannon? She won't want to snog smelly boy." He lunged at her, but she dodged his blow.

"Enough!" Maggie shouted. "Get the skis off and let's go."

As they walked through the outskirts of the town, Maggie thought she glimpsed the watching man in the window of a pub, but whoever it was turned away and spoke to someone as they passed.

"Don't get paranoid," she muttered. "She's not coming back. In any shape, or form."

3

Zelah organised lunch on New Year's Day. Jack had returned late in the morning from his party, clearly hung-over and looking sick, with traces of alcohol and vomit on his shirt. Maggie sent him to bed, forbidding Alice to say anything, before they set off for lunch.

"Rite of passage," Nick said when she told him, out of earshot of Alice – the lover of any opportunity to wind up her brother. Maggie was determined that Alice wasn't going to use her sharp verbal repartee on Jack in his current vulnerable state. "He's going to feel terrible for a couple of days. But you didn't get any panicky phone calls in the middle of the night, so it must have been OK. You'd have heard soon enough if it wasn't."

"I suppose so," Maggie replied. "You think it'll be easier when they grow up. I hadn't thought about this bit. We'll just have to get through it." She paused for a moment, then said, "These are the times when his father could have stepped in."

"I didn't have a father, growing up. I managed." This was the first time Nick had mentioned his father. She knew that his mother was dead, and his older brother. "You're a good mother."

"Not too sure about that, all things considered."

"Not too sure about what?" Zelah asked as she came through the kitchen door with a tray of coffee. They were sitting in the deep, white leather armchairs in Zelah's living room, looking through three ceiling-height picture windows at the spectacular view of the Mynnedd Maen, snow-capped in the sunshine like a classic Christmas card.

12

Maggie put her finger to her lips, indicating to Zelah that she didn't want Alice to overhear. "Nick said I'm a good mother. I'm not so sure. After… you know."

Zelah let out an exasperated sigh. "Still blaming yourself? It wasn't your fault, but I suppose we can tell you that until the cows come home, and you still won't believe it. Anyway, she seems fine," she said, looking over at Alice who was transfixed by a giant computer screen at the far end of the room. "Don't you think?"

"Honestly, I don't know. She's been quieter since she started at senior school. Lost some of her energy. Maybe. I'm not sure. It could just be the change of environment. She's never liked crowds."

Nick spoke in a low voice, "I think you may be right. She's struggling with something. Would you like me to talk to her?"

"Oh yes, please," Maggie replied. "You and she have an affinity and she trusts you. See what she tells you and let me know?"

"If I can," Nick said, staring at the mountains. Maggie knew he had a sixth sense that could pick up signals that eluded others. A delicate and sharp intuition. That, to a lesser extent, Zelah shared, but unlike Nick, she didn't keep it to herself.

"So, back to work Monday, and lots to talk about. We have a new client," Zelah told them. "An interesting one. Canadian. Thinks his great-grandfather emigrated as a child. Can't find any trace of his relatives." She banged her cup down on the saucer. "Maggie, did you listen to any of that?"

"Sorry, no. I heard 'new client.'"

"Name of Morgan Sturridge and he's very charming. I've spoken to him a couple of times. He's coming over to the UK in a couple of days, to meet us. He's sent some details. I'll fill you both in on Monday."

"OK. So, a couple of days left before we start again. I'm going to the Frost Fayre at Llanyrafon Manor tomorrow. Either of you fancy coming? Nick?" She addressed her comment deliberately to him. He shook his head.

"Busy."

"Really? Truthfully?" This was unfair, she knew. Nick was a poor liar. He shrugged. Clearly, untrue.

"Look, why don't you just come into the grounds? There are stalls outside. You don't have to actually enter the building."

He was still gazing out of the picture windows, sitting on his hands now.

"Come on, Nick. Alice says it's too cold for her and Jack's unlikely to have surfaced. I'd love to have your company." Again, unfair. She knew that he was fond of her. More than fond. She didn't know yet whether she could return the feeling.

She waited. Then, reluctantly, he said, "Well, if I don't have to go inside. Can't talk about it, not yet," this last part, mumbled.

"Definitely not. Great. See you there around eleven. And afterwards perhaps you can come back and speak to Alice?" Maggie could see that Zelah was scowling, but she turned away. If Nick had a concern about the manor, he was the person she could confide in about her experience there when she was growing up. She just needed to get him there. "So, meeting up on Monday morning, in the office? What time?"

"Nine o'clock," Zelah said. "Lots to talk about."

"Before we head off, just something I need to tell you both about," Maggie said. "Probably nothing really. But yesterday, when I took the kids skiing, there was a man watching me. When he realised that I knew he was watching, he hurried off."

"Did he approach you, try to speak to you?" Nick asked, frowning.

"No, just hurried off."

"Then you're probably right, it was nothing." Zelah stood up and whisked away the coffee cups.

"Yes. I'm off then," said Maggie and, turning around,

"Come on Alice. Time to leave the nice big screen alone. Let's get back to Mr Grumpy."

"I like it here," Alice said. "I like to look at those mountains, and when you get tired of that, you can go to the kitchen and look at the sea. And I like everything white. I'd like to live here when I get older."

"I'll leave it to you in my will," Zelah said with a wide grin.

"Really?"

"No, Alice. She's joking," Maggie said grimacing at Zelah.

"Don't be so sure," Zelah said under her breath, as Maggie closed the door behind them.

4

Cwmbran, South Wales
January 2017

Maggie found Nick waiting at the gates of the manor just after eleven. He was shifting his weight from foot to foot, occasionally glancing up at the building, then back down at the ground.

She took him by the arm. "Come on, then. Let's see what's here. It's good to support the community, isn't it?" She smiled at him, but the smile didn't reach her eyes. She could see his concern, but she was using him and she needed him inside the grounds.

There were a dozen or so stalls set up around the abandoned, roofless outbuildings, selling food and drink and homemade crafts. All of the stallholders were in nineteenth-century costumes and there were performers at the entrance, juggling and dancing.

After twenty minutes of visiting stalls and buying a few knick-knacks, Maggie suggested they get a hot drink and sit on the straw bales that were scattered around.

She waited until Nick seemed settled, blew on her drink, and tried to initiate a conversation. "Hot chocolate, lovely. Just what we need." Nick had only grunted a couple of times so far. He didn't comment.

"OK. I know you didn't want to be here and you only came because I asked you, and you aren't comfortable. I can see that." *No point in leading up slowly.* "I want to talk to you about this place. I've been fascinated by since I was in school. I visited once and something strange happened." She paused for a moment and saw him staring straight at her, his expression both puzzled and fearful. He nodded for her to go on.

"When it was first opened, it was in a bad state. I don't think many people visited, and it was soon closed again; health and safety, I think. You could only visit the ground floor because the stairs were dangerous.

"There was a woman looking after the building and she must have sensed that I was an impressionable teenager, because she told me it was haunted and that sometimes at night there was a red glowing light from a small room or cupboard, or something, behind a heavy door. Then she laughed and said she was just teasing. But I was scared. And she said something else, what I can't quite remember, but that I think I *need* to remember. Anyway, I ran out and haven't been back here, not until last summer. But when I was in the butchers'," she pointed across the road to the row of small shops, "I thought I saw a red glow. It took me by surprise. But it was gone in a second. At first I thought it was my imagination. But I'm not so sure now. And it's connected to whatever it was she said to me that I can't remember. I've been wracking my brains, but it won't come back. So, what do you think?" As she was speaking, she looked over at the porched entrance to the building, trying to recall. When she turned back, Maggie was horrified to see that Nick had tears in his eyes.

She instinctively took hold of his hand, but he pulled it away from her abruptly. As usual, it was gloved.

16

"Oh, my God, what have I done? Nick, I just wanted to get your take on this. I didn't realise it was so personal. I'm so sorry."

"Let's get out of here," he whispered. "Alice is waiting. And I'll tell you as much as I think I can."

5

Cwmbran, South Wales
January 2017

Maggie busied herself, lighting a fire in the living room, while Alice and Nick sat in the kitchen, chatting. After a quarter of an hour they were still there, so she decided to go upstairs to see if there were any signs of life from Jack's room. She knocked and put her head round the door. He was propped up on one elbow.

"Good party?" she asked, resisting sarcasm.

He nodded, winced, and sank back down onto his pillow.

"I'm assuming you remember most of it?"

"Enough," he groaned, eyes fixed on the ceiling.

"Did you embarrass yourself?"

"A bit." He thought for a moment. "I don't think Rhiannon fancies me. Not anymore."

"Such is life, son. Maybe she wasn't the right girl for you. Or maybe, she prefers men who can hold their drink. Anyway, lessons learned, hopefully."

He nodded again, carefully. "I'll get up soon. Can you keep the mini-witch off my back?"

Maggie laughed. "Of course, but she'll find a way to get you alone. Ignore her. If she doesn't get a response, she'll get fed up. We both know she has a low boredom threshold."

He smiled, and she backed out and closed the door. First rite of passage negotiated without too much damage. Many more to come.

On her way down the stairs she found Nick at the front door, about to leave.

"Well?" she whispered.

"Tell you tomorrow morning. Be here at nine." Then he left.

Maggie had planned to go back through some of her files, catch up on the research she had left a couple of days before Christmas. In the end, she just cooked a meal and watched a film. But only with half of her attention on the plot. She had to think about how to tell Zelah and Nick what had been proposed to her and what she was going to do about it. It would have to be delicately handled.

* * *

The following morning, both Zelah and Nick arrived early. Maggie had been up early, too, getting the office tidied up and, over coffee, rethinking the speech she had prepared the previous evening. She dressed up, abandoning baggy jogging pants and trainers that had been her uniform over Christmas. Today she had smart trousers and a shirt. If news was to be delivered, she should feel smart.

"No sign of Jack or Alice yet?" Zelah asked as they walked into the office and sat around the conference table.

"They don't go back to school till Thursday. Alice has a friend coming over, and Jack's ramping up his teenager cred. Probably won't appear until lunchtime."

"Which friend?" Nick asked intensely.

Maggie was surprised. "Janine. They don't get to see much of each other in school, because of that stupid system of splitting up friendship groups. To get them to meet new people, the school said. But it seems to me that in such a huge place they'd be better off with people they know. Anyway, that's me off my soapbox. But why do you ask?"

"Just something she said yesterday," Nick replied. "I'll tell you later."

Maggie was about to reply, but Zelah interrupted. "Right, let's get on, please. Lots to do. Nick, you want to go first?"

He sighed. "OK. First of all, I've got sign-off from the two US cases, from the reports you sent them, Zelah. Both are delighted and Maggie can report on the stories. They want to know if they can get a recording of the radio pieces?" He glanced up at Maggie, who nodded.

"Next, I've found the link in the Liverpool case, Mrs Uffingham. She was right, her three-times-great-grandfather was the embezzler. He changed his name several times. But it was him."

"Brilliant!" Zelah shouted, making Maggie jump. "I don't know how you do it but... are you sure, quite sure?"

"Yes," Nick replied in his usual monotone. "I'll show you the paperwork."

"Excellent. Anything else?"

"No. My other four are progressing, but a way to go yet."

"Maggie, what about your little snippets of research. Making progress?"

Maggie bristled. Patronising, even for Zelah.

"Surprisingly, yes, Zelah." Her tone was sarcastic enough to make Zelah look questioningly at her.

"Something I said?"

"Just remember that I did get quite a long way on my own when I first started researching genealogy, Zelah. I know I have a lot to learn and I'm grateful for yours and Nick's guidance. But I'm not a complete novice."

"I didn't say you were!"

"Oh really? Snippets of research?"

Zelah had, inadvertently, touched on the very topic that Maggie had been working up to talking about. Perhaps this was the time to get it out. Maggie could see Zelah was bristling. No time to hang around. Nick turned his head between the two of them.

"What's wrong with that?" said Zelah. "It's what you've been doing and it's very profitable. And you're good at it."

"But it's just the 'bits'. OK, I know there's a lot of it. And yes, I enjoy it. But I don't own it, do I?"

"Is that corporate speak for something?" Zelah leaned across the table.

"Sit back, Zelah, and let me explain. Don't get on your high horse with me. We're friends, remember? I'm one of the few people you get on with, so don't get arsy with me."

Zelah retreated, but said, before Maggie could speak again, "I know there's been something on your mind, Maggie. You need to tell us. I don't like this kind of tension. So, speak."

"Good. I will." She looked at them in turn. "I love researching genealogy. I think I'm good at it and I'm getting better, learning more, applying more. The people we do this work for recommend us because they like the service. But the problem is that what they like isn't *me*, Zelah, is it? It's *you*. It's how you write it up for them."

Zelah nodded, Maggie hoped she understood. Since they had started Maze Investigations six months earlier, they'd had a good volume of strange, difficult, complex cases, and, apart from one failure, had come through on them, with delighted clients and excellent stories for Maggie to tell. They had decided early on to keep away from heir-hunting. Zelah had decided, and Nick had agreed, that it was too much diversification. So Zelah sought out, found, and struck up a relationship with a specialist heir-hunting probate company, to whom they referred cases that came to them. And the probate company reciprocated with cases that were genealogy-based. The arrangement worked well.

But they were increasingly asked to undertake basic research, thanks to one particular outcome. A few months back a client had asked for a little more than just a report. More of a story. So, Zelah had written up the results of Maggie's research in detail, adding local colour, a bit of social history and no small amount of surmising around how these people's lives might have been lived. The outcome had been a mini-novel, charting the history of an ordinary family over ten generations. The client loved it. Maggie's name was on it and she told the story on one of her weekly radio slots, which led to a new avenue to their business and brought out a whole new range of talents in Zelah who, it turned out, was a gifted writer. She could write a story as if the people were living and breathing. Clients felt so close to their roots after reading Zelah's story about their family's history. It was an increasing area of business and Maggie was the chief researcher. But no more than that.

"Two things I need to tell you about. First, I'm happy, which I wasn't in my old corporate life, not at all. But – I'm not really progressing. And the way things are going, I can't see how I can. I can't write like you do, Zelah. And I don't have your intuitive skills to get past brick walls, Nick. But I am good. And I want cases of my own. Something I can get my teeth into, be responsible for. We can hire another researcher to take on some of my current work. I think I'm ready."

She paused, to see their faces, see how this was going down. Nick nodded slowly. But Zelah's expression hadn't changed. She looked miffed, lips pursed, neck stretched, head tilted to one side.

"The really big cases are few and they're very complex, Maggie. You need a lot of knowledge. You know how much time we spend around the country. In libraries and records offices, all sorts of places, looking for impossible-to-find information. Each case worries me when we take it on. I think: *Will this be one the one that beats us? Will we look foolish?* It's going to happen at some point and I don't want it to happen to you if you make mistakes and mess up because you aren't ready."

"But when will I be ready, if I just keep on doing the same thing?" Maggie flashed back at her. "And there's the second thing." She took a deep breath. "Before Christmas, you remember I did the TV piece, about the Dickensian characters? It was just meant to be a whimsical thing."

Zelah and Nick both nodded.

"I went down well, I've been told. 'Impressive.' By someone who wants to talk more to me. An agent, in fact.

Wants me to think about moving into some TV presenting. She's going to speak to me this week. She gave me over Christmas to think about it."

Maggie folded her arms and sat back. No one spoke for a couple of minutes.

"What does this mean?" Zelah asked.

"I don't know, yet. I just want to hear what she has to say. But if you're thinking that I want to move away from this," she swept her arm around the office, "I don't. But, I do want more out of it."

"Are you giving us an ultimatum?" Zelah's voice was rising; Nick decided it was time to intervene.

"No, she isn't," he said, firmly for him. "Stop now, Zelah. Think about it. You put Maggie forward as the front person. She's succeeded so well that there could more in it for her than we ever expected or dreamed of. So, it's quite right that she should explore this... option... whatever it is. You know that Maggie is good at whatever she does. Maybe, it's inevitable. Success leads to more success." He paused for a moment, reflecting. "Perhaps we should have thought about it. But we've been so caught up in our success that we didn't. Think about it. Maybe." He seemed to have run out of words, like an engine slowing down to a stop. Maggie had never heard him say so much at once in all the time she'd known him.

"Look, I've told you what's going on and how I feel. I don't want to break this up. I love it. Really. I just want to move on a bit faster. Is that too much to ask?"

Zelah still looked angry, but gave a small nod. "OK. We should talk more about it. But not now. We have another big case coming up and I've given the client my assurance that Nick and I will deal with it. He asked for us, me and Nick. Sorry, Maggie."

Maggie looked away as Nick stood up and pushed back his chair. "Let's leave this for now. I have to go to the records office in Cardiff. Let's talk again tomorrow." He walked around the table and whispered to Maggie, "Go for it!"

She turned to speak to him but Zelah said, "And he's mentioned a local place, in passing," but she could see that they weren't listening. She stood up and snapped shut her briefcase. "Things to do," she muttered and walked out of the office. Maggie heard the front door slam.

She went to follow, but Nick held her arm. "Leave her be. I'll speak to her." He grabbed his coat and left.

Well that went well. Great start to the New Year, Maggie grimaced as she walked into the kitchen, *and it's only nine-thirty. What am I supposed to do now?*

She looked outside the front door, but both Zelah's and Nick's cars had gone.

* * *

Maggie tried to get on with some research, but, two hours later, neither of them had called her and she kept thinking about the conversation and how badly she had handled it. At lunchtime, she gave up.

During the morning, Alice's friend Janine arrived. They scooted straight up to Alice's bedroom. Maggie thought Janine looked thinner and paler than the last time she'd seen her. But when she went upstairs the door was closed, with a homemade 'Do Not Disturb, Especially Parent' sign on the door. She could hear whispering, but left it and half-heartedly went back to her office.

Late afternoon, Janine's mother called to take her home. Jack and Alice were sitting in front of the fire, still in pyjamas, watching TV and eating mince pies.

Maggie was about to switch off the computer when the doorbell rang. Hoping it was either Zelah or Nick she ran out into the hall and flung open the front door. It was neither of her colleagues, but it was someone she recognised immediately. It was the man who had been watching her in Abergavenny, and he looked furious. Maggie jumped back.

"Who are you and what do you want?" she demanded.

"My name is Bob Pugh. That's Detective Inspector

Robert Pugh, South Wales Police. We spoke some months ago, you may remember. About your daughter. I need to talk to you about a case. Urgently."

6

Maggie didn't speak for a moment, trying to pull her thoughts into line. This was not just unexpected; it was bizarre.

This man had spoken to her after Eira Probert had failed to take Alice and had been revealed as a malevolent fake. It had been clear from their phone conversation at the time that he didn't believe in the supernatural and was angry and frustrated with Maggie for what he perceived as her lack of co-operation with the police to find a dangerous criminal. To now find him standing on her doorstep asking to consult with her was… yes, bizarre.

"Can I see some ID?"

He was prepared, his warrant card already in hand. Maggie kept him waiting, examining it for longer than was necessary. She handed it back with a suspicious glare, but said, "OK. You'd better come in and tell me why you're here."

She led him into the kitchen, indicating that he should sit in one of the armchairs in the glass-fronted extension and took his overcoat.

"Drink?" she asked.

"No thanks, Mrs Gilbert."

Maggie sat opposite him, appraising. He sat still and upright. She could see now that he had a close-shaved his head. Was this what policemen did to seem more formidable? His head was round under his flappy hat and he was thickset, muscly under jeans and a smart, roll-collared jumper.

"You aren't in uniform. Is this official?"

"I'm a detective, but this isn't official. It's about… a friend of mine." And before she could ask, he added, "And it's nothing to do with your daughter exactly, but..." he trailed off, seemingly stuck for how to continue.

Maggie was so relieved that she missed the hint contained in the hesitation, and interrupted with, "Why were you following me on Saturday?"

"Sorry about that. I thought I might be able to approach you outdoors, more informally, like. I was here at first, sat outside and trying to decide whether to come in, when you and your children came out with snow gear. I followed you. There wasn't an opportunity to speak to you, so I went to the pub instead."

"I've been known to have that effect on people."

He smiled. "I think you saw me, in the window. You gave me a right look. I was expecting you to come in and call me out."

"I might have done if the kids hadn't been with me. Anyway, why are you here? I'd have thought I'd be the last person you'd turn to if you needed help. Our last conversation gave me the impression that if you never spoke to me again, that would be a good thing."

He nodded, and looked out at the garden. After contemplating the snow for what seemed like an age, he looked back at her and said, "Yes, I thought you weren't just crazy; I suspected you might be dangerous. I couldn't understand why you weren't yelling at the top of your voice about that person. It made me suspicious of you."

He swallowed, as Maggie's expression turned from curiosity to anger. "What, you thought that I was involved… colluding?"

"Yes," he replied, without expression.

She was stunned. Knowing what she knew, about the evil entity that was Eira Probert, fury swelled up inside her and she was about to say something, when he said, "So, I went to my boss. I was angry and upset, beyond upset, actually. I wanted to arrest you. At first, he listened intently. But he didn't react like I expected. He asked me to repeat bits a couple of times. He just sat there nodding. Then… he told me to leave it alone. Just that. Well, I was shocked, then outraged; I was yelling loud enough for the whole station to hear. But he just sat there, sat through my outbursts against you and him; let me rant until I ran out of steam. Then he said to me, 'I know what she's talking about'. Just that. I had him repeat it. Again, 'Leave it alone, Bob. You won't get anywhere.' I asked him how he could possibly know that. He just shook his head and said, 'There are some things best left, better not to know.' Then he threw me out of his office."

He prickled with the memory, which gave Maggie, who had calmed down a little, the chance to ask, "And did you? You never spoke to me again. So, you left it?"

"Of course not." He smothered a chuckle. "My colleagues call me Persistent Bob, or just Persi Pugh. I never give up on anything. I went back to the school, spoke to the head and the teachers. Found out none of them liked the woman and the class teacher had asked that she not come back to the school."

"They never told me that," Maggie said.

"Wouldn't, would they? They were struggling with it. Just decided to keep it to themselves. Head still half thinks you're a nut job."

Maggie's turn to bristle. "And you? If I'm a 'nut job', why are you in my kitchen?"

He didn't respond to that, continuing with his story. "Met dead ends. Everywhere. The woman had no history. In the end, I had to give up. My chief found out what I was doing. But, by that time, I had nothing anyway. Summoned me to a meeting. He asked what I had found. I shrugged. He nodded. That was it. Didn't discuss it with anyone else. Not for ages. But then something happened, in my family. Something that's shocked the hell out of me. Still don't know entirely what to think of it."

Maggie looked curiously at him. She saw that he was clenching his knuckles. "Family history thing?"

26

"Yes," he nodded. "A story told to me at a funeral. By a cousin, not a real cousin, a couple of times removed. But a Pugh." His breathing had increased. Something had deeply touched him. Maggie let go of her anger. The reason he was here had to be because, somehow, there was a link to her, why he needed her help.

"So, what's it got to do with me?"

He ran his finger around the inside of his collar and pulled at it. "Eira Probert," he replied. "Turns out she's in my family, too."

7

Newport, South Wales
2017

As soon as she reached her car outside Maggie's house, Zelah wanted to go back in. But she was torn between conflicting emotions – fear that she had gone too far and anger that Maggie's news had so shocked her that she would start up an argument as soon as she set eyes on her. Standing undecided at the car door, she felt an arm on her shoulder. Turning in expectation, she was disappointed to find it was Nick.

"Slow down, Zelah. This was not intended to upset you."

"Well it has," she snapped back, regretting her intensity as he recoiled. Too late to stop now, Zelah was never one to not have the last word, whatever the cost.

"Then it shouldn't" said Nick. "Think about it. Maggie has uncomplainingly done our donkey work for six months. She's really good at it. Is it so surprising that she wants to do more?"

"It's not that. She should have said something before Christmas. Letting us sit there, eating and drinking, knowing that she might be about to stab us in the back." Inappropriate words, but unable to hold them in.

"If that's what you think, then I'm very sorry for you," Nick replied.

"Don't you dare feel sorry for me!"

Nick turned away. "I'm not going to argue with you," he called over his shoulder. "Call me when you've calmed down and you're thinking straight." He got into his van and drove off without looking at Zelah again.

* * *

Just after midday, Zelah scuttled into the foyer of the Celtic Manor Hotel, late, out of breath, and agitated. She had arranged to meet with the new client but, after leaving Maggie's house, had driven around for an hour, to try to suppress her anger. Then she had gone home and paced around her flat. So much so, she had lost track of time.

Glancing around, she could see that there was no one waiting in the grand reception hall. Perhaps he'd gone back to his room. Damn! She was about to head to the reception desk when an arm on hers made her jump.

"Mrs Trevear?"

Where the hell had he come from?

She turned to find a man of average height, thick, black well-cut hair, dark grey eyes, wearing a designer three-piece black suit and matching shoes. He held out a pale, manicured hand that, as Zelah grasped in her usual firm handshake, was quickly withdrawn.

"Mr Sturridge?"

"Yes. And my given name is Morgan, which I hope you will use. Shall we?" He indicated a couple of armchairs opposite a low table on the far side of the reception area. As she followed him across the high-gloss floor, her jewelled high heels clicked methodically, while his shoes made no sound. Zelah could see the two receptionists surreptitiously watching them.

"Coffee, tea? And I do like the shoes. *Jimmy Choo.* This season's, I think?" he said.

"Coffee please," Zelah replied.

He raised a finger and gave a slight nod, whereupon a

28

waiter appeared and took their order. Zelah noted that his manner towards the waiter was respectful, his order given in a warm voice. And he'd recognised the shoes. Most men, even the well-off ones, would never have done so, never mind knowing that they were new season. She'd been stroked, she knew that, but it was a pleasant sensation.

"Well, Morgan," she began, "so far you've told me very little. I know that you are, or you believe yourself to be, local and that your family emigrated to Canada in the mid-1840s. You know your mother's family's name, but little more. You want us to find out about her, who she was, where she came from. Is that correct?"

"Pretty much," he replied with a smile.

"And you're in a hurry. You want to get this research completed in a couple of weeks?"

"Very important," he nodded, leaning towards her. "I have a seminal life event coming up. I must be clear about who I am. Where I came from. How I got to where I am." He sat back. "So that's why I chose Maze Investigations. You've established yourselves as the go-to folks for enigma solving. And, I can assure you, Zelah, I am such a one." Again, a warm smile.

The coffee arrived. He paused to pour them each a cup, black for her, no sugar. *How did he know that? She wondered. She said,* "You're right, we've developed a formidable reputation, considering we only started back last year. And we have an almost one-hundred-per-cent success rate. But you want quick results and we aren't cheap."

"I can assure you there is no problem with money. Name your price. And I'll pay a bonus if you can get me the information I need by the end of this month."

Zelah didn't even stop to consider Maggie and Nick. "Done." She scribbled on the notepad she had extracted from her bag. "This is what I believe will be the cost, based on what you've told me and the timescale you're looking for. We'll have to throw everyone at it." She pushed the paper across the table. He barely looked at it. "Fine," he said. "Draw up a contract and send it to me here. I'm staying in the hotel for the foreseeable future. Fifty per cent up front, the balance and the same again as a bonus if you succeed. That OK with you?"

Again, Zelah's response was instant. "It's a deal, Mr… ah, Morgan. The paperwork will be with you by the end of this afternoon. Now, please tell me as much as you can: names, dates, locations to start with."

8

Cwmbran, South Wales
2017

Maggie stared open-mouthed at Bob Pugh. Then "How could she be in your family?" came more as an accusation than a question.

He saw her aggression. "Let me explain, before you go for me." He paused, but Maggie didn't interrupt. "I was at a family funeral just before Christmas. At the eats and drinks afterwards the grandson of the deceased, about ten years older than me, introduced himself to me and we got talking. Turned out we have the same great-great-grandfather. A man also called Robert Pugh. A Baptist minister, who was based here in Garth Hill."

"Just a moment," Maggie interrupted and ran out of the room. In the office, she went to the 'Probert' file, rummaged around and found a document, then ran back to the kitchen.

"I have a letter inherited from a relative, Louisa Jenkins. From a family called Morris. The husband referred to 'our dear Mr Pugh', but didn't he go to Hereford?"

"Yes. And it was because of what happened here. At the school. When he was the minister and Eira Probert was the teacher." He stopped and asked, "Does the letter give you any idea of what kind of man he was?"

Maggie scanned through it quickly. "Not really," she

replied. "But they call him 'our dear Mr Pugh,' and they offered to be of whatever help they could be to Ruth, my great-grandmother. Suggests that he was a decent sort of man."

"Well, according to my three-times-removed cousin, that couldn't be further from the truth. Says he was a pompous, arrogant little shit. Hated the Welsh; thought they were beneath him. And he particularly hated a man called John Jones. Ring any bells?"

"Oh, my God," Maggie exclaimed. "That was Ruth's husband. My great-grandfather; the man who built this house. But why? Do you know?"

"Yes. But that's not why I came here. I said I have a problem with a case. It's to do with a friend of mine who just died. And I need your help."

Maggie almost stamped her foot. "Don't think you're going to get away without telling me the whole story! How could you possibly think I'd help you, given what my family went through?"

He growled back at her, "But I have no idea what you went through, do I? I just know that a woman called Eira Probert has affected both of our families. I know what happened in mine. But I have no fucking clue what happened in yours, apart from Alice's kidnapping."

Maggie thought she was being manipulated. Led to a point where there was information that she craved, but to get it she would have to tell him everything. But could she trust this man? He had wanted to arrest her, had followed her, and had now wormed his way into her house. She felt a frisson of fear. Was any of this genuine? Had he just made it all up, to satisfy the curiosity of 'Persistent Bob'? But that would be outrageous. And he was a real policeman. But how much was that worth, these days?

She made a quick decision. "What's the problem with your friend? If that's why you're here, tell me. I will tell you the whole Eira Probert thing and you will tell me your story. But not until I know the friend thing."

Surprisingly, he smiled at her. "You'd make a good

detective. OK. I'll tell you. Any chance of a cup of coffee?"

"In a minute, but start talking."

"Right. So, my friend, my old pal, was called Jerry Allen. Died at the end of November. He was ninety-eight, but clear-headed, right up to the end. No real illness. Just kind of wore out, like. He lived up outside Pontypool on some land on the side of the mountain, looking after animals; horses and donkeys mainly. People took them to him, and he was quite well-known locally. Bit of a scruffy old eccentric.

"Anyway, he told me a story, about his youth. Amazing, as it happens. He was a real lefty, in the 1930s. Communist, he was. Decided to go to Spain in 1938 when he was nineteen, to fight for the Republicans against Franco. Seems there was a lot of young men went from Wales. You know anything about it?"

"I've read Orwell's *Homage to Catalonia*," Maggie replied. "That's about all. Orwell didn't make it sound like a walk in the park, either. It was all quite hopeless and sad, I think."

"Yeah. Jerry went out there full of enthusiasm. Came back less than a year later, a broken man. A broken young man. Still only twenty."

"Broken by what?"

"The politics, he said. The ugly reality of factionalism. Supposed to be on the same side, the Communists, the Socialists, the Anarchists, whatever, but really all of them were just trying to gain the upper hand over each other. All for when the glorious victory over fascism came, and it mattered who was going to be in charge. I didn't know too much about it. But I know now.

"Anyhow, it was the politics, but there was something else. He spent time close to a small village south of Barcelona. Met a local girl, another communist, called Lola. He was nineteen, she was eighteen. They fell in love and got married. Whirlwind romance. It must have seemed logical at the time. Convinced of course that they were going to win. And next thing, she was pregnant. Then, at

32

the last big battle on a river called the Ebro, Jerry got wounded and was sent back to Barcelona. Just like Orwell did.

"Then it really fell apart and he had to leave Spain. Got back to Wales and tried to send for Lola. Hoping, see, that she could get out too, before Franco's troops took over. But – long story short – he couldn't reach her. When he finally gets news from her village, from another comrade who had made a run for it, he finds that it had been overrun. Someone in the village gave her up, because she had supported the commie foreigners, and they took her away. Desperate, he was. Then World War Two started, and he was stuffed. He enlisted right away. Thought that, wherever he was, he would eventually get to Europe, somehow go to Spain, and somehow find her. Daft plan. Never even got close. He was wounded at Dunkirk."

Maggie's resistance had dropped, she was interested now.

Pugh continued "Eventually, after the end of the war he got a private detective to go over. Couldn't go himself because Franco had made all the fighting foreigners *persona non grata*. Couldn't get into Spain for the next thirty-odd years. The bloke he sent over found out a few things. Found that no one had seen her since she'd been taken away. But Franco was kingpin, and people enquiring into a disappeared commie wife were not welcome. So, he was thrown out too.

"Once it all changed, in the seventies, Jerry couldn't bring himself to go; thought he couldn't bear to see it all again and to find out first-hand that something terrible had happened to her. He knew about Franco's abducting his opponents and the torture and the labour camps. So, he tried again with a different private firm, but the trail had gone cold. And that was the end of it." Bob Pugh paused briefly, and leaned towards Maggie. "He made one visit, when he was eighty. Went on a battlefield tour around the Ebro. But it was too emotional. And no-one would speak to him about personal details, even after all that time. He tried to put it all behind him, until he realised he was dying. Then it all came back all over again, and he wanted to find out, before he died, if she and the child had survived. But he'd left it too late. He wrote it all down and asked me to see if I could find out. Because I'm a copper he thought I was going to be able to find out something. But the end came quicker than he expected." Pugh stopped, taking a deep breath.

"So, he died without knowing?" Maggie asked.

"Yes. Shame."

"Why does it matter then?"

"Two reasons. One, I made a promise. Two, he made a will, one of those things that you buy off the shelf. Wanted to leave everything he had to his descendant, if he had one, and he gave me three months to find out."

"What if you can't?"

"Then it all goes to another family member. An American from New York. Jerry wrote to his American cousins a couple of years ago, told them the whole story and asked them to use their considerable resources to help. They said they tried, but couldn't find anything."

"Sounds to me like there's nothing left *to* find," Maggie mused.

"Maybe not," he nodded. "But I want to try."

"Why? Because you're Persistent Bob?"

He shrugged. "Yes, that, I suppose. And because he was my mate. And because I don't want his estate to go to the American."

"Hmm. Does any of it go to you?"

"No!" he shot back at her. "I'm not doing this for personal gain."

"Just asking," Maggie soothed. "Don't get fired up. I need to understand why it matters, so much so that you've come to me, of all people, for help. Sounds more like a case for heir-hunters."

"The American already hired one of those. And he's pushing for probate. But I was able to show the will at the court in Cardiff. I – we, if you'll help me – have a month left."

"But if Jerry was just an eccentric old man, living on his own, is it worth the effort? He wanted to know before he died, but that's over now. Why can't you let the American have the estate? I still don't get what the big deal is?"

"The big deal, as you say, is just that. The American says he couldn't find anything, but I think he's lying. Either he didn't try, or he's sitting on some information that he's not sharing. I've met him. I'm a detective. I can smell it," he tapped the side of his nose, "when someone is telling great big porkies."

"What am I missing here?" Maggie asked. "What's making you keep going, apart from the fact that he was your mate, and you promised, and you don't like the American?"

"It's this," he replied. "Just because he was a scruffy old git, don't mean he was a poor old git. The land is extensive, inherited from his dad and his dad's dad before that. And he wasn't a layabout. Jerry retrained as a vet after the war. He was a clever man and he had nothing else to spend his money on. He never married again. His estate is worth over half a million pounds. And the American isn't the big smooth Mr Financial Wizzo he claims to be. He's desperate to get his hands on the money. I know, I've checked him out. Detective, isn't it?" He grinned, tapping the side of the nose again.

"Wow. So, assuming the American is a nasty piece of work. And assuming – and this is a big leap –that we can trace a descendant, how do you know that the Spaniard won't also sell everything for whatever he or she can get for it?"

"Good question," he said. "I don't. But there's a paragraph in the will that says the Spaniard can't sell the land. He'd have to donate it to an animal charity if he didn't want it. Hopefully he or she won't want to. But we'll only find out by finding him or her."

Maggie nodded.

"Look, Mrs Gilbert, I want to try. I think you're the best person to help me. I've listened to you on the radio and I like the way you think. What do you say?"

Maggie bit her top lip. The story *had* fascinated her, she had to admit. But she didn't know what Zelah and Nick would say. Strictly-speaking this was heir-hunting, which they had decided to steer clear of. But, was this the case that would prove to them that she was capable of more?

"I need to speak to my colleagues, but I'm interested. I'd like to read what Jerry wrote. Can you let me have that?"

He reached into his pocket, brought out a folded, brown envelope. "Here is it. When can you let me know, do you think? The clock is ticking."

"I'll speak to them tomorrow. And I'll call you. Do you have a mobile?"

He gave her a card. "You can get me on this, leave me a message if I don't answer. I'm in work tomorrow, but I'll call you back if I can't answer right away." He stood up. "Thanks for taking the time, and for letting me in. Wasn't sure if you would."

"You can't go! You haven't told me yet about Eira Probert."

"And I want to hear your story. But, I must go. I'm working tonight. Let's talk tomorrow. Another reason for you to call me," he replied.

At the front door, he turned to shake her hand. "Here's to a good working relationship, despite the bad start." He strode purposefully away, through the gate to the end of the lane.

Maggie watched him go, then closed the door and stood for a moment with her back to it.

Well, she thought, *you knew when you got into this that life wasn't going to be predictable. But this is much more fun than I ever expected.*

9

Catalonia, Spain
1939

Lola knew that she should have left the village, but she couldn't bring herself to go. Some days she was hopeful, others desperate. The International Brigaders had been sent home, and not a word from Jeremy since his last message in September saying that he was alive and well and would come to get her. Now she didn't know if he was alive or dead. But they had been so close, she was sure she would have known if he had died. Something in her would have died, too.

But not the baby. She had the baby.

The winter had been harsh. She and her aunt had managed to survive on very little. Everyone had worked together. The priest, one of her most-loved people despite his calling, had managed to bring food each time he returned from another village. He was a man who never judged. The food was always divided evenly.

The people had helped each other, or most of them had. Hardship certainly separated the sheep from the goats. They had always known difficult times, but nothing like this. Some people had turned inward, no longer sure of the outcome, and afraid of the consequences of what they had done. The landowner would return. There would be punishment and retribution.

At first Lola had refused to believe what she was hearing. She never had any doubt the Republic would win. It had to, right was on their side. But yesterday they had heard that the Nationalists had crossed the Ebro and were heading in their direction. The fear in the village had been tangible. Some families, fearing the worst, had left overnight, taking with them whatever they could carry.

She went to visit friends close by. They had two children, whom they were struggling to feed. She would take them bread. Their son, nine-year-old Lluis, had a crush on her. She knew that, but she was compassionate. And the boy was always hungry.

She knocked on the door. There was a short pause before it opened a crack, to show half of a woman's face. The door was flung open.

"Lola! I thought you would have gone. Why are you still here?"

"He might be hiding. Come back. I can't leave."

"But you know that all of the boys were sent home."

"I have decided to wait until the weather is better, then go to Barcelona and find out how to get to France."

"You think he'll allow that?" the woman answered, pointing at Lola's stomach. "You can't leave it any longer. You should go now."

Lola shook her head and held out her hand with the bread. "For Lluis."

"He'll love you even more now," the woman said with a wide smile. "Come in, warm yourself."

Lola shook her head. "I'm going to find more firewood."

The woman shrugged. "Don't leave it any longer." She closed the door.

That evening, Lola talked to her aunt. They reluctantly concluded that their neighbour was right: Lola had to go. Jeremy had said to wait for him, but this was too dangerous now. They decided to leave the following night, after dark, when everyone was in bed. She would let the priest know she was going, and her neighbour, but no one else.

The following morning, they packed a small bundle each, some bread and olives and water, and waited for darkness to fall.

At five o'clock there was a rumbling that got louder. Something was coming. Anyone who was outside ran into the nearest house.

Within minutes three trucks arrived and parked in the

small square in front of the church. Soldiers got out. An officer barked out instructions. They went from house to house, breaking down doors, dragging out the young men and herding them onto the trucks.

Lola and her aunt watched from their window, peeking from behind the drawn curtains, lights extinguished. Women ran out to the square, screaming, begging the soldiers not to take the men and boys away. They were knocked down by the gun butts. The officer took out a pistol and fired a shot into the air. There was silence.

"I want the girl," he said. No one moved.

"Where is the girl, the pregnant girl, the wife of the foreign fighter? Bring her out."

Still, no one moved. The officer grabbed the nearest woman and put the pistol to her head. The priest ran out from the church.

"What are you doing?" he shouted at the officer. The officer cocked the gun, ready to fire.

Lola walked into the square.

"I'm the one you're looking for," she said, facing him, showing him no fear.

"You're coming with us." He pushed the weeping woman to the ground and lifted Lola into the truck. Her aunt came out sobbing.

The trucks drove off.

The people came slowly from their houses into the square, looking at the priest and each other. There was a traitor amongst them. The girl had been betrayed. But there was nothing anyone could do. They returned silently to their homes.

The next morning, half of the villagers had gone.

10

Zelah was feeling pleased with herself. A new client, a wealthy one – not that the money mattered to her – and a good, weighty project to get into. She buzzed around her small kitchen, grinding coffee beans, humming, retrieving a large cup and saucer from the shelf, thinking about how they should divide up the tasks to make sure every angle was covered. After all, time was pressing on this one. Then, abruptly, she stopped.

She hadn't told Maggie and Nick anything about it. How was she going to explain what she'd done? Well, it was for their good, much more than hers. But she should tell them.

She was still irritated by Maggie's news, but now willing to forgive and move on. She had agreed at the start to listen to what they had to say, adjust her own ideas, be part of a team. Not easy, but she was trying. What did they expect? That she would just agree to everything all at once? No chance.

She poured the hot water into her cafetière, and stood on the balcony to wait for it to brew. Although it was cold, the sun was shining and it was one of those days of sparkling arctic air, so that the view across the Bristol Channel from her luxury hilltop apartment was spectacular. She could see the contours of Exmoor, the shades of brown, green, and purple. And the coastline weaving in and out of the small towns and harbours that lined the coast below Portishead. She never tired of this view.

But how to approach her colleagues? This new, more self-aware Zelah knew that she had not given Maggie time to explain, had just reacted in her old way; aggressive, unforgiving, unbending. Not how she wanted to be. She valued their friendship more than she let on. And she admitted to herself that her reaction was one of fear.

40

Maggie was her friend as well as her colleague. It was quite a shock to realise that she, who had always been so independent and self-reliant, had come to rely on another so much. She would have to phone and arrange a meeting. Explain herself. Put things right.

The smell of the coffee brought her out of her reverie. She went into the kitchen and picked up her phone.

* * *

Nick pushed the button to end the call with a sense of relief. He had felt sure that Zelah would come round. He knew that Zelah, without explicitly saying so, was relying on him to make her peace with Maggie. Well, if that was his role, he was glad to do it. He had accepted from the beginning that he was the link between two strong women, neither of whom was good at climbing down once they had taken a position. Compromise was difficult for them both.

Over the months they had worked together, Nick had come to know that underneath the soft, attractive exterior was a core tougher than the strongest steel. It had got Maggie through the tragedy of losing her husband, and discovering that he had left her bankrupt. Had pushed her through selling her beloved home, moving back to South Wales and starting afresh with her family. But sometimes, he felt, she needed to allow herself to see an alternative view. He remembered his own mother, an uncompromising woman, a controlling woman who never listened to anyone, who saw only weakness from considering of the feelings of others. He had never had the kind of conversation with her that he could have with Maggie. He could propose his own point of view without being despised or humiliated for daring to have his own opinion. He hoped that Maggie appreciated this in him. She trusted him completely with Alice, that was clear; she hadn't questioned why he and Alice had such a rapport. Soon, he would have to explain and reveal something of his own life, his 'oddness', that he had seen manifest itself in Alice when the girl had struggled with Eira Probert.

But, for now, his role was as intermediary. Still feeling a sense of relief, he dialled Maggie's number.

11

Cwmbran, South Wales
2017

Maggie was in the kitchen, thinking over Nick's call, pleased that they were coming back together to talk. The previous evening, she had skimmed through the information that Bob Pugh had left for her. And she knew that she was smitten with a story that was agonisingly sad, but intriguing. She wanted to accept Bob's offer, to find out if Jerry Allen had a surviving child, and whether there was a living ancestor. The meeting Nick had arranged for tomorrow morning would be her chance to explain to Nick and Zelah why it was important to her to take on this case, but for now she wanted to go through Jerry Allen's information thoroughly.

She went to the office and was about to bring the papers out of the envelope, when Jack burst in.

"Got a few mates coming over, if that's OK with you Mum?"

It was the last day of the Christmas holidays. They would be back to school tomorrow. And he would be straight into mock GCSE exams.

"How many is 'a few'?"

"Four or five. Depends who can get a lift. We're just going to play some games, check out some stuff, you know." He was smiling, but the smile had a pleading look.

"Anyone from the New Year's Eve party?"

"Yeah, all of them."

"Do I know them?"

He thought. "I think you've met a couple before. They're OK, you know. We all like gaming. And music."

42

"OK," she replied, and saw his look of relief. "When are they coming?"

"On their way," he grinned, exiting the office speedily, knowing that she wouldn't be pleased to discover she'd been 'managed'.

Maggie sat for a moment, looking at her envelope. She couldn't really be cross with Jack. He wasn't a bad boy. She should let him have some space. But she couldn't concentrate with half-a-dozen raucous lads in the house. Nor would Alice be pleased.

An idea came to her. She stood up and went to look for Alice.

An hour later, after the boys had arrived and she had organised a pizza lunch for them, and read the riot act to Jack about what she expected to find when she came home, she and Alice were seated in the café at Llanyrafon Manor. Alice had reacted just as she expected when told that Jack's friends were about to descend on them. She couldn't get out of the house quickly enough and accepted Maggie's offer of lunch.

Maggie had also phoned Bob Pugh. He was working, but agreed to a quick meet with her in the café.

Alice and Maggie ordered and while they waited Maggie took out her envelope and began to read through Jerry Allen's notes again. Alice had left in such a hurry that she hadn't brought anything with her. With nothing to do, she asked Maggie if she could go and look around the manor. Maggie agreed, suggesting that she explored the museum on the opposite side of the entrance hall, and go up the small staircase to look at the rooms above.

"Don't be more than ten minutes," she said. "Food won't be that long. Just a quick look."

Alice nodded and walked out of the café.

Maggie began reading through the account of Jerry's time in Spain. She was struck again by the sadness of the story. The man had met the love of his life, had abandoned her and their child, and died not knowing what had happened to them. Reading in depth this time, Maggie began to understand the guilt he carried all his life, which had turned him into a recluse and an eccentric. She got the impression that he felt like a coward for not going back, for not trying harder.

She had spent time the previous evening reading about the Spanish Civil War. There were many accounts online, from factually historical to personal. There were societies for the families of the fallen. She had discovered that a contingent of Welsh miners was one of the largest groups from Britain that went out to Spain to join the battle against fascism. She was surprised at how many monuments and memorials existed in Welsh towns and villages to remember those who never came home.

Maggie had been shocked and horrified to discover about the viciousness of the revenge taken against the Republicans after the victory of General Francisco Franco. How homes and property had been confiscated. How hundreds of thousands of men and women had been detained, imprisoned, and executed or had been sent to labour camps for the 'sin' of being a communist or a socialist, and never heard of again. How the families were never able to look for them, and how they had been forced by the tyranny and repression of Franco's government to grieve silently for the missing, for fear of the same fate befalling them. Then the final horror of Franco's policy to punish his opponents by taking away their children.

She discovered that this decision removed an estimated thirty thousand children from their Republican parents over a period of over thirty years, starting in 1939. This was an ideological choice as well as a punitive one.

Franco believed in and supported the Nazi ideology of racial purity, believing that true Hispanicity represented racial purity. And he theorised, together with a state psychiatrist, that politically active women were, by definition, morally degenerate and should not be allowed to raise children. As a result, their children were forcibly taken away, some to orphanages, some to families sympathetic to the regime, to purify them and remove their so-called 'contamination'.

With mounting disbelief Maggie read of the involvement of the Catholic Church, which supported and encouraged the removal of the children, many of them going to Catholic orphanages, from which came evidence from the survivors of humiliation, abuse, and starvation, as reparation for the sins of their parents. Although she now rejected it, Maggie had been brought up in that religion and found this cruelty towards children hard to swallow. She had been taught by nuns, one of whom was her most favourite and revered teacher, known for kindness, her love of teaching, and empathy towards all the children in her classes. But Maggie remembered the others, from her time at secondary school. The ones at the opposite end of the scale, who seemed to gain a heightened excitement from the humiliation they inflicted upon innocent girls.

The stories of the horrific treatment of the 'red' women in Francoist jails gave her no optimism whatsoever that Jerry's Lola could have survived. Nor did it give her any hope that a missing baby, even if it had survived, could possibly be traced.

She understood why Bob Pugh wanted to help his friend. Although she truly believed they were about to undertake something with a miniscule chance of success, nevertheless, if she could play some small part in righting a wrong, then it was worth trying. This was how she would explain her decision to Nick and Zelah. She was sure that Zelah would understand.

A cough at her shoulder brought Maggie back. She expected it to be their lunch, but she looked up to find Bob Pugh standing next to her.

"You were well away there," he remarked as he sat down in the chair opposite Maggie. "I called your name a couple of times."

"I was thinking about what I read last night," she replied. "About the war and the outcome and the children. It's a horror story, isn't it?"

"Yes. I feel guilty that I bought an apartment in Spain, and I've spent years lying in the sun, enjoying myself with the cheap food and the plonk."

"You didn't know. You acted in good faith."

He fell quiet for a moment, then said, "In this country we don't know what it's like to be defeated in war. There's hardly anyone alive who knows. Just the last few men who fought in Spain. What they did has been ignored, and covered up. Inconvenient."

Maggie mused "Well, if we can find out what happened to Lola and find a living heir for Jeremy, then at least his fight for what he believed in won't have been in vain. Assuming the heir is a decent person, of course."

"That's the risk," Bob acknowledged. "If the baby did survive and was given to a fascist family, the descendent could be a real bastard. Worse than the American."

"Maybe. But if the American is hiding evidence, doesn't that suggest what he found was not to his liking?"

"Good point."

"And you will have done the only thing you were asked to do. To fulfil a promise to a friend. You can't be held responsible for the outcome."

He nodded. "So," he leaned towards her across the table, "have you decided?"

"Yes. I'll help you. But, I think I'd like to meet this American, as the first step."

Bob rubbed his chin. "I can try to set up a meeting with him. Don't expect anything good to come of it."

"I'm quite capable of making up my own mind, thanks. How soon can you arrange it?"

"Couple of days, probably. I don't think he's gone back to the States. Cardiff OK for you?"

"Fine. But not tomorrow. We have a Maze meeting and I'm going to explain to my colleagues why I want to take on this case. It's not what we usually do. It should be an heir-hunter thing. But I want to help. They'll understand." She said this firmly, to herself as much as to him.

46

A waitress approached them with two plates of food. She saw Bob look quizzically at the second plate.

"It's for Alice, my daughter. She's wandering around the museum. I'd better go find her. I told her only ten minutes."

As Maggie stood up, Alice appeared in the doorway and raised an eyebrow at Bob. Maggie reached out and put an arm around Alice's waist. "This is a new colleague, Bob. He and I are going to work together on a case." Alice was sufficiently reassured to sit down next to Maggie.

"What have you been doing?" Maggie asked her. "You've been away a while."

"I met a boy upstairs. He's called Tommy. His sister is coming to get him."

"Will she be long? Should we offer to stay until she comes?"

"No, I think he's OK," Alice replied. "He said he's expecting her very soon."

"I'll have to go in a minute," Bob interrupted. "What made you chose this place, by the way?"

"I'm attracted to this building," Maggie replied. "Always have been. It's a very comfortable place to be. Although, once it frightened me."

"If you'd like to know something about the history I can introduce you to the manager," Bob said. "I know them here." Without waiting for her reply, he called the waitress over.

"Is Stella here today?" he asked.

"She's upstairs, doing some paperwork," the girl responded. "Shall I call her down for you?"

He nodded and the girl headed out of the café towards the staircase.

"She'll be thrilled that you're interested," he said to Maggie. "She had lots of curious tales to tell. And some cracking ghost stories." He winked at Alice, but was surprised that neither she nor Maggie showed any enthusiasm.

Then he remembered. "Oops, sorry. I forgot why we

47

know each other." He stood up abruptly. "I have to go. I'll let you know about the meet in Cardiff."

He strode to the entrance, but stopped and turned back in the doorway. "But they are very good stories." And, with a chuckle, he left the café.

12

Newport, South Wales
2017

Since speaking to Nick, Zelah felt better, felt that things could get back to how they were before. She started on the research for Morgan Sturridge and sat down in front of her laptop.

From what he had told her, Zelah knew that Morgan was born in Canada in 1965. She had been surprised when he told her, as that made him around fifty years old; she would have put him at no more than mid-thirties. *Wearing well,* she thought. *Must have had a good life.*

He had told her his parents were John Sturridge and Maria Hammill. His father, he knew, was an orphan, the only son of a James Sturridge, a bank manager who had been killed with his wife in a freak accident leaving their only child, John, to be brought up in an orphanage.

Morgan had told Zelah that he had researched his father's ancestry and was happy with it. It was his mother's side that he wanted to pursue. So, she began by looking at Canadian records and quickly found the birth of Maria Hammill to John Morgan Hammill and Maria Hammill, née McKay in Nova Scotia in 1937. So far, so good. Then she found the marriage of John Hammill and Maria McKay, again in Nova Scotia, in 1936. From there she found that John Hammill, whose middle name was Morgan, was the son of another John Hammill. This final one, or first in line depending on which way you looked at it, had married Abigail Parry in 1885. He was forty years old when he married. The marriage confirmed that he was born in Monmouthshire, England. Funny. She thought Morgan Sturridge had said that his ancestors might have come from Glamorgan. Another example of why you shouldn't take anything a client said for granted.

This would mean that John Hammill was the ancestor who was born in South Wales and taken to Canada as a small child.

She puzzled for a few moments. Why hadn't Morgan Sturridge been able to find this out himself? It had been too easy. All she had to do now was to locate the birth of John Hammill in South Wales, probably Monmouthshire, somewhere around 1845. It wasn't a typical Welsh name so it shouldn't be too difficult to find. Of course, it didn't help that John Morgan Hammill was the first John Hammill's only surviving child. There had been five sisters, but all had died at birth or in childhood, so no chance of looking further out at other family lines.

Three hours later, in a fit of frustration, Zelah slammed down the laptop cover and marched into the kitchen.

She had searched throughout the country, on many name variations, and ever-increasing time periods, and had come up with only three possible Hammills – all women and none of them in Wales. This was why Morgan Sturridge had come to Maze. He too had probably got this far, but no further.

"Well, it would have saved me a morning if he'd just said so," she muttered as she slammed the kettle down on the kitchen top. "Idiot."

What next? As Zelah calmed down she thought through her next steps. There were plenty of possibilities. She could check passenger emigration lists to find the Hammills on a passage from the UK to Canada. She could also check public ancestry boards, to see if anyone else was looking for the same family. It might have been that John Hammill Junior served in the Canadian armed forces in World War One. There was a lot of Canadian information available online. She could also get in touch with a genealogy researcher that she knew of in Nova Scotia.

But this was all the time she could give this case today. She had three stories to write up and they were due imminently.

She took her coffee and went back to the laptop.

* * *

Maggie and Alice had just started to eat their lunch when a woman arrived and the waitress pointed her in their direction.

"Hi, I'm Stella Bell," she said as she walked over to their table. "I look after the manor. I was told Bob was here?"

"He had to go," Maggie replied. "But do take a seat."

The woman took the seat Bob had vacated. She was around Maggie's age, tall, slim, and well made-up.

"How can I help you?"

Maggie put down her cutlery, as Alice leaned over and shovelled salad from her plate onto Maggie's.

"I'm not really sure if you can," Maggie replied. "I'm about to help Bob with some research, family history stuff, and I mentioned that I liked this place. I grew up just up the road and I've always liked the building. He said he would introduce me. How do you know Bob?"

"He's helped us out a few times, with some petty damage and break-ins. He knows the local suspects," Stella grinned. Her smile turned to a questioning look. "Is this by any chance about Jerry Allen?"

"The research, yes." Maggie confirmed. "But I also have an interest in the manor. A friend of mine does, too. Although he is a bit wary of the place. I'm not sure why. Bob said that you have some good ghost stories?"

"We certainly do! But I'd really like to hear about what you're doing for Jerry. I used to take my pets to him when I was a little girl. I heard he died before Christmas. He was a lovely man. A bit odd, but kids liked him. He didn't talk down to us." She nodded at Alice, who emphatically nodded back. "Bob told me that something in Jerry's past needed resolution."

"He had an interesting past, with an unresolved mystery. I'm going to try to help Bob solve it. Bob promised Jerry before he died."

Stella clapped her hands and sat back. "I know you!" she exclaimed. "You're Maze Investigations. You're Maggie Gilbert, yes?"

Maggie reddened and nodded. She still couldn't get used to this.

"I loved that thing you did about the Dickens' characters at Christmas. You were really good. Are you going to do more TV?"

"Good question," Maggie replied. "I'm not sure yet. But anyway, looks like Bob and I will be working together."

"Good stuff. So, what can I tell you about the manor? It has an interesting history."

"I know a bit of it," Maggie said. "But I'm really more interested for my friend. His name is Nick Howell."

"How do you spell that?"

"H-o-w-e-l-l" Maggie replied. "Is that important?"

"The original family to own the manor, as far as we can trace, was called 'Hywel'"; she spelled it out. "But the name did change over the years. They started off successfully around 1680. But about a hundred years later there was a tragedy. The manor's original owner was Morgan Hywel. He had a son and three daughters; but his son died young, so he wanted to leave the manor to his eldest, Morgana, who was about to be married. But they were both drowned on the same day. Morgan Hywel's body was eventually recovered, but not his daughter's. The manor passed to his brother, Gwyllim Hywel and down through his line. But they didn't manage the property well. We don't really know why, but a lot of the successors died young and as time went on the property deteriorated, until the last Hywel – who by then was a 'H-o-w-e-l-l' abandoned it, around 1875. It was eventually sold to pay off his debts. The new owners took better care of it, but it wasn't the gentleman's manor house it had been. It was downgraded to a farm."

"I think I know the story after that," Maggie intervened. "Are any of your stories related to the Hywel family?"

"Loads," Stella responded with a smile. "Finish your lunch, and I'll give you a tour, if you'd like."

"I'd love it," Maggie enthused. "Can my daughter come, too?"

"Off course. Let one of the girls know when you're done eating and I'll come down for you." She stood up and started to walk off. "Enjoy your lunch," she added. "We're very proud of our catering here."

As soon as they finished, Maggie and Alice found Stella and they were escorted around the ground floor museum. Stella was in her element describing the rooms, how they would have been set up in the manner of the seventeenth- and eighteenth-century manor. Maggie was pleased to see inside a small room off the parlour the remains of a turret staircase, apparently leading nowhere. A reminder of the story she had been told as a girl.

"We don't know where it went," Stella replied to her question. "We think there might have been a cellar here once, but there's no sign of it now. We think it probably collapsed and was filled in. And the staircase led down from above to this floor, then into the cellar. But it's a mystery. You can see that the top of the staircase isn't level with the floor. Perhaps something you can look into?" she asked in a mock-hopeful tone.

"Buildings aren't really our thing," Maggie replied. "But I agree, it's intriguing." She moved away from the small, enclosed space. Standing inside she had felt an uneasy shiver. Perhaps that was what she remembered from the past.

Out in the entrance hallway Stella led them up the

wooden staircase that divided right and left, and turned left into a large chamber. This was, she explained, the Great Chamber, part of the original Tudor building. After Maggie had looked around, they descended the four steps to the platform and took four steps now ahead of them, up again into another, bigger room.

"This is the Tudor Hall," Stella explained, sweeping an arm around the impressive space. "We think it was once divided into bedrooms."

Maggie gazed around, fascinated. As well as an impressively large carved stone Tudor fireplace, there was a blocked-up door on the back wall, and all of the windows were very small. She asked Stella about these.

"We think there was once another floor above this one. There's another floor on the other side of the building, but not here. The door might have led to a staircase. The windows date from the Civil War. Dangerous times, so they were defensive, not decorative."

Maggie nodded. "I guess you don't have enough written history to be sure."

"Let's go this way," Stella said, leading them to an open doorway close one of the front windows. Through the doorway, she turned left and walked down three steps into a bedroom.

"Here's the site of one of our stories," she said with a gleam in her eye. "The bedroom of Dewi Tomos Hywel. He was the only son of Morgan Hywel, the one I told you about downstairs. He died when he was eight years old. Another accident… apparently." She gave them a knowing look. "After the deaths of Dewi's father Hywel and sister Morgana, the new master, Gwyllim, Hywel's brother, turned his sister-in-law and her remaining daughters out of the manor. People who have spent time here say that the boy is still here, in this room, watching his mother leave and calling out to her."

Maggie and Alice peered into the small, neat room with its embroidered bedcover and window hangings.

"Well, he's not here now," Alice said. Maggie frowned, but Stella laughed. "No, he's not and personally, I'm not a believer, although I like a good story. Let's carry on."

She led them out of the room, back up the three stairs and along a narrow corridor. At the end she turned to yet another staircase. "Upstairs are the old servant's quarters and a small room that we use as an office. It's the oldest part of the manor."

At the top of the short flight of bare wooden stairs that leaned over to the left, they found themselves at the corner of two passageways, one they could see was leading to a landing with rooms off it, but the other was a short, narrow, low passage leading to a wide, heavy, dark wooden door, which was closed.

"That door," Stella pointed out, "is the oldest artefact in the manor, we believe. Probably sixteenth century and part of the very first building." She went to turn back to the landing, but Maggie asked, "Can we go into the room?"

For a second Stella was hesitant. But then she said, "Yes, of course, why not?" She stopped, took a deep breath, and opened the door the way you might when you were concerned about what might be behind it. This heightened Maggie's anticipation but she was disappointed when she saw that it contained nothing more than a desk covered in papers, a computer chair and a filing cabinet. Pushed into the corner opposite the door, against two of the sloping walls, was an antique chair with ornately carved arms and a seat covered in ancient fabric.

"That looks old," Maggie said, walking past Stella into the office and to the chair. She was so focussed on the chair that she jumped in surprise when Stella shouted, "Don't touch that!"

Maggie quickly withdrew her outstretched hand. "Another story?" She looked quizzically at Stella.

"We call it the psychopath chair," Stella said in a low voice. "We do use this room as an office for community groups, but not many people like to work in here."

Glancing round, Maggie could see that there was a single window, high up in the wall that faced the door and, she guessed, looked out over the front of the building. It was above the height of the tallest of human heads. The only other light was artificial, giving the room a gloomy feel.

"It's a bit depressing," she agreed. "But what's the problem with the chair?"

"It moves," Stella whispered. "We don't touch it now, but we found it in an attic room when we first moved in. It was separate from the other furniture. Apparently, the last inhabitants and the museum trust had a problem with it. When they closed the building they moved it up to the attic and stacked it up. But we found it on the other side of the room. When we put it in this office, no matter where it was at the end of a day, it was always back in that corner the next morning."

She shrugged at Maggie. "I love this building and I've never had any funny experiences here, even when I'm working on my own at night. The staff have lots of the usual stories about grey ladies and moaning sounds. All a bit convenient for an old house, if you ask me. But that chair... I don't know."

Maggie glanced at Alice, who remained silent in the doorway. She saw nothing to be alarmed about.

"But it's OK, you didn't touch it," Stella added. "Let's get on."

She showed them around the remaining attic rooms, low-beamed and brightly lit that were being used as storage for the café, then took them back downstairs.

"We need to get home," Maggie said when they were in the entrance porch. "But this has been great. Thank you so much."

"My pleasure," Stella replied. "Tell your friend that if he wants to get in touch, we'll be happy to show him around too. And give my regards to Bob. Good luck with your research."

"Let's go," Maggie said to Alice. "Time to get back to work for me. And you've got some homework to finish tonight."

As they walked down the path towards the car, Alice asked her mother, "Why didn't you tell her you touched it?"

"How do you know I did? You were behind me. You didn't see my hands."

"You touched it," Alice said, matter-of-factly.

Maggie grinned at her. "Yep, I did. No big deal."

She turned to open the car door, so Alice couldn't see her grin turn to a troubled expression. She was wondering what she had brought upon herself, but she wasn't going to tell Alice that she had, for a fleeting second, felt beneath her hand, the cold skin and bones of another hand, gripping the chair's arm so tightly that the skin and flesh was stretched.

13

Cwmbran, South Wales
2017

When they returned home they could hear the music booming from the back of the house.

"We'll have to put up with it for a little while," Maggie said to a scowling Alice. "I can't just throw them all out. Not for a couple of hours, anyway."

"Can I go to Janine's house?" Alice asked. "I can see if she's finished her homework. If not, we can do it together."

"OK, let's call her mum."

Janine's mother was happy to have Alice for the afternoon. "It might cheer Janine up," she told Maggie. "She's not looking forward to tomorrow."

In the car, Maggie asked Alice what was the problem. Janine had been such a happy girl in junior school.

"There are a couple of spiteful bitches in her class

56

picking on her. They sit either side of her and push her about."

"Has her mother talked to the school about it? And mind the language, please."

Alice shrugged in response to the rebuke and answered Maggie's question, "She tried. Just made it worse. They put Janine at the side of the class on a desk on her own. Now she doesn't have anyone to talk to, or work with."

At Janine's house, once the girls had gone off together, Maggie asked Janine's mother what was going on.

"The school doesn't really care," she replied. Her shoulders were hunched and she looked deflated. "They talk about zero tolerance of bullying, but when it comes to doing anything about it, they treat you like you're a nuisance. Janine is trying to deal with it herself. But those girls are not nice."

"Let me know if there's anything I can do," Maggie said. "I've noticed that Alice has been quieter since going there too. Jack seems to manage. I might talk to him about it, later." She paused. "But it's hard for kids who don't want to have to fight everyone and everything, just to get by."

"Janine can't," her mother said. "It's not in her. I'll be honest with you. I'm worried about her."

Maggie squeezed her arm. "As I said, let me know if there's anything I can do."

"Alice is her only friend right now. The others won't go near her while this is going on." She was close to tears.

"Alice is going to stay her friend," said Maggie. "She won't be put off. And if anyone tries it on with her, I'll be up there!"

"Watch out for the head if you do," Janine's mother replied. "Bullying starts at the top in that school."

* * *

At home, Maggie closed the office door, put on noise-cancelling headphones, gritted her teeth, and got on with her research. If she was going to go to Spain she needed to get a lot done in the next week.

After a couple of hours, she had made good progress, confirmed a visit to the Cheshire archives in Chester, and written up another level of the chart she was working on.

By six o'clock she'd had enough – of research and the booming background beat. As she shut off her computer the noise stopped abruptly and Jack appeared, to say that his friends were leaving. She smiled through pursed lips and went to the door, expecting to be bowled over by a bunch of savages. What she found was a group of lads, putting their shoes on, and politely saying thanks to her for putting up with them.

"No problem at all," she smiled at them, as she waved them off. She turned to Jack. "Surprising, son. I expected to be clearing up a load of mess."

"Teenagers don't all conform to your stereotype," he said loftily, turned, and went back up the stairs.

Well, that put me in my place, she thought. *But at least I should be able to trust him when I have to go away.*

That evening, over dinner, Maggie asked Jack about the atmosphere in the school. She wasn't surprised when he confirmed what Janine's mother had been saying.

"Survival of the fittest. You have to let people know as soon as you get there that you aren't to be messed with."

"What if you are to be messed with?"

He ran a finger across his throat.

Maggie decided not to comment further, as Alice was looking stricken. She changed the subject.

"I may have to go away for a few days, on a work project, probably next week. Do either of you mind?"

Jack shook his head, but Alice asked the inevitable: "Does that mean Aunty Fee?"

"Yes," Maggie reluctantly confirmed, "but it's only for a couple of days. I'll see if she'll come and sleep here. Would that be better?"

Alice nodded, but with a tragic expression.

"What's the project?" Jack asked.

Maggie told them about Jerry Allen and the Spanish Civil War.

58

"Sounds interesting," Jack commented. "What if you can't find the descendants? And what if there's more than one?"

"We might not," she agreed, "but Bob wants to try. And I'm going to help. I can't guarantee anything, but he knows that. And if there's more than one, there will be a way of working out how to share."

"Why can't Nick come and stay here?" Alice asked. "He can work from the office."

"I'm not ready for that, yet. And I don't think he is, either. He still doesn't use the key I gave him or come in if I'm not here. But I can ask him to call in, if you'd like?"

Alice nodded. Then she took herself upstairs. An hour later, Maggie went up to Alice's room, to find her video messaging with Janine.

"Time to pack up," Maggie said. "Get your things ready for tomorrow."

As Alice signed off Maggie sat on the bed. "How do you feel about going back to school tomorrow?"

"Alright, I suppose. But I don't like it much."

Maggie was shocked. "You've never said."

"You didn't ask," came the reply. "You ask about homework and stuff, but you've never asked me if I *like* it there." Alice sighed. "It's alright. I'll cope."

"What don't you like about it?"

The reply was immediate. "Everything. You have to be 'one of them'. You mustn't stand out. So, I can't put my hand up to answer questions, even when I know the answer, which I always do, because they make fun of you. You just have to keep your head down."

"But the school gets excellent exam results," Maggie said. "They must be teaching well."

Alice shrugged.

Downstairs, Maggie sat for a long time, pondering. Had she once again ignored obvious signs because she had become so fixed on her work? Life was never straightforward.

14

Catalonia, Spain
1939

There is a golden moment on first waking, in half sleep, a place where there is no memory, only sensation. With her eyes still closed, Lola felt the warmth of the sun, the warmth of her body and the warmth of her happiness. But, as she grew to full consciousness, it fell away. Then came despondency, as memory bubbled in her gut, worked its way up to thick bile in her throat.

Bite on it. Push it back. Determination. Get through the day. A day at a time. That was the way. Just one day. I can do it. Again.

Background noises; shouting, screaming, abusive, vitriol. Other women waking around her; moaning, crying. *I will not cry.*

She had been dreaming, of course. Of Jeremy. Their baby. Together and happy. In a world they had made fit for themselves and the people. Warmth and love. How had it all gone so wrong? And where was Jeremy now? She knew – no, she felt – that he was still alive. Not far away. Once she got away she would find him. He would take them all to Wales. Another precious second to remember happiness. She stroked her stomach and felt responding tiny movements.

But she had taken too long. A rough hand dragged her from the bed onto the floor, kicked her in the back where the bruises wouldn't be seen.

"Get up, filthy bitch! Stand."

She stood. The hand slapped her hard across the face. Her ears rang. She wobbled. *Keep your eyes down. Shoulders down. Deferential. She'll move on.*

This time, she was lucky. Better prey further down the line. One who couldn't stand. She risked a glance. Saw the profile, the eye gleaming with the prospect of pain, the rictus of suppressed excitement. Taking the girl by the arm, dragging her up, punching her repeatedly until she fell back onto the bed.

"Get up, filthy bitch! Stand. Stand, I said." But the girl curled up on the bed in the foetal position, to protect her baby and herself. Not possible, Lola knew. No direct violence to the baby, of course. They needed the baby. But the mother? Expendable. The black-clad arm dragged the girl to the floor, then to an upright position.

"Any of you want to help her?" It was an invitation to get the same. No one moved, just looked at the floor. The was girl thrown back onto the bed. "Ready for work roster in five minutes. Don't be late."

Lola's eyes quickly returned to the floor as the figure swept past her. Relief. Then it paused, turned, and walked right up to her. Inches from her face.

"You, whore, you took up with the foreign invader. He'll be dead by now. Or somewhere where he's learning to understand his sins." The words spat out, then another slap. Lola knew she shouldn't but she couldn't help herself. She looked up. Defiance. Lola saw the maniacal light in her eyes.

"Yes, Sister Angeles. You know best," said with contempt that she couldn't disguise. This would earn her another beating, but she could bear that. The wimpled head nodded in agreement. Then the nun turned abruptly and walked out of the dormitory.

The other women said nothing. They didn't look at her. Didn't want to be associated with her today. Got on with their bed-making.

Lola picked up her blanket and folded it. Not looking, not speaking. She knew what was coming. But she could bear it. *Just get through today. Don't think about tomorrow. I am alive. It is enough.*

15

Sunk into the front passenger seat of Bob Pugh's opulent, sleek, black Jaguar staring out of the window, Maggie knew that he was becoming increasingly irritated with her lack of response. On their way to the hotel in Cardiff Bay he had done most of the talking and hadn't seemed to notice how quiet she was. Probably assuming she was taking in what he was saying about the meeting they were about to have with the American, Mason Haussmann. It turned out that he was Jerry Allen's nephew, the son of Jerry's father's sister who had gone to the States after the war.

As soon as they left the hotel Bob had begun to talk, at first an angry rant, then settling down to a dissection and a destruction of each argument that Haussmann and his lawyer had put forward in support of their view that Jerry Allen's Spanish family simply did not exist. But now he had run out of anything to say, and noticed that she hadn't responded at all.

He abruptly turned the steering wheel hard left and pulled into a pub car park. Maggie didn't react.

"I'll book the tickets, shall I?" he asked. "We'll go via Jakarta and Timbuktu. Should be an interesting journey."

"I would have thought Madrid, if we have to go via anywhere. Although straight to Barcelona is probably best," she said.

"You have been listening, then? I thought you'd lost interest and hadn't wanted to tell me."

"Of course," she replied. "And I'm sorry. It's not been a good couple of days."

Glancing at him, she thought he was about to say something sarcastic. But the sun caught her face as she turned and he must have caught a glint of moisture underneath her eyelids.

"Oh. Let's talk. But inside. Nice fire in this pub."

Maggie nodded. She knew the pub. It wasn't far from the company headquarters at which she had first accepted, then reneged on, a job last year. She had made the decision to join Zelah and Nick, and Maze Investigations was born instead. A decision whose wisdom she was doubting for the first time.

The snow was slushy on the ground, but melting fast. It had been so attractive over the Christmas holiday, but now it had lost its magic, had become dirty and a nuisance.

Inside, the pub was cosy and inviting, with a big log fire blazing in a two-way hearth in the centre of the room. They chose a couple of armchairs with a small table in-between. Bob went to the counter to buy hot drinks and Maggie tried to push from her mind the abysmal altercation that had taken place the previous day when she had told Zelah and Nick about the Spanish case, trying not to think about what had been said to her, and the shameful words she had spat back in return. Her face prickled hot as the memory refused to be deleted.

Bob returned with two cups of hot chocolate and put them on the table as he sat down in the chair opposite Maggie.

"So, what did you think of him?"

"He's lying," she replied, staring into the fire. "All that posturing and threatening, but he kept glancing at his lawyer too often. I saw a lot of that in my previous profession. It put me in front of a lot of liars. But you must know that."

"Knew it the first time I met him. It's like a smell, is lying."

"And I know about bad smells," she continued as he looked at her questioningly. "It's what first alerted me to Eira Probert's presence, and you still haven't told me the rest of your story. I think it's time."

"OK, fair enough," he acknowledged. "Do you want some lunch, by the way?"

"Are you avoiding telling me? This is the third time

that I've asked you to tell me and you've either left or used some kind of distraction."

He didn't speak. Now, it was Bob's turn to stare into the fire. Maggie waited.

"Yes," he conceded. "I *am* avoiding talking about it. Don't know why really. I think..." he paused, still not looking at her. "It makes me uneasy... I never believed in anything, see, not anything I couldn't explain. Then I heard your story, which, you will recall, I dismissed as the ravings of a mad woman. Then I found that you weren't mad; and the same thing had infected my family."

He sat forward, held his hands towards the fire and rubbed them together. He turned back to her. "How did you deal with it, when you found out what it was?"

"Depends on what you mean by 'deal with it'," she replied. "I've never tried to explain it to myself or anyone else. I just accept that I don't understand it, and leave it at that. If anything happens, well I deal with the consequences."

"Are you ever frightened?"

"No, emphatically not," she replied. "If I fear it, it wins. It's not difficult, you know. Yes, the universe has shifted, the ground under your feet isn't the same, so you adjust your thinking around it. But if you can't, then I think you'll be in trouble. So, tell me the story."

He nodded his head in a gesture of resolution. "At the funeral, my cousin told me about Robert Pugh. Stories passed down from my great-grandmother. He was the minister over at the Two Locks, just up the road from you. He'd been sent there to take over from a man called Robinson, or so he thought. When he checked later, no one in the ministry knew anything about it. Anyway, seems he was a sycophant. Loved being praised. Some obliged, some didn't. Your great-grandfather was one who didn't. Seems he told the truth, as he saw it. Robert Pugh didn't like that. Pugh was an easily manipulated man. And the schoolteacher who arrived just after him understood him just right. His story was that John Jones's daughter disappeared because she was a bad girl from a bad family. Probert encouraged it. Things started to go wrong. Stuff happened that didn't add up."

"Like what?" Maggie was excited. This was the other side of the story, at last. She knew the basic facts, but none of the detail as to why it happened. The last few missing pieces of the jigsaw. The human side.

"Well, the teacher said that Pugh had appointed her, but he hadn't. He had no idea who she was or where she was from. But he never contradicted her, because he didn't want to look stupid." He paused for a moment. "I'm interpreting some of this, you know. I've taken the story and put a spin on it, based on what my cousin told me."

"You're a policeman," Maggie countered. "Your job is to read between the lines, make sense of things. Get to the truth. But every story is told with a bias."

"Yes. So, when the girl went missing, Pugh wouldn't encourage help. Bastard. The teacher told him he was quite right. But then he found out that she herself had been looking for the girl. Next, he found out that she had lied about being at his house, using him as an alibi. And then he saw something, according to my cousin, something that affected the rest of his life, probably cut it short."

"He saw what I saw," Maggie interrupted. "He saw her disintegrate, fall apart in a stinking sulphuric slime."

"You saw that? Really?"

"As did my daughter," she said quietly.

"Fuck. That's why you didn't want to speak to me or do anything."

They were both silent for a moment.

"And you really aren't afraid? That she might come back, try again?"

"I don't think she can," Maggie mused. "We beat her, this time. But I don't know what she is or what she can do. So, I wait and watch. But, no, I'm not afraid. I believe that's how I keep her away. Fear seems to energise her, so I don't allow her any. Think about it, Bob, your boss must have seen something similar."

She could see he was far away inside his head, searching for an answer, which she knew he wouldn't find.

"What's it like?" he asked.

"Strange question," Maggie replied. She paused for a moment, to think of how to respond to this. She hadn't really thought about it in depth, that wasn't her way. But here was someone who needed to know more, who needed something tangible.

"I know she hasn't gone away and I don't know how to make her go away forever. I suppose it's like there's something out there, malignantly toying with you. Waiting for its opportunity. So, I stay vigilant. But I never, ever obsess about her. That's the route to paranoia, I think."

"Like a stalker," he mused.

Maggie felt it was time to change the subject. She didn't want to spend any more time thinking about this. Too many other things to obsess about right now.

"So, Bob. Here's what we know. Your great-great-grandfather knew something that might have helped find a missing child. I say 'might', we'll never really know. Instead of sharing this information, he kept it to himself and ran away. But he couldn't rid himself of the memory and, eventually, it caused his death."

"Fucking bastard," he said, loudly enough for people at nearby tables to glance quickly in their direction. Then, in a quieter voice, he said, "And that's not all. She was at his funeral. And she was at your great-grandfather's."

"How do you know that?" she blurted out.

"Because she visited my great-grandmother. They exchanged some information."

So, Maggie thought, *that's how Ruth came to know, why she tried to warn us all.*

"She didn't win," she added, and he looked quizzically at her. "My great-grandmother's daughter, Alice, didn't die. She found a new home. In her attempt to escape she suffered catastrophic injuries and lost her memory. She thought she was the niece of the housekeeper at Knyghton House. And she was happy there. Became the housekeeper

66

herself, in time. Married one of the footmen. But eventually she remembered and knew her original self and was reunited with her mother."

"Good," he kept his voice lower. "But, what can *she* do, really?"

"*She* can't do anything to you, not now that you know about her. You seem like a strong man, Bob. Yes, you've been shaken by this. The world isn't what we think it is and this is difficult knowledge to absorb. But, I think you'll be OK. My advice: just go with it."

They were conversing so intensely with each other that the arrival of a waitress with plates of food was a welcome distraction, until Maggie said, "I didn't order anything."

"I did," Bob said. "I thought it would help us to concentrate; focus on what we need to do next."

"Is this a steak sandwich?" It looked very appetising, but she couldn't help herself. "Vegetarian," she said, and pushed the plate away, and immediately felt guilty at his panicked look "OK, not really. But you should have asked. I might have been."

"You're an awkward bugger," he flashed back, picking up his sandwich and shoving it angrily into his mouth. The gravy from the steak dripped down his chin and he didn't stop to remove it.

"Yes, I am. Now, what comes next? You said something in the car about booking flights?"

Throughout the rest of lunch, they discussed timetables, agreed that they would need five days to make arrangements, and started a tentative plan on how they would go about their search in Spain. Maggie offered to look for hotels, but Bob said that they should stay in his apartment on the coast.

"It's only about an hour's drive from the Ebro. It has two bedrooms with en suite bathrooms. And it's on the seafront."

"It's January," Maggie countered, "and this isn't a holiday."

"Agreed. But we should use it anyway. Keep the costs

down. Which we haven't discussed. I'm paying for the flights and meals in Spain. Unless you want to have another argument?"

"No," she threw him a grin, "that suits me. At least I can tell my colleagues it isn't costing the company."

"Problem?" he asked, sensing something tentative in her tone.

She shook her head, hoping he would not push it.

"Time to go." She stood up. "I have arrangements to make, as do you."

They sat in silence as he drove her home. Maggie could see Bob's lips moving, asking internal questions as he drove, probably working on the plan.

She became pre-occupied once again with the disastrous meeting with Zelah and Nick, wondering if things stood any chance of being put right, or was this the end of Maze Investigations?

16

Newport, South Wales
2017

Zelah was feeling panic in a way that she hadn't felt for many years. Despite her best endeavours, she had found out nothing further about the origins of Morgan Sturridge's mother. She was beginning to get suspicious. She knew that she was a good, no, an excellent, genealogist. But she had rarely come up against a brick wall like this.

She gazed out of her kitchen window, at a hazy Channel. What next? She had taken his money, got him to sign a contract. Guaranteed him success. But she had found... nothing.

Maybe, it was the result of the sleepless night she had endured. The terrible row with Maggie unnerved her. A feeling she was not used to. Zelah Fitzgerald – the woman who always got her own way. Always knew what she was doing. Always succeeded. But not this time. And the way they had parted! She realised that she was also feeling frightened. Something she hadn't experienced since childhood.

It was time… to step back and think things through. To try to look at the world from someone else's perspective. She smiled ironically at the thought. She believed she had achieved that, but her reaction to Maggie's news about the Spanish project had revealed the old, cantankerous, bossy, angry, Zelah. The person she didn't want to be any more. The part of her that her deceased husband Martin had disliked. That thought brought her up sharply. Maggie had said she was a harridan, a selfish bitch. Terrible words. But now that the anger had died down, could there have been truth in those words?

Of course, she saw from Maggie's expression that as soon as the words were out of her mouth she had regretted them. But they couldn't be taken back. Only forgiven. The old Zelah would never had considered forgiving or speaking again to the person who had said such things, called her such names. But the new Zelah? Well, yes, she was a different person. It had taken the sleepless night after the showdown to bring her to the realisation that she had played her usual part in provoking the row, and that there was *joint* responsibility to make it right. Humility. Another new sentiment.

She wasn't going to be able to solve this Morgan Sturridge mystery alone. With neither reluctance, nor forethought, Zelah picked up the phone.

* * *

When Bob dropped Maggie at her house, she was unsurprised to find Nick sitting in his van. Wordlessly, she opened the front door and he followed her into the kitchen, where she put the kettle on and waited in silence for it to boil, her back to him. But she couldn't keep it up.

"So, Nick, where do you stand, in this mess?"

69

He didn't answer and she turned round.

"That's better," he replied. "I can't talk to your back."

Maggie held back a smile. One of Nick's quirks was being unable to look at the person he was talking to, often appearing to be talking to a wall or the furniture.

"Where am I? Difficult to say. Somewhere between the two of you, I think. Although, last night I thought we were looking at the end of Maze. A short, sweet venture, but doomed to failure because two hard-nosed women couldn't listen to each other's point of view." He held up a hand to stall her protest and went on. "But this morning, and I've spoken to Zelah already, I think we can retrieve this... this mess. She wants to, if you do."

"I didn't expect that. But she can't have it all her own way, all of the time. She just didn't listen to what I was saying, how I was trying to explain."

"You asked me where I stand. I can see both sides. In part I agree with Zelah. Don't pout at me! We're running a business. I agree that the Spanish case is fascinating, and yes, compelling. We all agreed to keep away from heir-hunting. You agreed to it. But there's no money in it. I know there's no out-of-pocket costs, but there is the cost of you being away and unable to do paying work."

"It wasn't quite like that. I did try to explain."

"You had made up your mind," Nick said, firmly for him. "And on top of your news about your TV offer, an impartial observer might think that that you're the one going off to do your own thing."

Maggie turned back to make the drinks. She was stunned by Nick's lack of support. She knew that she had been aggressive and rude, but she believed that she'd been right. Now she could see his point of view. She had accused Zelah of being selfish and domineering. But had her own behaviour provoked it? It looked like it might have done.

"So, what do we do now?" She wasn't going to admit her culpability just yet.

"I don't know, if you're asking me to stand between the two of you. It's up to you. But, you've both gone and landed Maze with a problem, because of your behaviour. Zelah went and signed up the new client, with a challenging time limit, with which she's now struggling. She needs help. And you're about to take off for Spain."

"I'm not... we aren't going until the end of next week. I have to make arrangements for the kids, and Bob Pugh has to arrange time off work. I can work until then."

"Actually, Zelah has decided that she's going to Nova Scotia. I'm going to pick up the research here, see what more, if anything, I can find out." He paused, sensing that now she was upset. "Maggie, you've had a lot going on. And... I could do with your help, but on a personal level, not with Maze."

She nodded, having turned back to the window again, so that he couldn't see her tears. But he knew they were there.

"Why don't you dry your eyes, and we can sit in the office and talk everything through."

She sniffed, nodded, and walked through, sitting at the head of the meeting table. Nick sat opposite her.

"Shall we start with your Spanish trip?"

"We'll be gone for about five or six days, I think. I'm leaving the flight bookings up to Bob. It's quick because the American is pushing his case at probate court. He was threatening when we met him this morning."

"Why? What's his motive?"

"We think he knows something he doesn't want us to find out. We did say we had some more information from Jeremy and that Bob has some new leads to follow up. He didn't like that, which made us suspicious."

"What's this man like?"

Maggie considered what she had seen earlier in the day. Her first impression of Mason Haussmann was that he was intimidating. But she quickly realised it was all show. Maggie had been pleased to get away from her corporate life, but it had given her plenty of experience of Americans like Haussmann and she had learned a great deal about what lay behind their corporate behaviour. She had wryly

71

thought, when she was working for them, that they must have had training sessions in bluff, bluster, bullying, and arrogance as part of their job preparation. They saw others in only two categories: ally or enemy.

Mason Haussmann was physically imposing. Around fifty, she guessed, and about six-feet tall, heavy-set, but not healthily so. She had thought he would likely run to fat and flab as soon as he ran out of energy. He already had signs of a paunch that he tried to suck in. He had thick, cropped, reddish hair that stuck up on top like a shaving brush, an outsized square face with cheeks that puffed out as if they had been artificially enticed to do so. A small, wet mouth. But his eyes were what had held her. They were lizard-like, hooded, a rheumy, pale blue.

"He was agitated," she replied. "He threatened us from the minute we walked into the room, even before we sat down. There was no attempt at discussion, never mind politeness. We were there to be dictated to. And he had his lawyer with him."

"Was he prepared to share anything you didn't already know? What did you get from it?"

Maggie considered. "Know your enemy? I can think more clearly when I have something to focus on. And no, he wouldn't give anything away. As I said, he just dictated to us. Didn't work with a policeman." She grinned, but Nick didn't react.

"What happens when you get to Spain?"

"We're going to visit the area where the battle of the Ebro took place. We know that Lola's village has gone, but, just before he died, Jerry gave Bob two names that he hadn't remembered previously. We're going to try to follow them up, see if we can get any leads on who they were and what part they might have played in Lola's story. And," she added, "I think Bob is getting in touch with a Spanish genealogist who's been involved in searching for lost children, who can hopefully give us a head start, or at least fill in some background."

Nick turned to look out of the window. "It's snowing

again. Jack and Alice are about to come in."

Maggie got up to go to the front door. She opened it to a blast of snow and quickly closed it again after the children were inside.

"More skiing this weekend?" Jack asked, his expression hopeful and he pumped the air and shouted "Yes!" when Maggie nodded.

"Can we bring Janine?" Alice asked. "She's never skied. I'd like to teach her."

"Of course, if her mother's willing, which I'm sure she will be."

Alice smiled, put her head round the office door to greet Nick, then went up to her room. *Probably to get Janine online to tell her the good news*, Maggie thought. Well, if they were happy, she was happy. She'd have to tell them more about the trip to Spain during the week, after she'd made the arrangement with her sister. But, for now, peace reigned and that was OK with her. She returned to the office. Nick was still staring out of the window.

"Do you have any thoughts about Spain? About what we're doing?" she asked.

"No," he replied. "It's your show. Let me know if there's anything I can do to help, but I'm mainly going to help Zelah with this Canadian problem."

"Can you tell me about it?" She asked tentatively. She was beginning to accept that her behaviour had sunk below an acceptable level. It also occurred to her that Nick had become more assertive, more confident. When did that happen? It was time to look at many things in a new light, from a more humble, insightful perspective.

"Zelah took on our new client, Morgan Sturridge, without talking to either of us about what he wanted from us. Now, we must find out what he wants to know. Problem is, and I think Zelah realises this now, he may not have been honest about what he wants. I suspect he may already know."

"So why has he come to us?"

"Well that's the question, isn't it?" he mused. "Zelah

found that she could quite easily trace his family to his great-grandfather, John Hammill. He's supposed to have been born around 1845 and arrived in Canada with his parents at the age of five, from South Wales. But there's no John Hammill born in South Wales in 1845. Only two girls with that surname in the whole of the UK." He stopped and stared out of the window again, at the driving snow.

"Not that long after civil registration," Maggie said. "Perhaps he wasn't registered?"

"I don't think so," Nick replied. "No baptism either."

"So, he got his age wrong? Widen the parameters?"

"It's the name," Nick responded, ignoring her obvious suggestion. "Too unusual. Bound to come up somewhere."

"How widely has she searched?" Maggie asked.

He turned back to her. "She's done everything. Used all her contacts. Even tried people in Canada. There's a lot of information available online in Canada. More than here. Free information, too. She's traced the line without any problem, but not the beginning. And he married late, to Abigail Morgan, in 1895 when he was forty. Zelah's traced the marriage certificate. It says he was born in Wales."

"OK, that is a mystery," Maggie replied. "But that's what we do. It must be why he came to us. He was having the same problem. He wants us to get around it. I can't see why you're so concerned. And you are concerned, Nick, aren't you?"

He nodded. "It's just not right. A feeling. Zelah got the impression that Sturridge's ancestors came from Glamorgan. But the certificate says Monmouthshire."

"Look, Nick, I'm just trying to be devil's advocate here. That's a mistake easily made. You know that we don't take anything a client says as accurate. We have to be sceptical, to check it all out. That's why we've succeeded. We're thorough. We check every fact, everything. What's so different about this?"

He was staring at her, wide-eyed, twitching. She recoiled. "What? What did I say? Why are you looking at me like that?"

74

He hesitated. He looked like he'd just had one of those nasty little electric shocks that come off a shopping trolley. "Nothing special. A moment of almost-insight. Not sure what it was. Can't grasp it." He shook his head, as if he was trying to shoo away an annoying insect. "I want to talk to you personally. About Alice, and about me."

"Yes," she replied. "I've been expecting you to. Shall we go into the sitting room?"

"No, not here. It's late and the kids are around. I want to be somewhere else. Somewhere neutral. I was thinking, Knyghton House? Tomorrow? I'm doing a stint of archiving there tomorrow."

"OK," she replied, "I can leave the kids here. They should be OK on their own for a couple of hours. What time?"

"Eleven. In the coffee house."

"Can you tell me anything now?

"No," he replied and stood up, put on his coat, and walked out of the office and the house, leaving Maggie to wonder all day what revelation Nick had to tell her.

17

Newport, South Wales
2017

On Saturday before breakfast, Zelah booked her flight to Halifax, Nova Scotia and found a hotel. She was leaving on Monday. This gave her another day to research, to see if there was anything she had missed. She knew there wasn't, but this was such a conundrum that she felt compelled go over it all again, anyway.

She had tried to call Morgan Sturridge the previous day, to let him know that she was going to Canada. But the hotel receptionist had told her that he had checked out a few days ago. Also that they were keeping his room available for him, as he was expecting to come back in the middle of the following week. That was when she realised that she had no mobile phone number for him. How could she have missed that?

Over breakfast, looking out through her picture windows at the snow-covered mountains, she thought again about the information he had given her, and what she had learned. Why had he told her that he hadn't been able to find anything, when the information in Canada was so readily available?

That was still annoying. But, the true problem lay with John Hammill and the marriage certificate that said he had been born in Monmouthshire, not Glamorgan. A mistake? Maybe for anyone else, but Sturridge was a clever man. He wouldn't have deliberately misinformed her. Would he? Had she been taken in by his smooth manner, his business savvy, his smart suit? Reluctantly, she realised that she might have been... and despised herself for it. Well, she could play him at his own game. She was going to go to Canada, to where he said his roots lay in Shelburne, Nova Scotia.

Don't think you can mess with me, Mr Morgan Sturridge. I'll find out what your game is. You asked us to do a job for you, and by God we are going to do it.

* * *

Maggie arrived early at Knyghton House on Saturday morning. Both Jack and Alice had been happy to stay in bed with computers, TV, and food.

She had given herself an hour to wander around the house. It had become one of her favourite places to visit, a place to which she felt a strong connection. This wasn't just because she and her sister Fiona had been at school there, during the days when the house had functioned as a private girls' school, but also because of the connection to her great-grandmother Ruth's story, of her missing child, Alice, who had become the housekeeper here. And the mystery that she and Zelah had solved, that had brought Eira Probert into her life and back into her family, but had also been the catalyst for setting up Maze Investigations.

She had last visited the house in mid-December, when it was festooned with Victorian-themed Christmas decorations. There had been hundreds of visitors enjoying the atmosphere, costumed guides, mulled wine and mince pies served in the kitchen and eaten in the medieval dining room, which had been her school canteen.

Now, as she wandered from room to room, she thought about Zelah, what she must be thinking at the moment. Nick had said that she was wanting to put things right. Well, if that meant Maggie picking up the phone, then she would do so. She had already decided that. What Nick had said had shocked her, but had made her look at herself with a critical eye. She concluded that she had changed, had settled, but that she might be about to do again what she had always done – react and run. Nick had asked her an interesting question the previous day: "Are you having fun?" to which she had immediately replied, "Of course." Then he asked, "So what's better about the new thing than the present thing?" She hadn't been able to answer.

She paused in the housekeeper's parlour, the former domain of Moira Davies, who had found a girl she believed to her niece and nursed her back to health with the aid of another of Maggie's great-grandmothers, the Irishwoman Honora Fitzgerald. She closed her eyes for a few moments, trying to feel the atmosphere when Moira Davies would have sat in the armchair in front of the fire, knowing that the girl she called Esme was probably not her niece, but deciding to continue the deception. Then she realised that an hour had passed and she was now late for her meeting with Nick. It was only a few minutes, but he would be fidgeting.

True to form, Nick was sitting at his usual window table in the coffee house, peering anxiously out of the window. He looked relieved when she walked in, bringing a gust of snow in with her. She waved to him, ordered a drink at the counter, then joined him at the table.

"I've been thinking," she said before he could start.

"I'm going to call Zelah to see if she wants to get together to talk before we both head off. I don't think it can do any harm, but then again, we are talking about Zelah. What do you think?"

"Worth a try," he said, gazing over her shoulder. "Are you going to explain?"

"Explain what, exactly?" Her tone was sharp.

"Why you're scared to stay in one place for too long?"

Maggie had raised her cup to her lips, but slowly lowered it to the table. Her instinctive reaction had been to refute what he'd said, give him a Jane Austen-style high-handed 'set down'. But she stopped herself. Nick was the most intuitive person she knew, and he was right. She sighed.

"I don't know if I can be that honest, yet. I'll see how it goes. Now what are you going to tell me?"

He was still gazing over her shoulder. "I have a lot to talk about. I've decided that I can't encourage you to speak about innermost feelings if I don't tell you about mine. About why I am like I am. So, I trust you enough now to hear what I have to say. If you want to ask a question," he added, "try not to. Not until I've finished."

He spoke slowly, measuring his words as if with a calibrated lexicon. "I'm different. You know that I'm quirky. I've spent most of my adult life doing my utmost not to connect with people. Not to form relationships. People usually avoid me. They do here." He glanced at the counter, where the waitress was watching them, but immediately looked away. He frowned and returned to the spot over Maggie's shoulder. "I don't know where to start on my story, but maybe… here."

He had been wearing driving gloves and had as usual taken off the right hand, but not the left. Now, he slowly pulled at each of the fingers of the left glove, in small tugs, releasing each finger from its prison. When the glove was on the table, Maggie saw that he had screwed up his hand, curled the fingers around into his palm. Again, very slowly, one by one, he uncurled them and held up his palm to her.

Maggie felt her pulse racing, knowing she was about to see something fundamental to understanding Nick. But was she saw caused her only puzzlement. In the centre of his palm was a jet-black circle, about three centimetres in diameter, perfectly formed. The black was so dense that it obliterated his palm lines. It could have been a burn, or a birthmark, she thought, except that it was too perfect. She looked up at him, waiting for an explanation.

"It's a curse," he said, "and I was born with it."

18

Newport, South Wales
2017

Maggie sat back and folded her arms. Said nothing, staring at Nick.

"You don't believe me?" Her expression and her lack of reaction surprised him. "What? Are *you* cynical now?"

He was still holding his hand towards her. Suddenly, she sat forward and firmly took hold of it; the movement was so fast that he had no time to stop her. She put her thumb firmly on the mark.

The look of horror on his face told her immediately that she had crossed a line. But that was what she had intended. If they were ever going to get to the bottom of what had happened in Nick's life, and move him on, shock tactics were needed; so she had gone with a gut reaction.

He yanked his hand out of her grasp and started to put his glove back on. Maggie could see that he was shaking. But still she said nothing. This was the moment of make or break. It was entirely in his hands, literally and metaphorically.

He pulled at each finger, tugging each one so hard that Maggie thought the next one was bound to break through the fabric. But he was slowing down. Taking deep breaths.

When the glove was in place, Nick put his hand on the table, palm down. He went to speak, but Maggie got in first.

"That's the second time in two days that someone has said '*don't touch*' and I've gone ahead anyway," said Maggie.

Now it was his turn to be surprised. And curious. "What else did you do?"

"It's to do with the manor. But, first, the time has come to talk. So, talk. That's why we're here, isn't it?"

Nick nodded, then they sat for several minutes whilst Maggie sipped at her drink. His eye movements said that he was mentally going through his story. Zelah would have been prodding him with a sharpened finger by now, but Maggie waited. She finished her drink and set the cup down, with a louder than necessary bang. Nick's head shot up.

"OK," he said. "There are three things to talk about. They are interlinked, so some of this won't make much sense."

"That doesn't matter," she said. "Just get it out. God, I can't believe I just said that. I'm turning into Zelah!"

"You could do with learning from each other. Anyway, here goes." He sat forward and rested both elbows on the table but still looked at a spot over her shoulder. A habit too hard to break yet.

"My parents didn't want me. My father died in a plane accident, before I was born. My mother made it very clear that he would have been horrified if he knew about me. Which he didn't. He died without knowing that I existed. I had an older brother and she adored him. He was enough for her. He died because of me. Don't interrupt." He didn't have to look at her to sense the uncomfortable signs emanating from Maggie. She folded her arms tightly and obediently sat back.

"When I was six, my brother and I were playing near a pond, sailing boats. We were pushing and shoving each other and we fell in. We both drowned. He didn't recover, but I did, if that's what it was. I didn't breathe for almost an hour. My mother was told I was dead. Two sons lost. Then, as I was being taken away in a plastic bag, I moved. Someone screamed and they undid the bag. I asked what had happened to me. My mother was told, 'One of your sons is still alive.' She asked which one. When she heard it was me, she banged her head on the ground. She screamed 'Not him!' From that day onwards she blamed me for John's death. She didn't abuse me, not physically anyway, but she isolated me. Rarely spoke to me. I think…" he paused for a few seconds. "I think that if it hadn't been for her all-consuming fear of what the neighbours would say about her, she would have put me into care. Because *she* didn't care. Not a bit."

Maggie had inched forward as he spoke, her expression altering from incredulity to horror, to pity. She wanted to take hold of his hand again, make some kind of gesture of compassion. But she could see that he was still immersed in his memories, so she waited for him to speak again.

"They let me out of hospital after two days. It seems I was unscathed. Or so I was told. But, I knew that I was somehow *different*. It wasn't the grief of being without a brother. I was grieving, of course. But something had happened to me. I was six and I didn't understand it. Everyone I looked at from then on crackled. That's what I called it at the time. Now, I know that I was seeing an energy field, each person's. Different in so many ways from person to person." Again, he stopped.

"Do you mean, like an aura?" Maggie couldn't help herself.

"That's a stupid word!" Nick glared unnervingly directly at her. "A fairground medium word. Fakers and charlatans talk about being able to see an 'aura'." He spat out the word with contempt.

"Sorry."

Realising that he had shouted, Nick rested his elbow

on the table, cupping his hand and shielding his brow. He closed his eyes.

"This is hard," he murmured. "But there's more you need to know."

"So, tell me."

"Alice has it too. She can see the 'crackle'. Call it whatever you want. She sees it. You didn't realise?"

Maggie slowly shook her head.

"She sees shades of colour," he went on. "Right now, she's worried about her friend Janine, who is apparently getting darker."

Maggie froze. "Should I ask her? Talk to her about this?"

He shrugged. "That's up to you. You're her mother. You know what's best. Not for me to say. But she knows she'll have to talk about it sooner or later. Up to you if it's sooner, or later."

"Oh, God." It was the best she could manage. He had thrown her into a frenzy of conflicting thoughts. What to do next? What was right or wrong? What would do good, what would do harm?

"You'll figure it out. But beware of being away too long."

Maggie nodded. She was sweating with fear. She felt her throat, constricting, twisting. How could she not have realised?

"Are you blaming yourself again, like Zelah says you always do?" It was Nick's turn to sit back now.

Maggie took a deep breath. "Of course. I should have taken more time with her. I've been so caught up in my own stuff that I ignored any signs that were there. I'm going to talk to her. I just need to calm down. Can you give me five minutes?"

He nodded as she stood and went to the door and into the grounds of Knyghton House.

19

From the courtyard, Maggie stumbled through a small, arched gateway into the lawned garden in front of Knyghton's original entrance, across the grass past the sunken garden and to the low wall that edged the lake. She sat on the wall with a thump and concentrated on controlling her breathing.

She had always known that there was something different about Alice, but she had put it down to character. She was a bright girl. Maggie had been told more than once that Alice had a high IQ. And she had always known, from conversations and comments, that Alice didn't see the world as other children of the same age did. Ever. But she had thought it came from the way in which the higher level of perception in the little girl's genius mind caused her to interpret her surroundings.

What Nick had told her took her understanding of her daughter to a new level.

Oh God! she thought. *Nick. He's just told me one of the most important things in his life and I've walked out.*

She stood quickly and ran back across the lawn, through the archway and into the coffee shop. Nick was, thankfully, still at the table.

"I'm so sorry," she gasped, sitting down opposite him. "It was the shock. Not just about Alice; your story too. I'll deal with what you've told me about Alice, but please carry on, about your... stuff. Sorry, I don't know what else to call it yet."

Nick smiled. "You're right. It's my 'stuff'. So, I've been able to see more of people than they realise for almost all of my life." Then his smile died. "But it doesn't end there." He paused, breathed deeply, nodding to himself, and continued.

"I left home as soon as I could. I've drifted, mainly. I

didn't keep in touch with my mother. But then, a couple of years ago, I heard she was dying. Cancer. I decided to come home. I spent three months with her. Nothing changed in her attitude to me, or in her view of the world. She had a few periods of feeling better. But finally, when she knew that there was no hope, in her last moments of lucidity, she called me late one night. And she told me a story." He stopped and took another deep breath.

"She told me that my father would have killed me if he had known about me. Literally," he added, watching Maggie's expressions of disbelief and horror pass.

"She told me that the Howell family had suffered generations of a curse: a curse that brought about the death of second sons. The mark was the sign for me. The story was that the father should never allow a second son to live. If he did, the father would die a horrific, painful death.

"I didn't believe her, of course. I said that was ridiculous, a stupid family story made up to frighten children. And anyway, my father was already dead, and had died a horrible death, burned alive in a plane crash, without knowing he had a second son. She said it was cruel fate. I shouted at her. Asked her how she could say such things to me when she was dying." He stopped again, looked down at the table. "It was like a dam burst in me. I said a lot of terrible things to her. Cruel, vicious things. She told me to find out, if I didn't believe her, but that I should keep away from the Howell family and where they came from. Then she said it was my fault that John had died. That she had always hated me. Then she died."

He looked up at Maggie. "And there you have it. Nick's story."

"Have you ever told anyone else about this?" Maggie asked.

Nick shook his head. "I ran away again. But it's time to find out. I want to know what she meant. I want you to help me."

"How can I help?"

"Do the Howell family research for me."

84

Without hesitation she replied, "Of course I will. You'll need to tell me some names, of course. And anything else you have. Do you know where your ancestors came from?"

"Can't you guess?" He looked archly at her.

It took Maggie seconds to realise what he was telling her. She slapped her hand to her forehead.

"Llanyrafon Manor," she said.

20

Cwmbran, South Wales
2017

Maggie had resolved as soon as she got home to talk to Alice, to have an honest, open conversation about her... what? Gift? Curse? She had no idea how to approach it. And she didn't want to talk in front of Jack. Instinct told her that this was information to be kept to as few people as possible, for now. She waited until bedtime.

Alice was in a good mood, anticipating the skiing trip the next day and being able to take Janine and teach her how to ski. Maggie decided that this was a good opening.

"Is Janine really excited?" she asked as they tidied away the usual heap of clothes on the floor.

"She can't wait," Alice replied, sitting on her bed, hoping to get out of helping.

"If you don't put your clothes where you want them to go, I'll just put them where I think they should go. Then, you'll never be able to find anything."

"I like them on the floor. I can find everything."

"But then I can't tell the difference between clean and dirty and I wash everything. Which leaves you at crucial moments with nothing to wear." It was one of those circular arguments that got them both nowhere.

"Whatever," Alice shrugged.

"So, tell me about Janine," said Maggie, deliberately stuffing clothes into the wrong drawers.

"What do you want to know?"

"Well, I know that she's being bullied by girls in her class. And that you help her as much as you can." She decided to confront the thing head on. "Tell me what you see when you look at her."

Alice's eyes narrowed. "What you meaning?"

Maggie ignored the deliberately incorrect grammar. "Look, I know that you see more than other people see. Nick has told me about himself. And he said that you and he have something in common."

Alice didn't reply. She scowled, looked up to the ceiling, then back to Maggie. "Why does it matter?"

"If I understand you better, Alice, I can help you more."

"Don't think you can," came the stiff reply.

"So, explain it to me. I'm not making any assumptions, or judgements. I just want to understand. I thought that if you knew that I can understand, then you'll talk to me when you've got a problem."

More hesitation. Then, a simple sentence that was so shocking to Maggie that she felt winded.

"I knew something very bad was going to happen to Daddy."

Maggie gaped at Alice, fighting for enough control to stem the mass of questions. She said simply, "How?"

"Because when he left the house that day, after you had the big row, he was so covered in dark that I couldn't hardly see him. Just the dark."

There was only one thing Maggie could do. She put down the armful of clothes and crossed the room to the bed, and threw her arms around Alice and hugged her tightly. "How horrible and upsetting for you."

"You're crushing me!"

"Sorry," Maggie replied, letting up on the bear hug. "Is that what you see, increasing darkness?"

"People go dark when they're in trouble," her daughter mumbled into Maggie's T-shirt. "You've been a bit grey lately. Janine is getting blacker."

"Then we must look after her as best we can. Do you see any other colours?"

Alice sat up straight on the bed. "Of course I do. Jack's usually red. That's because he's crazy-boy. You were sort of gold and orange last summer, when you decided to give up the horrible job and work with Zelah and Nick."

"I remember," Maggie reminisced. "I was happy."

"Miss Bigbutt Probert didn't have any colour, but she wasn't a real person, the bitch."

Maggie frowned, but decided information was preferable to another argument about language.

"Nothing at all?"

"Nope. Nick explained that there's energy that lives around people. He sees them crackling, I see their colour."

"Why didn't you ever talk about this before?"

Alice gave Maggie her full-on 'you're a stupid parent' look. "Duh! I thought everyone could see it. Until Nick explained." She mused for a moment. "Explains why other kids looked funny at me when I said they were looking green, or grey or black. 'Spect they thought I was a weirdo, so I stopped saying it."

"When was that?"

"Nursery, I think. Can't really remember. Where did you put my skiing things?"

Maggie judged that, although Alice seemed nonchalant, it had taken a lot for her to explain, so she decided not to ask more any questions for now.

"Can't remember," she said. "You'll have to find them in the morning." Maggie walked to the door. "Don't be too long, please, it's going to be an early start and a long day tomorrow." She stopped in the doorway. "Lights out in ten minutes. And Alice…" she paused and Alice looked questioningly, "…please don't ever feel that you can't tell me about worries you have about people and their colours. I only want to help."

Alice nodded, but she was already on her hands and knees on the floor, looking for her library book and pyjamas.

21

The skiing was a great success. They reached the slope early and Maggie was relieved to find that the lift was still operating, although it didn't look like there was going to be enough snow to last beyond the weekend. The skies had cleared and the temperature was already climbing above zero.

Janine was surprisingly adept. After spending the first hour with her on the bottom of the slope, Alice took her further and further up the hillside and after a couple of hours she was making her way down unaided, with Alice at her side shouting encouragement.

Jack had decided not to accompany them, preferring gaming instead, and Maggie had left him to it, feeling that he was now sufficiently responsible to look after himself.

At lunchtime Maggie called a halt. The snow had become slushy and the girls decided they'd had enough. On the way home Maggie expressed surprise that Janine had never skied before.

"No, never, Mrs Gilbert. But I like sport."

"You're really well-balanced and co-ordinated, Janine. And skiing isn't the easiest. Do you take part in anything else?"

She saw the girl's head go down and she bit her lip.

"I like netball," Janine said quietly. "We played in junior school. But no one wants me on their team, now."

"She was the top scorer on the junior school team in her last term," Alice added, giving her mother a 'shut up' glare.

Maggie caught a glimpse of Janine's miserable expression and changed the subject. The bullying problems were deep and, for the first time, Maggie felt a real sense of worry.

Janine stayed for lunch and into the afternoon. As the

girls had ensconced themselves in Alice's room and Jack was still on his computer, Maggie decided to make a start on Nick's research.

As always, she became hooked immediately. She decided to follow her usual method, of tracing the line of descent, making sure that she had the right people and places, and not to go into detail until she had as much as she could find on the confirmed direct line. Nick had been able to give her a few details about his father and his grandfather, both of whom were called John Howell. He knew that his grandfather had been a miner and had lived locally. And he knew that his grandparents were called John and Cecily.

First she decided to see if there was a connection with the manor. The census records were easily accessible. With such a prominent property to search for, she found the family on the records from the first census in 1841 up to and including 1871.

In 1841, the inhabitants of the manor were John and Alice Hywel, aged forty-one and forty respectively, no children, but four servants. His profession was given as 'Gentleman Landowner'. They confirmed that they had both been born in the county, which was the only information required at the time, the county being Monmouthshire. By 1851, John and Alice had been joined by their son John, born in 1845, now aged six, and two servants. At this time, John and Alice were both aged fifty-two, a year or so out from the previous census, but this wasn't unusual. Again, he was a 'Gentleman Landowner'. But here there was the major change. On this census, the family name was 'Howell'. Was this a mistake by the enumerator, or a deliberate decision by the family? Maggie knew from previous research that names could change slightly from census to census. She had seen 'Griffith' become 'Griffiths' and vice versa, and 'Groves' become 'Grove' and back again over three census records. But 'Hywel' to 'Howell' was a more significant change and if the gentleman landowner had been an educated man he would have known how to spell his own name. Puzzling.

By 1861, Alice had gone; Maggie guessed that she had died in the intervening ten years, but the old man was still alive, now sixty-two, and his son John, now sixteen, was still with him. Now, just 'Farmer' was listed as the profession of them both.

In 1871, John, aged twenty-six, was living at the farm with his wife Mari and three daughters. There were no servants. John's own father was no longer there. Again, probably having died in the intervening ten years.

However, on the 1881 census there were no more Howells. The manor, listed as a farm now, had been taken over by a different family.

Now it was time to work backwards from the present day. Maggie decided to start with the 1939 register, where Nick's information, meagre though it was, should give her a head start. This document had been released in the previous year or so, and was proving to be particularly useful to genealogy researchers. It was taken as a record of the entire UK population at the outbreak of war, to ensure national security and the distribution of identity and ration cards and other wartime documentation. It proved a vital source of information, as the last published census was in 1911, the next one, for 1921, wasn't due to be made public until 2021 because of the hundred-year rule. The 1931 census had been completely destroyed by a fire in 1941.

On the wartime register she expected to find Nick's family and, in particular, his father, who would have been about twenty years old. She knew that he must have joined the Royal Air Force soon afterwards, but she was hoping that he would have still lived at home with other family members. She wasn't disappointed.

The Howell family lived in Pontypool and, apart from John and Cecily Howell, and their son John, there were four others present, two women, a nine-year-old boy, and a redacted name. Nick's father, John, was twenty-one years old and his profession was given as 'Apprentice Engineer'. She speculated from what Nick had told her about what little he knew of his family that he didn't know he had two aunts. Could one or other of them still be alive? Maggie considered, but dismissed the idea. The elder, Cecily Morgan, was given as thirty-seven years old and was born in 1902, so no chance. The younger, Mari, born in 1920, might still be alive. But then Maggie remembered that if Mari had been alive her name would have likely to be redacted, as the publication of the register ensured that anyone under one hundred and still alive could not be identified. So, she had also died. And the nine-year-old boy, named Robin Morgan? He was probably Cecily's son. Cecily Morgan was recorded as aged thirty-seven and a widow. She could have been Cecily Howell before her marriage. The fact that the boy was named meant that he was dead, too. But when did he die? If he made it to adulthood he might have had family. And finally, the redacted name. Could this have been another child? The fact that the name was not visible could mean that this child was still alive, or was at the time of publication.

Maggie decided she would follow it up later, but for now she had to concentrate on the main line of descent, to find out the full history of the connection with the manor. And the birthmark.

She was pleased to find that Nick's father was indeed living with his parents, John and Cecily. That now made three generations of the male family named John Howell. From what she had seen of the early census records this was a consistent pattern of naming the first son John. At least it gave her a potential lead when looking further back. This John Howell was a miner, as Nick had told her. At the time of the pre-war register, he was sixty-five, so he would have been born around 1875. His wife, Cecily, did not have a profession listed. But it gave a clue to the naming convention in the family. This couple had named their first two children after themselves. Was the third child's name, Mari, also given a family name? If so, it was likely to be a grandmother. Another potential clue. There had been a Mari Howell at the farm on the 1871 census.

She then began the search for Nick's grandfather, John Howell. She found evidence that a John Howell had married a Cecily Hughes in 1900. There were no other couples named John Howell and Cecily who had married in Monmouthshire in 1900. She would have to go to the local registration office tomorrow to get a copy of the certificate, to find out the name of his father, but she suspected that it would be John Howell, again.

In the meantime, she went back to working on census records and found John and Cecily, in 1911 with daughter Cecily, then aged nine. And further back in 1901, in the same cottage on the hillside near Pontypool, newly married. John was then twenty-six years old, which confirmed his birth year of around 1874 or 1875. But from there, with increasing frustration, she found nothing, on both the 1891 and 1881 registers. She did extensive searches with all versions of the family name, but nothing showed up.

Outside, the afternoon light had faded to darkness. It was nearly five o'clock, but Maggie hadn't noticed. She was sitting in front of the computer screen, puzzling, when she was snapped back into reality by the overhead light coming on.

"Janine has to go home," said Alice, walking into the room, with Janine cowering behind her.

"I thought she was staying for the afternoon… oh my goodness!" She had glanced down at the time on the computer screen. "The afternoon's been and gone and I didn't notice. Sorry, Janine. I'll take you now. Give me five minutes to tidy my notes."

The girls went back upstairs and Maggie, having created a new file for both the online information and the paper notes, went around the house switching on lights and closing curtains.

Maggie intended to spend Sunday evening in the usual way in winter: dinner in front of the fire with a brief chat about the coming week; check homework done and if not, order it done; readiness check for the next day. This evening she had extra things to discuss. But first, she should speak to Zelah. It had been three days since they had last spoken and it felt like a supersized elephant in the room. With trepidation she picked up the phone. But it just rang and rang, not even an answerphone message. That was unusual. Disappointed, and slightly relieved, she cut the call. Then she called Nick. He told her that Zelah had left earlier that evening for the airport, to stay overnight at Heathrow, as her flight was early Monday morning.

"I'll give her time to get there," Maggie replied, "and I'll call her on her mobile."

"Send a text," Nick suggested. "Let her know you tried?"

"Good idea," Maggie said. She told him she had started on his research, confirmed his grandfather's information and found out where they lived, but hadn't been able to get any further. She decided not to let him know about potential cousins yet.

"So, I'm going to go to the registry office tomorrow morning as soon as the kids are in school, to get your grandfather's marriage certificate. See what it tells us."

"And the manor?" he asked tentatively.

"I've found a Howell family on the early records, but there's a gap. But leave it to me, OK? Early days." She didn't want to say too much yet, just in case she couldn't make the link between the Howell family of Pontypool and the Hywel/Howell family of the manor.

He offered to call her the following evening and asked about Alice and Janine. Maggie told him what she had learned, and how she was becoming concerned about going away and leaving them.

"I'll keep an eye on her," he said. "Make sure nothing worries her. And if it does, I'll get in touch right away."

She was grateful for that. She hadn't yet confirmed dates and times with her sister. She would deal with that tomorrow. In the meantime, she would try to convince Alice that she didn't have to deal with Janine's problems alone.

Over dinner she told Jack and Alice that she would be going to Spain, starting the coming Saturday. Jack, who had been interested in the story, was pleased. But Alice scowled.

"You said you'd help me," she shot at Maggie.

"And I will," Maggie replied. "I'm only away for five or six days. You can call me at any time. Are you expecting trouble?"

"Always," Alice muttered.

"Anything I can do?" Jack offered, kindly meant but received badly.

"You can mind your own business," Alice growled at him, then she got up and left the room. He turned to his mother, but she shook her head. "It's not her, it's Janine. She's worried, that's all."

"She's her own worst enemy; she's a pain in the ass," Jack retorted.

"I know," Maggie said with resignation in her voice. "But she's our pain in the ass, so we bear with it, OK? And she does have something to worry about. It's just a shame that she won't let any of us in."

Maggie felt her apprehension growing, a tenseness in the pit of her stomach. But she had agreed to the Spanish trip and couldn't back out now. Anyway, she didn't want to.

I can't give up on things, every time she has a hissy fit, Maggie thought before going to bed. But the worry didn't go away.

22

Cwmbran, South Wales
2017

Maggie decided to try Zelah again, but later in the day, allowing for the four-hour time difference and to be sure that Zelah would be in her hotel room.

She had gone to the registry office in Newport as soon

as it opened and obtained the marriage certificate of Nick's grandparents, John and Cecily. It confirmed that Nick's grandfather was the son of yet another John Howell, as she had anticipated. However, his abode was not at Llanyrafon Manor, but in Llantarnum parish, in a cottage. The marriage had taken place at the Church of St Michael and All Saints, in January 1900. His age was given as twenty-six, which confirmed that he had been born around 1875, as she'd surmised from the 1939 register. And his profession was 'Agricultural Labourer', not miner. Mining must have come later.

It still didn't tell her anything about the reason behind this research: the curse and the mark. But, of course, at this initial level of inquiry it wasn't going to. The internet was a great source of basic records but the interesting stuff came from diving into actual archives, which would come later.

She decided to find a nearby café where she could get online and see if she could find the birth of this latest John Howell. Once again, it didn't take long. She searched between 1873 and 1876, allowing for latitude in information about his age – people at this time could be uncertain about exactly when they were born – and came up with three possibilities. She noted the registration identification numbers for the certificates and went back to the registry office to order all three.

They were going to take about an hour, the clerk told her, so she decided to go back to the café and do more internet searches to see where else she could get to. Making an assumption that this John Howell would also be the son of a John Howell she set out to see who she could find in Monmouthshire. Without the birth certificate it was like looking for a small fish in a reservoir. Without more exact dates there were just too many possibilities.

After an hour, she got the three certificates. Two of them were clearly not the right man. But the third one was a possible lead. This was a John Howell, born in 1873 to – of course – another John Howell and a Mari Davis. The

1871 census had recorded a John and Mari Howell at the manor. But on this certificate the place of birth was given as number three, Crown Buildings, Stow Hill, Newport. This wasn't helpful. But she decided to go back to the 1871 census, to check out who lived at that address at the time. She found that it was a Mr Edgar Davis and two daughters. He was a lawyer. She breathed a sigh of relief. Assuming this was Mari Howell's father, then a child born at his house was feasible.

Intriguingly, the child's father's profession was listed as 'Gentleman'. And the name Mari did fit. Maggie had suspected that, as this was the name of Nick's aunt and the family was strong on convention it might have been the name of a grandmother, and she had been spot on. This must be the one. Next: the marriage of John Howell to Mari Davis. She went back to the café.

Having decided to have lunch there, rather than go home, Maggie reckoned that she had one last chance to get another certificate before she had to head back to pick up Jack and Alice. The marriage of John Howell and Mari was her next target.

Not knowing how many children John and Mari Howell had, she decided to use a wide date range. She started around 1870, but this yielded nothing, so she widened it out year by year. Finally, in 1865, she found the marriage of John Howell and Mari Davis in May 1865, and they were based in the registration area that covered Llantarnum. She just had enough time to get back to the registry office to get the certificate.

Maggie decided to wait in the registry office. It was only going to be half an hour. She tried to keep a hold on the agitation that crept up on her as soon as she found the marriage reference. She felt that at last she was going to find something significant.

When she got her hands on the certificate, she discovered that she'd been right. At the time of his marriage, in 1865, in St Michael's Church, Llantarnum, Mari Davis was the daughter of Edgar Davis, lawyer. She was nineteen years old. John Howell was twenty years old, the son of yet another John Howell, a landowner. This John also gave his profession as landowner. And his place of residence: Llanyrafon Manor. At last, the breakthrough. This was Nick's great-great-grandfather, the owner of the manor, in the direct line of descent.

But he was also the man who had lost the manor. Stella Bell had told her that the manor had been sold some time in the mid-1870s. The family weren't on the 1881 census. Maggie itched to find out why. But not today.

23

Cwmbran, South Wales
2017

Nick had said he would phone Maggie that evening, but he decided he couldn't wait and turned up in person at five o'clock, accepting Maggie's invitation to stay for the evening.

In the kitchen, as she cooked dinner, Maggie took him through what she had found so far.

"We've found your connection to the manor," she began and chucked at his expression. "You look like you've swallowed a wasp!"

"I didn't expect anything this quickly," he replied.

"Well, put it down to my knack," she smirked, ignoring his sideways look and frown. "Your great-great-grandfather, John Howell, was living there when he was married, in 1865. As was his father but his mother had already died. I found that out from the census records. I'll have to find the birth certificate to confirm that she was called Alice. But his father was John 'Howell', English spelling, and the birth would have been around 1845. I'll see tonight what I can find about his birth and get the certificate tomorrow. But his father was the person who underwent a change of name, somewhere between 1841 and 1851. It's a definite connection to your name."

She was surprised by Nick's lack of enthusiasm.

"I don't know how you're going to find out the real information though. It's all very well tracing this back, but there doesn't seem to be anything even a bit unusual about them. Being honest. It might all be a wild goose chase."

"Come on, Nick," she rallied. "You never know what's going to turn up. Once I've got as far back as I can I'm going to widen out the research to other family members, see what I can find. I haven't even tried deaths yet. Or siblings. There's loads still to do. Anyway, don't you find it odd that in just two generations your family went from landowners to poor miners?"

"I suppose so," he agreed.

"I've got until Friday evening. I don't have to do anything about the Spanish research, or to prepare for the trip. Bob's dealing with that and I'm happy to leave it to him. Anyway, I haven't finished yet. I was rechecking the 1841 and 1851 censuses just before you arrived. Here's the print-out of the records with John and Alice at the manor. They don't have any children in 1841, but in 1851 they only had John, then aged six. So, either they had early infant deaths, or John was an only child."

"Not unusual," Nick replied after considering the information.

"I think it may be right, though. Their ages are given in 1851 as fifty-two... both of them. Which means that there is an outside chance they were grandparents, not parents. But, I'll have to get the 1845 birth certificate. Shouldn't be too difficult. I'll do it tomorrow." She paused for a moment, then continued, "We've been very lucky, you know. Finding all of this out in two days. Seems like providence was guiding me. What do you think?"

He didn't react.

She paused for a moment to check the oven. "And I found that their local church was close by. It's St Michael and All Angels at Llantarnum. Know it?"

Nick shook his head. "Not a church person."

"But it might be that your family worshipped there and, if so, there may be graves. It's worth a look. I'll go there tomorrow, too.

"Nick, can you keep a close eye on Alice, please, while I'm away? She's getting grumpier and more distant."

"Janine?" he asked.

"I think so," Maggie replied. "But it's like trying get blood out of a stone. She says she wants my help, but she won't tell me anything. I don't know what to do, and if I try to raise the subject I get the scowl of doom."

"Is she eating with us tonight?"

Maggie nodded.

"I'll see if she'll tell me anything after dinner. But I won't push her, OK?"

"OK," Maggie agreed.

* * *

After dinner Maggie manoeuvred Jack out of the conservatory, to leave Nick at the table with Alice, but he joined her after five minutes, sitting down in front of the living room fire.

"She doesn't have much to say, but she's promised me not to be a pain, and not to guilt you about going away." He warmed his hands in front of the flames. "She thinks the nasty girls are planning something, this week. I've said to let you know, or let me know if you're away, if she hears anything, or if anything happens."

"Thank you so much," Maggie sighed. "I'm going to check out the Llantarnum parish registers, if they're available, see what I can find. Want to come through?"

"No," he replied, standing up. "Promised to do some research for Zelah. She's in Halifax tonight, going on to Shelburne tomorrow morning." He looked expectantly at her.

"Not yet," she responded. "But I'm going to call her later, when I know she'll be at the hotel. It's only four hours' difference, so I thought I'd wait up, call her about midnight here."

He nodded, walked into the hall, pulled on his coat and let himself out.

* * *

After checking that Jack and Alice were OK, Maggie went into the office and switched on her computer. This was one of the aspects of working for Maze that she loved: being able to work when she liked, fitting work around her family life. She remembered that she had to call her sister. She had already primed Fiona about a trip away. It was time to confirm that she needed her sister to stay for five nights. This wasn't going to be easy.

Half an hour later, when she had finally stopped swearing and throwing non-breakable things around the kitchen, Maggie calmed down enough to sit, although she was still shaking. She picked up the phone to call Nick, opening the conversation with a clipped: "Well, I think you can say that my sister and I are back to the same state of open hostility as last summer."

"Would you like me to step in?"

"How did you know what I meant?"

"If Fiona was just being a bit fussy you'd have been cross, but not needing to phone me. I feel your anger disturbing the air. So, she won't do it. Did she actually ever specifically say that she would?"

Maggie hesitated for a moment. But she was sure. "Yes, Nick, she did. Now she says it's not convenient." She stopped to reflect. "I knew that my sister and I were very different people, but I thought she'd still support me, even though she didn't approve of my rejection of the nine-to-five thing. But she's been very impressed by the TV stuff; and she encouraged me to follow it up. I thought she'd be there for me. Well, I was wrong, wasn't I? She likes to be associated with fame, she's told all her friends about my potential TV career. But when push comes to shove, she's still holding a grudge."

100

"People aren't always what you think they are. Families especially."

"Can you really stay here for me? Honestly, the kids prefer you to her anyway."

"Yes, I can. Saturday, is it? Until when?"

"Wednesday or Thursday, I think. Depends on how it goes. Thanks, Nick. I'll go and let them know. I'll put the phone down, but you'll probably hear the whoops of joy through the airwaves."

Jack and Alice were delighted. And sufficiently happy to sit through Maggie's warning speech about behaviour and not taking advantage. Alice danced like a disco diva around her room, much to Maggie's amusement. Then she stopped suddenly.

"Can he cook?"

"I have no idea. You'll have to find out."

"Five whole days of takeaways and chips. Cool."

"Thanks," Maggie replied in her best, most sarcastic, downtrodden-mother tone. "Good to know my efforts at healthy living are so appreciated. Lights out in five minutes."

Going back to her computer, she found that she wasn't unhappy at the outcome. But as regards taking advantage… wasn't that exactly what *she* was doing? *Oh well*, she thought, *it's done*.

In the middle of the night she woke up and remembered that she had meant to phone Zelah.

24

Cwmbran, South Wales
2017

Maggie's next challenge was to get the birth certificate for Nick's great-great-grandfather. *I'm going to have to give each John Howell a number,* she thought. *As soon as I start thinking about this, it gets confusing.*

Once she had delivered Jack and Alice to school, she set off to see what she could find. This time, she found five John Howells, born between 1844 and 1846, all in Monmouthshire. She'd have to get all five of them. The problem with the records of civil registration was that there was no confirmation of any other information. But, she decided, this was no time to worry about cost. Five certificates it would have to be. She noted the registration numbers and set off for Newport.

It was going to be a couple of hours before she got the certificates, so Maggie decided to fit in a visit to the Church of St Michael and All Saints, at Llantarnum. She knew the church by sight, as it sat on the road along which her bus had travelled daily to and from school. She had registered the presence of the church, but never thought anything more of it. Nowadays, there was a bypass and the hamlet had been left to snooze quietly.

She parked on the road outside and walked through the iron gates and past the graveyard, ignoring the tugging feeling that steered her towards the gravestones. There might be time afterwards, but first she needed to explore the church, check out its history and see if there was anything inside or out dedicated to the Howell family.

It was a bigger church than she had anticipated. Perhaps that was poor memory, but as she went through the Norman entrance and porch and into the main body of the church, she was amazed and fascinated. A communion service was just finishing so the church was brightly lit. Maggie took a seat in a pew at the back of the nave. The first thing she noticed was the stained glass in the windows, some of which looked medieval. Left of the main altar, she could see a small side chapel separated by thick, tall pillars. The carving and detail on these confirmed that the church was of medieval origin. The list of incumbent priests on the wall to her right dated back to the mid-sixteenth century. Memorial plaques on the walls showed early eighteenth century. Everything was well kept and cherished. It was a most beautiful church. But she couldn't see any obvious reference to a Hywel or Howell family.

At the end of the service Maggie was about to leave when a female member of the congregation approached her, and from her questions was obviously hoping that Maggie might be a potential new member. Maggie explained her purpose and for a few moments exchanged pleasantries and praise about the building and its history. As she was explaining about her research another member, an older man in his seventies, joined them.

"'Howell', did I hear you say?" he asked.

"Yes, the family who owned the manor in Llanyrafon at one time," Maggie replied, "I know that they must have worshipped here because there's a marriage certificate that names this church. I suspect that the christenings and burials took place here too, but I haven't looked at the parish records yet." Then she explained about the change of name.

"If anyone will know, Rob will," said the woman whose name Maggie hadn't caught.

Rob rubbed his chin, looked down at the floor, then up at Maggie. "I don't know of a Howell, but there's a couple of gravestones outside for the Welsh version, H-y-w-e-l. One's for a Gwyllim Hywel and a Herrick Hywel. It's basic but still standing. Rather odd inscription, actually. Always had me wondering. Would you like to see it?"

Maggie accepted with pleasure and followed him outside. The headstone was at the back of the church in a far corner.

"Are you the church historian?" Maggie asked, as she followed Rob around the path.

"Sort of," he grunted. "Still got quite a good memory and I've always liked history. You see that patch over there?" He pointed to the farthest corner, close to a large, spreading cypress tree. Maggie nodded. "See there's no stones, nor nothing?" She nodded again, not sure why a patch of bare grass would be worth pointing out, but didn't say as much.

"Can't dig there," he lowered his voice. "Plague pit."

"Wow!" Maggie exclaimed. "Can I stand on it?"

He grinned. "Course you can. Won't get anything nasty coming up now. But we don't dig. Anyway, here's this stone. Make what you can of it," and he turned and walked away.

"You said a couple?" Maggie called after him. "Where's the other one?" In reply he vaguely waved his hand in the direction of the line of headstones close to the old stone wall that separated the churchyard from the pub next door.

Maggie peered at the upright stone. It was quite simple; flat and not very wide, perpendicular and ending in an arch. It took several minutes to make out the wording, which had faded so much it was almost impossible to read all of it, but it was a simple inscription and, with perseverance she deciphered it. In the grave were a father and son. The father was Gwyllim Hywel with dates of 1699–1736. Nothing more, but the son was more interesting:

> *Herrick Hywel*
> *His son*
> *1729 – 1735*
> *Moste foully gone*

If this was part of the Hywel/Howell family, then maybe, just maybe, Maggie was getting closer to the family secret. She would have to research any contagious diseases prevalent in the area at that time, but something about this inscription suggested a more sinister end for the six-year-old boy. If it was more sinister, could this be the death of a second son, as Nick had spoken about in his story? Why wait until the child was six years old? Nick's mother had said that his own father would have killed him as soon as he was born.

Where could she find such information? This was over a hundred years before civil registration and, unless she was very lucky, it was unlikely that the cause of death would be recorded in parish records, if they even existed this far back.

She checked her watch and found that she had been there well over an hour. She had better hurry up, see if she could find the other Hywel grave. It wasn't far away, and even more difficult to read, but on this one she could see that there were three names.

The first, a boy of eight years. His first name looked like 'Devil' and he seemed to have died in 1735. A coincidence that it was the same year as Herrick Hywel? There was also Morgan Hywel. She couldn't make out the year or birth, but the death was 1735. Finally, Morgana Hywel, born in 1715, but this time no year of death. Why carve her name? And at the bottom of the stone, the words:

Alle sadly drowned.

Maggie took out her notebook and wrote it all down. The stone didn't explain how these three were related. Nor did it explain whether they had drowned together or separately. And the coincidence of 1735 was another mystery. But, she reminded herself, these people might be nothing to do with Nick's family. She didn't know how common a name Hywel was; something else to add to her growing list.

Almost two hours had passed, and the certificates she had ordered should be ready. With regret, she returned to her car, ignoring the many fascinating headstones and monuments lining her path. This was definitely a church to visit again.

Back in Newport, she signed for the five certificates, took them back to her car and sat to read them.

Although they were in the same registration district they came from a widespread area. She didn't have to go far to find the one she was looking for, although she meticulously checked all five before she was certain.

The second certificate she reviewed was for John Morgan Hywel, born 5th March, 1845, at Llanyrafon Manor. His father was John Hywel, 'Gentleman' and his mother was Alice Hywel, née Curtis.

This made it easier for her to search for a marriage for the parents. She found John Howell and Alice Curtis in 1840. She rushed back into the office and ordered it, knowing that she should have gone home and because there were so many things to do before she went to Spain. But this was going to be the last certificate before she had to delve into parish records, so it was a milestone of sorts.

She got the certificate a quarter of an hour later. John Hywel and Alice Curtis had married in 1840 at the Church of St Michael and All Saints. They were both forty, which meant that the next John probably had been an only child, born to a forty-five-year-old mother. And it also confirmed for her that they were they were indeed the parents, not grandparents. The final piece of information was that the groom's father was, inevitably, John Hywel, the 'Gentleman Farmer'.

Armed with this final certificate, Maggie drove home and drew up a family tree for Nick. After she passed this to him, leaving out the graveyard information for the time being, she planned to start the parish record search after dinner, hoping she would get sufficient information to get further back.

Just after eight o'clock, a phone call changed all her plans.

25

Llanyrafon, South Wales
1735
The First Visitation

He was the master now.

He had waited patiently for his brother's body to be brought back to the manor. He mourned with the rest. He waited again for the girl's body. It never came, but he didn't concern himself. It had been a strong, fast river, as high as it had ever been. She would have been washed away. All the way to the sea.

As soon as his brother had been put in the ground, Gwyllim had set about his plans. With a long face of mourning he sent his sister-in-law and her daughters to a relative of hers. Shortly afterwards he heard that they had gone to the poor house, because the relative couldn't feed them, which he knew would happen.

He made changes to the manor's way of operating. Increased the tenants' rents, something that his brother had refused, despite his own frequent urging. He argued with his neighbours over rights and land. But he wasn't worried by his increasing isolation. He was the master now.

He looked with great pride upon his two sons. Especially little Herrick. Youngest, but favourite. So much like himself. He would teach Herrick how to be a master. His elder son, John? He was his mother's boy. Small, whiny. He was disappointed that it should be John who would inherit after him. But, who knew, anything could happen. He didn't like the boy.

At first, all went well. The servants who had been lazy and stupid, soon learned to work harder. He reduced their wages, of course.

But. When did he first notice? A small doubt. A quick look over his shoulder at something that was never there. An uncomfortable feeling, as if he was being watched. He wasn't, of course. No one knew what he had done. Apart from Susan. She alone knew that he talked in his sleep. But she would say nothing. She had seen how he had dealt with his sister-in-law, who was now reported to be begging on the highway. A dutiful wife, Susan.

But slowly, it grew. He could not prevent it.

He bought himself two grand coats, made by the best tailor in South Wales. And he had a chair crafted, with a fine tapestry seat and backing, and wide arms so he could sit at the head of his table in all his finery, master of all he surveyed. Yet, he just couldn't stop it creeping up on him. His anger grew with the servants, and with his family. He had few friends, had no need of them. But now, he angered his business associates, who also began to avoid him. He had wanted to appear in public with important people; landowners, magistrates, lawyers, clergy, but they avoided him.

Then his land began to fail. He blamed his servants, of course, stupid, ignorant peasants. Obviously not working hard enough. He dismissed them all and hired more. It didn't improve.

Still it grew – sounds, whispers, rustlings. He shouted at where he imagined them to be. Family and servants looked at him with furtive, frightened glances. The servants gossiped amongst themselves.

Soon, it would be winter again. He wasn't as wealthy, or as influential as he wanted to be. Unlike his brother. Damn his brother! It was all his fault. As the weather became colder he kept to himself, wrapped up in one of his coats, sitting in his chair. As the noises grew louder he shouted at the foul spirits to be gone. He blamed his son John, and kept little Herrick even closer.

At the end of the year, approaching the anniversary of the death of his brother and his brother's daughter, the weather was strange. There had been a heavy fog for two days with no sign of it abating. The servants spoke of spirits in the mist and were afraid to go outside. Gwylllim's wife retired to bed, taking her daughter Susan and son John with her. He waved at them to go. Susan no longer conversed with her husband. Herrick was kept in the parlour and he soon fell asleep.

Gwyllim sat in his chair, listening. At six in the morning, before the sun was up, he fell asleep, but awoke immediately, when he heard the creak of the solid front door. He sat up, alert, stroking Herrick's hair as the boy lay sleeping in his lap.

"Who's there? Show yourself! Be you man or spirit?" he whispered desperately.

"I am not one nor other," came the soft reply and the hair stood up on the back of Gwyllim's neck as he recognised the voice. He had last heard it imploring him to spare her, and he had smiled at her before finishing the frenzied smashing of her bones. He hadn't stopped until she was unrecognisable.

Her footsteps made no sound as she entered the parlour. Gwyllim froze in his chair. She walked directly to him, stood for a moment contemplating him, then turned up her hood. Gwyllim opened his mouth to scream, but the sound died in his throat. The face was stripped of skin, a piece of raw meat and muscle. One eye stared, the other a blank socket. The lower jaw was at a right angle to the rest of her face.

"Pretty, am I not?" she said.

He twisted away in disgust, went to raise a hand to ward her off, but his hands were pinned to the arms of his chair. She was directly in front of him, so he was forced to look at what remained of her face.

"You cannot imagine the pain, the suffering, Gwyllim Hywel. But you will do more than imagine it. I will reduce you to this and more." A hand darted out and her broken fingers squeezed his throat until he was gasping for breath. "This is your fate, now." She eased the pressure a little and he choked. "Pain, torment, rejection. No one able to look at you, think how that will be." She saw terror and revulsion in his eyes. "And it will go on forever. Forever, Gwyllim Hywel. Death will not release you." She paused, looking at him, he imagined a smile on her contorted face, sucking in his terror, licking the place where her lips once were with her gross black tongue.

Bile rose in his throat. He closed his eyes, but her skeletal fingers moved to his eyelids, forcing them open.

"I have an offer for you, Gwyllim Hywel. You can avoid this. Keep your manor, keep your friends, such as remain, and your family. But I want something in return. Does this interest you?"

"Anything," he rasped.

"I want *him*," she said casually, gazing at Herrick still sleeping in Gwyllim's lap.

"No! No! Not my boy."

"You have another. This is just a second son."

"My boy." It was all he could say.

"Choose. Now. This boy… or everything."

Tears ran from his eyes. She picked up the child's hand. "See here." She pointed at a small round black mark on the palm of Herrick's left hand. "He is marked with my curse. You will take him to the river and throw him in. Do it now. And you will tell the son who will inherit from you that the curse must be known. Every second son born with my mark must be killed by his own father, lest the father inherit my fate. That is my offer. Do you accept?"

It was not a question. She knew the man and his answer. He looked down at the sleeping child, then back at her face, then around the room. He could not speak. He nodded with a look of defeat on his face.

"I will leave you now. But know that I will be watching. You are an abomination, not a man."

She looked at him again, with a gaze beyond revulsion. Then walked out as silently as she had entered.

* * *

In the months that followed, Gwyllim Hywel rarely moved from his chair. He had it moved to the upper floor. Servants and family thought that he was unable to bear the grief of the tragic drowning of his favourite son, Herrick. His wife knew better, but she did not speak.

He soon stopped taking sustenance. As his madness grew, all kept away from him. He ranted and raved about a demon. Until one morning, when a servant found Gwyllim Hywel dead in his chair, his hands gripping its arms, his eyes wide open and staring.

He was neither missed nor mourned.

26

Zelah threw her briefcase onto the floor of the hotel bedroom and sat down heavily on the bed with a snort of exasperation. She bent down and pulled at her furry snow boots, shaking the snow off and throwing the boots to a corner.

This was her second night of two she was spending at the Prince George Hotel in Halifax, Canada. Zelah hadn't spared expense. The hotel was one of the best in the city. Her room had all the usual luxury accoutrements, and gave her access to plush office amenities she had used to meet with her Canadian counterpart to discuss the history of Morgan Sturridge.

She put on the coffee machine and, whilst it whirred and glugged, she went over to the *chaise longue* in front of the full-height window. It was already dark outside. The hotel, in downtown Halifax, was surrounded by lights and activity, but she couldn't make out the sliver of water that she had noticed earlier, which she thought was the sea. It was only a five-minute walk to the harbour. Perhaps she would wander down there later, before dinner. Clear her head… again.

* * *

After several cups of creamy coffee and a long soak in the bath, Zelah felt ready to return to her research and review what had occurred during the three hours that she had been with the Canadian genealogist, a young man named Ben Alder. She had found Ben online and had sent him the details about Morgan Sturridge in advance of her visit.

She had waited for him in the hotel foyer, and spotted him immediately and been amused by his reticent entry. He stood nervously for a while, glancing around furtively through horn-rimmed glasses, alternately tugging at his small, straggly beard, and running his hand through his long, wet hair. She took pity on him, walked over to introduce herself, and led him and his oversized rucksack to the executive lounge.

Zelah had organised lunch, after which they went over what they had both found. Ben had done the same research in Canada as Zelah had done in the UK, and come to the same conclusion: Morgan Sturridge's genealogy was a mystery.

However, he had found plenty about the Hammill family. Morgan's great-grandfather had first come to light when he married Abigail Parry in 1885, when he was around forty. Ben had researched more widely than Zelah and in addition to their one son had found a further six children of the marriage, all girls. Three had died in childhood, three had survived.

"The boy, John Hammill, was the second youngest of the seven children," he told Zelah, "but I haven't followed up the girls who survived into adulthood. Would there be any value in that?"

She considered it for a moment. "Not for the moment, no. But let's keep the idea open."

He nodded. "The family founder turned out to be a bit of a stinker, I think," he went on.

"Why?" asked Zelah.

"Looks like he left her with the four children to bring up. There's no sign of him after the last one was born, but he didn't die for another ten years. And not in Shelburne, but here in Halifax."

"Do you know anything else about him?"

"He was a pauper when he died. He died in jail, by the way, and his given name at death was Jonathan Hammill. Apparently, mad as a hatter, as you English say." He smiled at his quip, but got a glare in return.

He moved on hurriedly. "His wife did quite well for herself. Must have been an enterprising women. She opened a shop in Shelburne selling baby clothes. Advertised them as handmade, which I guess she and her

112

daughters did." He handed her a copy of an advertisement from a magazine dated 1900, for *Parry's Baby Emporium, selling exquisite handmade baby clothes, for the discerning mother.*

"Can I have a copy? Why Parry's?" Zelah asked in her normal, forceful manner. She noticed that he was shrinking back into his chair. "Are you OK?"

"Of course. It was her maiden name," he quivered.

"Oh, don't worry about me. I can be a bit fierce. Nothing to do with you. Just my way."

He gulped, and smiled nervously.

"So, what about the son, the next John Hammill?"

"Well, he did very well for himself," he replied, sitting up. "He began his working life as an apprentice in a shipyard in Shelburne. But," he paused for effect but carried on quickly when Zelah frowned and waved her hand in a 'hurrry up and get on with it' gesture, "he married one of the boss's daughters. She was Maria McKay."

"What then?"

"Well, after he completed his apprenticeship it seems he was a talented man in demand. He was sent here, to Halifax, to work in the shipyard, then to New York. He managed an office there. Eventually, they came back to Halifax."

"Children?" Zelah demanded.

"Just one, a girl, named Maria, born in 1937. She was your guy's mother."

"She married John Sturridge from Shelburne," Zelah nodded. "I know this and I believe both died in a car crash, in 1967."

"Yes. Did you know they had two other children?"

"No, I didn't." Zelah sat up. "I was led to believe that Morgan Sturridge was an only child, and an orphan. I assumed in an orphanage. Where are they? Can we talk to them?"

"Sadly, no," Ben said. "They both died young. The elder, Maria, died in 2013. She was a spinster, no children. But the younger..." again he paused, regarding her with a look that it seemed he couldn't resist before imparting important information.

"Just tell me!" Zelah barked.

"Sorry. Yes, she didn't marry but she had a child. She was called Annie... your guy's younger sister. And she had a daughter, Louisa Sturridge, born in 1985, so she would be around thirty. And, according to the records I've checked, she's still living in Shelburne." He finished hurriedly and flung a handful of papers over to Zelah.

She briefly read through them. There was a report of the car crash in which John and Maria Sturridge had died. It said that they left behind two children. "Why two?" Zelah mused. "There were three."

"A mistake, possibly. The youngest, Annie, would have been a newborn. She never knew her parents and the other two would have been very young, four and two."

"Doesn't explain it," Zelah retorted. "Sloppy reporting. And, in my experience, it's rare that such a mistake is made. What happened to them after the crash?"

"There's no record in any institution, so maybe they were brought up by family. I haven't checked it out. But I can, if you like."

"Yes, I think so. And on second thoughts, can you get me some more information about the first John Hammill's other children, the ones he abandoned. You never know, might be something useful there."

"I'll work on it tomorrow," he assured her.

"What happened to Annie Sturridge?" she said, studying the papers.

"Died of pneumonia last year."

"Unusual."

"Not if you were a school dropout with a drug and alcohol problem. She was well-known in Shelburne, local entertainment." He turned down his bottom lip in what Zelah thought was a gesture of regret. But she wasn't sure if this was for the woman or because they wouldn't be able to question her.

She was silent for a few minutes, intensely reding the

papers, before her head suddenly shot up.

"You've done a great job, Ben. Thank you. I'm driving down to Shelburne tomorrow. I wasn't expecting to have a live person to speak to, so I guess I'll just have to knock on her door."

He blushed and went to stand, but Zelah pointed her finger at him to sit, which caused him to instantly drop back into his seat.

"I want to go back to the first John Hammill. You said he died in Halifax. Is he buried here? Is there a grave, by any chance? Not that I'm expecting there to be."

"Not that I've been able to find. He was a pauper, so there wouldn't have been anyone to organise it, and I suspect his abandoned wife wouldn't have been interested."

"So, we aren't anywhere near solving the mystery of the first John Hammill's origins."

"No, sorry."

"Not your fault. But what made you say he was as mad as a hatter?"

"Well, it's just surmise on my part, but there is a report from the jail. Because he died there, there had to be an inquest. One of the police witnesses says that he spent all his time muttering about revenge. Apparently, he kept trying to bite the skin off his own hands."

"Mad as a hatter, as we British say." Zelah smiled. "OK, you can go now. I think we're done here."

"I thought you would want this," he said as he stood up. "Morgan Sturridge's birth certificate." She took it without speaking, glanced at it and put it with the stack of papers he had given her.

This time he was quickly up and at the door, but Zelah accompanied him downstairs. She pulled on her boots and coat and walked with him to the lift.

"Please send me your invoice, Ben," she reminded him when they reached the foyer. He nodded, turned, and went out through the revolving door. As he tried to zip his coat as he dodged the moving door, he lost concentration and bumped into it, which made it stop abruptly. He blushed, pulled his coat together around him and exited the building.

Zelah decided to walk around the block to review if what she had heard had got her any further. But she already knew the answer. Peripheral details, but nothing concrete. And what of the original John Hammill, who seemed to have materialised out of nowhere aged forty? He must have been somewhere before Shelburne, with his Welsh parents. Halifax? Somewhere else in Canada? Or in the USA? But she'd found nothing in any Canadian and US census record, or traceable deaths. This was odd.

* * *

After dinner, Zelah began to feel the effects of the jet lag that she had been ignoring, but that had built up during the day. The earlier walk had helped, but the meal left her feeling drained. She decided against another walk. Tomorrow was going to be a long day, with a minimum of two hours to drive down to Shelburne to look around. There were several churches with graveyards to review, as well as the municipal Pine Grove Cemetery. And now she also had to fit in time to find where Louisa Sturridge was living. Fortunately, she had booked herself into a motel on the waterfront at the heart of Shelburne, as well as her room at the Prince George.

She decided to reread Ben's notes and make some of her own before she went to sleep. She began with another read-through of Morgan Sturridge's birth certificate. Nothing unusual there. Born in Shelburne in 1965, son of John and Maria Sturridge née Hammill. She put it down and picked up some other papers. But the jet lag went into overdrive and within five minutes she was asleep, so deeply that she didn't hear the buzz of her mobile phone ringing on the bedside table. The caller tried three times, then gave up.

27

After three attempts, it was quite clear that Zelah wasn't going to answer the phone. It was only 8pm in Halifax and Maggie couldn't believe that she was asleep. So, she had to presume that Zelah was deliberately not answering her phone. She had waited all evening to call, after speaking to Nick to rearrange the arrangements and she wanted to explain to Zelah. But if Zelah wasn't ready to talk to her… well, she'd just have to get on with her trip and deal with it when she got back.

Fortunately, Nick *had* answered her call. She explained to him that the trip to Spain had to be brought forward a couple of days and that she was leaving on Thursday morning.

Bob had explained that he was worried about a call from Mason Haussmann's weaselly lawyer saying that they were returning to the probate court with further evidence that would confirm that Jeremy Allen had no descendants and that probate could be granted to Haussmann as the closest relative. Bob had demanded to hear the evidence, but the lawyer had refused. He would produce it to the court. Bob would have to wait.

"We have to get to Barcelona," he had said to Maggie. "Pronto. There's a flight out on Thursday morning with seats available. Can you make it?"

She had hesitated, but, she reckoned that as Nick and not her sister was going to babysit the kids, and Zelah was doing her own thing in Canada, there was no reason why she shouldn't.

She didn't think Jack and Alice would mind. Nick confirmed that he could step in at short notice. She spent the rest of the evening between the calls and waiting to speak to Zelah, making sure that her absence would be as little-noticed as possible. School uniforms were available, there was food, not much but enough to go on with and she would leave pocket money. She would also write out a few instructions for Nick about how everything worked. They probably wouldn't notice she'd gone.

It did mean that she would have to put a hold on Nick's research, just as she was reaching the interesting part. But she had the whole of the following day, so there was still time to see if she could get something else significant.

After explaining to Jack and Alice that she was going earlier than expected, which, as anticipated, caused little interest, Maggie went into the office to see if she could fill the rest of her time with some parish record research to further Nick's family genealogy.

When she checked her emails, she found one from the agent who had contacted her after her Christmas TV appearance. '*Have you made your mind up yet?*' was the gist of it. She had barely given it a second thought.

Without thinking too much she replied that she had to unexpectedly go abroad for a week on business, but would give an answer when she got back. Then she sat back. *Was* she still interested? So much had happened in the past week, not just the cases but what she had been forced to confront about herself. Running away? Running towards? Was she being attracted to something bright and shiny that would lose its sheen as soon as she got her hands on it? Had Nick been right when he said that she kept moving towards an unachievable goal of perfect happiness instead of making the most of the good thing right under her nose? Most importantly: did she really want to repair the ruptured relationship with Zelah? It had always been a risk, she realised, always in the back of her mind that Zelah would be too fractious to work with, too overbearing. Perhaps time away in the company of someone who might be able to give her a fresh perspective would help her to resolve her jumble of thoughts. Maybe.

Knowing that she wasn't going to be able to sleep yet, Maggie turned on the computer and flicked the screen over to her favourite genealogy research site.

A couple of hours went by without her even looking at the clock. She wanted to prove the link in Nick's family line before she went away. There might be time to fit in a visit to the archives tomorrow – make that later today – but it would be satisfying to make more progress.

This was some of the easiest research she had done. Having become used to trying to trace names like Jones, Smith, Williams, and Davies, this was a doddle. The parish and Monmouthshire records were good. She had thought at first that the fact that every ancestor in Nick's direct line was called John would be a problem, as there were so many, but this proved not to be the case. Combined with the surname of Hywel, there were few and when you added in a prominent building, it was straightforward.

By 3am Maggie noticed she was tired, but she had achieved her aim. She had traced Nick's family tree back to a Morgan Hywel, who she guessed from the available information would have been baptised around 1670, although the records didn't go that far back. He was the first Hywel she could find at the manor. He was the father of three sons, John who died in infancy, Morgan and Gwyllim. The latter was the youngest, but the direct line of descent down to Nick came from Gwyllim. Gwyllim the father of the child 'moste foully gone'. She had checked that. And she had checked out the surname. Hywel was not a common name, being used more frequently in the nineteenth than the eighteenth century. There were other cases of its becoming anglicised to 'Howell' in the nineteenth century. That could explain the change of name between censuses. Perhaps Mr John Hywel felt pressurised by English influence in Wales into changing his family's name? She would check whether there was a formal process in 1845 or whether he could just give the new name to the infant who would then call himself Howell.

She switched off the computer. Now she could sleep. She was sure that she had the direct line. Next, she needed the detail. Time to branch out and see what else had

119

happened in that family. The interesting stuff. The stories that revealed themselves when you least expected them. Maybe what she had set out to find was now waiting to show itself, behind one of principals of the nine generations of direct descendants she had found.

28

It had taken Zelah almost three hours to drive from Halifax to Shelburne. Any concerns she had about driving in snowy conditions had evaporated as soon as she got out onto the highway. Snow was piled high on the sides of the roadway, but the roads were all clear and it was the same in Shelburne. Of course, this was a country where snow was a way of life for more than a quarter of every year. Not like the UK, where one day's worth of a slight fall could stop the entire country. In this small town there were some remnants of snow that was being removed to allow the normal passage of traffic.

There were few people out on the streets. Those who were had nothing showing of themselves apart from their eyes and were dressed in warm clothes that doubled their size. Zelah decided not to stop to ask any of them the way to the motel. Although the sun was shining in a bright blue sky, a sharp wind was gusting, moving trees and bushes. The car monitor showed that the temperature wasn't too low, but she suspected an icy wind chill and decided not to roll down a window.

There was little traffic around. She drove for about ten minutes to get her bearings, in which time she covered most of the town of Shelburne.

She had booked a night at the best-known accommodation in town, Coopers Inn, down on the harbour front. Parking as close as possible to the entrance, Zelah discovered in the thirty-second dash from car to reception that her fears about the biting wind were not exaggerated. She had specifically asked for a room with wi-fi and a desk and was charmed with what she found. The inn catered for year-round tourists and was more homely and welcoming than the Prince George. Not as sophisticated, but comfortable.

As soon as she was booked in, she decided to spend an hour with a hot drink and Ben Alder's notes. She hadn't really taken it all in yesterday in Halifax. As it wasn't yet noon she had the rest of the day to plan what she was doing and get out and about. Searching graveyards was going to be a challenge in the cold. But she only had one day, so she had to make the best of a probable frozen face.

Ben had discovered where Abigail Hammill was buried: Pine Grove municipal cemetery. She needed to find out the location of Louisa Sturridge's house.

The owner, who had greeted her and checked her in, was on hand to pinpoint both for her, but expressed surprise that Zelah was intent on spending so much time outdoors.

"Don't have much choice," Zelah replied heading for the door. She had already decided not to walk, although both sites were close by.

Her first stop was Louisa Sturridge's house. As Shelburne was laid out on a straightforward grid system, the street was easily located. She pulled up outside the house. It was, like many of the houses in the centre of town, made of cedar shingle, which in this case had been painted primrose. Zelah's pre-trip research had included Shelburne itself and she had found that it was one of the most important examples of this kind of historical architecture in the province of Nova Scotia.

Louisa's house had an open front porch, reached by six wide, shallow steps and the front door was half-glazed. Zelah walked up and knocked several times. There was no reply. After a minute, she walked along the porch to a window. Inside was a small kitchen, but there were no lights on and the room was empty. She was looking to see

121

if she could access the back of the house when a voice disturbed her.

"Can I help you?" The tone was more threatening than helpful. She looked up to find a man, probably in his sixties, standing at the edge of his own matching porch. He was dressed in a thick parka undone at the front, with a bright bobble hat sitting askew on his head.

"I'm looking for Louisa," Zelah replied, emphasising her English accent. "I've come from the UK to talk to her about her UK family history. Is she here, do you know?"

He stared belligerently at her for a moment. "Didn't know she had any."

"I don't know if she knows," Zelah replied with as much patience as she could muster in the biting cold. She felt as if her lips were about to solidify. "Do you know if she's here? I don't want to hang around if she isn't. Too cold." She tried a smile.

He looked puzzled. "Not that cold. Not yet. Gets worse."

"Well, it's bloody freezing for me. We Brits aren't used to this. Look, can you help me or not?"

"Gone away," he shrugged. But he must have seen Zelah's sigh and her shoulders sag. "Come on over, have some coffee, warm up."

She decided to take him up on it, despite her impatience to the get the information and move on.

On the porch, he introduced himself. "Richard Matheson. Call me Rick."

"Thank you, Rick. Zelah Trevear." They shook gloved hands and Zelah followed him into the kitchen, which was a replica of the one she'd seen next door. She showed him her passport, gave him a Maze Investigations business card, and explained what Maze did and her role as a researcher, as he made coffee in an old bubbling percolator.

"Interesting houses," Zelah said, cradling her hands around the warm cup. "Very traditional."

"If you mean the pink outside, my wife Prudence chose it. It was her favourite colour."

122

"I didn't actually," Zelah replied. "I meant the exterior, the cedar shingles. The construction must keep you warm in this weather."

"Well, of course it is!" His brows knitted together. "Did you think we make them pretty and freeze to death in the winter?" He seemed indignant. "We have storm windows for the wind and probably the best insulation in the world."

A catty response sprang to her lips, but, Zelah saw what this was. Herself, her own character, spurting out the reaction that she was used to giving. But now, on the receiving end, she was amused.

"Your wife," she asked, "is she around?"

"Died, two years ago. I might repaint in the summer."

"Know what you mean. My husband died a few years ago. I had to move house. Too many memories."

He nodded. "So, about Louisa, you say she has an English family?"

"Welsh, actually. You think she doesn't know?"

"I'm sure she doesn't. Only heard her speak about family, once. Something about her great-grandfather, or was it great-great-grandfather? Whatever he was, she said he was a real bastard." He paused for a moment. "But she never said he was Welsh. Or anything, other than Canadian."

"Well, I can't discuss details, but I'm keen to speak to her. This is about her uncle. He's from around here. Morgan Sturridge."

The man glared at her. "Louisa never had no uncle, not around here."

"Are you sure? I've met him. And he said he came from here, from Shelburne."

"Nope," he replied. "Not from Shelburne. Been here all my life. Know most folks. No Morgan Sturridge. What's he supposed to do?"

"He's a businessman," Zelah replied. "I believe he's quite wealthy."

"No," Rick Matteson said again, firmly. "Not from

Shelburne."

This was getting beyond fishy. "Well, thanks for the help, Rick. Do you know if Louisa will be back soon?" She wondered if she could extend her stay. She had to find out more about Morgan Sturridge, about anything that Louisa could tell her about the Sturridge and Hammill family history.

"She won a competition," he said. "Gone to Las Vegas for two weeks. Best hotel, money to spend. She was thrilled. Never been out of Canada before. Had to get a passport." He paused and laughed. "Didn't even remember entering the competition, until the guy from the magazine came to see her last week."

Zelah felt a tensing in her gut. "What did he look like?"

"Didn't see him, but she said he was a handsome kind of fella."

"Medium height, dark hair, dark grey eyes, immaculately dressed?"

"Exactly so, that's what she said." He paused and peered at her. "You know him already? You met him?"

"I think… maybe I have." Zelah put the cup down, pulled her coat around her. She needed to get out of this house. "Thanks for the hot drink, Rick, much appreciated. Very good to meet you. And actually… I like the pink."

He followed her to the door. "You're welcome, Mrs Trevear." He looked like he wanted to say more.

"Don't worry about Louisa, she'll be fine. Please let her know that I was here. I'll get in touch with her as soon as she gets back. Perhaps you could give her my card. Here's another one. I won't leave her a note, it might confuse her. Better for me to call and explain. Could you let me know as soon as she gets back? The man I met called himself Morgan Sturridge, which is a problem. But he's not dangerous. A conman, I think. I don't know what he's up to, but I'm going to find out. I'll let you know, too, Rick."

He nodded and she strode down the short pathway, to her car and drove away fast.

She drove straight to the cemetery on Victoria Street,

parked on the road outside, but didn't get out of the car.

For five minutes Zelah sat rigidly with her head on the headrest, controlling her breathing, letting her thoughts come.

I've been conned, she thought. *Taken in; duped; led by the nose. I wanted to believe him. He offered so much money.* The last part was a demoralising thought. *Seduced by money into selling my professional integrity.* Tears gathered.

Then she felt angry. Banged her hands on the steering wheel and shouted, "Damn, Damn! Fuck it!"

It didn't help, but it did make her realise that she had to suck it up. She had been fooled. She had to find out *why*. However, she had more to do here first. Whatever lay behind Morgan Sturridge's lies, there was a *bona fide* Sturridge family here in Shelburne. Anything she could find out might lead to an explanation of why the man she had met had used this family as a disguise. She buttoned up her coat, pulled on the ugly, but necessary, woolly hat, got out, slammed the door with enough force to shake the car, and walked into the cemetery.

Laid out in the late 1790s but not in use until a hundred years later due to the graveyard space available in the local churchyards, Pine Grove's fish-shaped layout necessitated the use of a map, which Ben had provided for her, together with a plot map.

He had located the grave of Abigail Hammill, which Zelah found quickly. It was a simple headstone, originally put up for two children, later joined by their mother. It read:

To the memory of Mari and Alice Hammill,
born and died December 25th, 1886.
Resting with God.

And their loving mother, Abigail Parry Hammill.
B May 26th 1860. D. Feb 1st 1930.
Dearest Mother of John Morgan, Mona Louisa, Sarah
Abigail, Christina Jane and Emma Mary.

Nothing much of note here. The first Hammill children, twin girls, were either stillborn or died just after their birth. Zelah noted down the names and photographed the headstone. Each was now a lead to follow. She would get in touch with Ben and get him to recommence his research for the survivors.

She returned to her car and drove slowly back to the inn. She had booked in for the evening and it was getting dark outside. There didn't seem much point in staying any longer, but she didn't want to drive in the dark. Zelah decided she could spend the evening making notes and searching the internet for further information about the Hammills.

After dinner, she logged on. Unexpectedly, there were a few articles about Hammills in Shelburne. She checked the online census records and found that prior to 1891 there was no one called Hammill in the town. There should have been the original family from Monmouthshire, from 1851 onwards. But there were none. She speculated that they might have died shortly after arrival. If the man who called himself Morgan Sturridge was at least telling the truth about this, they would have arrived after the birth of their child in 1845.

Zelah had already looked at the history of Shelburne, but without particular attention. Now, she checked again, and recalled that the original Welsh settlers had been from Carmarthen and Cardiganshire. A good number of other immigrant settlers had been from Scotland, during the time of the Scottish land clearances. But the bulk of Shelburne's early settlers were fleeing from the aftermath of the American Revolution.

To try to square what she knew, Zelah began to speculate about different scenarios around the first John Hammill. She had been told that he had been brought to Canada with his parents. What if this wasn't the case? Perhaps they had come earlier, to the United States, and moved to Canada from there. Or, was he orphaned in Britain, and sent as a 'lone child' by one of the

126

philanthropic agencies active at the time, sending orphaned children to Empire countries around the world, for the opportunity of a new life? She knew that the records were still available. If nothing else came up, she would have to get in touch with them to see if there were any records of a small John Hammill on any of the ships around 1850. The problem with that was that shipping records didn't begin properly until around 1890.

She was so immersed in reading that she jumped when the phone rang. It was Ben Alder.

"Ben, I'm glad you call–" Zelah began to speak, but he cut across her opening.

"I have something for you," he whispered.

"What?"

"When are you coming back to Halifax?"

"First thing tomorrow. I need you to do some more work. I've found out something unexpected and I need you to follow up some of the sibling leads."

"Me too," he said. "Very unexpected."

"What?" she barked into the phone.

"I have a grave reference for you to check out. It's something you need to see."

"Who is it? A Hammill?"

"No," he replied hesitatingly, "it's a Sturridge." He read out the grid reference.

"So… tell me who it is, then."

"I prefer not to. You need to see this for yourself, Mrs Trevear. I'll be available to meet you at the hotel tomorrow, if you need to talk." He hung up.

Zelah dropped the phone on the bed with a snort. Why couldn't he have just told her? Whatever it was, it couldn't be any worse, not after the day she had. She closed the computer. Enough was enough. It had been a long day and she was tired. Tomorrow she was facing a three-hour drive and now had to fit in another visit to the cemetery before she left. Time to sleep. Once again, she had meant to call Nick and Maggie, but she felt too wound up. Leave it until tomorrow.

The following morning Zelah arose early, breakfasted, checked out of Coopers Inn with thanks for the hospitality, and headed to the cemetery. It was another freezing day and again there was no one around. Heavily wrapped up, she strode into the cemetery, grid map in hand, and made her way to the far-left corner, where the headstone whose reference Ben had given her, was located.

Ten minutes later, after she had stood staring at the inscription in horror, she snapped back to reality, took a photograph and ran back to her car. Inside, she turned on the engine to warm herself up. She pulled up the photograph on her camera and stared at it.

Morgan John Sturridge.
Beloved son of James and Maria Sturridge.
Born March 3rd 1965. Died March 6th, 1965.
Resting in the Arms of Jesus.

* * *

The drive back to Halifax was three hours, this time all in daylight. The road was easy, not too much traffic, which gave Zelah some thinking and planning time.

She intended staying in Halifax again overnight. Was this the right thing to do? Should she cancel her room, see if there was an overnight flight back to the UK? What would be the advantage to her of coming home a few hours early? She was due out tomorrow morning on the daytime flight, which she had booked to try to minimise the jet lag on the way back. She was itching to get home and sit down with Nick and Maggie. Tell them what had happened, ask for help.

There was nothing she could do from the car so she spent the time going over the entire Morgan Sturridge story, to see if anything leapt out at her, from her new perspective.

She thought back to the first contact with the man. He had called her from Canada to ask for the help of Maze

128

Investigations in clarifying his family ancestry. He had already known their names. Or had he? She recalled that he had mentioned Nick. Why?

What was in it for him? Morgan Sturridge – she still had to call him that given the absence of a real name – said that he needed the information for a seminal event in his life. What did that mean? She had assumed marriage. But if that wasn't the reason what could he be trying to achieve by engaging Maze? The information he had given her was easily traceable in Canada. But the mystery remained in Wales. In Monmouthshire. With the original John Hammill. Therefore, there was a chance that the information he had given her about John Hammill was deliberately misleading. Again, why?

There was also something else that he had said in their first phone discussion. Something local. What the hell was it? It might have been insignificant at the time, but now, everything had to be looked at again. Forget that for now, come back to it later.

Zelah's years of researching and fact-checking were telling her that the answer lay with the original John Hammill and that she needed to widen the search for him. Decision made. She would stick to her original flight tomorrow. Tonight, she would go through everything again, set Ben off to search for young John Hammill's emigration to Canada. And hope that she would find that missing link.

She had been so pre-occupied that she hadn't realised she was almost back in Halifax. Shunting the teeming questions to the back of her mind, Zelah concentrated on getting through the midday city traffic and back to her hotel, where she handed over the keys of the hired car to the receptionist and went back to her room.

After dinner, she decided she would call Nick and Maggie before going to bed. She had to leave at 5am to get to the airport to check in for her flight. It was 9pm in Eastern Canada, so 5pm in Wales thought it was 4 hours earlier? She felt reluctant to start a conversation with

Maggie, not yet sure of the words to use. So, she dialled Nick's number. He answered immediately. That was when she discovered Nick's own family research had dug up a horror story, and that Maggie had left for Spain earlier that morning.

29

After her late-night vigil on the computer, Maggie had to drag herself out of bed on Wednesday morning to get Jack and Alice off to school.

A quick phone call with Nick, with some direct questioning, elicited that he had limited cooking skills and would be only too happy to take part in a chips-and-takeaway-fest. It was only for a few days. She could repair the dietary damage when she got back.

On the way back from the school run she picked up some necessities at the local store, then back to the house where she double-checked the uniform and other essentials, and was satisfied that she could go away without disaster occurring. Hopefully.

Bob Pugh was going to pick her up at 5am the following morning. Nick was coming over at lunchtime for a tour of the house and would be staying.

By half past ten every preparation that could be made, had been made. This gave her time for further exploration.

She decided to keep another read-through of the Spanish information until she was on the plane. It was a three-hour flight, which should give them enough time to refocus on the details of the case and plan how they would go about following the new information. They would arrive in Barcelona at 2pm, local time. Bob reckoned that it would take around one and a half hours to get out of the airport, get the hire car and drive down to his apartment on the coast. He had fixed a meeting over drinks in the early evening with the Spanish genealogist who had been finding out what he could about Lola and her family. Maggie was only taking a small carry-on suitcase which she could pack later and her briefcase with notes, notebook, and laptop.

With a couple of hours to spare before Nick arrived, she could go to the next phase of researching his family, concentrating her search on the generations before the registration act came into practice in 1837 that would only appear in parish records. Now she was going to widen out the search, looking for siblings of the principals in Nick's line, and as many births, marriages, and deaths as she could find.

Knowing that deaths were more difficult to find than births or marriages, she decided to start with marriage records of each John Hywel/Howell in the line of descendants. She had already seen that the Llantarnum parish records were reasonable. If she could find each of the marriages, that would give her a better idea of the births of children.

She had already traced the John Hywels/Howells back to the marriage of John Hywel and Alice Curtis in 1840. And from there she had each John in the line. The marriages would confirm the names of the wives, which might help in the search for children, although parish birth records could be inconsistent in naming the mother, often recording only the father.

Maggie knew that she had four generations in the parish records to go before she got back to the first Hywel she had found. Once again, the name of the property made the search much easier. The next generation had been John married to Mary Phillips. Before him, John married to Mary Price. And before him, Gwylllim Hywel, married to Susan Fletcher. This marriage had taken place in 1717. This was the one she was looking for. Gwyllim's father was John, but of his marriage and birth there was no trace. And she couldn't find the name of his wife. But this was the era that most interested her. She began the search for Gwyllim's siblings.

The first was John, born in 1693, but she had already found that he died in infancy. The next was Morgan, born in 1695, followed by Gwyllim in 1699, and two more daughters.

Out of interest, Maggie looked at records for Morgan Hywel, who had drowned in 1735. She found that he had four children, the first a girl named Morgana born in 1716, then a further two daughters, Mari and Jane, then a boy named Dewi Tomos, born in 1728. Assuming this was the right Hywel, the boy had died in 1735, along with his father and his cousin. Was this the boy in the cemetery that she had read as 'Devil'? With only three daughters, it was likely that the next living brother, Gwyllim, would inherit the property.

But three, possibly four, deaths in the same year was puzzling. Coincidence? Hard to believe, especially given that two drowned and one possible murder. Child murder was a terrible crime, even in the seventeenth century. And then there was the missing date of death on the gravestone for the girl Morgana. That was decidedly odd. Did it mean that there was a third body in that grave, or not? If she had Zelah to talk to, she might have been able to explain. Then there was the other dead child, Herrick. If it was foul play, then there should have been a coroner's inquest. The result of inquests were often reported in the newspapers of the time. That was something she could look up. She didn't have a date but she did have the year, and Welsh newspapers' archives were freely available online.

For now, she should stick to her original plan. As she had the dates of the marriages of each John Hywel/Howell, she could look for siblings, see if there was anything else out of the ordinary. It would mean looking for the deaths of each sibling too. That could be a hard slog. She decided that if there was anything to find it would be the death of another child under unusual circumstances.

She was still working at it, with no success, when Nick arrived. Over lunch she took him through the results of the research. He still wasn't particularly enthused.

132

"I don't agree," Maggie countered when he said that there was still nothing significant. "Three deaths in a short period of time, and what may be one missing, is too much of a coincidence. *Something* happened. I just don't know what or how... or why."

"Running out of time before you go to Spain," he said.

"Tell you what, why don't you go pick up Jack and Alice and I'll keep on searching? I'm a further three generations in and nothing interesting yet. But I want to keep trying."

"Don't think you're going to get anything."

She flicked her fingers at him in a 'clear off' gesture and tossed him her car keys. "Pessimist," she said. "You wait."

He phoned twenty minutes later to say that he and Jack and Alice were going for ice-cream.

"Hope it's OK. I thought we should have a chat before we came back."

"Yes, fine" she replied.

"You sound distracted, Maggie?"

"Tell you when you get back."

* * *

Nick brought Jack and Alice back an hour later, to find Maggie sitting in her office. Her warning look told him to wait until the children had disappeared. Once they were both upstairs in their respective rooms, she called him into the office and shut the door. In her hand, she had a sheaf of papers.

"You've found something." He sat opposite her at the conference table and Maggie spread out the papers.

"Yes, and I now have a theory, but it needs more examination. And Nick, I can't do any more."

He nodded. "Whatever it is I'll follow it up over the next few days. But, please tell me what you've got."

The papers were in a fan shape in front of him. Some were copies of parish records, but Nick could see that there were also excerpts from old newspapers. Maggie had sketched out his family tree, with the names of siblings at each generation now included.

"Right. It all begins here," she pointed to Gwyllim Hywel below John Hywel at the top of the tree. "Gwyllim was the second surviving son of the first John Hywel – the first I've been able to find," she added. "But the start as far as this story is concerned.

"You can see that Gwyllim had three children: a daughter Susan, named after her mother; a boy, John, named after Gwyllim's father; then a second son, Herrick, who died when he was six." She paused. Nick was still looking at the tree. His head jerked up and he looked directly at her when she added, "And I think that Gwyllim killed him."

Nick opened his mouth, but Maggie put up her hand and made a zip gesture across her mouth.

"You want to know why and how, but please wait. There's more. A lot more."

For a moment he didn't move, his expression frozen like a photograph that forever captured a moment of terrible discovery.

"I believe whatever it was caused this story of a curse started here. But I'll come back to that. When you went out to get the kids I was three generations further on and looking for another child death. Preferably – that's a horrible word to use about dead children – but preferably a second-son death. I found it... them. There are two. And a shocking story. Are you ready for this?"

Nick stared at her. She felt sorry for him, this was always the price that might have to be paid in researching family history. To find out that something profoundly traumatic had occurred, to which the researcher was linked. Yes, only by a bloodline and a line of descent. Maggie was about to break the news to Nick that he was the descendant of ancestors that had a heinous past.

134

30

Cwmbran, South Wales
2017

Maggie pointed on the family tree to Nick's three-times-great-grandfather, the John Hywel who had married Mary Smith.

"This was the one I was starting on when you left. I concentrated on second sons. The generations between this John Hywel and Gwyllim didn't have second sons." She paused. "Or, if they did, they were never baptised. Which may have been deliberate, we'll never know, but this one was."

She slid her finger along the line of names on the tree and stopped at the name of Peter Hywel.

"I haven't entered the birth and burial dates yet. The cause of death was 'suffocation in a ditch'. Now, ask yourself, how could a two-year-old die in such a way? There was a coroner's report, and I'll come back to it. But here's the big one."

Maggie took a breath and looked at Nick. "I did a *Google* search on the name 'John Howell'. Don't know why I didn't think of it before. What came up is… this." She pointed to the newspaper clippings. They showed a front-page story from 1875, of a double murder.

"This is your great-great-grandfather, the one whose name changed to 'Howell', the son of John and Alice, and who married Mari Davis. He murdered her." As she spoke she had moved her finger back across to the family tree. Nick didn't look up. "He stabbed her to death. She found him strangling their newborn baby, Edgar. She tried to stop him, and he stabbed her to death."

"Second son?" Nick asked, his head inches from the family tree.

"Yes," she confirmed quietly, "but there's more."

He looked at her. His eyes were filmy. "Poor little

135

baby. And poor Peter, and Herrick. Innocents." He shook his head slowly. "What else?"

"Well, the story dominated the press for some time. There's a lot of information. I printed off a few pages," she indicated the stack of papers on the table, "but I'll leave you to read it in your own time. The interesting one is in the story told by John Howell at his trial, in his own defence. He said he had to kill the baby, because of a curse on the family."

"What did he say about the curse?"

"All he ever said in court was that he had to kill the baby. That he had to kill the baby. He said he didn't want to do it, but that 'the beast' would destroy him if he hadn't. It's all in there. But..." again she paused. "Nick, something happened. He was sentenced to death by hanging, but it seems that he escaped."

Nick put his head in his hands. "Does any of this end well?"

Maggie put out her hand and cupped it around one of his. This time he didn't withdraw it. "No, I don't think so. I'm sorry, Nick."

"Was bound to be like this, I suppose. Wouldn't have passed all the way down to me, otherwise. Kept hoping it was just a silly story."

"Me too," she said. "We still don't know anything about the reason for the curse, and that takes me back to to Gwyllim."

"Yes, I forgot. You have a theory?"

"I think the curse started here. Now, this is only a theory, developed in my overactive imagination," she smiled at him. "But you know how we work at Maze – no theory too preposterous."

This time he smiled back. "Go on, then."

"Well, Gwyllim inherited the manor from his brother Morgan, who drowned. Shortly before his own death, Morgan's only son, Dewi, also drowned, and his daughter, Morgana, disappeared, also presumed drowned. I'm guessing her body was never found, as her name is on the family headstone but without a date for her death.

"Gwyllim was a third son. The second son was Morgan, but he survived into adulthood. If the curse was active, Morgan shouldn't have survived infancy. Right?"

"I guess so," he replied, staring over her shoulder.

"But Gwyllim's second son died. If the curse was something to do with Gwyllim himself, and his own second son died at the age of six, which remember was in the same year as deaths of Morgan and Dewi, *and* the disappearance of Morgana, doesn't that suggest that all of the deaths and the disappearance weren't coincidental and that Gwyllim might somehow have been involved?"

Nick didn't say anything for several minutes, during which time Maggie fidgeted in her chair, but managed to stop herself from interrupting his thoughts. Finally, she could stand it no more. "There are some strange stories about ghosts at the manor, Stella Bell told me. And I had a funny experience there."

He turned to look at her. "Something you touched that you shouldn't. You never told me what happened."

"We were in an office, on the second-floor landing. They have a chair that keeps moving. She told me not to touch it, but I did. I felt something there. It felt like a hand gripping the arm. It was cold skin."

Nick pulled a quizzical face. "You're enhancing your theory, I think. And it still doesn't explain a curse."

"Maybe," she shrugged. But it's something else for you to investigate. And you have to do it now." She glanced at her watch. "Bugger, it's almost seven. Need to feed those kids. I'm amazed they haven't come down to forage by now."

They both stood up. Maggie went to the kitchen. Nick leaned over the table, gathered up the papers, and took them through to the sitting room.

Half an hour later he was still there. Maggie glanced in from time to time and saw him making notes and drawing diagrams in the notebook he always carried with him. His face twitched as his thoughts, reactions and concerns reached the surface. She knew that inwardly the intensity of what he had set in motion was now blazing with ideas and qualms and uncertainties. Outwardly the only face he would show to her and the rest of the world was calmness. Unexpectedly, the thought arose that Maggie would be glad when Zelah was back.

After dinner, they all sat so Maggie could deliver one final lecture on behaviour and co-operation. The children nodded solemnly, and she suspected they had been told by Nick to comply.

Once the children had gone to bed, Maggie and Nick sat in front of the fire in the sitting room. Maggie had bought some scent for the logs and the room smelled of Christmas. She sat down on the sofa and tucked her legs up.

"When's Zelah back?" she asked him.

"Friday afternoon. Have you spoken to her yet?"

"No. I don't know if she's avoiding me, or I just haven't managed to catch her at the right time. How's she getting on?"

"Strangely," he replied. "The client is a mystery."

"Were you going to tell me about this before I left?"

"Why?" he replied. "If you'd spoken to her you'd know. Anyway, you haven't shown any interest in what's she's doing out there."

Maggie sat back with a huff. Nick was right. She'd been absorbed by his research, didn't that count for anything?

"We're in a bad place, Nick. Still." For a few minutes neither of them spoke. Then a log crackled and collapsed and the noise and movement raised Maggie from her reverie. "I was just thinking I'll be glad when she's back."

"Why?"

"Because it isn't right, like this. Do you think we can get together as soon as I get back from Spain?"

He rubbed his chin. "That's up to you. You know… she was upset. Your words were harsh."

Maggie nodded. "I know, and I regret them. But, regret's pointless. I can't unsay them. It's going to take a lot to get over what I've done, isn't it?"

Nick nodded. "She's difficult, yes. She provoked you. Sort it out when you get back. She's frightened, I think."

"I didn't think anything frightened Zelah Trevear."

"Neither did she. Thought any more about moving on?"

Maggie bristled. "I've thought about what you said. But you constantly move on, too. What are you looking for?"

"I don't move on. I'm not looking for anything special. I moved away. It's different."

"How?" She sat up. "Explain it to me, Nick. You're criticising me for something you do too. I don't get it."

He sighed. "It's not the same. I told you about my mother. I couldn't stay there. The atmosphere around her was toxic. Every time I drew a breath I sucked it in… I had to get away. That's all.

"But you must have wanted to go somewhere better?" she persisted.

"No," he replied quietly. "Just away. I never got any help, or support, or a vision of what life could be like. I didn't know how to imagine anything better. It was just… away."

They didn't speak for a moment. Maggie was about to say something, to reinforce her point, but Nick got in first. "It's not the same for you. Nothing wrong for you, but you think there's something perfect out there somewhere. There isn't. So, why?"

Maggie sank back on the settee and looked up at the ceiling, searching for words, knowing he was right.

"Guilt. I married a man I didn't know at all, and that's a terrible admission. Then he died. I want to make it perfect for his children."

Nick got up and threw a handful of chippings on the fire. "Jack and Alice are happy here. It won't ever be perfect for Alice, whatever you decide to do next. She needs people she can trust. She needs you."

"Do you really think I'm enough? Someday I'll have to detach her from me."

"Concentrate on that, just that. Make her confident. It's not easy."

Maggie cupped one hand around her face, her mouth covered, and decided she couldn't talk about this anymore. "I would like to hear about the client. Will you tell me some of it?"

Nick shook his head. "It's late. Call me on Friday evening. I'll run you through it when I've spoken to Zelah."

31

The Second Visitation
Llanyrafon Manor
1804

He lost his footing half way down the stairs, tried to cling onto the bannister, but missed and tumbled to the bottom, where he lay on the rush matting in the hallway. Lucky for him it was the final descent of stairs and he had fallen only a few feet. He checked his arms and legs; all working. He tried to sit up, but his head swam.

"Woman!" he screamed. "Come here and help me."

From the parlour a pale, mousy woman appeared, peering around the doorframe. She turned and signalled to someone behind her. A man joined her and together they picked up the drunk man, half dragged him into the parlour and sat him down on the settle in front of the fire. He leaned forward, belched, and spat into the flames.

His four-year-old son looked with mild curiosity at him from the floor, disinterested he turned away. His three daughters went about their business, heads down, exchanging fleeting glances of fear and revulsion.

The man stared into the flames until the mesmerising,

rhythmical crack and hiss of the wood caused him to close his eyes. He began to snore.

When she was quite certain that he was asleep the mousy woman slipped into the room, called to the older man to join her. They sat side-by-side on the opposite settle, watching him snore.

"Nothing to be done, daughter," the older man whispered. "He has brought us all near to ruin. Perhaps the little chap," he nodded at the child on the floor, "will bring us around in his time. If we can last 'til then." He leaned forward and rubbed his chilblained hands together in front of the flames. "He's a sturdy little lad. Unlike *that*," he nodded contemptuously at the snuffling man who had one hand resting on his great belly, the other flinging out in pursuit of something in his dream. He began to mutter, "Accident, not my fault. Accident, it was." He became agitated, then settled again.

"Do you believe him?" the woman asked.

"No more than you."

"I told him it was no more than a story. A family story. My father made me promise to pass it on. But I never believed it."

The woman shook her head. "He believed it."

The man shrugged and pulled a hand through his long, tangled hair. "There's bad blood in our family. It's come out in him. I'm sorry for you girl."

"He wasn't always like this." She had not intended her words to sound like an accusation, but the old man flinched.

"I had to tell him. It's been the way for generations. But I never expected… what he has done."

"My poor little boy," the woman moaned. "Just two years old. He may not have done it proper, but it was down to him. He was there. He could have done something. He could!"

"He says he could not, that it was too late before he saw it." The older man was trying to convince himself that his only son was not a child-murderer. But why else had the man's behaviour changed so much? Why had he let the farm run to ruin? He himself had not been a good manager, had lived the life of a country squire, lord of the manor. Had relied too much on others, who had cheated and deceived him. Brought him down. His honest guilt told him that he had contributed to the slow downfall of the once elegant manor. He had hoped that his son could change their fortunes. And once it had looked promising, he had hope. But, no longer. He glanced across at the red-faced, drooling, snoring drunk. He got up, sighed, bade his daughter-in-law a good night, and left the parlour.

The woman regarded the man opposite her. She had once admired his handsome face, his long, thin nose, his high brow. Now the nose was red and bulbous, the cheeks calloused, the forehead deeply scored. The hands that had once gripped with energy were lumps of clay, unused to work. The day he had set out to mend the fence next to the ditch, had taken little Peter with him, had he planned what would happen? He swore not. Swore to the constable, to the coroner. They had believed him, his grief seemed real.

Only she had seen him glance, narrow-eyed, over his shoulder, at her. That was when she knew. He could have stopped their child from drowning. She blew out the candles, dragged herself upstairs, leaving her husband sleeping by the fire.

The sound of the front door opening and closing again was what disturbed him, the rush of cold wind. "Who's there? Woman, is that you? Bring me a bottle!" He glanced around, saw the kitchen was dark. Footsteps were approaching from the hall. A figure came into the room, put a finger to its lips and said "Shh, John Hywel. No drink now." It sat opposite him.

He was bemused. Who was this? Then the figure pushed up strange-looking fingers, pushed back the hood. John Hywel, a scream in his throat, tried to dig himself back into the settle. He turned away, but she spoke. "Look at me, John Hywel. Did you think I wasn't real? That I wouldn't come?"

"What... what?" He couldn't get anything else out. He stared at what was in front of him. "I did it, I did."

"No, John Hywel. You let it happen. Not the same thing. Thy boy was marked. You knew what you had to do. But you waited two years."

"I could not kill a babe."

"Fortuitous, I think, that he fell. I know you could have reached in to pluck him out. I think you decided to do so, did you not, in the end? But too late."

He nodded slowly.

"Then you shall receive my fate. As the curse promises. I shall reduce you to this." She waved her hands around her face in a regal wave.

In response, he put his hands up to his own face and began to cry.

"Or, shall I be merciful?"

"Yes," he cried. "Yes, spare me. My boy is dead. Spare me."

One of her broken hands delved into her cloak and withdrew a length of rope and handed it to him. He clutched it, comprehension dawning.

"Five years from now, to the exact date of your son's death, you will hang yourself in this parlour. You will not fail. Do you accept my bargain?"

He nodded quickly, unable to look at what her smile did to her face.

"And be sure to tell your eldest son our story, John Hywel. This is a nice tradition. We mustn't let it die, must we? Not when there is still such a long way to go."

Without waiting for anything further she stood and walked out of the manor as quietly as she had arrived.

32

On Thursday morning Maggie left the house quietly, so as not to disturb anyone.

Alice had seemed quite relaxed, cheerful even, at dinner the night before. Maggie had told them she would check in every evening. Alice could speak to her if she wanted to, but the girl wouldn't feel like her mother was smothering her.

They left so early that they missed the usual morning queues on the M4 and reached Bristol Airport with plenty of time to spare. Bob hadn't had breakfast, so as soon as they checked in they found a restaurant airside. Maggie didn't eat, but watched him, her hands cupped around an enormous cup of tea.

"You're quiet," he said, after finally putting down his knife and fork. He placed them carefully in the centre of the plate, making a tiny adjustment.

"I've had a very intense couple of days," she replied. "I'm getting my head out of one space and into another. I'm going to spend the plane journey reading up about what we have to do when we get to Barcelona."

"Fair enough. The first thing we're going to do is get down to Sitges, then meet up with the Spanish genealogist I've hired to get the ball rolling."

"When is that?"

"Tonight, at six. We're meeting him in a bar close to the apartment. Then we'll have dinner. It's early to eat, but we need time to talk over what we know and whatever he'll tell us. Then we can make a plan."

Maggie grinned, her head cocked to one side.

"What?"

"Good plan. Sorry, this is your project much more than mine, so just organise what you think is right. But one thing…" She held up a warning finger.

144

Bob scowled, then laughed. "Don't order your food for you?"

"That's the one thing."

"Point taken."

Their flight was called. They made their way down a mile of corridor and boarded. Maggie elected to take a window seat. As soon as they were settled she fixed her attention on what was going on outside as technicians scuttled back and forth, loading luggage, food, and fuel.

"Anything special going on out there?" Bob asked, when she had been gazing non-stop for ten minutes.

"No, just the usual," she replied. "I love flying. Actually, I love travelling. All of it. I like airports, even the security checks. It's all part of the experience."

He made a *humpf* noise.

"Not so keen?"

"I prefer arriving to the mess of getting there."

"Does flying bother you?"

"It's an inconvenience. I'm not scared, if that's what you're asking."

"Calm down, I'm not suggesting that at all."

"Fair enough."

They didn't speak again until they were in the air and the seatbelt signs were off. Maggie noticed that Bob had closed his eyes as soon as the plane started to move and he'd definitely gripped the arms of his seat as the wheels left the ground.

Once daylight arrived, it turned out to be a cloudy morning, with little to see on the ground, so Maggie got out her new book and immersed herself in yet another account of the role of the International Brigades in the Spanish Civil War. Bob opened his eyes, once the plane had stopped climbing and was less noisy.

"I've read that one. It's good. Nice and simple."

She looked up from the book and raised a questioning eyebrow. He sighed. "No, I don't meaning you're stupid, so don't look at me like that. It's well-written and logical and gives a good understanding of both sides, especially the factionalism on the Republican side. OK?"

She nodded and went back to the book. He left her undisturbed for five minutes, then, "How's things going with your company work?"

"OK," she replied, not wanting to go into detail. She wanted to keep this trip separate from Maze cases. "There's always a lot to do. We attract a particular kind of client; ones who have something very odd in their history that they just can't understand. We're working with one right now." *Damn, hadn't meant to say that.* She waited to see if he would follow up, but he didn't.

"Do you believe in ghosts, Maggie?"

Maggie was taken aback by the question. She wasn't sure if he was being serious, flippant, probing, or just trying to make conversation.

"No," she declared. "I do not. But... I believe in a power of the human mind. The psyche. Whatever you want to call it. Most people who live a normal life, inside the curve, have a normal mind. Nothing outside the curve ever happens. Maybe it can't. I don't know. Maybe it's how they're wired. But, for those of who are wired differently – and I wouldn't have included myself in such a group, or even known that there was a group to be included in until last year – we have experiences. It's well outside the safe, comfortable curve. Do you understand what I mean?"

He nodded, reluctantly, no longer able to deny it. "But that doesn't explain anything. You don't believe in ghosts. You seem to be saying that the human mind has experiences, abnormal, paranormal, whatever you call it. But that explains nothing."

Now it was Maggie's turn to nod reluctantly. "I don't have anything else. We see things, and things see us. And they attach to us and to our generations. Like me. Hopefully not you. For now, it's just a story, for you."

"But now I know about something, does that mean that something knows about me?"

"Bob, I really don't know. I've said to you before, I don't obsess. And my advice to you? Don't think about it.

146

If something has found you there's nothing you can do about it. At least you know you're not alone." She smiled at him. He smiled back, then reached out and touched her hand. She thought that he was more concerned than he let on.

After that, they talked about Jeremy Allen and Lola and possible scenarios. Maggie pulled out from her bag excerpts from a book of testimonies written by Republican women who had been imprisoned from 1939 onwards.

"Have you read any of these, Bob?"

He took the papers from her, leafed through them. "No, I haven't seen them before. What do they say?"

"They say that they were treated harshly, abominably. They were beaten, tortured, and starved. Manny died, some of them as young as sixteen. Thousands of them executed by firing squads."

He started reading and for the next half an hour nothing was exchanged between them. He paused when the flight attendants served food and drinks, which Maggie refused.

"You do actually eat, I presume?" he said, tucking into an unrecognisable concoction of bread and some grey squidgy stuff that Maggie thought could be tuna. "It's just I've never seen you actually eat." He didn't look at her when he said it and she thought he was winding her up.

"I had food at the pub last week."

"No, you didn't eat what I ordered. Said you were a veggie."

"But then I said I wasn't, really. But I didn't eat the sandwich, that's true. I was upset that day."

"Anything you want to tell me?"

"No. Thanks, Bob. Not right now."

He finished what he was eating and went back to reading the papers. Half an hour later the captain announced that they were twenty minutes from landing and should do the getting-ready-to-land things. Food and drinks were cleared away, tables put upright, seat belts on.

As the plane descended, Maggie thought she could make out the sea below, not the usual Mediterranean bright blue, but a darker shade, duller, with a scurry of dark clouds making shifting patterns on the water. Then she saw the city of Barcelona and turned to tell Bob, but once again he was upright with his eyes closed, gripping the seat.

* * *

They retrieved their luggage and made their way to the car hire desk. The attendant greeted Bob like an old friend, in Spanish. Bob was fluent, or so it seemed to Maggie. He took the keys and led them out of the airport building, found the car, stored their luggage, and set off on what he said would be about an hour down to his apartment in Sitges.

Maggie waited until they were clear of the airport and on the motorway.

"Fluent Spanish, Bob?"

"My grandparents on my mother's side came to Wales in the 1930s, escaping from the poverty. He learned English, but spoke Spanish to me. My mother She became Mrs Pugh, but she started out as Julia Martinez Garcia."

"Bob, why do you need me here? You speak the language and I'm guessing that you have relatives here?"

"Actually, no. My grandfather's brothers all died in the war."

"Oh. I'm sorry to hear that. But then that means you know a lot about the civil war. And, you're a detective. Why do you need me?"

He paused for a moment as he concentrated on the road. "Always takes me a bit to get used to driving on the wrong side. I don't know that much about the war. My grandfather wouldn't talk about it. It broke his heart. I didn't know I had a cousin here until a few years ago.

"You're here because I need someone who understands genealogy. I understand investigating. But it's not the same. I know crime, I'm not subtle. In my world, I

148

know how to get information out of people. But I don't coax it out. You get what I mean?"

"I think so," she said. "So, when we meet the genealogist later you won't be giving him a slap to the head if he doesn't give you good info?"

"That's not what I meant!"

Maggie had meant it as a joke, but thought she might have gone too far. "Sorry, that was uncalled for. I'm sure you're really good at your job. But, you told me you're Persistent Bob, wouldn't you have got to the truth yourself? Just with the right questions?"

"Maybe, but I respect other people's special knowledge. That's why I asked for your help. Now, we're going to take the scenic route. Do you get travel sick?"

"Not usually," Maggie said, remembering the boat trip to Devon with Zelah and the kids the previous summer and her trepidation about not being on firm ground. "Why?"

He didn't reply, but grinned and speeded up. She quickly understood. The scenic route from Barcelona to Sitges was a two-lane road that hung over the edge of the Mediterranean. It was more like a Swiss mountain pass than a coast road. But the clouds had cleared overhead and, although she knew it was cold outside, Maggie was thrilled to be driving alongside an endlessly calm, deep blue sea.

It took just over an hour to reach Sitges. Bob steered the car along some narrow streets until they reached the promenade and a small road that ran next to the apartments and restaurants close to the old town. When they had almost reached the imposing apricot-coloured church standing out on a promontory at the end of the promenade he turned off and went around a block to the back of a building, where he used a code to open a barrier into a small, private parking area. They took their cases out and Maggie followed Bob into the lobby of an apartment building of high, wide proportions traditionally tiled on the floor and walls. A small lift took them to the fourth floor.

Bob opened the only door on the floor and led them

into a spacious, light, open-plan apartment with a wide balcony that looked out through full-length windows over the promenade and the sea. The curtains were open and the heating was already on.

"This is beautiful, Bob," Maggie said, looking around. She walked over to the window and looked down at the wide, palm-lined seafront. To her left she had a close-up view of the church. He joined her.

"It's called San Bartolomeu. It's the pinnacle of the old town of Sitges. Bells can be a bit noisy. Don't take your coat off yet. I'll give you the guided tour."

He showed her the two en suite bedrooms, then down the hallway to a door to a staircase; she followed him up. They emerged onto a roof terrace. It was bounded by the high walls of the taller buildings each side, and to the front and back a shorter wall topped with terracotta tiles, beyond which were spectacular views of the old town, the church and the sea.

Turning her back to the sea, Maggie could see the hills above the town, and the mountains beyond. The terrace had furniture and a barbeque, all covered, and a vast array of pot plants, all of which looked well cared for. Trailing plants crept up and around the walls at either side.

"This must be divine in warmer weather, when those plants flower. And I'm assuming they are aromatic?" she added, pointing to the creepers and some of the huge Alibaba pots.

"It's a haven," he said, gazing out at the sea. Very peaceful, even with summer traffic and crowds. And yes, nicely smelly."

They returned to the apartment and Bob locked the door to the terrace. Maggie went to her room to unpack. It was late afternoon and the sun was fading over the sea. She returned to the living area, where Bob was making tea.

"Be dark soon," he remarked over his shoulder. "Goes down quickly this time of year."

He brought mugs of tea to the sofa where Maggie had settled herself.

150

"Right, there are two things we need to do. One: go over what we have and what we know so we're ready for the meeting later. Two: make a plan for where we go tomorrow."

"I agree with the first one," Maggie replied. "But shouldn't we wait until we've met with your genealogist before we go too far into planning? Whatever he tells us may change what we need to do."

"I'd just like to get an idea of what tomorrow might look like," he replied, Maggie thought peevishly. He was a man used to leading, not being interrupted. So be it.

"OK," she agreed. "You talk through what we have and I'll give you my comments. If that's OK with you?"

He settled back into the settee, gazing at the ceiling. "History. Jeremy and Lola first met when he was doing his initial training in Barcelona. She was working at one of the hospitals. The brigade was sent up to Tarrega and she went too. In late February, he was sent across the Ebro to reinforce the British battalion fighting around Gandesa. It was a disaster. He had to swim back across the river with the enemy shooting at him. They got closer in those spring months. In June the battalion moved down near Falset, close to Lola's village, which was subsequently destroyed. Jerry and Lola realised that this was probably in readiness for a new offensive, so, they got married. The Battle of the Ebro began with the International Brigade crossing the river at the end of July 1938."

"Do we know exactly where the village was?"

"No, but I'm hoping that Señor Torrens will be able to tell me later. Anyway, Jerry was wounded in the battle, somewhere close to Gandesa, in early September. He was taken back to Barcelona. He tried to get messages to Lola to say where he was through comrades who had been wounded but returned to the front. He didn't think they ever got through".

"How did he know she was pregnant?"

"He heard from a soldier who had been wounded before him and taken back to the camp at Falset. She was there looking for Jerry, trying to get word to him somehow. The soldier told her that Jerry was alive and well, which he was at that point. The same soldier ended up in the hospital in Barcelona with Jerry and told him about the baby. Somehow, he assumed that she would know that he was in Barcelona, so he waited there as long as he could."

"But she didn't know," Maggie mused. "She was waiting for him, and he for her." She paused, then said, "Just a thought, but probably too late."

"What?"

"Is there anyone else he fought with who might have left some kind of testimony, someone who wasn't wounded, who stayed longer than Jeremy did?"

He looked irritated by the idea. She paused for a moment but started again before he could speak. "Do you want to hear what I have to say, or not?"

He huffed, "Yes. It's just that I need to talk through my bit in one go. It's how I concentrate and get the full picture, see?"

"Then you should have told me before you started. OK. I'll shut up and listen."

"Sorry, it was a good point. We'll add it to the list of questions," he scribbled a note on a pad. "So, we know that as Jerry was recovering from his wounds the decision was made to repatriate the International Brigades. He was sent back to Britain without being able to go back to the Ebro region. He got back at the end of November 1938. He was hospitalised for months back in Wales. By the time Jerry was sufficiently recovered, Franco had won the war and retribution was starting against anyone who had fought on the Republican side. There was no way back. In 1939, he joined up after war was declared and in 1940 he took part in the Dunkirk landings, got shot – again – completely buggered his knee and was invalided out of the army."

All the time that Bob had been speaking he'd been staring at the ceiling. Now he lowered his head to look at Maggie on the other settee.

"Anything important I missed?"

"Not for me. Keep going."

"At the end of the war, around 1946, he wanted to go back immediately, but found that wasn't possible. Effectively, he was a war criminal in Spain. So, he hired a private investigator. Suspicion and paranoia were endemic; anyone asking questions, especially a Brit, was a potential enemy. The investigator found out that the village had been destroyed. He also found out that Lola had been betrayed and taken away, but that was all. In the end he had to high-tail it out of Spain.

"Over the years, Spain was locked down. Few visitors, almost no tourists, but that began to change in the late 1950s. Franco died in 1975. Jerry was in his fifties by then. He decided to try again, but I think he was still afraid to go himself and that's something he blamed himself for, at the end. Called himself a coward."

Bob paused for a moment. Maggie thought that he'd reached into a terrible memory. After a moment's pause, he shook his head and continued: "Instead he sent another detective, but no luck. So, he gave up. But it kept coming back. He finally came back himself in 1999, when he was eighty. There were tours of the Ebro battlefields and he joined one. They went to look at the river, but all he could remember was the bodies floating in it. He didn't get much from local people. He felt disorientated, too. He thought he would remember exactly where everything had been. But he couldn't even pinpoint the site of the village. He gave up and went home, but it never left him.

"In 2014, he contacted the American relatives. Asked them if they could help. As you know, they said they couldn't find anything. Last year, he knew he was dying." Again, Bob took a deep breath. "It took a couple of months. Fucking awful, slow death. He wandered a lot in his head. Talked as if he was there. I asked him about it. That's when he told me the whole story and asked me to find her. And that's when he gave me a couple of names."

Neither of them spoke. Bob seemed spent. Jerry's story had affected him, perhaps more that he showed to others. She nodded, stood up, and went to look at the sea as the sun disappeared, to give him space and to arrange her ideas and questions.

"You OK?" he asked, breaking into some ideas that she was forming.

"Yes, I'm good. It's an immensely sad story, though. I have some questions and I'm looking forward to seeing your genealogist. What time did you say we're meeting him?"

"Six, at a local bar. It's just around the corner."

She turned around and went back to the settee. Sitting down again, her knees had wobbled and her head spun a little. Not enough sleep in the past few days.

"It's a restaurant, too. Serves good food so we can eat there."

"OK." She glanced at her watch. "Bob, it's almost five. Do you mind if I sleep for an hour? I'm really tired and I want to be alert for this meeting."

He shrugged. "Sure, no problem. I'll call you."

Maggie stood and walked into her room. She needed the sleep, but she also wanted to be alone to gather her thoughts.

* * *

Maggie had been deeply asleep, so when Bob knocked on the door and called her, just before six, she was disoriented and it took a few seconds for her to realise where she was. She had no time to think through what they were going to talk about, having fallen asleep as soon as she'd laid down.

The walk to the bar was undertaken in silence, as Maggie tried to pull together her thoughts. Bob pounded the pavement, hands in his overcoat pockets, head down. The atmosphere was, she felt, tense, but she didn't understand why. They had moved away from the tourist area and were crossing back streets. Bob came to a halt and nodded at a small, nondescript bar that looked closed.

"This is it." He didn't move, just stood in the street.

"Can we go in?" Maggie asked. He nodded, walked

154

across the pavement and shoved at the door.

At first, she couldn't see much, in the darkness within. There was one man sitting at one of the upright stools at the bar. He was as nondescript as his surroundings. He was staring at the mirror on the wall behind the serving area, a beer in front of him. As Bob walked up to him, the man jumped and turned and, seeing it was Bob, a wide grin transformed his dour face. They hugged each other, kissed once on each cheek and broke into a torrent of Spanish.

Bob broke off and turned back to Maggie. "This is Pepe, it's his bar. He's opened up early for us to meet Señor Torrens."

Maggie smiled at the man and held out her hand. He grinned, grabbed it, and shook it warmly. "Good to meet you, Maggie," he said in accented English. "What can I get you drink?"

She glanced around. "Just an orange juice," she replied. "Thank you for opening up for us. What time do you usually open?"

"About eight, or when I feel like," he replied, walking around the counter. He poured a beer from a tap into a tall glass for Bob and took another from a shelf above the counter, which he filled with orange juice and handed it to Maggie. One sip confirmed that it was fresh.

He nodded towards an area behind them and Maggie, turning her head, saw that there was an area of comfortable armchairs close to the bar. Now that she could see better she also spotted a dozen or so utilitarian tables and chairs further down the room, all made up and ready for diners. Then she noticed that the walls were covered with paintings. On examining them more closely, she realised that these could be original watercolour and oils. They gave the room a vibrancy, but at the same time an intimacy. Pepe saw her looking.

"My brother," he said. "An artist. He's good, yes?"

"They look beautiful," she replied. "I have a colleague and good friend whose husband was an artist. She'd love this." Recognising that her first thought had been Zelah, she pushed it to the back of her mind and turned back to the two men.

"What time are we expecting Señor Torrens?"

"Any minute, he knows the bar. Shall we sit?" Bob led the way to the armchairs, choosing an area with three separate seats. "We'll eat too. Pepe's offered to cook."

She nodded, accepting Bob's decision making. She was so used to having to make every decision about everything in her life that it was interesting to see how it felt to have someone else take the lead.

"What can you tell me about Señor Torrens? You haven't said anything about him."

"He's–" but at that moment the curtain at the front door swished and a man entered. He was short and round-shouldered. He stopped, blinked through heavy black-framed glasses, peered around, realised that Maggie and Bob were the only people in the room, and tentatively moved towards them. Bob stood.

"Señor Torrens?" Bob asked.

The man halted and nodded. "Si. Joan Torrens Diaz." He put out his hand. They exchanged a few words in Spanish, he nodded again and sat opposite them. He placed a battered brown leather satchel on the table and opened it. A small sheaf of papers spilled out onto the table between them. He stood again, took off his weathered brown Macintosh, folded it and laid it carefully on the arm of the chair, then sat down, on the edge.

Maggie gave Bob a quizzical look.

"Señor Torrens speaks English," he said. The man nodded. "Please, call me Joan. It is a Catalan name. It means 'John' in English."

"Pleased to meet you, Joan," she replied. "I'm Maggie. I'm looking forward to what you have to tell us."

"I have information for you, I think you will be pleased, Mrs Gilbert," he said.

"Maggie," she replied, "and that sounds promising."

He was about speak again, when the door at the back

156

of the bar flung open and Pepe appeared with tray. He swept over to them and placed half-a-dozen small dishes of food on the table. Joan quickly grabbed the papers and his bag.

"Tapas," Bob said to Maggie. "Appetizers, sort of. Thanks, Pepe."

Joan shuffled and organised his papers, whilst Maggie, who suddenly realised that she hadn't eaten all day, leaned forward to inspect the food. She didn't recognise anything, but didn't care, and took a selection. As she was putting the food into her mouth she wondered if that was the polite thing to do, but both men did likewise.

They finished their food quickly, and cleared the table and Joan laid out his papers on the table in small groups.

"So," Bob started, "did the names I gave you get us any leads?"

"Yes, they did, but I think that is not the place to start."

Bob shrugged. "You're the expert. Tell it the way you want to."

"Thank you. Well, first of all, the girl and the village. Records are quite poor, you know, from that time. If they existed at all, they were kept by the priest. Sometimes, if we are very in luck, the village records were deposited with the diocese. In this case, I had the name of the village and I have found the list of many inhabitants in 1938." He said this last piece with a beaming smile and a two-handed readjustment of his glasses.

"Wow," Maggie said. "How did you get that?" She looked at Bob but he was frowning in concentration.

"There was an estate, a big one, and many of the people worked on the land, before the landowner was thrown off after the war. Of course, he got back again, later. But he kept a list of the workers of the villages inside his estate, of 1937. There was only one Lola. The village was called Santa Rosa de l'Ebre. It does not tell us any more around her. For the landowner, she was a peasant, a worker. She had no other value. But this has been lucky, yes, to find her name. She was Dolors–"

Bob interrupted. "Dolors Maria Rosas LLorens?" he asked, leaning forward, turning his head to Maggie. "Lola is a diminutive of Dolors, the Catalan version of Dolores."

"Yes," Joan replied. "You knew this already? You didn't tell me?"

"No, I didn't. I kept it back for confirmation. In case there was more than one Dolors Maria Rosas. Wanted to be sure we ID'd the right one."

"He means identified," Maggie explained, scowling at Bob. "He's a policeman. They have their own language."

"Well, I found this name. I also found a descendant of a woman who lived there, who could tell me about the village. It was very small by the end of the war. About twenty people. I suspect they all knew about Lola's association with the International Brigade soldier. They did not keep secrets."

"Did the descendant know her?" Maggie asked.

"No, he knew very little, except that his grandmother lived there. She is dead now. She did not pass on names."

"And the village?" Maggie asked.

"Is gone. It was… what is the word?" he turned to Bob and said something in Spanish.

"Deserted," Bob answered.

"It was deserted when the army of Franco arrived. The people, they knew there would be no mercy. The stories of horror were spreading. Just half a dozen were left and they packed what they could and ran. It was never rebuild. Now, there is nothing; only a few very old people know where was the site."

"Did she have any recognisable relatives, on the list of names?" Maggie asked.

For a few seconds, there was silence.

"I found the record of her birth. It was still in church archives, in Reus. She was born in 1920. Her parents were married in 1919. Her parents were not on the landowner's list. I found her father's death in 1935 and her mother in 1936. I did not find brothers or sisters.

"But… I have traced many names on the list. And I

think that one might have been a relative. There is a woman with the same family name. This was maybe an aunt related to Lola's father. She was called Estel Puig Rosas, married to Tomau Puig. I have not been able to find her death. There was another of that family name, Carme Rosas. But her name had been crossed out. I think maybe she left the village before 1937, or retired, or died. I still try to trace her, but so far, I have no luck."

He passed across some of the papers to Bob, who handed them on to Maggie and they both quickly looked through them. She saw that they were copies of the landowner's list of workers on the estate and what she thought were the birth, marriage, and death notices of Lola and her immediate family.

"This is a great start, thank you, Joan. Further than anyone has ever got before," said Bob, still looking at the copies.

"But no, I am not the first to look," the man replied. "A few years ago, I think, someone viewed the same list and noted the same person and her family."

"What?" Maggie and Bob both looked up and spoke at the same time. "Who?" Bob asked, eyes narrowing.

"The estate did not give me a name. But they said they thought the person was from the United States. Does that mean something to you, Mr Pugh?"

Bob sat back in his armchair and rubbed his eyes with his fingers. Maggie could see that they were shaking. Expecting an explosion and not wanting the man who had done so much for them to feel intimidated, she said quickly "Yes, Joan, it does. We are acting quickly because of trying to find the possible heir, the child that might have survived. But there is another claim to the estate. An American. He has been saying that he tried a few years ago but found nothing."

"I see," replied Joan.

"We aren't interested in the money," Maggie clarified. "Bob was Jeremy's friend and Jeremy asked him to try to find out one last time if his child survived. He is redeeming a pledge. Do you understand?"

"I do," said the genealogist. "Then we must redouble our efforts. I have more information."

Bob got up and walked over to the bar to sit next to Pepe, who had been listening and he silently handed him another beer. Bob took a deep gulp, swallowed and walked back to the seating area.

"Sorry," he said. "I knew that American bastard was lying." He put his beer down on the table. If he had been honest, Jerry might have found out something before he died. That shit let him die not knowing if he had a child. All for money. Despicable bastard." His tone increased in vehemence as he spoke.

Joan moved back, staring wide-eyed. Maggie saw this and put a hand on Bob's arm.

"Sorry," he said, looking at Maggie and Joan. "What more information do you have?"

"You gave two names. Lidia Domenech and LLuis Portell. Well," he paused, "I have traced LLuis and also Lidia's descendant," he said triumphantly.

Bob nodded his head appreciatively. "That's excellent news, Joan. What can you tell us about them?"

The man picked up another sheet of paper.

"The first name you gave me, Lidia Domenech. Sadly, she is dead, but I think you would know that. She was imprisoned in 1940." He turned to Maggie. "Many women were, often for no reason, just that they had a husband or son who had fought and who had not been found, so the wife or mother, or both of them, was put in prison as punishment."

"I've been reading about it," Maggie replied. "I found it shocking."

For a few moments, the man didn't speak. He looked at the floor, swallowed, then looked up. "Yes. My grandmother was one. She has not spoken about what happened to her. I believe it was very terrible. She was in a

160

prison called Les Corts in Barcelona, for two years."

"I know of it," Maggie said, trying to convey sympathy and compassion in her tone. She had read of the beatings, torture, and starvation that thousands of women had endured in prison when the war ended, in this particularly notorious prison for women. The paper shook in his hands and she thought it was best to move on quickly. "So, what have you found?"

"Lidia was just twenty when she went to prison. Her daughter is still alive. She knows something of the story. She was not keen to speak, but I told her your story and she agreed that she will talk to you. I did not ask her what she knows. That is for you to ask."

"You have an address?" Bob asked. "When can we talk to her?"

"Tomorrow," Joan replied. She lives in Corbera D'Ebre now. She is in her seventies. Her name is Roser Sivils Domenech. She will meet with you tomorrow morning. You must be there at ten." He handed over a piece of paper. Bob nodded. "I know this place," he said. "And the second one?"

"He was a young boy in the village at the time of the war. He is now in his eighties. He lives in an old people's home, in Gandesa." He turned to Bob. "His language is Catalan, but they say he can manage Spanish. But you will need an interpreter?"

Bob shook his head. "I can manage enough Catalan." Maggie raised a quizzical eyebrow.

"My grandfather," he explained. "Catalan was his first language, but he also spoke Spanish. He spoke to me in both. I haven't used Catalan a lot since he died, but I can manage."

"Full of surprises," Maggie muttered.

"When can we meet him?" Bob asked, ignoring her.

"The following day," Joan replied. He handed Bob another piece of paper. "Here is the number of the home. Call them and they will arrange a good time. He is frail, but

he has a good memory still. Now, that is all and I will go."
He stood up abruptly, put on his coat and put the remaining
papers back into his satchel.

Bob and Maggie also stood, and shook hands with
Joan.

"This is excellent work, thank you, sincerely," Bob
said.

"I wish you good luck." Joan paused. "But a warning.
Be very… careful when you speak to these people. Some
of the memories are very bad. They may be, I think you
say, reluctant, at first. Many Spanish people do not want to
remember. It is too painful and too soon."

"What did he mean, 'too soon'?" Maggie asked when
he had gone and they had sat down again.

"There are still people alive today who lived through
it, quite a few. It's been called the Spanish holocaust.
Hundreds of thousands of Spaniards who fought against
Franco were imprisoned, beaten, tortured, and killed – by
their own countrymen. There were hard labour camps, lots
of Franco's opponents just disappeared. At the end of the
war, after the Allies won World War Two they turned their
back on Spain and let the madman continue because they
preferred the fascists to the communists. So, it went for a
long time. Today they live together. Some people prefer not
to know which side their neighbours were on. I think some
are ashamed of their country's past."

Maggie shook her head. What she was learning now
just didn't match her understanding of the country she had
partied in, in her wilder youth on the sunny Costas.

"We should eat," Bob said, interrupting her thoughts.
"Pepe's made us a local dish. It's good."

"I thought we had?" she replied.

"That was just tapas. This is a proper meal."

"OK," she said compliantly. She had given up on any
expectation of consultation. "We should make a plan,
though. How far is it to this place where the daughter
lives?"

"About an hour, hour and a half, from here," he replied, standing up and heading to one of the restaurant tables close to the bar. "We'll have to start early."

Over dinner they went over everything Joan Torrens had told them and discussed how much Mason Haussmann had found out and what he was likely to be keeping from them.

"He knows." Bob said, emphatically. "Whatever the truth is, he knows something, more than he's let on."

"But he may not have the full picture," Maggie said. "It may be that he knows that there was a surviving child, but not what happened to it. He didn't have the names that you had."

"Possibly," Bob agreed. "He found the village list, though. Couldn't have been another American, too big a coincidence, and there's no such thing as coincidence anyway."

"Agreed. It's all down to what we can get from the descendants. Big day tomorrow. Shall we go? I need to call my kids. Make sure everything's OK at home."

"Sure. You liked the food?"

She nodded, smiling. "Very good. Please thank Pepe for me. He's a great chef. What was it called?"

"Fricandó," Bob replied. He went over to the bar to speak to Pepe, who smiled and waved acknowledgement. Maggie put on her coat and they walked to the door.

In the street, it had become cold with a wind whipping in from the sea. She pulled her coat collar up and walked quickly. Neither of them spoke, both deep in thought.

Inside the apartment, the heating had fully warmed up. Maggie threw her coat over the arm of the nearest chair and dug out her phone. Bob picked up the coat and took it to the coat hangers next to the door. He signalled the letter 'T' to her and she nodded as she dialled.

Nick answered the phone and immediately told her that all was well. She didn't believe him.

"Tell me exactly what's happening. To each of them,

please. In detail."

Nick grunted. "Jack's fine. He's got homework and revision. Is it always this difficult to get him to do anything?"

"Yes," she replied, "and Alice?" The fraction of a second of silence before he answered was her cue to push.

"What's happened, Nick?"

"Nothing in particular, I think." His tone was measured and careful, but didn't give her any comfort. "She's quiet. That's all. She doesn't want to talk."

"Then push her."

"No," he replied, more firmly. "I believe she trusts me. I'm going to give her the space to tell me when she wants to tell me. You left me in charge, Maggie. Let me do as I see fit. Please."

Maggie was taken aback. The please wasn't a request. She gave herself a few seconds to think before replying. "OK. I trust you too. Do either of them want to speak to me?"

"No. I asked them earlier. I told them they can call you at any time and they both seemed fine with that. Is that enough?"

"Yes." She sighed the reply. "I'll call again same time tomorrow. Unless I hear anything back in the meantime. Thanks, Nick."

"Sure." He ended the call.

Maggie was still staring into space when Bob appeared at her elbow with a mug of tea.

"Everything OK at home? Only you look a bit phased."

"Yes, fine," she smiled brightly at him.

"Up to you. You can tell me to mind my own business. I'm OK with that. Hear it all the time."

"I bet you do. If I need to, I'll tell you. So, what do we do next?"

33

Early the following morning, they drove out of Sitges as the sun came up, leaving the sea behind and heading towards the mountains.

"I'm taking a roundabout route," Bob explained, although Maggie had no sense of direction in the mist that had enveloped them as they left the apartment. "We're heading for the city of Reus. Could have taken the coast road, more direct like, but I prefer the main roads. We'll get there in the same time. Just more kilometres."

She shrugged and he said nothing more until they reached the countryside and joined the autovía.

Bob looked at her scowling face and broke the silence: "Look, it was the most sensible thing to do."

Maggie shrugged again. "So why did you leave it until this morning to tell me?"

"Look, I know you want to be consulted, but it was a no-brainer, see? It's going to take us a couple of hours to get there. We have someone to see at ten, probably take an hour or more, then if we can arrange it, someone else to see today. Or tomorrow. So, what was the point in coming back two hours to the apartment, if we have to go back there again tomorrow?"

Bob waited a few minutes, then said in an attempt at a conciliatory tone, "I thought about what Joan said last night and the idea came to me. It was after you went to bed. I called the hotel in Gandesa on the off-chance they might have a couple of rooms. Which they did. I wasn't going to wake you up, was I, just to tell you that I thought it was a good idea to stay local for a few days. If I had and you hadn't got back to sleep you'd have been cursing me. So, are you telling me that you'd prefer to spend hours driving when we could be finding something out in the place where it all happened?"

"No, of course not," she replied, not looking at him. "I just… oh, never mind. I suppose I'll just have to get used to your ways."

"Good idea. Save us a lot of time."

Maggie glanced over at him, just in time to see him turn his face to hide a grin.

At Reus, they circuited the city and the road signs told them that they were about an hour from Gandesa at the rate they were travelling.

"Which means about three-quarters of an hour from Corbera," Bob said. "We'd better talk through what we want to get out of this visit."

"The most important thing, in my opinion, is to let Roser tell her story, with as little interruption as possible. I'm more concerned about how we are going to get it written down so we don't miss the details. Will you be able to translate unobtrusively so I can scribe?" Maggie replied.

"Good thought," he said. "Yes, I'll explain in more detail to her when we get there who we are and what we're doing here. And tell her that you'll be making notes in English." He paused. "Do you think it might have been a good idea to ask Joan to come along? I thought we could manage it between us, but now I'm not so sure."

"It will work," Maggie replied. "Let's trust ourselves to work with this woman, not upset her. Anyway, if we turned up with three of us, she could be intimidated. And I think we shouldn't go in with too many questions. Hopefully, they'll arise naturally from her story."

"As long as we are sure we get everything she remembers about Jerry and Lola."

"Of course, and whatever she can tell us about the village."

Bob's mobile rang. He answered on the hands-free and for a few minutes there was an exchange in rapid Spanish, or Catalan, Maggie wasn't sure which. As soon as the call

166

was finished he said, "That was the old people's home in Gandesa. LLuis isn't at his best in the afternoon, he likes to nap. They asked if we could come tomorrow morning, about eleven. That OK with you?"

"Yes," she said. "I presume you've told them that it is?"

"I told them to assume it's OK, but that I'll check with my colleague and get back to them if there's a problem. But if they don't hear from me, we get there at eleven."

"Good. What can we do this afternoon, then?"

"Well, it will give us plenty of time to go over Roser's information. See if that gives us anything special to speak to LLuis about tomorrow. And, if you like, we can go to the ruins of old Corbera. Give you a first-hand view of what happened during the war."

"How can it do that?" Maggie asked.

"It was bombed into ruins in 1938, after the Ebro battle, but it was never rebuilt. When Franco was in power nothing was made of it, but then, people realised that it was a symbol of the war. So, they deliberately left it as it was, and still is now. A monument. You have to pay to walk around, but it's worth it. And there's a very good museum in the town. Lots of information about the battle of the Ebro and the International Brigades."

"But there's still a town where people live, at Corbera?"

"Yes," he said. "After the war they started to rebuild below the old town. The old town is at the top of the hill, see. The new town built up around it, on the slopes leading down to the valley. You'll understand when we get there."

* * *

The sun had now burnt away the remaining wisps of mist. The road ran along the sides of hills and across plains, in and out of valleys that occasionally gave views of distant mountains. Maggie noticed the countryside and was attracted by the organisation of the agriculture. She knew

167

that Spain supplied a huge amount of olives, grapes, wine and fruit to the UK and other European Union countries, but she had supposed that this was done with an industrial-style organisation. Now, as she looked at the passing countryside, she saw how the trees and plants complimented the scenery. Everywhere she looked, vine and olive plantations were laid out in rows, in sectors, whose boundaries were nothing more than the next crop, growing on steep-sided hills as well as on the flat floor of the valleys. None was so big that it dominated. They were laid out like the patterns of a quilt, in all shades of green and brown. She thought that they must belong to small farmers, each producing his own individual crop. Maybe they were collectives. She had read already that collectivism had been the goal of the republicans during the civil war, but the majority of the land had been owned by aristocratic landowners who used the working people as little more than slave labour. Spain had its share of economic problems and the level of unemployment was worrying. But looking out over this scenery she felt that she was looking at something to which modern life had adapted, that had been in place for generations, maybe thousands of years. Here, tradition was more important that modernism. To Spain's advantage? She wasn't sure. But to look at it gave the impression of serenity and peace, and there was a lot to be said for that.

"What else do they grow here, Bob, apart from grapes and olives?"

"Nuts," he replied. "Almonds, pistachios, walnuts. And lots of fruit: apples, pears, peaches, apricots."

"I love the way they're growing right up the hillsides."

"Soil's fertile here. Good for almost anything. It's more intensive than it was back in the thirties. The estates and farms are mostly small. Lots of European grants for small producers."

They passed a sign that said ten kilometres to Gandesa. "Nearly there," Bob said. "Corbera is about five kilometres

168

from Gandesa. I've set up the sat nav already."

With that, he flicked the switch on the dashboard and a map appeared, followed by a voice in Spanish. Maggie could see more buildings and soon they lined the road.

"Up there," Bob pointed to what looked like a church on a hillside in the near distance. "That's the old town. There's not much else you can see from here."

The guidance voice spoke up again as they entered the outskirts of a small town that fell down the hillside to the valley floor. It was featureless; the housing looked around fifty years old. This must be the 'new' town, Maggie guessed. At the bottom of the hillside on the valley floor there was a small, new, housing estate. Like everywhere else she had seen in Spain, local planning didn't seem to have as much influence as it did it in the UK. It made the town look straggly, but perhaps that was more in keeping with how local people liked it.

The main road through the town ran in a straight line, bordered by a few shops, cafés and houses. There were several sets of traffic lights; Bob turned right at the second set, climbing a steep hillside. At the top, he turned right, then stopped and parked at the side of the road. Maggie climbed out of the car and looked down the street. It was steep here; the houses had been dug out of the hillside and were multi-levelled.

Bob checked a piece of paper, then marched off up the road. She caught up with him, but he didn't speak. He was looking at the names and numbers on the houses. He came to an abrupt stop. "This is it."

It occurred to her then that the personal nature of this quest was having more of an effect on Bob than she had realised. His face was set in grim determination, which she was thought was tinged with nerves. There was no bell, so he knocked loudly. In the distance an inharmonious church bell clanged out the hour. It was ten o'clock. Someone must have been standing behind the door because it opened before Bob's hand was back at his side.

A small woman dressed in black stood in the doorway.

Bob introduced himself in Spanish and presented her with a business card, whilst standing to attention. He introduced Maggie, who smiled. The woman put out her hand, which Bob took and shook gently and the woman beckoned them inside.

She led them along a dark corridor that ended in four steps, then along another short length of corridor and through a door that opened into a lounge. The far wall was all glass, with a balcony. The view of the valley below and the mountains opposite, was breath-taking. The room was pristine. The settee and chairs were backed with antimacassars. A glass cabinet held shelves of small knick-knacks. A highly polished, folded gate-leg table hosted portraits of dead ancestors. Larger portraits and religious pictures covered most of the walls. The room smelled of unremitting polishing. Maggie felt a frisson of memory of her late grandmother's house, of the 'best' room, reserved for guests and special occasions, denied to children with even a speck of dirt on their shoes or fingers.

Señora Sivils had put a plate of small cakes on a table in front of the chairs. Another, younger woman arrived with a tray of tea. Bob and Maggie took the armchairs offered and waited whilst the tea was poured and the cakes nibbled at, all the while with a flow of what Maggie assumed was pleasantries between Bob and the two women.

The second woman had taken the fourth seat and Bob began to speak. Maggie guessed that he was explaining their mission, who they were and why they wanted to find out about the past. Although she already knew all of this, he no doubt thought it best to explain in person. He then pointed to Maggie and said that she would be writing down the translation of the discussion. The woman smiled and nodded. Maggie thought she looked guarded.

"I've told her we don't want to cause any trouble, or to cause her any unnecessary pain," he said to Maggie. "Just got to convince her that nothing she says will have any repercussions."

170

He turned and simply said, "Señora Sivils…?"

Slowly, the woman began to tell her story, which Maggie captured as best she could from Bob's rapid translation, done in a low voice and not taking his eyes off the old woman.

"Lola and my mother were of a similar age… Lived in the village all their lives… Friends… Both had been young and idealistic, worked for the Republic. Took food to the men of the International Brigades, who were at a training camp nearby… Saw the relationship between the young Englishman and Lola… A hopeless love… Saw them married by the village priest."

Maggie interrupted, "What kind of man was he?" Bob scowled sideways at her, but the woman nodded emphatically.

"A good man. Padre Carles Rovira. My mother remembered his name. Said he should be remembered as a good man. Not like some of the others." The woman's eyes wandered away, lapsing into memory.

Maggie recalled some of the stories she had read about the convents that had been turned into women's prisons, the stories of the bullying, the humiliation, the cruelty inflicted by the nuns on the women prisoners.

The story continued and Maggie scribbled quietly. "The men left in late July… heading for the river Ebro… crossing somewhere, didn't know where. Lola was pregnant… frightened. Mother said she had never seen that girl frightened before… They all waited, hopeful, sure… eventually news came, terrible news. Failure… Much death, the international brigade defeated, driven back… across the river… not sure where. Then no news… The fascist army coming… retribution against villages… My mother decided to run. Begged Lola to go with her. But she wouldn't leave… wanted news of her husband. He had sent a message that he could come for her. Mother couldn't wait… The girl waited too long… Mother heard she was taken away… Someone in the village gave her up… Never heard any more about them. Mother was caught in 1940.

Sent to prison for thirty years... sent to a prison in Barcelona, then moved around. I cannot say any more."

Maggie thought that the Barcelona prison was probably Les Corts. She stopped writing and looked up. Once again, the old woman's gaze was far away. Her daughter had taken her hand. She spoke to Bob, who nodded and said to Maggie, "She says it's still very hard for her to talk about. Her mother's treatment in prison was horrifying; they were tortured and starved. Her back was damaged when a fascist interrogator stamped on it; she was never strong when she got out. But she was released early after five years. She died at the age of forty-five. But at least she survived, unlike so many others. Young girls, as young as fourteen were imprisoned and shot. They were just idealistic young people. To the fascists, they were traitors and sub-humans. Her mother saw horror that she could not forget, no matter how hard she tried. My grandmother was a woman filled with sorrow and anger and pain."

The pen was shaking in Maggie's hand, so much so that she had to put it down. Señora Sivils saw and leaned over to take her hand, speaking softly in Catalan.

"She says 'Write it all down'," Bob said. Maggie picked up the pen again, as he continued translating: "It's not made up. It all really happened. But people don't like to talk about it." He paused for a few seconds then said, "I think it's time to go, now. But, just one thing..."

He reached into his overcoat pocket, took out an envelope and handed it to Señora Sivils. She opened it, took out its contents, and gasped. It was a photograph, but infuriatingly, Maggie couldn't see what of. Señora Sivils' eyes filled with tears. She looked at Bob, nodded and ran her thumb caressingly over it, then handed it back to him, with a few words that to Maggie seemed beseeching. Without a word, he put the photo back in the envelope and stood up.

He made a short speech, which Maggie presumed was thanking her for speaking to them, that her information had been helpful, that she was a brave woman. Señora Sivils shook her head. Then she took each of their hands, squeezed them, and led the way back to the front door.

Neither of them spoke until they reached the car. By this time, Maggie was burning with curiosity and a little frustration.

"Are you going to share whatever that was with me? I felt pretty stupid right now."

"She didn't know you hadn't seen it before," he retorted. "I needed her confirmation." He handed her the envelope. She felt like throwing it back at him. But curiosity won out. The old, black and white photograph showed three young people. A man in the centre with blond hair, grinning at the camera. On each side were two young women. The man had his arm hung loosely on the shoulder of the woman on the left of the photo, a smallish dark-haired girl. She was looking sideways at him and laughing. The second girl stood with her arms folded, pursing her lips, but more in mock indignation than anger, Maggie thought. It looked as if they had all just shared a joke. They were all wearing bandanas around their necks and the man appeared to be in a shabby-looking uniform. Maggie threw Bob a quizzical look, but already knew the answer.

"Jerry, with Lola on the left and Señora Sivils' mother, Lidia Domenech, on the right," he confirmed. "I didn't know, but I thought there was a chance it was her mother, so I brought it with me. It was the only photo Jerry had. He left it for me, to help me. When I thanked her, I told her I'd send her a copy. She said she doesn't have many photos of her mother, and in this one she looks so animated. They all do."

"When was this taken, do you think?"

"Probably around early summer 1938. He couldn't remember exactly."

"It's in good condition."

"He preserved it. Only one he had."

"Lola looks… I'm trying to think of the right word… sparky. She must have been quite a personality." She examined the photograph again. "Doesn't her name have something to do with sorrow? She doesn't look like a sorrowful person. Quite the opposite."

"It's common in Spain and here in Catalonia. It's means something like 'Mary of Sorrows'. Jerry said that he was really scared of her when they first met. But that soon changed. He thought she was the most tender-hearted person he had ever met. And yes, sparky."

Maggie kept her eyes fixed on the photograph. "Señora Sivils' mother was imprisoned in 1940. She probably didn't look anything like this when she got out, from what she told us."

"I think she struggled on. Many of the women didn't, or couldn't. She survived sixteen years after coming out of prison. But Señora Sivils lost her mother when she was barely more than a child. Tough."

"I read something about the treatment of the women in prisons after the war," Maggie said. "Although until you hear it first hand, it's just another historical story. But it's so hard to comprehend, to accept that it happened in a country such as Spain. It's making me feel queasy."

"Let's walk. Clear our heads. Come on."

He put his arm through hers and led her along the street, turned left and headed further up the hill. Maggie didn't take too much notice where they were until she perceived that the buildings on either side of them were ruins and they had to pick their way over damaged cobbles. "Where are we?"

"At the start of the old town of Corbera D'Ebre," he replied. "You'll get a better idea of what the war actually did. It's a living museum, like I said."

It was now almost midday and the sun was high in a cloudless sky. But the temperature hadn't risen. Maggie reached into her bag and found her gloves and hat. She put them on while Bob went to a small kiosk and bought their entry tickets.

Maggie had only seen bomb damage before on news programmes. The reality was more shocking than she could have imagined. Not a single building had survived intact in this little hilltop town. It consisted of a few streets surrounding a flat central area.

"That used to be houses, too," Bob explained, "but they were annihilated. Bombed out of existence. Nothing left."

They walked slowly and silently around the ruins. All of the houses had their fronts blown out, revealing varying stages of internal destruction. In some, kitchens and bathrooms were just about recognisable. In others, everything had caved in, leaving just the shell of what had once been family homes in great piles of rubble.

When they drove into Corbera, the only building visible on the hill had been the church. It looked intact, but when they reached it, Bob pointed out that it had no roof. In fact, the entire roof had now been replaced by glass. The only sound was the twittering of a few birds that had found a way into the huge, hollow, echoing space.

Although it had been this way for almost seventy years, Maggie saw the similarity to what she saw daily on the news from the Middle East.

"Gets to you, doesn't it?" Bob said quietly as they descended the hill back to the car. He had tucked his arm into hers as they picked their way over the uneven ground and she found it comforting. "Lunch, I think. We can go over the notes, make sure you got it all down."

"I think I missed a lot," she replied.

Before they got back into the car Maggie looked out again over the soft fertile valley and the distant snow-capped mountains. "It's so beautiful," she said. "How do such ugly things happen in such a beautiful place?"

34

The drive into Gandesa took fifteen minutes. They checked into the hotel on the outskirts of the small town and met in the foyer once they had deposited their bags.

"How's your room?" Bob asked, as they headed out for the ten-minute walk to the centre of the town.

"Fine," Maggie replied. "It's rather quaint, but clean and the bathroom doesn't leak. That'll do for me."

They found a small sandwich bar on one side of a central tree-lined square. It was too cold to sit outside, although a few smokers were enduring the bite of the wind. Another man came in, looked around and sat and ordered.

"Probably nice in the summer, when those baskets and tubs are full and that fountain works," Maggie commented.

"Nothing remarkable about this place. Did you notice the museum on the way in?"

She shook her head.

"It's a civil war museum. Gandesa looks quiet and backwater now, but strategically it was crucial. Target of the International Brigades. They got as far as besieging it, but couldn't take it. Franco's troops took more of the hills and pinned them down. In the end, they had to retreat. The beginning of the end."

"Do you have a plan for this afternoon?" she asked.

"Are you really asking, or do you just want to know what it is?"

"Surprise me."

"I thought we could look at the museums. There are at least ten of them in the area. One's here and the main one for the battle of the Ebro is back in Corbera. And we need to go over the notes, make sure everything's written down. I'll need to use it in court when we get back."

"I hadn't thought of that. OK, let's do that. Not that you were expecting me to object."

176

They spent the next couple of hours in the museums of Gandesa and Corbera. Maggie gained a greater understanding of the course of the war, but all the time with a feeling of depression. She knew a lot about both world wars, with first-hand stories from her grandfather who had been in the RAF in the 1940s. But the feeling of being on the losing side was so different.

Why do I feel so melancholic? she wondered, as they left the museum at Corbera and headed back to the hotel. Probably because she had just seen the film records and read the reports and letters of hope of the men on the front line, but knew their fate. She had felt something similar when researching her own family history and when she'd read a report of the birth of twin girls in the nineteenth century, imagining the happiness of the parents, and knowing that ten years later one of the girls would be horribly drowned. She didn't speak until they got back to the hotel, where they sat in armchairs in front of a small table and ordered coffee. Bob nipped up to his room to get his laptop.

"You're right," she said, as he sat down next to her. "It gets to you."

He put an arm around her shoulders and gave her a quick hug. "You're doing well. This isn't easy stuff."

"But I'm a researcher. I'm supposed to be able to handle it. My own family, yes, there was a connection and I felt sad. But why this? Why these people? I didn't even know about them two weeks ago."

"Because they're real people, not historical footnotes, and I think that matters to you. That's why you're so good at your job."

She turned to look at him to thank him, but found that his expression was tender. The waitress arrived with a tray of coffee and biscuits, which gave Maggie the opportunity to turn away and he slipped his hand from her shoulder. By the time the drinks were poured and the laptop was ready to go, the moment had passed and they were business-like again.

It turned out that Maggie hadn't missed much. Bob's expertise quickly turned her notes into a statement.

"Will she have to sign it?" Maggie asked.

"I'm thinking about that," he replied. "It would probably help. I'll get Joan to call her daughter in a day or so, after we've met with LLuis Portells tomorrow. Let's see how that goes first, yeah?"

They decided to eat in the hotel restaurant. There were only a few other guests. The food was good and by the time they had eaten, Maggie felt a wave of exhaustion stiffening her neck and shoulders.

"Time to sleep," she said. "I think we did well today. A good start anyway." Bob nodded in agreement but seemed distant. "You OK?" she added.

"Just thinking about tomorrow, how to approach it."

"I would have thought, same as today. This guy is even older; and he was just a boy when he and Lola lived in the village. Just let him talk, to start with."

"OK. See you in the morning. Breakfast about nine-thirty?"

She nodded and stood. Bob remained seated. "Going for a walk," he said. "Helps me think." She left him at the table.

Maggie called Nick before retiring, but was told that both Jack and Alice were out and he was just leaving to pick them up. This time he asked her how her trip was working out. She explained briefly. He didn't comment, but said, "Zelah's back. She's coming here tomorrow."

"Was her trip successful?"

She felt him consider his answer, a heavy breath, or was it a sigh, coming down the phone. "Yes. If finding out that the client is a fraud is successful."

"What?"

"Calm down, Maggie. It's all OK. At least we know now. Look, I have to go. Alice is at Janine's and Jack is at a friend's. They're expecting me."

"Sorry you had to do this, Nick"

"I'm enjoying it," he said, then ended the call.

35

Zelah called Nick from the airport as soon as she had cleared customs and told him that she would be back in Newport in about two hours. He didn't bother asking if she intended to take a rest before starting work again. They agreed to meet at Maggie's house. By the time she arrived it was early evening and Jack and Alice were home. Nick had ordered pizza for all of them, including Zelah.

"You must be tired," he said, as she walked into the house and straight into the office where he had laid out a pizza, plates, and a tray of coffee. Zelah flung her bags down and started on the pizza.

"Need to regroup," she began. "Something very wrong with Morgan Sturridge. Considering he's been dead since 1965!"

Nick sat forward in his chair, put his elbows on the table and his fingers up to mouth and nose in a prayer-like gesture. "Can we walk this back a bit, Zelah?"

She stopped chewing. "Explain?"

"You say he's been dead for just over fifty years. The original Morgan Sturridge died then, that's a fact. You saw the grave. But who have you been talking to? There are two possibilities as far as I can see. One, an impostor. Two, not an impostor." He stopped there and looked at her. Zelah, who was about to start on another slice of pizza stopped with her mouth open, as the implication of Nick's suggestion hit her. She bit her bottom lip, went to speak, stopped again, closed her mouth in a grimace, and put the pizza down on a plate.

Her phone rang. She glanced at it, raised her eyebrows and answered the call. Nick watched.

"Well, hello. I didn't expect to hear from you so soon." She gestured to Nick, who moved in closer. "Yes, my flight was fine, thank you. Actually, I'm back at my office and here with a colleague, called Nick Howell. Do you mind if I put him on speaker?" The person at the other end must have agreed and Zelah pushed the button. The voice at the other end had a North American accent.

"Hello there," it said.

"Nick, Rick Matheson. He lives next door to Louisa Sturridge in Shelburne. We met a couple of days ago."

"Hello there," Rick Matheson said again but didn't wait for a reply. "Zelah, I've been thinking a lot about what you told me about this Sturridge guy. I was pretty sure I was clear, but just in case I did some checking with some local folks."

"Thank you, Rick. What did you find out?"

"I was right. No one of that name ever lived or worked in Shelburne. Not in any capacity. They checked around, too. No one at all ever heard of him. Except…"

They waited.

"Except, there's a lady works at the museum. 'Bout my age. She thought she recalled the Sturridges had a baby they called Morgan, but he died, just a coupla days old."

"She was right," Zelah said. "So that confirms that the man calling himself Morgan Sturridge and whatever he told Louisa his name was, is an impostor. Nick and I are just starting to try to figure out why."

"Louisa's due back Sunday. You want me to talk to her?"

Nick and Zelah looked at each other. Nick said "Rick, I think it's a bit early to tell her everything about this. We don't have enough information yet. Still more questions than answers. But… I'd be interested to know if she had a good time and if the trip was as good as it was sold to her. Because, if it was, someone has gone to a great deal of expense to keep her out of the way."

Zelah's head bobbed up and down at speed as Nick was talking. "Rick, this had been really helpful. Can we give you a call back next week, mid-week, after Louisa is back? We may have some more information by then. But if there's anything significant in what she says, call us as soon as you've spoken to her. How does that sound?"

"Sounds good to me," Rick Matheson confirmed. Nick thought the man's voice held a tone of real enthusiasm.

Zelah ended the call with more thanks and a promise to speak again. Then she gave a huge yawn that she tried to swallow, but not quickly enough.

"That's the third time you've done that since you got here," Nick said to her. "Look, we need to think this through, can we leave it until tomorrow?"

"No, we can't!" she replied, but yawned again.

"Zelah, you're tired and you can't think at your best when you're tired and jet-lagged. Please, go home. I think what we need next is as close as you can get to a script of every conversation you had with Morgan Sturridge. There's going to be a pointer in there, somewhere." He stared directly at her. "Come back first thing tomorrow and we'll start again."

She went to automatically object but thought better of it. "You're right," she admitted. "I'm knackered. I thought I could fight through it." She picked up her coat and briefcase. She looked, Nick thought, dejected.

"Chin up, Zelah. We'll get to the bottom of this. You'll see."

"Makes a change for someone other than me to do the pushing. Back here at nine?"

He nodded and she left.

Alice's head appeared around the office door. "Someone leave?"

"Zelah," Nick said. "Gone home to sleep. Go call Jack, please. Then we can get stuck into this pizza. Don't know about you, but I'm starving."

When Jack arrived, they took their boxes into the living room. Nick lit the fire and they sat down in front of *Netflix* for an hour, demolishing the pizza and hot chocolate brownies. They had eaten from the boxes, with their hands, not bothered with the plates or cutlery.

"Your mother's going to kill me," Nick said, as they took the boxes straight out to the bin.

"Don't tell her," Alice said with her best evil smile.

"She'll probably guess, but there's no need to lead her to it," Jack added.

"You two are leading me down wicked paths," Nick said sternly, as he pushed the pizza boxes to the bottom of the bin; at which they high-fived each other and went back to their respective computers.

Not really sure why he was doing it – surely he should be thinking about Morgan Sturridge and the possible reasons for his deception? – Nick also went back to his computer and began to research his own family history. He had made some progress since Maggie had left him with the news that he had a murderer in his line of descent. But it was mainly siblings and deaths. Yet, he felt a strong compulsion to go on. He couldn't do much about Morgan Sturridge until he had spoken to Zelah in the morning. He had avoided his own family history for so long that he was surprised to find such a great hunger to discover it all now. It was like the proverbial snowball down a hill, he thought. Once he and Zelah got together tomorrow he would have to put this work down. So, on he would plough.

Later in the evening Maggie called. He thought she seemed quite well, reassured that her children were also well. He decided not to tell her too much about the Canadian news. She needed to concentrate on what she was doing in Spain. He told her that the client was a fraud, which drew a screech of horror, but he cut her off with what he considered was a small white lie, that he had to go out to pick up Alice and Jack from friends' houses.

Back to his research, he confirmed what Maggie had discovered, that he was the only second son in his Howell line to survive infancy. Which, according to his mother, was purely by accident, due to his father's accidental death in a plane crash. Would his own father really have killed him? Of course, he only had his mother's word for that, and he never trusted anything she said. Or had he? He sat back in his chair, arms folded, staring at the screen, but seeing his mother's dying face. His head told him that the story of a curse was unbelievable. Nonsense. But his heart, or whatever organ outranked his head, kept the seed of doubt alive. His left hand was still gloved. He lifted it to his face and examined it. What would happen if he took it off? Threw it away? No, not yet. Not until he truly understood.

A couple of hours later, when he had gleaned as much information as possible through online resources on each generation of the Hywel/Howell family, Nick believed he had honed down to just a couple of important questions.

First question – was it possible that the story of a curse, handed down through generations, could have sufficient impact by itself to push fathers to kill sons? His head told him no. Perhaps, in times of superstition, a curse would have been believed. But to murder just for its avoidance? He couldn't believe it. There must have been more. This was partly based on the transcript of John Howell's trial, where he had been claimed to have been visited by a 'demon'. Of course, he wasn't believed, not even back then. He had been portrayed as a lazy, wife-beating drunk. But there had been no idea put forward as to why he had strangled his newborn son and then frenziedly stabbed his wife to death. He could have tried to pass it off as an intruder caught in the act, or some such story, but he hadn't tried. From the moment he had been found, sitting in a pool of blood next to the bodies, he had only talked about the 'demon'. There was something Nick didn't understand in this story. It required more thought, Zelah's as well as his.

The main question: what had happened to John Howell, after his escape from Monmouth Gaol prior to his execution in 1875? There had to be more stories in the papers of the time. These days, you wouldn't have been able to move for tabloid reporters and social media so-called news. But back then? Even back then this would have been newsworthy with a killer on the loose.

And, what had happened to his remaining children after John Howell was condemned?

Nick glanced at the screen, and saw that it was almost 3am. He was too tired to do any more. He turned off the computer, then went round the house, locking doors and turning off lights. He realised that he hadn't spoken to Jack and Alice since supper. He checked in each room, found that they were both asleep, Jack still in his clothes. He went to the guest room, got into bed, and fell asleep immediately.

He was awakened, what seemed like minutes later, by a loud banging noise somewhere in the distance. After a few seconds' panic he leapt out of bed and ran to the front door, where Zelah stood waiting.

She swept past him into the kitchen and filled the kettle. "Did you sleep in those clothes? You look like death."

"I'll tell you when I've woken up. I thought we agreed to meet at nine?"

She pointed at the clock on the wall, showing nine-fifteen. Nick turned and walked back to the hall and into the office, followed by Zelah with a tea tray. She put a cup in front of him and poured it out. "Extra sugar?"

"I'll be fine. I was up late."

"How come?"

"My own stuff. Couldn't start it for years, now I've started I can't stop."

"Are you getting somewhere?"

"Not sure," he glanced at her, a steaming cup at his mouth. "I don't know exactly what or where is the destination, except I'll know when I get there."

"I'm curious," Zelah said, sitting down opposite and putting her notebook and pens on the table. "What made you start this, after such a long time?"

He sat back in the chair and looked into the cup. "I don't know, something. Maybe it was Maggie deciding to go off and do her own thing. It just felt like… it was time. I knew the manor was involved. Maybe it was her going there, taking me there."

"No more to it than that?"

He sat up in the chair. "I think there is. But I don't know what. Like an out-of-focus picture. There's something to see, but I can't make it out. Nagging away at

184

me." He banged the cup back down on the saucer, causing the spoon to jump onto the table, and crossed his arms.

"Anyway, let's get on with your Canadian imposter?"

She was gawking at him as if he was an exhibit in a circus that had just performed a trick.

"What?"

"Never seen you almost break something."

"Drop it. Let's get on. Where do we start?"

"For me," Zelah said, "we go further into what you suggested last night. I've been thinking about it. Either he's a scammer and he's trying to get us to prove something for his benefit, or he's something else. We should examine each possibility to see what feels possible. And," she jabbed a finger at Nick, "no holds barred. We say exactly what we are thinking. Everything on the table. OK?"

"OK with me."

"Right. I'll start with the scammer angle. First question: why? He said he came to Maze because of our reputation, but he talked about you, and you're the least well-known of the three of us."

"Agreed. But did he push it?"

"No. Just said that he presumed he would meet you, eventually. Come to think of it, he didn't even mention Maggie's name. Anyway, he said he had an important 'life event' coming up."

"What was he like, as a person? What impression did you get?"

"Hmm. Rich. Well-dressed and staying at the best hotel. Well-groomed, smooth. And confident, but not ostentatious. A man it would be easy to do business with."

"Did anyone else see him or speak to him?"

She considered for a moment. "The staff at the hotel. And they did look at him a bit funny. Like they didn't quite understand something about him. But I didn't question it, did I? Didn't question anything. Just saw the big cheque." She put her hands to her eyes and rubbed them with her palms. "Idiot."

"If he's a scammer, then he must be a successful one.

Don't beat yourself up. You have to be well-off to stay at the Celtic Manor. What else?"

"Not much, really," Zelah replied, drumming her fingers on the desk. "Hell, I've tried to think. What did I miss? What else was there? But I can't think of anything. Except that he mentioned two counties. He talked about his mother's family coming from Glamorgan." She sat forward. "But at one point he said Monmouthshire. Could that have been a mistake?"

"Which one?" Nick replied. "And we've looked at both. "No Hammills in either. Ever."

"So, then he disappears. They're still keeping the room for him, all paid for, but he's not come back. And that's not cheap."

"Let's think about the research. It wasn't difficult to trace the Canadian line. And it all goes back to Jonathan Hammill, who is supposed to have come from Glamorgan or Monmouthshire – let's assume either may be right. And he's supposed to have travelled to Canada with his parents when he was a child. But you've checked, right?"

"Everything. Ben Alder, that's the Canadian researcher, and I have covered every passenger list from 1840 to 1870. Not that there were many at during period. But Ben has also checked the records at the entry ports. There was no one called Hammill."

"What assumptions did you make, when you couldn't find anything?" Nick asked.

"I thought the name might have been written down incorrectly. Believe me, I tried everything."

"I believe you," Nick mused. "What we have is a man who came to us asking us to trace a non-existent forebear, who turns out himself to be an impostor. Whatever his motivation, it wasn't an obvious one. He couldn't have been getting married, or doing anything normal, because he wasn't who he said he was. He was leading you in a direction that we can't understand, yet."

Zelah banged her fist on the table. "I'm so angry with myself!"

"Don't be," Nick replied. "Maybe you were doing exactly what he wanted you to do. You're a first-class researcher, Zelah. It took you a couple of days to find out all of this. He must have known that you'd go to whatever lengths were necessary to get to the true story."

"And what have I found out that's of any use?" she barked back at him. "Any genealogy researcher could have found out the same information."

"Quieten down. Yes, probably. But not as quickly. You hired help, and you went to Canada. Not many would have done that. But, I agree, there's nothing you found out that a good pro couldn't have. Time to change our focus."

"To what?"

"To us," he replied. "Maybe it's not about him. It's about us *and* him. And that brings us to the second possibility – not an impostor."

Zelah gave him a long, appraising look. "What do you think he could be?"

Nick stood up and paced the length of the table, then sat down again. "From what you've told me he's easily believable, yes?"

"Well I believed him," she retorted. "He didn't look ethereal to me."

"We both have different theories about ghosts. You think they're the embodiment of a memory, close enough and strong enough to an individual to be seen. I think they're the energy that remains after a person dies. It should dissipate with them, for some reason it retains the shape and form of the dead person, but imperfectly." She nodded. "But Morgan Sturridge has an individual personality, not of a person known to either of us and I believe not to Maggie. That makes him something else."

"What else?" Zelah asked.

"Something dangerous to us. Think about it. He targeted Maze. He met with you and gave you a believable lie, led you to a story. He mentioned my name. I don't think Maggie is involved. It's you and me he's after."

"Why? What have we done? Could it be a past case?

Did we upset someone enough for this? Is he trying to destroy Maze?"

Nick drummed his fingers on the table. "No, I suspect it's personal. You and me. You *or* me. And another question: why now? And anyway," he added, "if you and Maggie don't sort yourselves out you won't need his help to destroy Maze."

Zelah opened her mouth to remonstrate, but checked herself. "I don't want to destroy Maze. I can't speak for Maggie."

"I can, and she doesn't either. But that doesn't mean it won't happen if you two don't start talking to each other. Anyway, let's not get distracted. Did you manage to write down everything he said to you? What about when he first contacted you?"

"I printed off his email. Here it is." She reached into her bag, brought out some papers and slid them across the table to Nick.

"This says he wants us to explore local roots. What did he mean by that?"

"Well, that's where he made a mistake, he mentioned Glamorgan and Monmouthshire."

"When did he mention them? This could be important."

"I thought about it last night. On the phone, he said Glamorgan. But when I met him at the Celtic Manor he said Monmouthshire."

"Who phoned who?"

"He called me," she replied. "And that's another stupid thing. I never got phone number. He said he could always be reached at the hotel." She slapped herself across her forehead. "Why the hell didn't I take a mobile number?"

"I think if you tried he'd have found an excuse not to give it to you. Morgan Sturridge didn't want to be bothered with inconvenient phone calls asking for information he didn't want to give. He gave you enough information to set you off that was meant to bring you to a specific spot. And here we are. It's Monmouthshire, not Glamorgan. It's a big county, but it has good records. And there's no John Hammill at any relevant time in the past in Monmouthshire. So, what if that was an alias?"

Zelah went to reply but was interrupted by a series of loud bangs that startled her, but she noticed that Nick didn't react. Jack rushed into the room. "Morning Nick, I… oh, hello Zelah. Nick, a couple of mates are playing footy for the school team. Thought I might go and watch. Can I get a lift?"

"When?"

"Now, if that's not inconvenient."

Nick nodded. "Five minutes."

"Well at least he was polite about it," said an amused Zelah.

"That's because Maggie warned them to be polite. I'll have to go. Won't be long. It's probably somewhere nearby."

* * *

It turned out to be Ebbw Vale, and Nick was away for the best part of an hour.

"At least he's getting a lift back with one of his friend's dads," he said when he got back.

Zelah had just made a fresh pot of coffee and Nick helped himself.

"Just wait for the next one, now. Has she surfaced yet?"

"I think so, but she's keeping to her room. I heard her talking. Probably heard me down here."

"It's not personal," he replied, sitting down at the table. "She has a friend with a problem. Expect she's video messaging with her." He paused. "I'll just go up and see if she wants some breakfast."

Zelah heard him go up and down the stairs twice before he came back into the office. "Is it always like this?" she asked when her returned, slightly breathless. "I don't know how Maggie does it."

"You going out again, or are we OK for a while?"

"Alice wants to go out this afternoon, needs a lift to the cinema. We're OK for now."

Zelah pushed her chair back, stood up, folded her arms, and walked to the door, then walked back again. "Don't know why I did that," she said. "It's so frustrating. I want to *do* something!"

Nick kept his voice calm. "Do you agree with what we've said so far? That's its personal, it's you or me?"

"Has to be," she huffed. "If it was a scam it was a bad one. We were... I was onto it much too quickly. So, it has to be personal. But why, Nick? What the hell is this about?"

"What could there be in your background that might warrant this, Zelah? You've never talked to me about yourself. Could this be about you?"

"I don't talk about it!" she raised her voice and turned her back. "Nothing of my early life means anything to me now."

"What about your ancestors?"

She turned round, and leaned forward, putting both hands palms down on the table, glaring at him. "I have no idea who they were. And this is *not* the time to find out!"

Nick raised his hands, palms toward her. "OK. OK. Calm down, Zelah. I had to ask. If it's not you, then it's me. Shall we think about me as the target?"

"No harm in giving it a try, I suppose."

"As we have no other leads, I want to think about this. But there is something I need to do. Something I should have done already, but it's not too late. How about we leave it for now? I'll take Alice over to Janine, then I want to go and check something out."

"Fine with me," she replied, picking up her bag. "There's something I want to do too." She grabbed her coat from the settee and walked towards the door.

"Zelah, we aren't arguing, are we? We are working together on this?"

"Of course we are," she replied turning to him. "Why would you ask?"

"Because sometimes, Zelah, it's really hard to tell."

She stood in the doorway, regarding him, head cocked to one side, then headed out of the house.

Nick went to the kitchen to make a sandwich for himself and Alice for lunch, but found her there already. She blushed when she saw him. "I just thought I'd make some sandwiches for me and Janny. We don't want to spend money on food and…"

"It's OK," Nick replied. "But that's a lot of sandwiches," pointing to the heap already wrapped on the kitchen table that would feed a classful of kids.

"We're growing girls," she replied, wrapped the last one and threw it into a duffel bag. Nick noticed that she had to heave it onto her shoulder. Something was going on, but he decided not to ask.

"Time to go, if you want to catch the start of the film."

"What? Oh, yes. OK. We're meeting Janny outside the cinema. You can just drop me and go. We'll get the bus back afterwards. We think we'll go across to the shopping centre to take a look around."

"Does your mother allow that?" he asked, feeling increasingly suspicious.

"Yes, but she likes to know times and stuff. I have to say a time and not be late."

"Sounds good. What time?"

"I'll be back about five. The bus stops at the end of the road and you've got my mobile. If you like I'll call you when I'm on my way. You can meet me at the bus stop." She looked at him with such a sweet, innocent smile that he knew he was being bullshitted to.

"OK," he replied. "But Alice, just remember that you and I both have to answer to your mother when she gets home."

Her expression didn't change, although he thought he caught a glimpse of wariness.

Janine was waiting outside the cinema, as Alice had said. She waved to Nick and they walked off in the direction of the cinema entrance. The traffic was too heavy for Nick to wait to see if they went in, but by this time he had concluded that he had to trust her.

As soon as he drove away he forgot about the girls and gave his whole attention to where he was going to go and what he was going to do when he got there.

36

Gandesa, Catalonia, Spain
2017

On Saturday morning, they met in the hotel foyer where breakfast was being served. They both ordered tea and Maggie had a croissant. Bob didn't eat. He seemed twitchy.

"Ready to go?" he asked as soon as Maggie had drained her second cup.

They hadn't spoken much over breakfast. Maggie had commented on the change of weather. She had opened the curtains of her bedroom expecting to see the small group of houses on the incline and the terraces of vines behind them, leading away to the mountains in the background. But instead there was just fog and rain. Bob had just grunted and said "We'll drive round to the home. It would have been a nice walk through Gandesa, but not in this."

"I'm ready," Maggie replied. "Are you OK?"

"Of course, why are you asking?" he snapped at her.

"Whoa," she replied. "If I've done something to upset you, let me know."

He sagged into his seat and put his head in his hands. "Not you. I can't get that stinking American out of my head. It's making me angry."

"Then stop it now," she said. "If he's got into your head, he's winning. Surprised at you," she added. "I thought a police detective would know how to remain detached."

He jumped up from his seat. "Exactly." And he walked off towards the entrance. Maggie picked up her bag and followed him, shaking her head.

The journey to the home took five minutes. From outside the home was a bland, square, concrete building. But inside they found something quite different. It was busy and lively, well-decorated, with a homely feeling. Staff bustled about, some helping men and women with walking frames to move between rooms, others sitting in armchairs around the foyer, chatting to residents.

They were shown into a small side lounge by the manager, who said in good English that she would bring LLuis Portells out to them. He had just finished his breakfast and was looking forward to meeting them. A few minutes later she reappeared, pushing an old man in a wheelchair. They both stood up.

Maggie's heart sank and she wondered how much they were going to get out of him. He was sunk low into the chair, a blanket over his knees, only his hands showing, which were warped by severe arthritis. His eyes were glazed.

"Well, hello!" he exclaimed in a strong voice, in accented, but clear, English. "Lovely to meet you. Don't often get chance to speak English. Sit down, sit down."

He winked at Maggie. "I was an engineer, when I didn't need this damn chair. Worked all over the world, including five years in Coventry."

Any tension that had existed in either Bob or Maggie dissolved away. Maggie got out her notebook.

Bob began "Señor Portells–" but he got no further.

"First of all, my name is LLuis. In England, they called me 'Lewis' with the English pronunciation. Now, they told me that you are a policemen," he nodded at Bob, who nodded back, "and you, my dear, are a genealogist. Is that right?"

"Yes," Maggie replied.

"And you want to know about the Welsh Brigader, and my girl Lola, yes?"

"Yes we do, and–" but she was interrupted again.

"Why?" The old man's expression had changed; had become challenging without a hint of the humour that had been there up to now.

"That's down to me," Bob said. "Can I tell you the story, LLuis?"

"You better had," the old man replied. "Because I'm not saying anything until I hear it all."

Bob summarised the story of Jeremy Allen's life, his efforts to find out what had happened to Lola, his eventual acceptance that there was nothing he could do. He explained his friendship with Jerry for the past five years, with details that Maggie hadn't heard before. How he'd met Jerry after a break-in at his animal sanctuary, how he'd caught the two culprits, but how Jerry had asked that instead of being prosecuted, he speak to them and give them the opportunity to work with him.

"They were just young lads," Bob explained. "He wanted to give them a chance."

"Did it work?" LLuis asked.

"One of them still works there."

"And the other?"

"You can't win them all. He's in jail."

LLuis laughed "At least Jerry tried."

Bob then told him about Jerry's death, how his mind had wandered in his final weeks.

"At the end, there were times when I think he believed that he was in the village, in Santa Rosa de l'Ebre. Walking around the streets with Lola. He described it, and that's when he talked about people, with names. That's how I got to know about you."

"He remembered me?"

"You used to follow them around the village. And you went with Lola when she and her friend Lidia Domenech delivered food to the Brigaders."

LLuis laughed out loud. "Well, I'll be damned. I was madly in love with her, you know. Nine years old and smitten. She was a special girl." He paused, then turned to Maggie. "Do you know what happened to her?"

"No, Maggie replied. "We were hoping you did."

He shook his head. "After she was taken away I never

194

saw her again. I don't think she survived."

Bob and Maggie glanced at each other, each feeling the other's disappointment.

"But I often wondered what happened to her baby."

"We suspect it died with her," Maggie said.

"Oh, no," LLuis said confidently, "the baby survived."

37

Gandesa, Catalonia, Spain
2017

"What?" Maggie said, "How do you know that?"

The man went to speak, but Bob put up a hand to stop him. "Wait. We need the full story. And you may need to turn this into a statement for the probate court. Are you prepared to do that?"

"I suppose that would be OK."

"I'm sensing some reluctance?"

"You told me about your friendship with Jerry. But not *why* you are doing this."

"I made a promise, when he was dying; that's important to me. He made a will leaving everything to his heir, if he or she could be found. But if not it all goes to another branch of the family. Nothing for me, LLuis, if that's what you're thinking."

The man nodded. "Very good, yes. But when you say 'another branch of the family', would that be in America?"

"Why do you ask that?"

"As I think you realise, Inspector, you aren't the first person to be enquiring about Lola and her baby." He smiled, Maggie thought slyly. "The village may be long gone, but the people are not. Old ties persist. Someone was asking a few years ago and then again recently. And, offering large sums of cash for information. Before you ask, no, I did not give any information or receive any cash.

Not my… what's that English expression? Ah yes, not my cup of tea. So, you want the whole story?"

"Yes, with as much detail as you can give us, and Maggie will take notes."

"Well, I'll tell you as much as I can remember. But, you must be patient, I'm an old man. My memory is still good, but your court may have some questions if I can't remember enough details."

"Not a problem," Bob replied. Maggie had her notebook and pen ready, and LLuis began his story.

"As you know, I was born in Santa Rosa de l'Ebre. My parents worked on the estate. We were peasants and we supported the Republic. We were poor but I had a happy childhood.

"Lola was my friend. She was a wonderful girl, and so very kind. She never made fun of my obsession with her. She was a political fanatic, fiercely for the Republic. The thought of it made her eyes shine. The only other time such a light came into her eyes was when she looked at Jeremy. "He arrived in June, when the International Brigade moved close by. They were at a training camp near Falset. The people of the village helped out with food. He was quite a hothead, you know, and very handsome." He paused and grinned at Bob. "You knew the old man. I knew the young man. Anyway, everyone could see how much they loved each other. I was so jealous. I hated him. But, I was just a boy. In February, these new Brigaders had been sent away to reinforce the main battalion at Gandesa. Lola had no fear for him. But not long after she heard that it was a disaster. They had been defeated very badly. There were so many deaths. But, he got back. He had to swim across the river, being fired at by the fascist soldiers chasing him and his comrades. He made it, but not all of those brave young men did.

"When the Battalion came to Falset they decided to get married. I think they knew what might be coming, so they got married. The village priest married them. I was there, it was a simple ceremony.

196

"Then he went away again. The Republican army had been forced back. They were going to retake the land they had lost. That was the battle of the Ebro. It started in July 1938. They crossed the river. At first, the advance went well. But soon they were outgunned in every way. Franco had more planes, more weapons, and more troops, supplied from Germany and Italy. They held out as best they could. Gandesa was besieged, you know. The International Brigade held positions on the Sierra Pandols, you can see the mountains from here. They held out for some time, but they were bombed and shelled constantly. In the end, they had to withdraw. Eventually, they had to retreat back across the Ebro. It was the beginning of the end." He stopped and sighed.

"Do you need a break?" Maggie asked.

The old man's eyes had been darting from side to side as the memories came back. Now he looked straight at Maggie; she could see tears.

"Difficult memories," he said. "No, I will go on. Over the next few months, we heard little good news. By September Lola knew she was pregnant. Then we heard that Franco's troops had crossed the river and were coming towards our village. We were frightened. Stories were circulating about mass imprisoning and revenge executions. Lola had heard that Jeremy was alive and well back in August, but nothing after that. She tried to get news, but it was just rumours. She heard he was dead, then that he was injured, then that he had escaped. By November, still nothing confirmed.

"We knew that the Nationalists were very close, had taken over towns and villages, coming closer and closer. But we were just a small village and my parents thought we might be spared. Some of those who had actively supported the Republic decided to leave, to head to Barcelona. Lola's friend Lidia was one of them. Lola wouldn't go. She was showing her baby by that time. She said that if she went and Jeremy came back as he had promised, how would he know where to find her? Many people, including the priest, told her to go, but she was firm and she stayed. This was, I think, a big mistake."

A nurse came into the room. It broke the intense atmosphere that had built up as LLuis told his story. She spoke to him. He shook his head.

Bob said quietly to Maggie, "She wants him to have a break. I didn't realise, we've been here over an hour."

"Fine with me," Maggie replied.

"But he's saying no," Bob whispered. "Says he's waited a long time to talk about this and he's not going to stop now."

As Bob finished speaking, LLuis flicked his hand dismissively at the nurse, who left the room, muttering.

"They worry too much," LLuis said. "Just because I'm old and stuck in this chair, doesn't mean my mind is the same as my body."

"But you are frail," Maggie said. "We don't want to make anything worse."

"You won't," LLuis spoke firmly. "Now, let's continue. What's that phrase? Ah, yes, I'm on a roll!"

Maggie laughed.

"Where was I? Ah yes, Lola wouldn't leave the village. It was a tense time. People split apart, no longer as strong in their views or their opinions. My parents stayed loyal to the Republic but people they thought were friends and comrades, started to move away from them. Then the news came that the prime minister, Negrin, was sending the International Brigades away. Lola couldn't believe it. She was furious. Now, *that* was a sight to see!

"We waited and waited. Then, at last the Nationalist soldiers came. They took away the young men. They questioned and beat the older men. Women were questioned and beaten, too. My parents didn't give in, although they were beaten." He stopped and took a deep breath, but carried on quickly before either Maggie or Bob could interrupt him. "Some people traded their own safety for the lives of others. That's how Lola got taken. We didn't know at the time who it was gave her away. But she was a real prize for them. They seemed very pleased that she was pregnant, although it wasn't clear why. I mean, she was the wife of a foreign soldier. That should have been enough, but there was more to it. I think I need to stop for a short while."

LLuis' breathing had speeded up and he started to pant for air. Bob stood, walked to the door, and called the nurse, was still lurking in the corridor. She rushed in, quickly assessed LLuis' state of distress, and wheeled him out, spitting out some words at Bob. Before Bob could reply, LLuis, turned in his chair in the doorway, banged his stick on the floor and shouted at the nurse.

Maggie upset at the state LLuis was in, but desperately wanted to hear the rest of the story. Who had betrayed Lola?

"He's saying that he's going to finish talking to us, but later, after lunch," Bob said. "The nurse is saying it must wait a couple of days, but he's insisting we come back in a couple of hours. I think he's winning."

The nurse turned to them both and said, "Two hours, at least must wait. Then he can speak you again."

Bob nodded and Maggie stood up. They left the care home and headed back into the centre of the small town, where they headed directly to the café they'd visited he previous day. They ordered food and waited.

"Amazing man," Maggie said, "but why has it taken him so long to speak about this?"

"This creates a big conflict for many Spaniards, I think," Bob replied. "Franco's been gone a long time and they have a democracy, but the price was unbearable. So many people died during the war, and for a long time afterwards. Many feel shame, horror, unable to accept the outcome, but unable to change it. They suffered for years under Franco's regime and his repercussions against anyone who supported the Republic."

"Except those who didn't suffer." Maggie replied. "Franco had enough supporters."

"Of course, and that's the conflict. People who'd been

on opposite sides then had to live together after Franco was gone. Civil war, the worst kind. They couldn't speak Catalan here, it was Spanish only. For lots of the old people Catalan was their first language. But if they slipped in public they were abused."

"What do you mean?" Maggie asked.

"My mother had friends who went through it. They told her, much later, what it was like."

"Tell me, I'd like to know. It's horrifying and fascinating at the same time."

"For example, if you were caught speaking Catalan in the street, you could be arrested and imprisoned. People ratted on each other. For survival, or sadistic pleasure, or to settle old scores. Anyway, my mother's friend, LLora, slipped up one day on a tram in Barcelona. Just a few Catalan words, but it was enough for a Nationalist officer to beat her with a riding crop in front of the other passengers. He said 'Don't speak like a dog, speak like a Christian!' as he beat her. LLora went back to her family in a small village north of Segovia. She and her family had been thrown out of their house, which was given to a Nationalist supporter, a local family. They couldn't take anything with them. LLora had to work as a cleaner and every day on her way to work she had to walk past her own house and watch the woman who now lived there pegging *her* sheets and clothes. And there was nothing LLora could do about it. Whenever the woman saw her, she just sneered."

"That's shocking," Maggie said.

"Civil war, like I said," Bob shrugged. "Anyway, we're getting closer to the story we came here for. I can't wait to get back."

"What if that nurse has persuaded him not to speak to us again? Could she have an agenda?"

Bob mused for a few seconds. "Unlikely," he said. "I think she's just concerned about his health. He may be sicker than we know about. Come on, let's go back. Don't want him pegging out before he finishes telling us what he knows." Maggie looked shocked. "Joke," he added hastily. He turned away from her scowl just as another diner entered. Maggie saw that he was staring.

"What?" she said.

"Nothing. Let's get on."

* * *

LLuis was waiting for them in the entrance lobby.

"I was worried you might be patronising and nervous," he said, smiling at them. "I am fine, really I am. I just get tired more quickly than I used to. But now that I've started, I want to finish. The lounge is still there for us. Give me a push, will you?"

The three of them headed for the lounge where they settled themselves again.

"I've been able to remember more, over my lunch. I usually take a small nap at this time, so if I nod off, you must wake me."

"Will do," Bob replied.

"Let's go on. Lola was taken away in February 1939. The battle on the Ebro front was over, Barcelona had surrendered. There were some pockets of resistance, but it was losing momentum. The last of the troops of the International Brigades had crossed back over the Ebro at Flix. Some brave men, who could not go home, stayed to delay the fascist troops, they held them up along a thirty-mile front in bunkers and trenches, and the rest crossed back over the river and went back to Barcelona where, as I said, Negrin had decreed that they should leave Spain. Those men, I think around five hundred of them, all perished. Most of their bodies were never recovered. They still lie undiscovered along that front, many of them where they fell. The Nationalists would not give them a decent burial. Ayee."

Maggie wanted to ask questions, but held herself in check.

"That winter was hard. We were all hungry. Old people starved to death. Around Christmas, I think it was,

201

Franco began a big attack to take the whole of Catalonia, and he succeeded. The war went on for months, but the Republic was beaten, so Negrin conceded. But of Lola, we heard nothing. Or Jeremy, who I guessed was either dead or had got out of Spain." The old man's expression changed and his gnarly hands rubbed together. "Now, we have reached the time when something happened. I guess this is the part that you really want to know about."

"Yes!" Maggie and Bob said in unison.

"One day in April thirty-nine–" LLuis stopped. He clasped his hands together as best he could, but they still shook. "It had been very cold, there was still snow on the ground, but it was beginning to warm up and we had been burning furniture to make fires to keep warm. Around midday we heard a lorry approaching. Every stranger was a worry, we didn't know who it was or what they wanted. We watched from the window as it pulled up into our little square and stopped. Soldiers jumped out of the back, their rifles ready to fire. From the front passenger seat a priest got out. Our own priest appeared at the church door, and as soon as he saw this man, he went quickly to face him. He bowed deeply and we saw them talk. Our priest was a little man, quite young. He had sandy hair, I remember, and a pleasant, square face. The other was tall, round face, high forehead, balding, he wore wire-framed black glasses. He had black eyes, it was like being watched by a robot. You know, they seemed to move automatically. He walked with a stick. There was something very ugly about that stick, it was too big."

He paused and took a rasping breath. "He spoke to the soldiers and they ran around the square, shouting for everyone to come out. Banging on doors with their rifles. A few people opened their doors. The tall priest spoke again and a couple of the soldiers fired shots in the air. More people came out at this. My parents, my sister and I, we waited. A couple of soldiers smashed our door down, took my mother by the hair and pulled her into the square, my father tried to protest and a soldier hit him in the face with his rifle. My sister cried and was told to shut up. We stood together in the square. I was terrified, but I didn't want to show it. I clung to my mother's hand. More joined us, until everyone in the village was there.

"The soldiers rounded us up in front of the church. They lined up, facing us, rifles pointing at us. Padre Rovira looked grim, his face was white, but he didn't say anything. I thought they were going to shoot us. The tall priest walked in front of them, to face us. 'Where is it?' he said. We didn't know what he was talking about, so nobody spoke. He looked along the line of families. 'Where is the baby?' he said. 'Someone here has it. One of you knows.' We all looked at each other, what was he talking about? There was no baby in the village. Our priest stepped forward, head bowed and spoke quietly, respectfully, 'Father, we haven't had a child born here for almost two years. Who is it you are looking for? How can we help you?' The tall priest looked at him with a puzzled expression. Then, without a word he swung his stick and gave our Padre a blow across the head. I can still hear the sound of his skull cracking as I tell you about it. My God!"

"Stop there," Bob said. He reached out his hand and took LLuis's hands in his. The old man was weeping.

"I must go on," he whispered. "I've never told anyone apart from my wife."

"Then take as much time as you need," Bob said, also in a whisper, releasing the gnarled hands. He reached into his pocket, took out a tissue and gently wiped the old man's cheeks.

"The tall priest turned back to us. For all of the look on his face, he might have just swatted an insect. His eyes had no expression. 'A woman of this village, married by this man,' and he pointed to Padre Rovira. Lying on the ground with blood was spreading on the dirt '…to a foreign invader. She gave birth, now it is missing. Where is it?' My stomach turned over. I knew that he was talking about Lola. My father stepped forward. 'If you mean Lola Rosas she was taken from here months ago. She hasn't been back.

She has no family here. They have all gone.' My mother was squeezing my hand so tightly that I thought she was going to break my bones.

"'Where have they gone?' the tall priest asked. 'Her parents died a few years ago. She had an aunt, but when Lola was taken away, her aunt left. I believe she went to Barcelona. She had a cousin there. That's where she thought Lola would be,' my father replied.

"The priest demanded to know the name and address My father shook his head and told him that she didn't say exactly, just the district. A few in the crowd nodded in agreement. The priest looked up and down the line. He called out a name and a man stepped forward. That's when we knew who had betrayed Lola. The traitor. The priest asked him 'Is this true?' and the traitorous bastard nodded. I felt a shudder run through my mother. My father stepped back into the line. The priest told the traitor he had ten minutes to get his possessions and leave. The man and his wife ran off. I thought now the priest was satisfied they would go away. He turned to the soldiers and said, 'Burn it, all of it.'

"The soldiers ran from house to house, ransacking everywhere, setting every house alight. They had dynamite. The memory of that hour will be with me until my death. We all stood in silence, not moving, as everything we owned went up in flames. When it was all blazing, the priest ordered the soldiers back into the truck, and they left. The whole time he never raised his voice.

"As soon as they had gone, we all ran around like mad things. We tried to put out as many of the fires as we could, but it was hopeless. The houses collapsed. My family managed to get a few bits and pieces out. All the time the body of our Padre lay on the ground. Later that evening we buried him. Then we slept in the church, the only building that didn't collapse. My mother hardly spoke for a long time.

"The next morning, most people packed up the little they had and left. We were like the dead walking. We had family in Valencia, so we went there. Then we moved around, my father needed work to feed us. It wasn't easy for a supporter of the Republic, even though he wasn't a soldier, not even a trade unionist. Eventually we settled here, in Gandesa. Before he died, my father told me that he had expected to die that day. My mother recovered enough to live through the years of Franco's rule. She got me admitted to school and eventually, I managed to leave. That is my story."

In the silence that followed Maggie realised that the light had faded outside the building. She reached up and flicked a light switch behind her head. The overhead light came on and the atmosphere changed at once.

"Thank you, LLuis," Bob said. "It can't have been easy, reliving all that."

"No, it wasn't," the old man replied. "But I feel a lightness, now it's out. There is one more thing I have to tell you." He said this with a smile of what looked to Maggie like triumph.

"I found out much later why my mother was so terrified that she almost broke my hand as my father told the story of Lola's aunt going to Barcelona." He leaned forward in his chair. "It wasn't true. Oh yes, Estel had said it to a few people she knew would spread it around. She didn't know then who it was, you see, who had given Lola up. But to my father and mother she confided the truth. She was just five kilometres away, in Falset. That's where her cousin lived, near to a convent where he had found Lola was being kept with other women. Her cousin came to tell her and she went with him. It happened very quietly. My parents knew, but no one else, because there was a traitor. My father did a very good job of fooling that evil priest, yes?"

"Yes, he did," Maggie said. "I can understand why your mother was so scared. What if the priest went to look for the woman in Barcelona?"

"Huh. It was a big district, easy to hide away. Easy to make sure that someone would say that you were there, but had moved on to another part of the country. But the only thing was for the priest to believe that it was a true story. He may have gone to check the story, I don't know, but he never came back.

"But," he wagged a finger at them, "you know that someone else has been sniffing around Lola's story?"

"Yes, an American," Bob said. LLuis nodded. "Did you speak to him?"

"I spoke to him on the telephone. I very politely told him to fuck off," LLuis chuckled, then frowned. "I didn't like him, don't ask me why. He was offering money. I don't need money. He was insulting me, him and his big bucks."

"Do you have any idea who else he might have spoken to?" Maggie asked.

"He said he had talked to a few people. He said he was Jerry's relative. Is he?"

"Yes," Bob replied, "but he never met Jeremy; just wants his legacy."

"I got that impression," LLuis said. "I don't know who else he might have spoken to. If he found other family from the village he might have got the story I've just told you. I don't know if any are still alive who were actually there, apart from me. But if he found someone who had the story handed down, then he would at least know that Lola's baby survived, but probably with the story of going to Barcelona."

Maggie turned to Bob. "Why would he be claiming that he has evidence that they were both dead?"

"That's for us to find out." He turned back to LLuis. "If we get this prepared as a statement, would you be prepared to sign it, for me to use at the probate court?"

The old man nodded. "Do it quickly."

"Tomorrow," Bob said. "I'll come back. We'll leave you now. Again, thank you, LLuis. I'll let you know whatever we find out." He walked to the door and called the nurse, who came in to fetch the old man.

They all went to the entrance, where they each took LLuis's hands in theirs and gently pressed them. Just as she

206

was walking through the open door, Maggie said, "LLuis, you mentioned the young men who voluntarily died to allow the others to escape. Is there anywhere I can read about that?"

"Better than that," he replied. "You can visit the site of a grave, of sorts. Up near Fatarella, about twelve kilometres from here. There's a small museum. Go and read about Charlie." He waved and the nurse turned him around and took him back into the home.

"Wonder what that meant? Charlie who?" Maggie said to Bob as they got into the car.

"A tangent," Bob replied. "We don't need those now, though it's probably an interesting story. But, another time, yeah? We've still got a lot to do."

"Agreed, but reluctantly."

38

Falset, Catalonia, Spain
1939

Lola didn't know how she had got back from the bathroom to her bed in the eight-bed dormitory. The bleeding had eventually stopped, but not the pain. She had no chance to clean herself up. Her best hope was that Sister Angeles didn't notice the state she was in, or that she was no longer pregnant. She just needed a little extra time to think about what to do next. At least the baby, her beautiful boy, was safe.

She remembered how she had felt when she held him for those precious minutes. The sheer joy. How proud Jeremy would be to see his son. That thought gave her strength. Now, if she could just sleep for a little while she felt sure she could get herself up from the bed, try not to be noticed. She could do it for Jeremy and Hugo. She had named him after Jeremy's father, Hugh, although she couldn't pronounce the English name. It was what Jeremy would have wanted.

A few hours, but it seemed like seconds, later she was awoken by the sound of scurrying around her. She was being shaken. "Get up, Lola, she's coming."

Lola came to, not understanding. Then, panic. She looked frantically up at the girl who had shaken her.

"A shift. I need a clean, dark one."

The girl looked at her without understanding, until Lola pulled back the bed cover; the blood seemed to be everywhere.

The girl shouted to the others. The rough, one-piece garment appeared and three of them raised her up out of the bed, stripped off her blood-soaked one and put another on her. It was long. That was good, it would hide the blood on her legs. She had managed to wash it off her hands.

She dragged herself to the end of her bed and waited, knees straining with the effort of staying upright. She sagged and the girl in the next bed gave a small scream, but another rough voice told her to shut up.

The door opened.

Lola kept her head down. One hand was by her side, the other clinging onto the iron frame behind her. The other girls all had their heads down.

"Quiet this morning," said the scratchy little voice. The nun walked slowly up the line. Lola stopped breathing. The nun looked her up and down. It wasn't Lola's turn this morning, she passed by. Lola slowly exhaled as the sound of a slap echoed around the room.

"Don't like it?" The voice said playfully. "You're sorry? Not as sorry as you will be, believe me." Lola risked a glance and saw the nun cruelly pinching a girl at the far end on her cheek. The girl was squirming in pain. "Filthy traitor. Well, your husband won't see this brat." A kick to the shins and the girl fell to the bed moaning and holding her face.

Her fun over, the nun walked back down the dormitory

towards the door. Lola thought she was going to be OK but the nun stopped as she reached her.

"And you, filthy traitor. What do you have to say for yourself today?"

Lola kept her head down and said, "Nothing, Sister."

The nun went to walk on, but stopped and said "What's that smell?" She peered around, her long, rat-like nose twitching in disgust. Back to Lola. "Is it you?"

"Maybe, sister. I didn't get to wash yesterday, or the day before. There wasn't any water."

"Stinking slug, do it now."

Lola knew she couldn't leave the bed, she wouldn't be able to hold herself up, let alone walk. "I'll do it straight after breakfast, sister. There will be water left over."

"There's something not right about you today." The nun moved in and carefully looked Lola up and down, then caught hold of her chin and wrenched her face up. "What has happened to you?"

"Nothing, Sister. I had some pains in the night. I think I am just tired, it will pass."

The nun threw Lola's chin down and turned to walk away. The baby was not due for a few weeks yet, and she seemed satisfied.

"What is that?"

"What do you mean, Sister?"

"Is that blood?"

"I… I don't think so. I just need to wash," she rushed the words out.

The nun hurried back. "Pull up your shift."

Lola stood still.

"I said, pull up your shift," the nun screamed at her.

Lola had to do it. Her legs were stained reddish brown. The nun put her hands on Lola's abdomen and squeezed it roughly. Lola screamed and collapsed.

Too late. Too late now. She was surprised at how resigned she felt.

The nun dropped down beside her and put her hands around Lola's throat. "Where is it?"

Lola smiled.

"What have you done with it?"

"Gone, Sister. Gone to a better place," she mumbled through the pain. *Let them think my baby might be dead. What could they do to me now?*

The nun got up and ran out of the room, shouting "None of you touch her."

One of the girls ran over to her, but Lola shook her head. They heard footsteps in the corridor and a rhythmical thumping on the wooden floor. The girl ran back to her bed.

The nun entered with the priest. Lola knew then what they would do to her. What he would do to her.

"Where is your baby, Lola?" he appealed to her.

"Gone, Father. Gone to a better place."

"Is your baby dead, Lola?"

It would have been so easy to tell him that Hugo was dead, but where could she say the body was to be found?

"No, Father. He has gone to a better place."

"Who helped you?" the quite voice came from above.

"No one helped me, Father."

The kick was sudden. She screamed with the pain and knew that she had begun to bleed again. In that moment, Lola understood that she was not going to survive. She felt immeasurably sad. She had so wanted to see Jeremy again, to travel to Wales, to set up her family in the place that she had imagined so often, on the hillside. Was it as green as Jeremy had described?

"You are a lying Communist whore. You have one chance. Who helped you?"

"God helped me, Father. One day you will need His help, too, but I don't think He is going to help you." A last effort at defiance.

"Stand up."

She tried to get to her feet, but collapsed and fell to her knees. The blood was pouring out now. The room was swimming in front of her eyes. She made out the priest's disgust as he looked at her blood.

"Filthy creatures, women," he remarked to no one in

particular. "Look at me, Lola. That's right, look at me."

She looked up, but she couldn't see his dark, mad eyes. She saw Jeremy instead, and her ears were singing with the beautiful sound of the baby snuffling, exactly as she'd fed him for the first and only time. She smiled.

With a sudden, sweeping movement the priest the swung the knobbled end of his walking stick into her head. There was the sound of a nut cracking. Lola collapsed.

A few seconds of silence and then the other girls began to howl and cry. A few collapsed on their beds.

The priest looked up, observed them as if they were misbehaving children, then looked down at Lola's body.

"Get rid of *that*," he said to the ashen-faced nun, "and clean up its mess." He turned and left.

The nun called out and was joined by another, who must have been listening outside. They each took one of Lola's legs and dragged her across the floor and out of the room, leaving a thick trail of blood across the wooden floor.

39

Gandesa, Catalonia, Spain
2017

As the light faded over the mountains the drizzle turned to steady rain. It was getting colder. Bob opened the car door for Maggie and she got in. He stared back at the mountains for a few seconds, then shook his head and got into the car as well.

"Might snow tonight," he remarked as they got out of the car at the hotel. "How about we get together in the foyer in half an hour?"

"Fine for me," Maggie said. "Just remind me, it's Saturday, isn't it? I've lost track since we got here."

Bob gave her a sarcastic look, but nodded.

"Good," she replied, taking no notice. "I need to call

home, check everything's OK with my kids."

By the time she got back to the foyer he had already ordered tea and cakes for them both.

"How are the family?" he asked.

"No one home," she answered glumly and sitting next to him. Her mood changed at once as she eagerly eyed the plate of pastries. "They look good."

"Help yourself. Tea is for both of us. So, your thoughts?"

"Well, my first thought is that somehow Lola got her baby out of wherever she was being kept, and I think she died there."

"Evidence?"

"The priest. A sadistic, murdering psychopath. He was only interested in the baby. If he had been trying to find Lola, he would have questioned the village about *her*. That told me that he knew where she was. Whether she was dead at that point, who knows? But she never shows up again, anywhere, on any record. So, she gave birth to a live child and died, maybe in the process. What do you think?"

"She died, definitely. I would say the priest had already killed her, or knew she was dead, when he went to the village."

Maggie frowned. "Why are you sure about that?"

"I can spot a pattern of behaviour."

"Do you come across many murdering psychopaths in your line of work?"

"If you're being sarky, don't. Of course not, but I've studied them. I've come across murder, yes. But most murders aren't planned, or if they are, not in great detail."

He stopped to take a swig of tea, picked up a pastry but instead of eating it, sat back. "I've dealt with people I believed were psychotic and capable of killing if it suited them. And I've interviewed one who got away with it. It was a game, to him. You can see the traits, see. No empathy, no understanding of social norms. He really believed he was cleverer than all of us, which he probably was. Charming when he needed to be, and knew exactly

212

what he was doing, right from the start. We couldn't even charge him."

"Wow," said Maggie, "and how do you equate that to this priest?"

"Well, he turned up accompanied by a lot of soldiers, not just a small armed guard. So, one, he was influential and two, he had something planned before he arrived. He never raised his voice, psychopaths are almost always in control. They don't need to shout or lose their temper. He already knew that the village priest had married a local girl to a foreigner, and he killed him without asking further questions. He'd pre-determined his guilt and there was no question of listening to what the priest had to say.

"Next, he was happy to identify the turncoat, make sure that the whole village knew. He let him go, then punished the rest of them without conscience or reason. If he was a sadist, he might have tortured a few, for pleasure. But he wasn't interested in that. He was only there to find out where the baby was. However, first, he didn't know the sex of the child, he said 'it'. That's unusual in Spanish. That tells me that Lola's baby got away immediately after it was born. Second, he wasn't interested in her at all, just her family, and he needed information about the whereabouts of her relatives. If he had known already he would have followed them up, not gone to the village. Which means that he didn't get that out of Lola."

"Couldn't he have obtained the information some other way?" Maggie asked.

"Think about it," he replied. "This was chaos in 1939, no rule of law. Few telephones. No convenient means of communication. If something wasn't in writing, you had to find people and ask. That's what he did. He didn't have to worry about someone reporting him to the authorities. He *was* authority, with a white collar and a big stick."

"Do you really think he killed Lola?" Maggie asked.

"I think it's a strong possibility. He wanted that baby. He didn't get it. He'd killed a member of the church without raising an eyebrow. If she had somehow managed to get her baby taken away and denied him, I can believe that he'd kill her. If she was no more than a baby producer to him, then he had no more use for her. I'm not sure we'll ever know for certain, but that's my theory."

"Oh, God." Maggie tried to pick up her tea cup but her hand was shaking too much. It rattled in the saucer, which seemed to break Bob's concentration. He reached out and took her hand.

"What are you thinking?" he asked.

"If she got a blow like that village priest; now I'm hearing the sound, like LLuis described. If that's what happened, thank God Jeremy never found out." She started crying, and withdrew her hand to wipe away the tears.

Bob stared for a moment, unsure of what to do. "Um, more tea?"

Maggie laughed out loud. "Absolutely. The answer to everything. So, what do we do next?"

He started munching on a pastry. "I've been thinking about that," he said between bites. "We've got a few more leads, now. I want to find out about this nasty priest. LLuis's father told him that the aunt went to Falset, because she believed that Lola might have been taken there, to a convent. Was there a convent? If so, did they take women prisoners there? That should be a matter of record. And who was the relative that Aunt Estel went to stay with? Should be able to find that out, too. I think I should call Joan back and get him working on this. He knows the Spanish internet sites, so he can start right away.

"And, if it's OK with you, we'll stay here tonight, go back to see Roser and LLuis tomorrow, get them to sign the statements. We can talk it over tonight if there's anything else we can do here, but I don't think so. If Joan finds out something, Falset is an easy drive from Sitges. OK with you?"

"Fine with me, but you'd better check that we can keep the rooms."

He didn't move, took another swig of tea.

Maggie sighed. "You already have."

214

He had the grace to look a little sheepish as he tipped his head. She sighed again, grunted theatrically without looking at him, and stuffed a pastry in her mouth.

They split up for an hour before dinner. Maggie called Nick, who told her that Jack was fine and gone to a party. As for Alice, she seemed OK, but was already asleep in bed.

They exchanged quick news about what they were doing and Nick mentioned that Zelah had been there all day and was coming back again tomorrow.

"How is she?" Maggie asked tentatively.

"She's OK. Cross with herself. Thinks it's her fault that the Canadian fooled her."

"I can guess," she replied. "I look forward to hearing more about it. And your family history?"

"Ah, that's another story," he said. "Tell you all about it when you're back. But it doesn't make sense."

"Which part?"

"All of it. Anyway, speak to you tomorrow."

* * *

Over dinner Maggie and Bob agreed that the next move was to go to Falset.

"That's where the trail leads," Maggie said. "But I don't know what we can do on a Sunday."

"Go to church?" Bob said with a smile. "Guaranteed they'll be working on a Sunday. A priest may be able to give us information about a nearby convent. And I've already called Joan, asked him to get on with trying to the trace the aunt in Falset from April 1939 onwards."

She nodded and he went on, "Is everything OK, otherwise? You seem distracted."

"No, just my daughter's friend is having problems at school."

"Which school?" he asked. She told him.

"Oh, there."

"Do you know something about it?" she demanded.

"Um, not really, not as such," he replied. "Good

academic record. But for the kids who don't fit it, there can be problems."

"What kind of problems, Bob?"

"Let's say, there's not a culture of support for kids who can't stand up for themselves. I've seen quite a few fall by the wayside. End up on the wrong side of the law."

"I'm getting that," she mused.

"OK, I have to go get the statement ready for LLuis to sign tomorrow. At least I can do this one in English. Meet in the foyer about ten tomorrow?"

40

Falset, Catalonia, Spain
2017

The following morning Bob was ready in the foyer, his coat on, bouncing on the balls of his feet. "Ready to go?" he asked, heading towards the door as soon as he saw Maggie coming out of the lift.

"No! I haven't even had a cup of tea yet. You said ten. It's only half-nine."

"We can't waste time. I've been to see LLuis and Roser already. They've signed their documents."

Maggie sat down at the bar where a waitress was filling cups from a steaming machine, and dropped her bag on the floor. "I want a hot drink before we set off," she said, giving Bob a mulish look. He huffed and folded his arms. "I can ask them to put it in a takeaway cup for you?"

"No. Why are we suddenly in such a rush?"

"I need to get on with it."

"OK, you twitch for a few minutes while I drink my tea, then we'll go." She turned her back on him, but drank the tea quickly, then jumped up from the bar stool.

"What are we waiting for? Let's go," she said, "and please, don't drive like a lunatic, no matter how twitchy you feel."

216

He ignored her and headed to the door at a run. Maggie watched him go, suspecting that she was going to have to do quite a bit of teeth-gritting during the day. By the time she joined him in the car he was already revving the engine. As soon as her door closed he pulled out, not even giving her time to put on her seatbelt. Maggie decided there was no point in asking him to explain, or in telling him to slow down. She was just going to have to put up with this sudden change of mood, and try to find what was behind it.

They drove out on same road they had taken coming into Gandesa, and after about half an hour, Bob turned the car off the main road and headed uphill. Another five minutes brought them to the small town of Falset. Or, as Maggie considered, a large village. It was set on a hillside below a vertical escarpment, one large church, many traditional houses set into the hill, with the now-familiar terraces of vines and olives both above and below, to the edge of the rock-face. Bob pulled the car to a screeching halt in a narrow, cobbled street next to the church.

"OK, let's go," he said, simultaneously unfastening his seatbelt and opening the door.

"No. Let's not go." Maggie was staring ahead out of the windscreen.

"What?"

"Either you treat me with some respect and intelligence, or I'm getting a taxi back to Gandesa, packing my stuff and heading to the airport." She continued to stare straight ahead.

"This is not some kind of game," he shouted.

"Exactly," she replied, still not looking at him. "And it's certainly not a child's game, despite your acting like one. Either you want me here to help you, or you don't. Make a decision, please."

"Oh, for God's sake," he muttered, getting out of the car and slamming the door. He started to walk towards the church at a fast pace, head jutting forward, arms swinging. But, as he reached the high wooden door, he stopped dead. Maggie saw his chin go down and his shoulders sag. He stood for several seconds. Then his head started to move around slowly. She wasn't sure if he was stretching out the tension in his neck, or talking to himself. Whichever it was, he turned around, walked back to the car, got in, and sat in silence, also staring through the windscreen.

"We have to go home, first thing tomorrow," he said.

Whatever she *had* been expecting, this wasn't it.

"Why?"

"My leave has been cancelled. Two incidents at home. A dead body and a missing child, probably just a runaway, but I have to go back."

"Detective shortage in Cwmbran?" she asked, turning to look at him. She saw the corner of his mouth twitch, but he replied "My team, they need me there."

"So be it. But, can we agree it's not my fault, and you should have told me as soon as you found out?"

"Not a good sharer," he said. "Sorry."

"Better," she replied.

"And I do have enormous respect for your intelligence."

"Thank you. So, when do we have to go?"

"Tomorrow morning is the first plane back to Bristol, from Reus, not Barcelona. We might as well stay another night in Gandesa, if that's OK with you?"

"Fine with me, but what about your flat?"

"One of my neighbours has a key. She'll lock it up."

"So, just one day left. We'd better make the most of it. And I have an idea, which I would have shared with you on our way here, and particularly before you went barging into that church to buttonhole the priest. I *am* a good sharer," she added.

This time she saw a smile. "Go on, then."

"Let's get out of the car and walk around this little town. Fresh air might help to clear our heads."

"Fair enough, but not for too long. I... *we* don't want to miss the priest. There's a service going on in there, but he might have to go somewhere else afterwards. They sometimes cover a couple of towns."

218

They decided to stick to the area around the church, which turned out to comprise of just a few narrow streets. There were a couple of closed shops and an open café, which wasn't doing any business. It was close enough to the church to spot people leaving.

They ordered coffee and Maggie began, "We've heard a story of two priests, one very good, one beyond bad. And a lot about what people had to do to live in some kind of harmony after the war, and how some of that still lingers. Now, you don't know anything about this priest, not even how long he's been here or how old he is. He may be friendly and helpful, but there's an equal chance that he isn't. Remember, Bob, this is not a police investigation. It would be good to have him on side, but, if he's hostile, then we can't get any further. So, I was thinking, he will at least know about the people in this town. Introduce yourself as an amateur genealogy researcher, trying to find out about your Spanish family. Ask him who the oldest people in the town are and get their names. With any luck, there will be a nonagenarian who might be able-minded enough to remember people and places from the thirties. *Then* you can ask him about the convent. If he's co-operative and helpful, fantastic. If he isn't, or he just doesn't know, we have someone else to try. What do you think?"

"Good idea, Maggie. Are you going to come with me?"

"I think so. Introduce me as your wife."

He looked surprised.

"That way, he'll think we're on holiday, not investigating something. Remember, someone else has been asking questions too, let's try to keep it sounding low-key," she explained.

"It's January. Not a lot of tourists in January."

"Yes," she conceded. "But I'm sure you can convince him. Tell him I'm allergic to heat. Look, just say whatever you must to get him on side. You're used to interrogating witnesses, you have the skills."

He sat for a moment drinking his coffee, staring into

the cup. Then he said "People are coming out of the church. We have to go now, let's do it." He looked grim, but excited. They headed out of the café to the church. As they got there, he took hold of her hand. "Mrs Pugh."

Together they walked from the bright sunlight into the dark interior of the church. Maggie shook her head and coughed at the incense that floated in the air, its smoky-sweet smell evoking memories of her childhood. The priest was still at the altar. She glanced round, but he was alone. They walked down the aisle and stopped at the bottom of the three steps that led up to a small altar where the priest was fumbling with something unseen in front of him. From behind he was a tall man, dressed head to foot in green embroidered robes, he had a tonsure, Maggie thought due to his age, rather than devotional preference. The remaining strip of hair was grey. She'd somehow expected an old man, but when he turned around, he was younger than she anticipated.

He spoke softly, and the tone was deep. "Si?" He raised his eyebrows, waiting for them to speak.

Bob began to speak in Catalan, but the priest raised his hand in a sharp gesture. "Español, por favor."

Bob apologised and switched to Spanish. Maggie looked from the priest to Bob, trying to assume the countenance of an admiring wife who thought her husband was very clever, although she couldn't understand a word he was saying.

Bob had taken on a new persona. He was slightly hunched, subservient. He asked his questions in a respectful voice. He even looked older. *Must have gone undercover before,* Maggie thought, killing the smirk that almost slipped onto her face.

The conversation went on for some minutes. Every now and then she felt her hand squeezed tightly. She wasn't sure if it was a signal, or a reaction to something Bob had heard and didn't like. She soon found out. She understood enough to know that Bob was thanking the priest, who had ignored Bob's outstretched hand and turned away. She caught the priest's eye and smiled at him as he turned. He ignored her and swept out towards a door at the side of the church.

"What do we do now?" she whispered as they walked into the sunlight and Bob paused to take a deep breath.

"Two choices. One, go back in and beat him to a fucking pulp. Two, back to the café and I'll tell you what the bastard said."

They walked back to the café and ordered more coffee from the puzzled owner, who served them then leaned on the bar, watching them.

Bob spoke in a whisper. "Definitely not one of the good ones. Your plan was good. He didn't have a good word to say about anyone, or anything. But he has given me the name of an old woman. A Señora Amalia Balaguer. He said she was almost a hundred. If we can find her, maybe she'll talk to us.

"Anyway, he asked why my grandad had left Spain. I told him poverty. That's when he looked down his pointy nose."

"I guess that's one of the times you squeezed my hand," Maggie said.

"Sorry, had to keep control somehow. Then he said he couldn't help me. He's not a local, see. He's just filling in for the regular bloke, who's sick. But then, I asked him about the convent. Said he'd never heard of such a place and why was I asking? I know he's lying." Bob tapped the side of his nose.

"Policeman," Maggie cut in before he could say any more. He laughed out loud.

"So, I asked him who might know. That's when he dismissed me. He was angry, not sure why, but I smell something fishy."

"Indeed, but Señora Balaguer is a lead."

"The only one we've got. We'll have to ask around, but that's not easy on a Sunday. We'll have to wait until later this afternoon. Families may go out for a stroll after church." He sat back and sighed, "Not enough time."

"Come on," said Maggie, standing up, "let's not wait. Let's see if we can find people in the street."

Bob huffed again, and stood up. He went to the bar to pay. Maggie stood by the door, looking out into the street. It was empty, nor was there any sign of activity in any of the windows. It occurred to her that Bob was taking a long time to pay, and she looked around. He was talking at great speed to the bar owner, gesticulating madly, but with a smile on his face. She watched as the bar owner, still leaning on the bar, paused for a moment staring at Bob as if trying to decide something. Then, he nodded and motioned for Bob to sit back down.

"Back to the table," he called across the café to Maggie.

She joined him. "What?"

"Under our nose all the time," he whispered. "We don't have to search out Señora Balaguer. She's upstairs. She is *Feliu's*," he nodded over at the bar "the owner's, grandmother."

Maggie mouthed oh, with eyebrow raised and a smile.

"But," he went on, "she really is almost a hundred. Ninety-eight, actually, which means she was born in 1918. It gets better, she's from Falset. Never left. And, she's not lost her marbles. Feliu just told me she talks a lot about the 'old days'. But, she's pretty frail and he wants to talk to her, to tell her who we are and what we are looking for, to see if she'll talk to us. So, now we just wait."

Maggie nodded slowly. "This might take some time, Bob. You'll have to go very slowly. Ask her about this priest," she nodded towards the church. "If there is something fishy, see if she knows what it might be."

He nodded briefly, then sat back and folded his arms. Then sat up again, and looked around, walked to the door, looked up and down the street, scowled at something, then walked back to their table. Maggie prayed that he could keep himself in check. This might be the breakthrough that they had been hoping for, but if Bob didn't hit the right note from the start, Señora Balaguer could just shut down. He had to win her trust.

41

Cwmbran, South Wales
2017

Nick parked his van, but it took a few minutes to bring himself to get out. He trudged across the car park, avoiding the puddles where the snow had melted, and stopped, facing the footpath that led to the manor. The thumping in his chest had increased that of a galloping horse and he took a moment to steady himself before putting a resolute foot on the path and starting to walk.

As he approached the building he put his gloves inside the pockets of his parka and rubbed his palms. He didn't want to present a sweaty hand to Stella Bell.

He stopped in front of the low, wide front door and looked up, taking in the whole of the façade. He thought he glimpsed a face at the window above the door; for a moment, he thought it was smiling at him. Instinctively he looked away at his shoes, but when he looked up again a second later there was no one there. The door was ajar, and sounds of chattering voices were coming from inside.

Just one step, he thought, but the weight pressing down on his shoulders was gluing his feet to the floor and he couldn't move. Then, the door opened and a middle-aged couple walked out, nodding to him. He had to move aside to let them pass.

"Nick Howell?" A woman stood smiling in the doorway, holding out her hand. He shook it. "Do come in," she said, turning around. He moved forward. The step was taken. His heart was thumping, but the weight was gone.

He followed her through the porch-way, into the

entrance hall, and then left into the café, glancing quickly around, taking in the open door to the right that led into the museum, and the wooden stairs that went up and then divided into two, leading to closed doors.

The café was busy, but Stella had reserved a table for them. She ordered hot drinks at the counter and came to sit with Nick.

"Thanks for meeting me," he began.

"No problem," she replied. "Maggie told me you might come here, one day. So, you're one of the original Howell family?"

"Yes," he replied, staring at the stone fireplace. "Maggie and I have traced my ancestry and I seem to be the last male Howell in the direct line of descent of the original owners."

"Well it's great to have you here. What can I do for you? Would you like a tour?"

"Yes, that would be interesting, but I'd like to know what you can tell me about the history, as far as you know it. Not particularly about my family, but about what has happened here."

"Delighted. Let's start in here." Stella stood up and began to talk about how the community project had taken over the building and what changes had been made.

Then she led him out of the café and across to the museum. "This was probably the original house, or a large part of it. The kitchen through there at the back was added later, but this part we are standing in was Tudor era."

Nick looked around. From where he was standing he could see into each of the areas and he took only a cursory look at them. One door was closed. "What's in there?" he asked.

"We think that was a small office, perhaps where accounts or wages were paid," she replied. "But it's interesting. There's half a spiral staircase and we've never been able to find out where it started or where it originally led."

224

Nick walked over and opened the door. He looked up at the suspended stone staircase and turned back. "Perhaps to the cellar?"

"There's no cellar in this building, which is unusual. If there is, it must have collapsed or been filled in. Anyway, we've never found any evidence of there being one."

He walked back into the hallway, a puzzled Stella following behind him.

"These aren't the original stairs," he said.

"No, we can't say exactly where they were, although it doesn't look like that old spiral staircase was part of the main staircase either. As I said, it's a puzzle. Would you like to go up?"

He nodded. At the top of the first flight they turned left into a chamber with a stone fireplace and decorated walls. "We use this for community meetings, now, and the same on the other side." She turned to lead him back down the few steps and up the other side into a similar, but larger, room. Again, Nick gave it only a cursory glance.

"Are you looking for something in particular?" Stella asked.

"I'm not sure," he replied, examining a small bricked-up doorway in the back wall. Then he turned to face her. "What I really want, Stella, is any stories you have of past owners and anything supernatural associated with any of them."

"Oh, I see. Can I ask what this is about?"

"Of course. I've found some strange stuff in my history that I want to know more about. Maggie told me about the chair, upstairs. I think that could be something significant." She seemed uncertain. "Look, I'm sorry if I sound a bit weird. Actually, I am, but I just need to know."

She bit her lip a couple of times, then said, "OK. Look, we happily tell people about some of this stuff, because it's just imagination. Grey ladies haunting the corridors, that kind of thing. There's supposed to be a little boy looking for his mother in the room next door. We have a spooky

225

week at Halloween. But honestly, I often work up in the office in the attics late at night, on my own, and I've never heard a thing. Of course, there are creaks, rattling, you know. But… but it's just not frightening."

"Or, you aren't easily frightened," he replied.

She acknowledged his comment with a wry smile. "I'm not easily scared," she replied. "I really don't know anything specific, about your family or any supposed hauntings on the premises. The only thing that I will say I'm wary of is that chair upstairs. That, I can't explain."

"So, Stella, if you are a rational person, very sensible and grounded, which I think you are, what is it about the chair?"

"Why don't you come up and see for yourself?" she said, and swept her arm in the direction of a small doorway on the opposite side of the room. Nick nodded, and she led them through the door and down three steps.

"This is the oldest surviving part of the building, as far as we know. Probably seventeenth-century." She pointed to her left to a small doorway and into what looked like a bedroom. "It overlooks the front door. It's where the little motherless boy is supposed to be."

Nick stopped and poked his head through the doorway. "I don't feel anything," he said.

"Me neither," she replied, "no matter how many times I've been in there."

She turned right, walked along a narrow corridor, and turned back on herself, to another flight of stairs. Nick followed her up. At the top was a landing and a choice of two directions. One led into doorways beyond which Nick could see boxes and general storage. The other was a small, slanted corridor leading to a closed wooden door.

"Maggie told me about this," he said. "This is the oldest original door."

Stella stopped in front of it. "That it is," she said, turning the tarnished metal ring that raised the latch and opened the door. It swung open to the wall inside. As he looked across the room Nick saw the walls move in and out and was sure the floor was also moving around beneath his feet. Bile rose into his throat, but he swallowed it back down.

"Are you OK? Stella Bell's voice was full of concern.

"Yes."

"Only your face is white as a sheet, and if you grasp that door ring any harder you're going to break it."

"Sorry," Nick couldn't get his voice above a hoarse whisper. He let go of the door handle. He was looking the chair and what was in it. "Just a bit... not sure what. Have to go." He turned and half-ran down the corridor and out of sight, leaving a bemused Stella Bell staring at the empty chair as the sound of Nick's footsteps faded.

Back in the hallway Nick looked around, trying to locate the front door. It was right in front of him, but he didn't recognise it until a woman opened it from outside and came in. When he didn't respond to her cheery greeting she gave him a quizzical look and held the door open. He ran out, and down the path without looking back or stopping until he got to his van. Once he was in the driving seat he grasped the steering wheel to steady his hands, and stared into the rear-view mirror.

It was ten minutes before his legs stopped shaking enough to be able to drive away. He drove back to Maggie's house, let himself in, ran into the cloakroom and stared at himself in the mirror above the sink. He pulled at the skin on his face, down from his cheeks, across and up. Then he let his hands drop to his sides, and just stared. And realised that no matter how he tried to amend his expression, the face he was looking at was the same face he had seen on the figure in the chair. It had been hardly visible. Not see-through exactly, just... vague. He could see it, but it couldn't see him.

Or rather, 'he' couldn't see him. The man in the chair; the man in the long gown, with his long dark hair parted in the centre, hanging to his collar; long hair that he flung from side to side with each wild shaking of the head. Dark, malicious eyes that saw nothing, but felt a presence. A wide mouth with thin lips, from which whispered and wailed, over and over 'Be that her? Is she come again? Show yourself, demon! I killed them. I killed my boy.'

Although Nick could not see an energy field, so he knew this was not a living person, he felt something emanating from the body. Something that made his gut pulse with terror. He knew that whatever this was, he was inescapably connected to it.

42

Cwmbran, South Wales
2017

Nick was jerked out of his reverie by what turned out to be the ringtone of his mobile phone. It took him a few seconds to recognise it. He took it out of his pocket, expecting it to be Alice, but it was Zelah. He caught it just in time.

"You took your time. What are you doing? We need to talk!" No reply from Nick. "Nick… Nick! Are you there?"

"What? Yes, I'm here." He glanced at his watch, then remembered that he was supposed to meet Alice at the bus stop. It was already getting dark and wasn't she supposed to text him when she was on the bus? The film had finished an hour ago. "I just need to track Alice down. Call you back."

"But–" He ended the call.

He checked his phone to see if he had a missed call or text from Alice. Nothing. Something caught his eye flashing past the window and he walked to the kitchen to check the garden, but at that moment the front door banged.

"I'm back!" called Alice.

Out in the hall she was divesting herself of outdoor clothes and hanging them up. "Your mother warned me that you usually drop those on the floor," he remarked.

"Trying to get better," she replied with a half-smile.

"How was the film?"

"It was OK. Not brilliant, but OK. I think I'll go to my room now."

"Where's Janine?"

"Gone home," she replied, scooting up the stairs. "She got the bus." And she was gone.

His phone rang again. "Don't bother calling me. I'm coming over now." Zelah cut the call this time, leaving him no time to object. He didn't think he was up to talking, but, as usual, Zelah had given him no choice. Ten minutes later he heard her car pulling up outside. Another car pulled up too. No one came to the door, so he checked through the window, to find Zelah laughing, with Jack and his friend sitting at the wheel of her red sports car. After a couple of minutes she turfed them out. Jack's friend went off in the second car and Zelah and Jack walked up to the front door, which Nick was waiting to open for them.

"Soon, I promise," Zelah was saying over her shoulder. She went to say something back in response to a comment from Jack, but stopped when she saw Nick. "OK, Jack, go and sit in it for five minutes," she said, throwing him the keys. She closed the front door. "Let's talk. In the office."

He sat down, not at the table, but on the settee, where he threw himself and stared at his hands, wringing them together as if trying to wash off something filthy. Zelah spotted that he didn't have his gloves on. This was the first time that she had seen his bare left hand.

"Where shall we start?" she asked him, taking a seat at the table.

When he didn't answer, she said, "Let's go back to our two theories. I have something to add, as I can see you do, too. OK, Nick?" This time he nodded, but still looked at his hands.

"Can I get you something first? Tea, coffee, whiskey, Valium?"

Nick looked up at her, his expression grim. "This isn't a laughing matter."

"Then it's just as well I'm not laughing. Look, you're supposed to be the calm one, the one who keeps us grounded. I'm supposed to be the unreasonable one. Or am I? Hell, I've lost track. Strange times, eh?"

"I don't need anything, thank you. At least we can all see that we've changed. I suppose that's something." He lapsed into silence again. Zelah turned her chair and pulled it forward until she was sitting in front of him.

"Well, I'm going to talk and you can listen. For now. Where to start? Yes, back to Theory X and Theory Y. The first one was that he's just a nasty conman, a fraud with an objective that we can't yet understand. What do conmen usually want? Money, or something valuable. I'm the only one of the three of us who's got any. But *he* paid *me*, not the other way round. So, unless I am very stupid and have missed something blindingly obvious, I can't see that that is his intent. I checked at home, if he was trying to get me to go to Canada to get me out of the way so he could rob me, that hasn't happened. But he was leading me, to where I don't know, but so far it seems he was leading me right back here, to the start. I've learned nothing about his history. I can't see how I was his intended victim. And you haven't got anything he'd want. Nor Maggie. Nothing financially valuable, anyway.

"Now, Theory Y. He's not a conman, he's... what? Some kind of... metaphysical aberration? I have observations to make here. And I've got some back-up. Have you heard anything I've said?" She stood up. "Nick, if you aren't going to listen to anything I'm saying, then I might as well go home." She moved to pick up her coat, but he stopped her.

"I heard what you said, and I agree. Sit down, Zelah, please. I'm nearly ready to tell you what happened to me today, but finish your piece first." He was holding his hands together in his lap, and his face had regained some normal colour.

"Well," she went on, putting her coat down and sitting again, "you remember I said that when I met him he was

230

very smooth and that he crept up on me? That the hotel foyer seemed to be empty, but then he was at my shoulder." This time Nick nodded in acknowledgement. "Good. I didn't think any more about it, until we started considering this... angle. I did notice that the staff were, what should I say, wary of him? I saw a receptionist give him a funny look. So, I went back there today and said I was due to meet him."

"And? Why is this important?"

"It's important, Nick, because not only did they have the same impression I got, but it seems they've been speculating. I got the one girl talking. She told me that he had a habit of seeming to appear at the desk. There'd be no one, they'd glance down and up again and he'd be standing there. She called it 'spooky'." She looked at him, but he didn't comment so she continued, "And she told me that when he went out a couple of times he would say he'd called a taxi, but he walked out of the front door and just disappeared. No taxi, not that they could see."

Nick pursed and bit at his lips. Then he said, "He's not right."

"What does that mean?"

He sighed. "Not right, not normal. Acting in a way you'd expect for what he'd asked us to do. Put it all together, it's way off. I think," he paused, searching for words, "he's leading us to something, trying to get us to see something he needs us to see, but to find it ourselves."

"That makes no sense," Zelah muttered.

"It makes no sense in the normal way of things. That's what I said: this is not right or normal. It's way off. Everything is way off."

"What do you mean? What happened to you today?"

Nick drew in a breath so deep that Zelah thought he was going to implode. "Please just listen, don't interrupt."

For twenty minutes, he went through the work that Maggie and he had been doing about the story of his family and the association with the manor. He told her about the curse, the story passed on by his mother, and, at last, showed her his hand. She was about to speak but he stopped her. "Not yet. There's more."

He told her about his visit to the manor and what he had seen there.

When it was clear he'd finished, Zelah said, "So, Maggie was right," she said. "There was someone, some *thing*, sitting in the chair?"

"Not just someone, Zelah. It was me. I was sitting there. The hair was longer, the face was wild, but it was my face. The eyes were the same blue as mine, too."

"Are you sure? Sorry, stupid question. Of course you are. Any idea who it might have been?"

"Yes. I think it's whatever's left of Gwyllim Hywel. He inherited the manor from his brother, Morgan, when Morgan drowned. Morgan's son, Dewi, also drowned. I think he killed them both."

"Why?"

"Because the thing in the chair said, 'I killed *them*. Then added, '*I killed my boy*'. That fits in with the grave that Maggie found, Gwyllim's son Herrick, '*most foully gone*'. I think he may have killed his brother and his brother's son, to inherit the manor. But then, he killed his *own* son."

"Hang on," she interrupted. "Didn't you say Morgan's son went first? Gwyllim would have inherited anyway."

"Yes, but Morgan might have lived a long life, and he may have decided to leave the manor to his eldest daughter, Morgana."

"No," Zelah insisted, "girls didn't inherit."

"What if she was betrothed? He could have decided to leave it to her and her husband."

"Unlikely, but not impossible," she conceded. "There might be a will. We can check that."

"But he was no more than middle-aged. Would he have left a will?"

"Yes," she said. "Quite usual, where property was involved. He may have suffered an illness. Decided to make his intentions clear, especially as the son who would have automatically inherited was dead. And another thought, if Gwyllim killed his son, given that the headstone indicates it wasn't an accident, there may be a coroner's inquest report."

Nick looked dubious. "A report dating back to 1735?"

"A long shot," she agreed. "Very long. But not impossible. I've seen plenty from the early nineteenth century. If it was foul play, then there must have been reports somewhere. No newspapers at the time," she mused, sitting back in her chair, rubbing her hands together slowly. "Earliest local paper for this area was about 1810. But, I think there was one in Gloucester that reported some South Wales news. I'll have to check."

"Exciting for you."

Zelah looked puzzled for a few seconds, then said, "Sorry Nick. I'm getting carried away. This is personal, and you're upset. I apologise."

"Another first," he murmured.

"The sarcasm is not necessary," she bristled. "I'm trying. I did actually listen to what Maggie said."

"I know," he conceded. "Can I go on with the story?"

"Please do," she said, mollified.

"There was one more second son a couple of generations later, and he died of 'suffocation in a ditch'. That was probably recorded as an accident."

"When was that?" Zelah asked.

"In 1806. And the next one, the last second son before me, was Edgar Howell. The baby murdered by John Howell in 1875, when he also killed his wife when she tried to stop him. He never gave an explanation, but he talked at his trial about being visited by 'the demon'. Same as Gwyllim Hywel in his chair." He held out his left hand in front of her face. "This is what I hide. My mother told me it's a curse, exclusive to second sons. Do you think Herrick, Peter, and Edgar had this, too?"

Zelah examined Nick's hand. "It's a birthmark."

"You think?" he replied, pulling his hand back and searching for his glove.

"Has Maggie seen it?" Zelah asked.

"Yes."

"So why the hell bother putting that glove back on? Time to face up to it, Nick."

Nick's left hand hovered in mid-air. He turned it slowly, flexed his fingers, brought it up in front of his face until it was almost touching his nose. "Right," he said to his hand. "Yes. New beginnings."

"Good for you. Great. But, we still haven't got anywhere with Morgan Sturridge and his bloody ancestor, John Hammill. That man is the key to cracking this case. I just know it!"

Nick had put his hand back in his lap and was staring at the floor, muttering.

"Something. What is it? There's something." He shook his head.

The phone rang in the hall. Nick sighed, stood and went out to answer it. Zelah waited in the office, but, as the tone of Nick's voice became increasingly agitated, she went out to stand beside him.

It was a friend calling for Jack. Nick called him down and he and Zelah went back into the office. After a few minutes of conversation Jack appeared and looked at Nick with a half-quizzical, half-begging smile.

Nick stood up. "When and where?"

"Now, over to Ben's house. It's only five, ten minutes away."

"OK. When are you coming back?"

"Probably tomorrow morning. It's not a party, his parents are there. Just a few of us, some gaming."

Nick shrugged as Jack ran out of the room to collect his stuff and he turned back to Zelah. "Want to wait? I shouldn't be more than a quarter of an hour." She looked at her watch. No, I'm going home. I'm tired and I want to think some more on… all of this."

Jack reappeared with a rucksack and a duvet. Nick called up to Alice to let her know that he was going out and would be back soon, but that she was on her own. She appeared at the top of the stairs. "What are we having for dinner?"

"I'll bring something in, if you like. What do you want?"

"Pizza?"

"One between us?"

"One each please. I'm hungry." She went back into her room.

Zelah, Nick, and Jack left together, Zelah telling Nick that she would call if she thought of anything else, but to expect her again in the morning.

When he got back with the pizza half an hour later, Alice asked if she could eat in her room. She explained she had homework to do that involved a lot of reading. Nick agreed reluctantly, knowing that Maggie wouldn't like it, but it would at least give him chance to eat in front of the computer in the office. He didn't hear from Alice again. He thought he heard her in the kitchen later, but when he went up to check on her just after nine, she was already asleep.

He tiptoed back downstairs and went round to make sure the house was locked up. The door from the kitchen to the garden was open, which surprised him as he didn't remember unlocking it. He locked up and went back to the office.

Shortly after, Maggie rang.

He told her that Jack was staying with a friend overnight, with parents present. He wasn't sure whether or not to share his concerns about Alice, and decided against. Alice was asleep in bed and it wasn't worth disturbing her. Maggie picked up something of his concern, but he assured her it was nothing to worry about.

"Any idea yet when you're coming back? Not that I'm concerned, but, you know."

"Minder, cook, taxi service, gets a bit wearing, doesn't it?" He could hear the suppressed laughter in her voice. But then, "Do you really think she's OK?"

"She and Janine went to the cinema this afternoon. She came back when she was supposed to."

"Well, I suppose that's good enough for now. I think we'll be back by Wednesday at the latest. Anyway, thanks for what you're doing, Nick. I really appreciate it." They discussed how their cases and Nick's own research was going. Then she was gone.

He went back to the office, and had just sat in front of the screen when the phone rang again. For a moment he considered ignoring it, but decided that it might be Maggie again, or Jack. It was Janine's mother.

"If you could just get her for me; I wanted to check she's OK. She isn't answering her mobile. I was going to leave it, but she was upset after school yesterday. Difficult, isn't it, to know whether or not to leave it, give them some space, or just check. I was hoping she enjoyed the cinema."

She was speaking so fast that it was hard to keep up, but Nick's stomach was churning. He couldn't let her go on. "I don't really understand, Mrs Morgan. Janine isn't here. Alice was back at five, but Janine wasn't with her."

There was a brief silence at the other end of the phone. "I don't... I can't... what do you mean, Janine wasn't with her, of course she's there!"

"She really isn't, Mrs Morgan. Alice got the bus back from town, on her own. Could she have gone to someone else's house?"

"She doesn't have anyone else!" Her voice was shaking. "Where is she?"

"Look, isn't there someone else you could try? I'll wake Alice up, ask her what happened when she left Janine. Give me five minutes, then call me back." He put the phone down and went upstairs.

Alice sat up as soon as her bedroom door opened and he suspected that she hadn't really been asleep.

"Janine's mother just called," said Nick, "and she thought Janine was here. Why would she think that?"

"She caught the bus, same as me," Alice said. "What's the matter?"

"The matter, is that she isn't home. Where is she?"

Alice shrugged. "She got on the bus."

The phone rang again. "Come downstairs, *now*." Alice had never heard Nick so stern. She got out of bed, pulled on a hoodie and tracksuit bottoms and followed him.

Janine's mother was now panic stricken. "I've tried her cousin. She's not there. There isn't anyone else."

"Alice is here," Nick said. "She says they both got their buses home. That's all she knows." He shot Alice a piercing look.

They heard the sound down the phone of Janine's mother bursting into tears. "I'm calling the police," she wailed, and the phone went dead.

43

Falset, Catalonia, Spain
2017

After ten minutes, Feliu, the bar owner, came back down and spoke to Bob, who nodded emphatically and motioned to Maggie to stand up. "She'll talk to us," he said. Feliu went across the door, locked it, and put up a closed sign.

He gestured to them to follow him through the bead curtain behind the bar and up a flight of stairs. At the top they turned left and walked down a corridor and into a room overlooking the street. Maggie guessed that it used to be the apartment's living room, but had been turned into a bedroom. A fire was burning in a grate. In a huge, old-fashioned carved wooden bed there was an old woman the size of a child.

She was wrapped in a black lace shawl, so that just her hands and face were visible. The hands were lined and claw-like, and wrapped around the bedsheet in the way a bird might wrap its feet around a narrow pole. Her remaining strands of white hair, parted in the centre, had been gathered in a bun behind her head. But the most noticeable feature was her black eyes. Although sunken into the shrivelled face, they shone with a fierceness that suggested anticipation of excitement and pleasure. She lifted a hand and beckoned them towards the bed, next to which Feliu had placed two chairs. Maggie and Bob sat and Feliu stood behind them.

Bob was starting to explain his story when Señora Balaguer interrupted him with a derisory wave of her spiny hand and imperious speech given in a surprisingly strong voice. Maggie gathered that Feliu had already explained their intentions.

"She says she doesn't have time for useless civility," Bob said. "Just ask what we want to know and she'll tell us what she can remember."

For a few minutes, Bob spoke to the woman, who nodded vigorously from time to time. Then he stopped. The woman began to speak and Bob translated in a low voice as Maggie wrote.

"I have a lot of stories. You want the story of the baby that didn't fit, right?"

Bob said "Yes."

"They were always suspicious of us in Falset.... with the Brigaders, the foreign boys, having a camp not far... We saw them from time to time... She helped out... They were nice boys, good looking, some of them." She winked at Maggie, who smiled back after Bob had interpreted.

"She wasn't political then... or her family. That changed when they saw what was happening to those who opposed the regime... Terrible things. Terrible things. The convent you want to know about... about two kilometres from here, south, between Marca and here. A couple of women from Falset worked there... Just a few.... Run by the crows... nuns," Bob was concentrating on translating as accurately as possible.

"The women didn't talk about it, but there were rumours." The woman paused and Feliu stepped forward, but she waved him away. "Girls, but only pregnant ones... in dormitories... Not able to get out. One woman who worked there was our neighbour... Virtudes. She was midwife, not real one. She helped the local women... and

238

she did cooking and cleaning. She and her husband were close with each other, didn't speak much to anyone else. She was ordinary middle-aged woman… She talked to my mother sometimes… I overheard some of it. I remember she said there was a priest in charge. Virtudes was fearful of him. One day, Virtudes told my mother that first the babies disappeared, then the girls."

"Did anyone know what was happening to them?" Bob asked, then told Maggie what he'd said.

Amalia Balaguer shook her head. "Never heard that. One minute they were there, they gave birth, then they were gone."

"Does she know anything about the girls, why they were there?" Maggie asked. Bob translated the question.

"They were prisoners… expect they were captured Republican women... Many children disappeared."

"We know," Maggie said. "Tell her I've read about it."

"Ayee, dones pobres!" Señora Balaguer sat back in her bed, but kept talking, Bob keeping pace with his translation.

"But, here's the story, now. One day… Virtudes came home upset, very upset. Told mother a relative was at convent… Her husband's cousin's niece… about to have a baby. Married to one of the foreign boys…. He'd gone, probably dead in fighting. Girl told Virtudes that the priest would take her baby. Virtudes' husband went and got his cousin."

Maggie interrupted, "Does she know where from?" Bob shook his head and told her to write it down the question to ask later, as the woman glanced at Maggie, then began to talk again.

"Between them, they hatched a plot. They were brave… took courage." She pointed a wizened finger at Bob. "People think they brave now, they don't know… They just don't know."

He asked her a question. She gazed past his head again, into the fire that was spitting burning wood. "The aunt, whose name was… can't remember now. It may come back. They decided to see if they could force baby to come early. Virtudes would hide in the convent... stay with the girl... when it was delivered, bring them both out. They had to climb through a narrow window and drop down a floor... dangerous plan... it was all they could think of. They couldn't get the girl out... didn't fit through window in her condition... baby due anyway, so she couldn't have travelled far. Aunt went away for a few days... when she came back, had her own daughter with her... She was about to give birth too... so they pretended. Good what you can do with a bundle of rags stuffed up your dress." She stopped to cackle, which ended in a hacking cough. Feliu stepped forward to support her back. When she finished coughing, she asked for a drink. Bob asked a question.

"Of course I knew... they were next door. This girl had arrived at night... they kept her hidden. But I met her. She already had small child, little girl... playing together in kitchen when I went in and some of the rags fell... She was terrified... I assured her I was a friend... Put out story she had come to be with the women of her family, to bring her baby safely. People believed it... it was a good story.

"One day Virtudes didn't come home after work... Mother guessed what was happening... We sat in kitchen all night, hardly able to speak. Finally, at dawn, Virtudes came back... only with baby." She stopped again. Her voice had started to crack. Book looked relied to catch a breather too. Maggie felt that something dreadful was coming.

Amalia breathed in and out a few times.

"This is hard... hadn't thought about it for a long time. It makes me sad, even now. Virtudes had the baby, but the birth went wrong... She had given medicine to the girl in the morning, by late in day, pains were coming. Virtudes hid in bathroom... when girl could cope no longer... and nuns all gone to bed, she went to the bathroom. At first, it went well. Virtudes knew enough about birthing babies. But it was too quick.... Pain must have been terrible for poor girl, but she said she never uttered a sound. Once, another girl came... saw what was happening... shook head and went away. There was too much blood. Baby was born... just before morning. Girl had lost much blood... she could hardly move... begged Virtudes to take the baby and get away... She would consequences. Asked for him to be baptised. His name... Hugo Jaume. It was almost dawn... Virtudes said that she could see... acceptance, of her fate, in the girl's eyes... knew what would happen to her. She asked Virtudes to get the boy to his father... but then heard sounds. Girl pulled away and out the door. Virtudes spent some minutes trying to wash away blood... Wrapped the baby, put him under her coat and ran... arrived here mid-morning. They went through the little play they had set up. Husband's cousin's daughter pretended to give birth.... Baby still new enough for people to believe he was born that morning. Virtudes even remembered to bring some of the bloodied rags with her and she made a show of burning them later... Then, we all waited.

"Virtudes sent message to convent that she would not come to work day because of birthing in village... Next day she went back. She had to pretend that nothing had happened. The girls cried when they thought no one could see. They were shocked... but no one told her anything. Lola gone, just gone. Only thing she saw was blood stains, a lot of it, where it should not have been. She had to keep going to that place for a few months more. Then suddenly, it was all over... girls were taken away. Her work was gone. She made fuss.... where would she find more work, you know, like that? She was happy to know that she never had to go there again. Baby was baptised the day after he was born. Girl's husband turned up. He was in on the act, too. Surly, bad-tempered. Probably terrified. Once the baby was baptised... husband took his family away... including V's husband's cousin... Never saw them or heard from them again."

She sighed and lay back into the heap of pillows. She said something to Bob and looked anxious and in need of reassurance. He replied, and she looked relieved. He spoke again and she nodded.

"I asked if it was OK for questions. I'm going to ask her if she can remember any of the family names, and he translated her response:

"Our neighbours were Virtudes and Felip Oliver Lopez. Felip's cousin was called… Estel… can't recall her family name. She can't remember any more."

She pulled the blanket up over her face. Maggie, who looked up briefly from her note-taking realised that this was an unconscious gesture of hiding something. She suspected something important.

Feliu was stepped forward again, when Maggie tugged on Bob's sleeve. "There's something else she's not telling us – something important. Ask her. Tell her she has nothing to fear from us. Tell her anything, but get it out of her!"

He cocked an eyebrow at her, but Maggie squeezed his arm. He spoke again, but there was no response. "I told her what you said."

"No more," Feliu said, stepping forward to stand between the chairs and the bed.

"Tell her, I understand," Maggie said to Bob. "Tell her, we all do things we aren't proud of. But if what she knows is of use to us, then we'll just be grateful to her, whatever it is. Tell her it's always best to get it out, no matter what the consequence might be." Bob repeated Maggie's words to the small lump in the bedspread.

Feliu was fidgeting, anxious to end the discussion, his expression of worry turning to anger as Bob and Maggie played this last card. He put his hand up in a barring gesture and was about to take Bob by the arm, when a voice came from the bed.

"I was ashamed of my thoughts," Bob said for her.

"Tell her our thoughts always sound worse when they echo inside our own head. They are smaller, more understandable… and forgivable when they reach the outside." Bob repeated this.

Slowly, the blanket moved down. Maggie felt a rush

242

of compassion for this ancient woman with so many painful memories. They had to lean forward to hear the words whispered like a breath of wind on the breeze.

Bob listened carefully and then turned to relay what she'd said to Maggie.

"She says she remembers his name, always remembered it, although they didn't want to tell her. She made them. Because she was frightened. She thought the troops would come, and torture us for names. She would have given him their name. To save herself. She was not brave."

"No, Maggie said firmly. "That may be what you thought, Señora, but you didn't have to do it, and you don't know what you would have done. None of us do. But we often find that we are better than we think, when we are faced with a tough choice." Bob spoke quietly to her, his face softened with compassion that Maggie hadn't seen before.

One of the hands unclawed itself from the bedsheets and reached out to Maggie's hand. She took it in hers. It was cold and dry, but Maggie put as much feeling into her squeeze as she could.

"Mateu Vilaro Roig. Estel's daughter... Carme."

"It's enough," Bob said, standing up to speak in an official way to the grandmother and grandson. Maggie assumed, once again, that he was thanking her. She looked touched by his words, as did her son.

"What did you say?" asked Maggie.

"I said we both thank her from the bottom of our heart. That right now, a wrong is being perpetrated, by a greedy, corrupt man. If the information she has given us can help us to trace descendants of the child christened Hugo Vilaro, we may yet do a very good thing, and honour the memory of a brave man who came to Spain to fight for freedom."

The old woman smiled, closed her eyes, and lay back on her pillows. The bar owner led them down the stairs.

"What are you feeling, about that story?" Maggie asked Feliu as they descended the stairs.

"I won't say it's not a shock," he replied. "I knew she was alive during those times, but she has *never* spoken of it. My family leaves it all well alone."

"She shouldn't think she's not a brave woman," Maggie said as they parted company. "She knew about the baby's origins and she kept the secret all through the regime. That cannot have been easy."

Feliu took Maggie's hand. "Thank you. I don't know how much she'll want the family to know, but I think what she did was honourable. Let me know how you get on, eh? I'm glad you came to my café."

"Just a final question," Bob said. "Can you tell us anything about the priest here? I tried to talk to him about the convent, but he wasn't forthcoming."

"Not surprised," Feliu said quietly. "I don't have anything to do with him. It was a bad day when he came here. He's a fanatic, you know. Do anything for the church." He leaned even closer to them. "I heard he was even prepared to arrange the provision of church documents, in exchange for a big donation."

"Not the best image for Catholics," Bob agreed. "Let's go, Maggie–" But she cut in and asked Feliu, "What documents? To whom?"

Feliu turned out his bottom lip and rubbed one ear. "I heard he organised some documents to a guy a couple of months ago, just local stuff, in return for a big donation to the church."

"He just asked me for money," Bob said to Feliu, but then to Maggie, "But I know what you're thinking."

"Yep," she replied. "Let's go."

They stood outside in the crisp sunshine, recovering from the heat of the fire in the room.

"If those records are here, and the priest is willing to sell them, shouldn't we try to see if we can find the baptism of Hugo Vilaro?" Maggie asked. "You probably don't want to speak to him again, but I think we have to try."

"Yes, I can put on my tourist face and try again. Worth it. Come on."

244

They walked back to the square and up the steps to the front door of the church, but it was locked. An old man was walking across the square and Bob called out to him. They exchanged a few words, then Bob, waved to the man and said under his breath, "Damn. He's gone. To the next church for another service. He won't leave the keys with anyone, and he's not back until tomorrow."

Maggie started to walk back across the square but Bob didn't follow her. She turned back and saw that, once again, he was staring into space.

"Bob?" she went to go on, but she shushed her. He walked up to her and whispered, "Get your camera out and make a big display of giving it to me. Point around the square, then stand in that corner, by the church."

Maggie was puzzled but did as Bob asked. Once she was by the church he took the camera and took a series of shots. They he took a few shots around the square, and walked over to her.

"What's going on?"

"Keep smiling. I didn't take photos, I just used the zoom. To check something out. Keep looking at me. We're being followed."

"What! How do you know? Who is it?"

"Done enough undercover myself. Same guy here today as in the café in Gandesa twice, and at the home."

"That's what you were looking at. What are you going to do?"

"Nothing, I think. I don't want to alert him. But we can guess who's put him onto us."

"Absolutely. What do we do now?"

"We leave. Just don't be tempted to look at him."

They walked slowly, hand-in-hand across the square like the perfect tourist couple, found the car, drove out of Falset and headed back to Gandesa, where they went back to their favourite café and ordered sandwiches and tea.

"Did he follow us back?" Maggie asked.

"Yes," Bob replied. "He's sitting in a car outside."

"Should we confront him?"

"Definitely not. Let him think he's done a good job. Nothing to be gained from confronting him. He's not likely to tell us anything, besides that he's been paid to follow us around and report back."

"So Mason Haussmann will know who we've seen and what we've done?"

"He'll find out anyway. It doesn't matter. The thing is, if he was so sure of the information he has, he wouldn't have needed this. We must have him rattled. We carry on, fast as we can. Now, where were we? Right, find out about the baptism of Hugo Vilaro."

"We can ask Joan to go back and check the registers," Maggie said, sandwich in hand. "It's not really necessary, though, is it? We've got enough to go on. They only stayed to baptise the baby, then left. It won't help to find out where they went."

"They would have had to name the village they came from," Bob replied. "It might have been a start. Although…" he paused, drank a mouthful of tea. "I guess they knew that if anyone came after them they'd be in trouble. So they might have moved on. Or lied. Would have been safer."

"Could that priest be Mason Haussmann's source, do you think?" Maggie asked, looking through her notes . "How do you want to deal with these, by the way?"

"It's the closest we've come to figuring it out," Bob said. "We need everything we can get. I suspect that Haussmann has information that he believes is secure enough. Maybe, he knows that the child might have survived, through other sources, but doesn't know anything more. We've still got the advantage, I think. As for the records, they are usually kept together at the diocesan headquarters. But I'm not sure where that it. If there are records from the civil war there, it would be useful to find out more about the psycho priest."

"We'll probably find that he went on to bigger and better things. Fate doesn't always do the right thing," Maggie mused.

246

"I'm going to call Joan. Get him working on tracing the baby. Probably not much available during the war period, but maybe afterwards."

"You know, Bob, he may still be alive. We might be able to work backwards, now we have a name."

"Yes, I had thought about that. Would be amazing, wouldn't it. But let's not hold out hope. He'd be in his late seventies. Give me the notes, I'll type them up tonight and send them to Feliu. Hope she will sign it," he added.

"I think she will," Maggie replied. "Now she's got it off her chest. I just hope she lives long enough to hear the outcome."

44

Cwmbran, South Wales
2017

"Look at me," Nick demanded, replacing the receiver. "Where is Janine?"

"No idea," Alice replied.

"I said look at me!" he shouted. "Where. Is. Janine?"

"I don't know. She got on the bus. That's all I know."

"That was over four hours ago and she's not home. Where is she?"

"I said I don't know and you aren't allowed to shout at me," she cried, and turned to go upstairs.

"Do you realise that something bad could have happened to her?"

"Like what?" Alice was fiddling with the strings of her hoodie.

"Don't play innocent with me, Alice. You're showing absolutely no signs of surprise or concern... or fear. If you really didn't know where she is, then I'd see all of those."

Alice said nothing, went on wrapping and unwrapping the cords around her fingers.

"Look," he continued. "Her mother is calling the police right now. They're going to take this very seriously because of Janine's age and they're going to want to talk to you. Doesn't that worry you?"

Alice shrugged, but she couldn't hide the strain.

"Look me in the eye and tell me you have no clue where she is."

"She was really unhappy," Alice said, her eyes on the tie.

Nick ran his hands through his hair. "You had better go back upstairs and try remember anything she said that might be useful. The police will want to know. They'll be here, tonight or first thing tomorrow."

Alice nodded, wiped her eyes with the back of her hand, sniffed and started to walk back up the staircase. He watched her go, uncertain about what to do next. He had thought it had been going well, but this had turned into a nightmare. He considered calling Maggie. But what was the point? It was now almost 11pm in Spain. What could she do, except panic? He decided to wait and see what would happen.

As he expected, two police officers turned up just after midnight. He told them what Alice had told him, that the girls had caught their respective buses at around 4.30pm, and that they hadn't spoken since. Then he told them that Janine had been talking to Alice about being unhappy. They said that there wasn't much they could do given the lateness of the hour, and that someone would be back to interview Alice first thing.

"How is Janine's mother?" he asked. "Does she have someone with her?"

"Her sister is there," one of the officers replied. "Don't think she'll sleep much tonight. I expect CID will take this over now. Young girl, and all."

He saw them out. Again, he wondered if he should call Maggie, but rejected the idea. He had to speak to someone. He'd never faced anything like this before. Then he hit on the idea of calling Zelah.

248

At first, she was groggy with sleep and therefore grumpy. But, when she heard what he was telling her, she became immediately alert. "I'm coming over."

"There's no need," he remonstrated. "Leave it to the morning."

"Fat chance of that! You don't call someone at one in the morning, get them all worked up, then tell them to leave it. I'll be there in half an hour."

Zelah was in a no-arguing mood, so he didn't, and being honest with himself, he was glad that she was coming. Someone to share the burden with. It was feeling heavier with every minute that passed.

* * *

Zelah's sports car ensured that she never arrived anywhere quietly. Half an hour later they were sitting in the kitchen, each drinking hot chocolate with a whisky chaser. He had explained everything to her.

"Unintended consequences," she said. "Kids do these things. They think they know everything. Bet they never gave a thought to how it would actually feel. Poor little things."

Nick raised an eyebrow at that.

"Come on, think about it, Nick. Janine's been having a terrible time by the sounds of it. She's been horribly bullied. Her mother is a wimp, so the kid reaches the end of her tether. Alice is just trying to help her."

"That's not fair," he interrupted. "Maggie told me that they don't want parents going to complain. Just makes it worse. Anyway, I'm going to call Maggie first thing. She has to know."

"I agree," Zelah replied. "Let's both get some sleep. We'll need to be on the ball in the morning. Alice is going to need a lot of support." She yawned. "I presume you're in the guest room. I'll sleep in the attic. Let's meet back down here at eight. OK?"

"Yes," he muttered.

"Come on, Nick. It's not your fault. It'll work out OK.

Stay positive. Not your normal way, I know, but give it a try."

"Good coming from you," he replied.

The next morning at 8am Nick walked into the kitchen to find Zelah standing in the conservatory looking out over the garden, cradling a teacup.

"I hate days like this," she said. "I preferred the snow. It's proper winter. This drizzly grey is so drab, like people who can't make up their minds."

Nick poured a mug of tea and joined her. The mist hung low enough to obscure the mountain and even the canal in the foreground.

"Brace ourselves for the day," he said, staring at the mist.

They were both startled by the sound of something crashing to the floor behind them. Spinning around, they found Alice bending down to pick up a smashed cup. "Sorry," she said, head down, picking up the shards.

"Let me do that," Zelah said, putting her cup on the low glass table behind her and hurrying forward. "You haven't got anything on your feet. Go and put some slippers on."

"Don't have any," Alice replied, not looking up.

"Then find something else, just get away from here in bare feet."

Alice stood and walked out of the kitchen. As she went, Zelah caught a glimpse of a white face and sunken eyes darkened by shadows. But she also saw the implacable set of her mouth. She fetched a dustpan and brush and began to sweep. Nick joined her.

"Damn, Nick. This isn't going to be easy. She's going to be very difficult to get anything out of."

"Psychological approaches from me, I think. Direct from you."

"Each to his own style," Zelah muttered, sweeping across a large expanse of the floor.

Alice came back into the kitchen wearing Maggie's slippers and Nick went to answer the phone. Zelah poured tea for Alice, who took the cup and went to sit in the conservatory and stare out at the mist. Zelah was just contemplating what approach to take when Nick came back. "That was the police. They're on their way. Alice, it's time to explain what's going on."

"I can't see the summer house," she said, then sat back on the settee, putting her cup on the table and folding her arms.

"It's still there," said Zelah.

Alice jumped up as if she'd suddenly remembered something. She picked up her cup, in the kitchen, walked back into the conservatory, unlocked the door, and marched off down the garden. It happened so quickly that Nick and Zelah didn't have time to stop her. They heard the sound of a car pulling up outside the house.

"Police," Nick said. "I'll let them in."

Zelah was agitated. She had never had children, but something told her that this wasn't right. She opened the glass door and called out Alice's name. There was no reply. When there was no reply to the second or third calls, she stepped out into the garden and walked down the path towards the canal at the end of the garden and the summer house. Half-way down she met Alice coming back up. The girl halted suddenly, looked around quickly, then back at Zelah. "Were you following me?"

"Yes, I was. Because I don't trust you." In reply, she got a scowl and pursed lips. Alice walked past Zelah into the house, where two uniformed police were waiting. One man and one woman.

Nick led them into the sitting room. Zelah had lit the fire, which was now crackling and shooting out flames.

"Nice room," the policewoman said to Alice. "Shall we sit?" She turned to Zelah and Nick. "Are you Alice's… family?"

"No," Zelah replied. "Her mother is away on business and her brother stayed at a friend's house last night. We," she indicated Nick, "run a business with Maggie, Alice's mother, from this house. She left us in charge."

251

"Me," Nick interrupted. "She left me in charge."

"Well, I suppose you'd both better stay. Does her mother know about this?"

"Not yet, I'm going to call her later," Nick said. "She's in Spain."

"How old are the children?" the male police officer asked, brusquely.

Alice spoke for the first time. "I'm eleven. Jack's sixteen. Nick's looking after us while Mum's away."

The female officer frowned at her colleague and waved him back. She sat forward in front of Alice.

"Hi Alice, I'm Sarah. We really need your help, Alice. We have a lot of police officers out looking for Janine, but we have no idea where to start. I understand you went to the cinema with her yesterday. According to the CCTV you left there around four-thirty. You got on buses. We're tracking down the drivers to see if they had CCTV on board, so we can see what Janine might have done if she didn't get off at her home stop."

Alice sat expressionless throughout, but Nick saw her pupils dilate when the officer mentioned the CCTV. *They didn't think that one through*, he thought.

"So, what else can you tell us?"

Alice shrugged and shook her head. "She got on the bus."

"Did you see her get on the bus?"

"Yes."

"And then?"

"I came home."

"Did you hear from her after that?"

No reply.

"No calls, no texts, no messages?"

This time Alice replied assuredly, "No, none of that."

"You said she was talking about being unhappy," Nick said. "What was that about?"

It was like a dam bursting. Alice jumped up, waving her arms about and shouting, "None of you listened! They were making her life a misery. No one did anything. Not anything. Not one of you helped her. She couldn't bear it anymore." She sat down.

This time Zelah spoke. "Your mother begged you to tell her more, Alice. You pushed her away. You kept saying there was nothing she could do. So, shouting now that no one did anything… you didn't really help either, did you?"

Alice looked at her in disgust. "I'm the only one who did anything to help. If we hadn't done... if we hadn't. She'd have gone."

"What did you do Alice? So far you aren't in any trouble, but you will be if you don't tell us what you did." Sarah reached out to take her hand, but Alice pulled back. She sat back on the settee, curling herself into the corner, arms folded over her chest, head down. The male officer pitched in, "We have two other serious cases to deal with today and we're wasting precious time and resources that could mean someone else's life. Now, what do you know?"

Alice didn't move.

"OK, let's take her down to the station. We'll have to speak to her mother, too. Phone number, please." He stood up.

"No! I'm not leaving the house. I can't leave!"

The police officer took no notice and went to stand in front of her. Nick jumped in. "Wait, please. There's things not adding up." He started to pace around the room, muttering to himself: "Think, think, think."

The two police officers looked at each other, then at Nick when he stopped and clicked his fingers in the air. He turned to them with a smile, and said. "Wait here, please." He walked out of the room and left them all standing staring at the doorway. They heard a door opening at the back of the house.

"Oh. Shit," Alice muttered.

After what seemed like an age, but was no more than two minutes, they heard the door at the back opening and footsteps in the hall heading their way. "You can call off your search," said Nick, appearing in the doorway. He stepped back to reveal Janine, wrapped in a duvet, sniffing, tears running down her face.

"She was in the summerhouse, where I think she spent last night." Janine nodded.

"Sorry, Alice," she whispered.

"We'll have to get her to hospital, get her checked over. And call her mother, let her know she's OK." The policeman spoke to Janine. "Your mother's out of her mind with worry. Did either of you consider that?" Janine burst into tears, but Alice stood up and faced him. "Yes, we did, and only now you're listening. If I'm in trouble, well, OK. It was my idea. But Janine was going to run away. I couldn't let her do that."

The policewoman smiled. "Let's get Janine to the hospital. We'll come back and talk later."

"I'm OK," Janine interrupted. "I don't want to go to hospital."

"Sorry, it's what we call protocol. You have to be checked out. I don't think it will take long. Then we can take you home."

"I don't want to go home! They'll make me go back to school."

"Sorry," said the policewoman, and they led Janine out of the room. She turned in the doorway. "Alice, don't go anywhere. We'll be back later."

Nick saw them to the door, then returned to the sitting room.

"What happens now?" she asked. "Will they take me away?"

"I don't think so," Nick replied. He piled a few more logs on the fire. Without looking back at her he asked, "Did you have this planned when you knew your mother was going away and I would be here?"

"No, of course not. It was Friday. School was terrible. They embarrassed her in front of the whole class and the chemistry teacher just laughed. He's a knob. They'd been

254

planning it. So, we worked it all out at lunchtime. We knew what we were doing."

"No," Zelah interrupted. "You had a plan, but with no idea of the consequences. Look, Alice, I get that you wanted to do your best for Janine, I really do. But it won't stop here."

Alice stared at her. "What do you mean? You've found her. She's back. I don't think she'll go back to school and I hope someone actually does something now. What else is there?"

"Something that eleven-year-olds can't imagine – your mother. What do you think she's going to feel when she finds out what you did behind her back? Do you think she'll trust you again? Do you think she'll trust Nick again? Janine's mother. Don't think she won't blame you. Do you think she'll let you be friends again? And as for putting her in the summerhouse, I wouldn't be surprised if your mother has it knocked down."

"Zelah!" Nick remonstrated. "Too much."

But Alice had begun to cry. "I'm sorry," she babbled, wiping the tears with the back of her hand. "But I couldn't let her run away. I really couldn't."

"But your solution hasn't made it any better, has it?" Zelah said. Alice shook her head. "And as I pointed out earlier, your mother wanted to help but you pushed her away."

"She wanted to do it her way. It wasn't the right way."

"What was?"

"I don't know," Alice sobbed.

"Then try trusting the people who love you and care about you. You hold too much back. Trust me, it doesn't work." Zelah's expression was grim. "I was the same as you. All it ever did was get me into trouble. And I didn't learn the lessons either. I've spent my life thinking I knew better than everyone else. But I don't, and neither do you."

"Enough," Nick said. "That's enough. I tried Maggie earlier but her phone was engaged. I've asked her to call."

Alice turned to him. "How did you know?"

He smiled. "I put the pieces together, eventually. Each one, on its own, was unremarkable. First, the sandwiches. Growing girls, remember. There were enough to feed an army. Then I saw something go past the cloakroom window last night, just before you came in. It was small, so not an adult. Then, the pizza. You ate in your room, but there was no box. And Alice, you can't lie. Your mother's done well there. You kept saying she got on the bus. But you didn't say which bus. This morning you went out to check the summerhouse, with a cup of tea. But when you came back you didn't have a cup. And when you said, very confidently, that you hadn't had a call, or a text or anything from Janine, that's when I realised that you had to have spoken to her, face to face. And, as they say, the rest is history."

"Clever," Alice acknowledged.

"That's Maze Investigations for you. It's what we do," Zelah said. "Not a difficult one. Not for someone like Nick."

"Let's dial this down," Nick said. "What would you like to do until the police come back? This time you're going to tell them the whole story. Nothing left out."

Alice agreed. "I think I'd just like to sit here, in front of the fire. Can I watch a film?"

"Yes," he said. Nick and Zelah walked to the kitchen.

"Nick," Alice called to him. "Do you really think Mum's going to be angry?"

"Furious," he replied. "Absolutely steaming. Get ready."

* * *

After lunch, the police officers called back. They told Nick and Zelah that Janine was fine, no health issues and no after-effects, except that she was steadfastly refusing to go to school the next day.

"Time she stood up for herself," Zelah remarked.

"Harsh," Nick said. "That girl hasn't got an aggressive

bone in her body. And while I don't agree that her mother is a wimp, I do think she's a woman who lives in fear of everything. Not a great role model. But still, what do we know? Other people's lives…" He trailed off into a thought.

Zelah led the officers into the sitting room, where Alice was lying on the settee watching a DVD. She sat up. "OK, I'm ready to tell you everything."

Nick and Zelah sat impassively as Alice went through the story, leaving nothing out, giving a blow-by-blow account of the bullying that Janine had endured. A couple of times she wavered, and Zelah got ready with a box of tissues, but she pulled herself together and went on, shaking the tissues away.

When she reached the point of Janine's discovery, she stopped, waiting for them to tell her what came next. There was a short pause.

"OK," said the policewoman. "We won't be taking this any further."

Alice's upright stance collapsed. "You won't be taking me to the station?" Her voice trembled and the policewoman said, "No. But don't ever do it again, OK?"

If Alice had nodded her head faster it would have been a blur. The officers left, satisfied that their work was done.

After they had left, Nick stood up. "Lunch, anyone?"

Before they could answer the front door opened again. Jack came sauntering in, looked at everyone and asked, "Did I miss something?"

At which they all burst out laughing.

Nick took him by the elbow. "Come into the kitchen. I'll tell you all about it."

* * *

After lunch Alice fell asleep in front of the film she had been watching and Jack took the opportunity to say some abusive things out of her earshot.

"Not too hard on her, please," Nick said. "She was desperate. They both were."

257

"But I offered to help too, and she told me to get lost!" Jack exploded.

"Well, I don't think she'll be so quick to do that again. She's dodged a bullet. The police frightened her, they made her believe that they would arrest her. Hopefully scary enough to make her think twice before doing something so stupid next time, which I hope there won't be."

"Then you don't know her, she has a talent for stupid."

"Don't we all?" Zelah remarked.

Nick took Jack away and challenged him to a game of chess. They were well into in when the phone rang.

"Your mother," Nick said. "Don't move anything, I'll know."

He spent five minutes on the phone, then came back into the office, where Zelah and Jack were waiting. He handed the phone to Jack, covering the mouthpiece to say quickly, "I've just told her the basics. No police. Just tell her you're both OK."

Jack did so, finishing with "Yeah, see you tomorrow."

Zelah looked glum. Nick explained to her, "But it's nothing to do with this. The detective has had his leave cut short. They're on the first plane home tomorrow. All being well she'll be here shortly after nine."

Later that evening, after Jack and Alice were asleep, Zelah and Nick took coffee and chasers into the living room and sat in front of the fire's dying embers. Zelah was yawning, but keen to talk.

"How did you put it all together so quickly, Nick? I mean, it could have gone on for days. That little girl has guts, I'll say that for her. She could have held out against a lesser adversary."

"I'm not her adversary," he replied, staring into the fire. "But I have learned something from this, for the three of us. The business, I mean."

"Interesting," she replied. "Like what?"

"We've become genealogists. Yes, I know, you already were. But Maggie and I were amateurs who wanted to be more professional. So, we followed traditional paths, and I think we began to lose what we were good at. We started to rely more on the conventional, rather than the unconventional, which is what we are."

"I don't get it, Nick."

"We need the basics, yes. But what's made us different? And successful? It's just us. Who we are, together. We have brains that are wired differently to other people. None of us has ever been normal, whatever that means. But we have the ability to think around corners. We don't just see, we feel. Based on what we feel we take chances. So far, so good. But, when did we become so afraid of not being successful that we stopped being who we are?"

Zelah contemplated the last crackling log. "Or did we try to run before we could walk?"

"No, I don't think so. We just got afraid of running fast."

"What's your solution?"

"I think that will take the three of us to work out. Are you up for a discussion tomorrow, when Maggie gets home?"

She nodded. "Yes. It can't wait. I can't wait. But you haven't answered my question. How did you figure it out so fast?"

"I cut out everything down to the basics. I thought about it from Alice's point of view. It's a long time since I've tried to think like an eleven-year-old, with no holds barred. I thought about who she is and that told me what she would do. I'd seen the signs, but they just flitted through my mind, until I stopped and thought about her. Just her. Then, the pieces all fitted into place."

"Interesting." Zelah stood up. "I'm tired and I need a good sleep before Maggie gets back tomorrow. Shall I lock up?"

"I'll do it. I want to think some more around your Canadian case and my own family history. See if can apply some of what I've just said. See if it gets me anywhere. There's one particular area of my story that I want to do some more research on."

"OK, see you in the morning."

When Zelah had gone, Nick went back to do a couple of hours of researching, followed by a lot of sitting on the sofa staring at the ceiling. A couple of ideas flashed through his mind. Crazy stuff, but what if it was true? But it would need three brains to work on it. He went to bed with fingers crossed, hoping Maggie and Zelah could work out their differences, and see how good a team they were… are, and give Maze another chance.

45

They strolled back from the centre of town to their hotel, studiously ignoring the watcher in the car. The morning fog that enveloped Gandesa cleared, leaving the sun bright but ineffective in a clear blue sky.

"We've just got this afternoon left, then," Bob said, once they were out of the cold and in the hotel foyer. "Any thoughts about what we might do? Shame to just sit around."

"We can't go far; there's only a few hours of daylight left. But, I agree, it's a shame to waste it."

Bob called across the foyer to the waiter behind the bar, who replied. Maggie heard the word 'generalissimo' in the response.

"There's an ancient monument about ten minutes' drive from here and there's a great viewing point, *and* it's historically relevant. Franco stood on the very spot before the battle of the Ebro. Worth a look?"

"OK with me," she replied.

They drove out of Gandesa, turned off the main highway and climbed a winding hill. At the summit a

260

signpost pointed to the monument, the Coll de Moro, which looked like a brick bell jar. It was fenced off. There was a small parking area, and she could see a short distance away a viewing platform.

It was colder up here than in the town, but the brightness of the day made up for it. They walked over to the viewing platform. Maggie rested her hands on the rail that guarded her from the steep drop into the valley below.

"This is quite magnificent," she said to Bob. "Look at the way the hills on the other side fold up higher and higher to the mountains. And down there," she swept her hand down towards the wide valley floor, "all those vines and olives and whatever. It's... I don't know the right word. It's luscious. And abundant. Look, you can see for miles down the valley where the road leads off."

"I don't think Franco could have stood here," Bob said, glancing around. "Don't see how he could have seen enough. But, who knows?"

"I can't understand how anyone could have stood here and only thought about death and destruction. I could look at this all day. It's peaceful; it's one of those sights that makes you think of eternity."

Bob shot her a puzzled look. "Quite nice, yeah. Do you want to look at the monument?"

She nodded and turned back to where they had parked the car. "It's called a *poblat*," Bob explained, looking up at the dome-like structure. It's about three or four thousand years old. Old Iberia." They stood for a few minutes.

"Once last look at the view," Maggie said, and walked back to the platform, Bob following behind her. "It's been a productive couple of days, hasn't it?" Maggie said, leaning over on the fence rail.

"More than I could have expected," Bob replied. "Pity we can't stay. I'll call Joan tonight and give him the name. But, you know it's our last chance. We've followed one lead. I want to think about whether we've missed anything. Need to think it all through. Early dinner, then I'd like to just sit and think."

"Works for me," Maggie replied. "I need to phone home, let them know the change of plan." She glanced up at the sky, which was darkening rapidly. "Time to go."

Back at the hotel, they reserved a table for dinner. Not that they needed it. The restaurant had been sparsely used the previous evening. Maggie went to her room, switched on her phone, went to call Nick, and saw that she had missed four calls from him. She dialled and he answered on the first ring.

"What's wrong, what's happened?" she asked without any preamble.

"Alice and Jack are fine," he replied. "But there's been some more Janine trouble. Bit more serious this time."

"Oh no," Maggie said. "What now?"

"School problems. She tried to run away–" he started but got no further into the explanation because Maggie interrupted.

"My trip's been cut short. We're coming home tomorrow." She thought he sounded relieved. "Put her on the phone." Nick said, "She's asleep on the settee at the moment. Look Maggie, she's fine. Janine's fine and back at home. Probably best if you talk to her face to face with you tomorrow."

"Did she run away too?"

"No, of course not."

"Can I speak to Jack, or is he out?"

"No," Nick replied, "he's here. We've been playing chess. He's a good lad."

"I didn't know he could play chess."

"I taught him. He picked it up quickly. He says it was better than twenty-four-seven computer games."

She didn't know what to say, but was saved from having to comment by Jack speaking. The conversation was no more than a few sentences. She got the impression that he was not telling her something, but he assured her that he and Alice were both OK.

"Well, I'll see you tomorrow," she ended.

"Yeah. OK, Mum, have a good flight."

And he was gone, cutting the call off without handing the phone back to Nick. *Not even a 'We've missed you',* Maggie thought.

At dinner, Bob confirmed that he'd had a conversation with Joan, but otherwise he spoke little. He was mentally elsewhere, so Maggie didn't press him for details. But she did want some information.

"How are you going to handle this when we get back, Bob?" she asked.

"Not sure," he replied. "Not sure how long we have. I told Joan that we need information quickly. He'll do his best, but… we probably don't have more than a week."

"What can I do?" Maggie asked.

He shrugged his shoulders. "Not much either of us can do, now. Just wait. It's going to be hard." He paused for a moments. "You've done a great job, Maggie. Thank you."

"I don't feel like I've done very much at all," she said. "I've just taken notes and followed you around."

"No. You've countered my way of thinking, got me to look from a new angle. Got us some good information. We've made a good team. You OK?"

"Trouble at home," she said. "My daughter's friend tried to run away." She stopped. "Surely not the case that you've been called back for?"

"Not unless her friend is a fourteen-year-old called Gavin, who's had a massive row with his mother's boyfriend and been missing for three days."

Maggie shook her head and smiled. "I think there's more to it than they're telling me. They're all telling *exactly* the same story and I have a nose for bullshit when it comes to my kids." She yawned. "Guess I'll find out tomorrow."

With that, they said goodnight and went back to their rooms, agreeing to meet at four the following morning.

As she packed her bag Maggie thought about the last time she'd heard that phrase 'a good team', when Maze Investigations was first proposed by Zelah. She hadn't thought too much about Maze for the past two days, but now it was time to go home and face whatever was coming. One thing she knew: she had made up her mind about what *she* wanted to do next.

* * *

The following morning, they landed in Bristol just after 8am, were quickly through passport and customs control, and onto the motorway. They arrived back in Cwmbran at 9.30am and Maggie remarked that she would have a quiet day, as the kids would already be in school. So, she was surprised to see both Nick and Zelah's cars outside her house. Oh well, get it over with, she decided.

Bob took her suitcase out of the boot and carried it to the front door. He went to shake her hand, but she leaned forward and kissed him on the cheek. "It's been an amazing experience, Bob. Let me know as soon as you hear from Joan, yes?"

"Will do," he replied and jogged back to his car.

Maggie fished her key out of her bag and opened the front door, expecting the usual echo of the tiled hall floor. Instead, she was rushed by a tearful Alice, with Zelah standing, hands on hips and a fierce expression on her face, and a worried-looking Nick hovering in the office doorway. *Welcome home.*

46

Cwmbran, South Wales
2017

Alice had begged not to go to school the following day and after couple of hours Nick had caved in. Jack had no such qualms, ardently keen to get out of the firing line.

"Not many times when I prefer school," he explained to Nick and Zelah, "but this is deffo one of them."

Zelah had decided to stay overnight again. She explained to Nick that she thought the sooner she and

Maggie spoke face to face, the better. Also, that Alice might need some support. "She was only trying to do the right thing, in her world. She's going to get a pasting. Perhaps between us we can deflect some of it."

Nick was also expecting a pasting, as he explained to Zelah. "She left me in charge. I've done a bad job." Nothing Zela could say allowed him to take a less dismal view. So, at 9am the following morning, after Nick had delivered Jack to school, the three of them waited in the office for the coming onslaught.

Having expected a couple of quiet hours at home, Maggie was so surprised by being rushed by Alice as soon as she got through the door, and the sight of Nick, and Zelah, that she just stood speechless for a few moments, patting Alice on the back, giving her colleagues puzzled looks.

"We have some explaining to do. All of us," Nick said.

For fifteen minutes Maggie sat in silence and listened to the full story of what Alice and Janine had done. She didn't ask questions. At the end, Nick said, "Do you want to talk to Alice, or me, now? Just one at a time?"

"No."

"Anything you want to say?"

"No," and with that Maggie stood up, went out to the hall, picked up her suitcase and took it upstairs, leaving the three of them sitting in the kitchen, speechless.

"Is this normal?" Zelah asked Alice, who was a picture of misery.

"No, she usually shouts. Then she stomps around, then she gets over it."

"Oh dear. Who makes the next move?"

Neither answered. Alice sat slumped in her chair, arms folded. It began to rain and the three of them sat and listened to the steady beat against the conservatory walls. Once, Zelah stood up, but she shook her head and sat down again.

"Whatever happens next will be the most natural thing, so just let it happen," said Nick, to no one in particular.

265

Maggie unpacked without noticing where she put anything. She chased thoughts like skittering moths inside her head, just catching one before another zoomed past to take its place. In the end, she sat on the bed and let her feelings overwhelm her. When she opened her eyes, she wasn't sure how long she'd sat there, but decided it was time to go back downstairs.

At the bottom of the stairs she saw Nick sitting in his chair in the office. Moving to the kitchen she found Zelah, still sitting at the table and Alice now curled up on the settee in the conservatory.

"Alice." As she heard her name Alice leapt off the settee. "Please go and ask Nick to come in here."

Alice walked past without looking at her mother. When they reappeared, Maggie pointed to the table. They sat. She walked to the sink and put the kettle on and started to speak. "Well, I thought I'd become used to your behaviour, Alice, but this is something new, isn't it?"

She didn't say anything. Maggie continued "You're expecting that I'm going to say how I feel, how angry I am. But I don't know how I feel. At the moment I'd win a prize for the biggest number of conflicting emotions in one head. Angry, furious, sad, puzzled, astonished, shocked. Lots more. But, most of all, disappointed. I have just one question. Did you wait until I was out of the country, until Nick was here, who you knew you could get past better than you could get past me, to do this unbelievably stupid thing?"

Alice started to cry, but stopped instantly at the sound of a crashing chair.

"For God's sake, leave her alone!" Zelah had sat up so quickly that she had knocked her chair over. "Don't you dare take out your anger on her. She saw a friend in trouble and she did what she thought was the best thing to help. Of course, we all know it was the wrong thing. But she's eleven. You aren't, so get off your high horse, Maggie. None of us here has any claim to the moral high ground."

Maggie, at the other end of the table, stood up to face

Zelah. Both were breathing deeply.

"Before you get into a scream-off," Nick's bored voice interrupted, "I have something to say. Sit down, both of you." For a few seconds they both stared at him. Then Zelah sat down. "You too," he instructed Maggie. She breathed deeply, but obediently plonked herself down in her seat and folded her arms.

"I am very sorry that Alice chose not to confide in me. But she didn't confide in you either, Maggie. Alice thinks she can do better than all of us. This experience has told her that she can't. Right?"

He looked at Alice, who nodded and put her head in her arms on the table. "She almost got taken to a police station and, for now, if I'm right, Janine's mother won't allow her to speak to Alice." Alice's head agreed. "Your daughter, Maggie, stood up for her friend when no one else did. You should be proud of that. And she doesn't need you to tell her how stupid she's been in the action she took to defend Janine." A long sniff came from the head slumped on the table. "You're going to have to speak to Janine's mother because, right now, taking away the only friend Janine has is foolish. But she's not thinking straight either. She's had a shock."

He turned to Zelah. "You've been an idiot, too. Don't bristle at me. You know you have. Between the two of you you've almost cost us the work we all dearly love. Right here, right now, decide if that's how it's going to stay." He sat down.

Maggie and Zelah stared at each other down the length of the kitchen table. Alice raised her head up and looked at each of them in turn. Nick stared straight ahead.

"I need some time to think this through," Maggie mumbled.

"No, you don't. And you're not getting it. Do you want to go on with this venture or not?" Nick wasn't taking prisoners.

For a few seconds, it seemed like no one in the kitchen was breathing.

Maggie gave Zelah a glare, then said. "I do want to go on with it. I'd already decided not to take up the TV offer."

Zelah threw her head back and, to Maggie, Nick and Alice's amazement, burst into tears. Alice rushed up to her with a bunch of screwed up tissues. "Nick gave me these, but I think you need them."

Zelah took the tissues and blew her nose with a loud blast.

"Come on, Alice," Nick said. "Let's go and watch a film. They need to talk. But," he added as they left the kitchen, "do not for one minute think that you're off the hook."

Half an hour later Alice popped her head around the kitchen door. Maggie was making a pot of coffee and Zelah was looking considerably more relaxed.

"Nick says can we have some lunch?"

"No," Maggie replied. "My decision is that I will starve you to death." She pulled a monster face at Alice, who grinned, walked into the kitchen and put her arms around her mother. Maggie hugged her back. "Don't ever do anything like that again," she whispered into Alice's hair. "We'll talk some more later."

"Time to go, I think," Zelah said. "I'll take Nick with me. But we'll get together tomorrow morning, to start on the plan?"

Maggie nodded. "Give me an hour first, yes?"

"OK," Zelah replied. "We'll be here about ten-thirty." She went into the living room to tell Nick what was happening and they both left the house quietly.

"Are you and Zelah friends again?" Alice asked.

"Yes, we are," Maggie replied. "We may dance around each other a little carefully for a few days. That's what happens when you're getting over a big argument. But, we both want to keep Maze going. And we have a puzzling case to solve. And," she said, pausing for a moment in buttering bread, "I'm going to the school tomorrow. You are not going to argue with me, that time has gone. It may not make a difference, but I'm going to say it, anyway."

268

Alice gulped. "OK," she replied in a small voice. "Are you going to speak to Janine's mum?"

"Of course I am. I'll do it this afternoon. I may even go over and see her later." She could see that Alice looked relieved. Maggie was touched by Alice's faith in her. She only hoped she could convince the woman to let the girls be friends again. "And you are going back tomorrow." Alice opened her mouth to protest, but closed it again and gave a tiny nod.

Before driving to the school to pick up Jack, Maggie called Janine's mother. At first she was met by a monosyllabic response, but she persevered and when she pointed out that without Alice, Janine would be utterly friendless, the woman started to warm up. Then Maggie clinched it by saying that she would call in on her before picking Jack up, just for five minutes. She ended the call before there could be any refusal.

* * *

Although she was kept on the doorstep when she got to Janine's house, Maggie came away fairly confident that the friendship wouldn't be forbidden, not at school at least, but that it would be some time before Janine would be allowed to visit Maggie's house again. She could understand that. If it had been the other way round, would she have acted any differently? Probably not.

* * *

Waiting outside the school she phoned to make an appointment to see the Head of Year the following morning. She asked for the Head Teacher, but was told by a snooty secretary that she was not available. Maggie got the impression that she was not an accessible person, certainly not to parents. She recalled that she had been wary of the woman when she had attended the pre-admission meeting, when she had announced, with more than a little pleasure, how she liked to frighten pupils caught in wrongdoing. It surprised her now that it hadn't meant more at the time. *She was proud of that*, Maggie thought, remembering the way the woman's eyes had glowed as she told the story of young children quaking outside her office when they had been sent to retrieve mobile phones confiscated during the day.

Then Jack came striding up the drive, saw her, lit up with a big grin and ran to the car. He got in and hugged her. "Missed you."

"Missed you too," she replied, surprised but happy.

"How's the mini-witch?"

"Subdued," Maggie replied. "Repentant."

"Well, that's a first," he said. "Is she going to turn over a new leaf and start listening to other people?"

"Probably, for a couple of weeks. Don't expect miracles, though."

That evening, she talked to Alice as she got her school uniform ready for the next day. Alice sat on the bed cross-legged. She had been relieved to hear that Janine would be allowed to speak to her in school, but was apprehensive about Maggie's visit.

"Alice, it has to stop somewhere. I do think I understand why you've been so reluctant to let me go before. I'm not expecting it to make much difference, but this is a start and we'll see what happens next. Ripples on a pond?"

"Will I get into any more trouble?"

"If anyone tries anything, I'll be back," Maggie said. "They will understand that I am not to be swept under the carpet." She said this with as light a tone as she could manage, "and I'll tell you all about it when you get home."

* * *

The following morning, Maggie was in the kitchen when she heard Zelah and Nick letting themselves in. She went to greet them, and pointed to the office where hot coffee and pastries were waiting. Zelah piled in without being needing to be asked twice. "How did the school visit go?"

270

she asked through a mouthful of croissant.

They settled themselves around the table. "Not well," Maggie replied. "The Head of Year thinks it's just a case of 'girls being girls', as if girl bullying is acceptable behaviour. I told her that I didn't agree and that if something wasn't done I'd take it higher, outside the school if necessary. She didn't like that. But, she didn't seem at all bothered when I said at first that I would go to the head. That was worrying."

"Why?" Nick asked.

"Because I'm getting a stronger and stronger sense that there's a culture of bullying in that school and it starts at the top." She sat back in her chair. "Anyway, I've done what I can. I've told Janine's mother what I've done. I called her earlier. Now we'll just have to see what happens next. Anyway, let's get on, shall we?"

She glanced over at Zelah who had just picked up a pain au chocolat. But before putting it into her mouth she said, "Why don't you tell us about Spain?"

Maggie went through the story of what she and Bob had achieved. "And now we're waiting to see if Joan can track down this man, or any of his descendants."

"Fantastic outcome, if you get him," Nick said. "Well done, Maggie."

"We still have a way to go. Even if we find him alive, we then have to tell him that he isn't who he thinks he is and get his permission for a DNA test. It will be a lot to take in. And for his descendants if he's dead. And your case?" she asked.

Nick ran through the details of the appearance and disappearance of Morgan Sturridge and his family history.

"It's not your fault, Zelah," Maggie said when he had finished. "Is there any more sign of him at the hotel?"

"No," Zelah replied. "I called again this morning. He's rung in a couple of times to hold the room, but he hasn't come back yet."

"But he must plan to come back. He's paying enough for the privilege. And it all seems to come back to where it

271

started. His ancestor John Hammill, of Monmouthshire. Or not. What have you done about similar names?"

"Everything I can think of," Zelah said. "But there's nothing close."

The paperwork was spread out over the table and Maggie stood up to read it all through. She had just begun to ask a question when the doorbell rang. It was Bob Pugh. Maggie welcomed him into the office and introduced him to Zelah and Nick.

"Pleased to meet you," Bob said, shaking hands with each of them, before turning to Maggie. "I just came to say that I had a call from Joan this morning. He's found a shedload of men called Hugo Vilaro. With a load of different second *apellidos* – that's the second surname that comes from the mother," he explained to Zelah and Nick. "And we don't know what she was called at all."

"But we do know that his father was Mateu Vilaro Roig, his mother was Carme and his grandmother was Estel," Maggie interjected. "Not much, but better than nothing. What's Joan doing?"

"He's gathering addresses and telephone numbers. Then he's going to start calling them. If he doesn't get lucky on the phone he'll write to them. That's assuming that Hugo Vilaro is still alive."

"Let's hope he gets lucky with a call," Maggie said. "Surely there isn't enough time for letters?"

"I'm going to report back to the probate court," Bob said. "Tell them what we've found. Hopefully enough to stall a bit longer. Maybe I can find out what evidence Haussmann has to prove the baby died. Anyway, just thought I'd let you know." He turned to leave but Maggie asked, "How are your cases going? The one's you got called back for?"

"Not good," he replied with a frown. "No sign of the kid. And the body looks like a suspicious death. Going to be busy for a while."

"Got time for a coffee?"

He hesitated for a moment, then said, "Yeah, why

not?" She led him into the kitchen. As she made coffee she told him about the case they were looking at. "Got a few minutes to look at it for us?" she asked. "There's a mystery about a man who appeared to be born locally but turned up in Canada. Story was that he went as a child, but there's no evidence. He's first found in 1890 when he gets married at the age of forty-five."

"So, born around 1845?"

"Yes, but there's no birth of anyone of that name. Zelah and Nick have checked everywhere they can and over a long period before and after, in case he lied about his age. There's nothing."

"Then that wasn't his name," Bob replied.

"But he said he was born here in Monmouthshire," Maggie said. "He somehow got to Canada. He would have needed documents. Nothing like a modern passport, mind you. And money. That's assuming he didn't go as a child, but an adult."

"Can I see what you've got?" Bob asked. She led him back to the office, explained to Zelah and Nick that she'd given Bob a summary of the case and asked whether they would mind if he looked at the papers.

Bob walked around the table, coffee cup in hand, skim-reading each document. "What are these?" he asked, having walked to where Maggie was standing.

"Something separate," Nick replied. "I've been tracing my family."

"Any ideas?" Maggie asked.

"Bit bloody obvious to be a coincidence."

"What do you mean?" Maggie asked.

He gave her a 'dumb' look, pointed at a spot on Nick's tree, then back down to the Morgan Sturridge paperwork. "I'd check this out, if I were you."

They gathered around him. "Look here, this guy, Hammill, born in 1845 in Monmouthshire, turns up in Canada in 1890." He walked back down to the other end of the table and they followed him. "This guy, John Howell, born in 1845 in Monmouthshire, disappears in 1870 and never turns up. What happened to him, do you know?"

"He murdered his wife and child, got convicted of murder and escaped, but was never found."

"Maybe because he was in Canada?" Bob said. "Worth checking out." He chuckled at their expressions. "It's what I do. Look at everything that's even slightly possible. Follow the evidence and see if there's a trail. There usually is. Anyway, got to go. Thanks for the coffee Maggie, I'll call you as soon as I've heard from Joan."

She accompanied him to the door. "Thanks, Bob. Good luck with your enquiries. I look forward to hearing from you."

"Will you?" he asked.

"Yes, I will," she said, smiling and trembling just a little. She closed the door as a thought occurred to her. She ran out to the road where his car was leaving and waved her arms at him to stop. He pulled up and wound down the window.

"Bob, would you be able to find out about someone coming into and going out of the country?"

"Not personally," he replied. "But I know someone who could. But I would have to be asking for a good reason, which means a link to a case."

"Well, we know this is a conman. We don't know what or why. He hasn't taken anything yet, but he could be leading up to it. Is that enough?"

"Maybe. I'll see what I can do. What's his name and when did he arrive?"

"Morgan Sturridge. He would have arrived from Canada sometime in the past month. He may have gone back there again. We think he turned up in Nova Scotia a couple of weeks ago."

"Leave it with me."

He wound up the window and Maggie ran back into the house. Zelah and Nick were staring wordlessly at the papers on the desk. As Maggie came back into the room

Nick said, "I'd begun to wonder. Just, something."

"He mentioned your name, when I first met him," Zelah said.

Maggie told them what she had just done.

"Excellent idea," Zelah said. "How long do you think it will take?"

"He didn't say. We'll just have to wait. He has a lot on, enough for him to be brought back from a holiday. I think he'll make a call, maybe today."

"He likes you enough to make it a priority," Zelah remarked. "Nick, sorry, you were saying?"

"I had spotted the coincidence, and I *was* wondering but they didn't match the dates. The only Jonathan Hammill was born seven years after our Canadian guy and he's on every UK census up to 1911. Zelah had already checked him out," said Nick.

"What else can we do?" Maggie asked.

"We can look for more information on the murder. Your detective said follow the trail. How about we see what we can find online, then go to the archives in Ebbw Vale? There must be a description of what happened after the trial. Usually, when they were sentenced to death it happened quickly, weeks not months. So, he must have escaped almost immediately."

They each agreed to investigate a different aspect. Nick was sticking to his family history, to find out anything he could about other members of his family who had made the press. Zelah and Maggie divided up the Welsh newspapers for the relevant period. It had been significant news at the time, so it had spread beyond Wales, and Zelah checked some of the English national papers to see if there was any difference in reports. The best result came from the archives of the *Western Mail*, based in Cardiff, which had covered the story in detail, giving its readers glimpses into the mind of the murderer, based on what the man had said to police before the trial.

"I don't think we'll get any more from the net," Zelah

said. How about we go to the county archives?"

"Now?" Maggie asked. "I can't. Not enough time to do it properly."

"They're open until five."

"But I have to pick Alice up from school. I can't not be there and here. Not right now."

"Fair enough," Nick said. "But Zelah and I can go. We'll tell you later what we find."

* * *

Maggie decided to spend the afternoon writing up her notes from the trip to Spain. Bob had agreed that she could begin the story in her weekly radio spot as long as it was hypothetical and completely anonymous. By the time she left to pick up Alice she had enough written for a five-minute talk and emailed the notes to the radio station, who always liked to check in advance what she was going to say, especially on anything that even hinted at political content.

After the school run, with Alice and Jack safely in their rooms, Maggie went back to the office, but couldn't summon the energy to begin anything new.

She took out some files that she had been working on from less than a week before, but it seemed like a year. For a couple of hours she forced herself to check biographical information on a case based in Chester, going through the online archives. But, unusually, she had no enthusiasm and a couple of times her head nodded. Giving in to the inevitable, she got up from the computer, lay down on the sofa, and was immediately asleep.

Two hours later she was awoken by the sound of a key in the front door, and she jumped o her feet. Zelah and Nick strode in.

"You found something?" she asked, stifling a yawn.

"Did we wake you?" Zelah asked.

"No matter. I'll have to start dinner soon. What have you found?"

Nick sat down at the table. "Not that much there, on the trial, but we widened our search. Coroner's report," he said, pulling papers out of his bag and putting them on the table. "He strangled the two-week-old baby, then stabbed his wife. Didn't try to make any of it look like an accident."

"OK, anything else?"

"Yes, I looked for the other deaths. Nothing from 1735, too much to hope for. But the death of Peter Hywel, who died of 'suffocation in a ditch', that was recorded. But, sadly not the inquest, only mention of the coroner's expenses." Maggie shot him a quizzical look. "The coroners travelled around," he explained. "They got expenses for going to the place where bodies were found. They would set up an inquest in a local hall or inn and assemble a local jury. They recorded their expenses and a short piece of information about the victim. Peter Hywel, aged two years..." he stopped to look at his notes. "He 'drowned by accident by suffocation in a ditch.' It was the parish of Llanvihangel Llantarnum, May, 1806."

"But we already knew that, from the burial record," said Maggie.

"But there's more," said Zelah. "Nick kept looking. Five years later, the father, John Hywel, was also the subject of a payment to a coroner. He 'wilfully murdered himself by hanging himself by a cord.' Same parish, different coroner. No inquest, so I got into the newspaper archive where there was just a small piece, but it said that he had expressed great remorse for the death of his young son some years previously. That he felt responsible and had left his wife and eleven-year-old son, John, and four daughters. She must have been a strong woman, because she ran the manor after him. But first son John, well he didn't marry until he was forty, and then he produced a murderer."

"So this was John Hywel... the murderer's grandfather," Maggie said. "He probably did the suffocating, don't you think, Nick?"

He didn't reply, but shook his head.

"Any mention of a demon?" Maggie asked, expecting the answer to be no, expecting a no.

"Before he died, he said that the 'demons of hell' would punish him," Zelah said. "The paper then proclaimed regret for a man who felt so strongly about the accidental death of a child, etcetera, etcetera."

"Maybe it *was* an accident," Nick said, staring at the wall. After a pause, in which he sat with his mouth open, head to one side, Zelah asked, "Why would you think that?"

"Two years. John Howell killed a two-week-old baby. This child was two. Why wait? If the story of the curse was passed on, he would have known from his childhood, since his father died when he was seven. He said that the demons would punish him. Why? Maybe because it was an accident. He didn't do it. It just happened."

Maggie sat up. "Or maybe he didn't hang himself. Or if he did, was he forced to?"

"Which just points to the fact that this so-called demon doesn't give up easily, and carries out its threats," said Zelah.

Her mobile rang. She raised her eyebrows and walked out into the hallway to take the call. After a few minutes, during which Maggie and Nick occupied themselves with their own thoughts, she came back.

"That was the Celtic Manor. He's back. He checked in, then went out again."

"How long ago?" asked Maggie.

"Half an hour. That means he's on the loose, and he's close."

47

"I think I'd like it if you two hung around this evening," Maggie said. "I'm going to make dinner for all of us. OK?"

"'Keep calm and make dinner.' We could put it on a poster."

"Not funny Zelah," Maggie said as she went to the kitchen. The last of the afternoon light had faded. The garden was disappearing into gloomy darkness. Usually Maggie left the curtains open, but tonight she closed them carefully, making sure that no light could seep out. *If he's out there, at least he won't be able to see us. I doubt whatever he is, he can see through curtains*. She double-checked each join anyway, overlapping them again. She heard voices from the office as she prepared food. It was going to have to be ready-meals. Best she could do, she didn't feel like making an effort.

After twenty minutes she called everyone to eat. She whispered to Zelah and Nick that they shouldn't talk about Morgan Sturridge in front of Jack and Alice, which made the conversation stilted, and after five minutes Alice asked what they were trying to hide.

"Work stuff," Maggie said, frowning a caution of silence at the other two adults.

"Something funny going on?" Jack asked.

"Just a difficult client," Maggie replied.

"What's difficult about him?" Alice's antenna was picking up intriguing signals.

"We think he's a conman," Zelah said. "Not a nice person. Someone to be wary of." She gave Maggie an 'is that OK?' look, which Maggie ignored. "Lying for profit," Zelah went on.

This led to a conversation about lying, which kept them occupied until the end of the meal, when Maggie packed Jack and Alice off.

Alice stopped in the doorway. "Are you both staying again tonight?"

"Yes. We need to talk over our strategy some more," said Zelah.

"Must be a really bad person," Alice remarked and left them to it. They moved through to the lounge with coffees and waited to be sure both children had gone upstairs.

"What are we going to do next?" Maggie asked.

Nick was watching the fire. Zelah had her tablet on her lap.

"Aha!" she shouted, making Maggie jump, although Nick appeared not to notice.

"What?"

"There's a very good police archive at Kew. They keep the notes of procedure. I've just checked it on *Discovery* and it looks like the investigation notes are there. That's me, tomorrow."

"I'm going to do what Bob suggested, try to pick up the trail after John Howell escaped from prison. See if there's anything that might suggest that he went to Canada. He would have gone from Liverpool, right, Nick? Nick!"

"Yes," he replied, not looking up. "Liverpool."

"What are you going to do?" Maggie asked him.

"I'm going back to the manor, poke around a bit. Stella won't mind."

Maggie decided to go to bed. She had already checked the entrances to the house several times, despite Zelah saying that Sturridge was not going to attack them in their beds.

"I'm putting the alarm on, so don't anyone go out in the morning before I turn it off again. It'll wake the road."

She didn't sleep very well, every hour or so thinking that she heard something outside, but telling herself not to be so panicky. Nick stayed up late. Maggie heard him walking as quietly as possible up the stairs just after 3am.

The next morning, she was up and about early, having been woken by Zelah at seven, ready to set out for London.

"Good luck," said Maggie, as she saw Zelah off.

She took Jack and Alice to school. By the time she was back, Nick had gone.

She got down to looking at shipping lists and other archives to see what she could find. John Howell had escaped in December 1875. If he went to Canada or the US, she was unlikely to find anything. No reliable passenger lists existed before 1890. Try another tack.

He'd have had to make his escape quickly. Most of the constabularies in the country would be looking for him, his description circulated by telegraph. He would have needed clothes and money and a disguise. She began to look for reports of petty crime from December 1875 onwards.

Almost immediately she found a report of a break-in near Brecon, clothes stolen from a cottage washing line. They were trousers and a shirt and a coat that had been left close to the front door. The report hadn't reached a newspaper until a week later and there was no speculation that this was linked to the escaped murderer. It didn't take long to find out why.

A murder had taken place in Newport, just twenty-four hours after the escape. The victim was a man of around thirty years of age. He had fallen into the river and was found to have a serious wound to the back of his head. He had been drinking. At first it was thought to be an accident, but when it was discovered that he had been boasting of having ten shillings, which was not found on his body, this was immediately considered to have been the work of John Howell. A wide search was made in the area and there were high hopes of catching him, but nothing came of it. Maggie's opinion was that the hunt had, at this crucial point, gone in completely the wrong direction. Much to John Howell's fortune.

She leaned back in her chair, arms folded, looking at the screen but seeing a man on the run, in the countryside in December. Cold, hungry, desperate. If caught he would be hanged. Not a stupid man. A man who would know that there would be a widespread hunt for him, that his likeness would be known everywhere. What would such a man do? A series of trivial incidents, petty thievery, nothing to raise much more than annoyance. Keeping himself covert, but inexorably making his way north to a port to get out of the country. Would such a man have formed a plan before escaping, or was he making it up as he went along? Maggie decided that he would have had a plan. Or that someone had helped him with a plan. At this point, she thought, it didn't matter if he had help. *How* didn't matter as much as *what* and *where*.

Next step – how long would it have taken him to get from Monmouth Gaol, where he had been held before execution, to Liverpool on foot? Probably about four or five days. And, when he got there, he couldn't look like a common criminal. He would have to have the appearance of a respectable man, if he was going to buy a passage on a ship. A single, working man, looking for new life. How would he assume such a persona?

She turned to the white board on the wall and began to write a potential timeline between the day on which the guilty verdict was returned, the escape, the journey north to Liverpool, to a departure on a steam ship.

The trial had begun on 24th November, 1875 and ended on 29th November, when the jury unanimously returned a guilty verdict. The judge passed sentence of death and the prisoner was led away to await his fate. Maggie saw that the date of execution was to be 20th December, 1875. She knew it would be after three Sundays following sentencing. That meant almost two weeks in the cell to John Howell's escape on 12th December.

Four to five days at least to reach Liverpool, so that took it to around 17th December. He would have needed to get out of the country as soon as possible, which meant the first available steam ship; steam ship because the journey had gone from thirty-five days by sail to seven to ten days by steam.

282

He would have had little or no money. *How could he buy a passage*? He would have to steal it. She would look for crimes around 16th to 20th December, of theft or worse to see if she could trace the money.

But what of the ship and where would he go? At first, she assumed directly to Canada, but back at the computer she checked again and found that she had been correct; there was little information before 1890. Up to then, evidence was random. Second, the main port of entry to Canada was Quebec, and the emigrants would have been firstly taken to Grosse Ile, in the St Lawrence estuary, to be quarantined and checked for disease before being declared healthy and allowed to go onward. But, in December the river became unnavigable because of ice. Could John Howell have waited? No, absolutely not. Where else? It had to be the United States.

A conflicting thought occurred to her. Could he have gone to one of the European ports to take passage from there? Hamburg or Amsterdam, for example. But she decided against. One attempted sea crossing was perilous. Two would be madness, risking identification the longer he exposed himself. She also discounted him going via Ireland because there were no transatlantic steamships from there.

Once again, no passenger lists. This was frustrating. Back to the drawing board. *Not easy to keep inside the head of a murderer.* Maggie thought she was doing well enough. But, time for a break.

Putting the kettle on coincided with the sound of a key in the front door. Nick called to her and she told him to come on through.

"How was your morning?" she asked, then stopped to look more closely at him. "You look a bit haggard."

"Late night," he said, turning away and taking cups from the cupboard.

"And this morning? Anything new at the manor?"

"Maybe, not sure," he said, putting the cups down and staring at the kettle. "I went to see Gwyllim Hywel again."

"Oh," Maggie said. She wasn't sure what to ask next. How was he? felt flippant. She settled for: "What happened?"

"Office," he said, and walked through. She followed him with the tea, set the cups down on the table, and waited.

"That's interesting," he said, pointing at the whiteboard.

"Trying to narrow down John Howell's journey, so I can match it to reports of petty crime along the way. So, what happened at the manor?"

"He can't see me," Nick began "But I think he knows someone's there. He asks if it's *her*."

"That's the second time he's mentioned a female. Should we put some time into seeing if we can identity who it might be?"

"Feasibly," Nick replied.

"Did you try asking him some questions?"

"I did, and I think I set something off. I asked him who else he had killed. He said 'I loved the boy, but she made me do it.' I asked him again, and he said, 'She did not deserve it. None of them did. It was mine.'"

"So... someone didn't deserve what happened to them?" Maggie asked.

"Maybe," Nick replied. "Or it could mean that some people were going to get something they didn't deserve to have, in his opinion."

Maggie jumped up. "Visitors!" She rushed out of the room and was back in a few minutes, tapping out a text on her mobile phone. "I'm just asking Zelah to check if there are prison records for the time between John Howell's conviction and his escape. If there's any record of him having any visitors."

A few minutes later her phone beeped and she checked it. "She says she'll see what she can find."

She sat back down at her desk. "Well, I've got half an hour before I have to go pick up the kids, so I'm going to carry on seeing if I can find a feasible story for John

Howell's escape. What about you?"

"I'm going to walk around your garden."

Maggie glanced out of the window. It was raining, not heavily, but a persistent drizzle and mist. "Not much to see out there now," she said.

He ignored her, walked into the hall to pick up his coat and let himself out of the conservatory. Maggie left him to it. Twenty minutes later, when he hadn't come back, she went to check through the window.

Nick was walking slowly around the garden perimeter, head slightly to one side, lips moving, and gesticulating an explanation to someone who wasn't there. Or was there?

She knocked on the glass to get his attention, pointed to her wrist, and then made a driving motion with her hands. He gave a thumbs up, but continued walking.

When she returned thirty minutes later he had gone, a note said he would be back later.

48

The Third Visitation
Monmouth Gaol, South Wales
1875

He was furious. How dare they not believe him? He had done what he had to do, had explained it several times over. Of course, he hadn't expected to have to explain. His plan had been for the death to be natural. So many small children died, who was going to notice one more?

It had been unfortunate that his wife had walked in just as he pressed the pillow on the child's face. She had screamed. He had only meant to frighten her with the knife. Unfortunate that he had caught her neck. Even then, he had thought quickly. He'd planned to call for help, to claim they were being robbed, but his father-in-law arrived too soon. He'd been found with the bloody knife in his hand, the pillow still in place over the child's face. There was no point running, so that only left the truth. The curse, the demon, why he had to do it.

They had found him guilty of double murder. Sentenced to death. How dare they!

John Howell sat in his cell in Monmouth Gaol, staring at the granite stone walls, bent forward, elbows on his knees. He had just a bed and a threadbare blanket. It was cold. He had asked for another blanket, but was denied. Asked for food and drink, again to be denied.

Three weeks to plan how to get out and get away. He knew he could do it, he was cleverer than all of them, despite the bad luck that had caught him in the act.

He had always known how clever he was. Growing up on that filthy farm with those two stupid old people, he had known that he was better, destined for more. He had married Mari Davis because her father was dying. Plenty of money there, soon all to be his. But the old man had survived. How did anyone survive typhus? The others had all died, including his parents. John and Alice Hywel, who had changed their name to Howell. Did they think they could avoid it like that? He remembered the day, when he was fifteen, when his father had told him about the curse, and that he should never do it. His father was quite adamant. He should never attempt to carry it out. A good, church man, his father.

He sat back, hands cupping his head against the cold wall, remembered being fascinated by the thought of killing another human being. He had killed animals, of course. Watched how they twitched and squealed as he dug knives and other instruments into their bodies, learning which points shortened the agony, which prolonged it. At some point he had turned his attention to how to kill people. Future experiments.

But now it had all come crashing down around him. He needed to get out.

He had been watching his guards, looking for the weak points. The small moments of inattention. Where the keys

286

were kept. Thinking about what distractions might work. He had been quiet, co-operative to make them think he was no trouble. An easily managed prisoner. Luckily he was kept apart from the other prisoners. That meant no one to get in his way, tag along with him, slow him down, or inform on him.

After they had fed him the usual nauseating breakfast, which he was quite sure they were spitting into, he was surprised to hear he had a visitor. This both interested and alerted him. There had been no visitors. He had no siblings. Mari's father had taken the children, and had let it be known that he would never see any of them ever again. At which he laughed. He had never wanted to burden himself with them in the first place.

As he was pondering who this might be, a man entered his cell. A well-dressed man in a long grey overcoat, a top had and leather gloves. The man had dark hair, a well-trimmed beard and deep, dark grey eyes.

"Do I know you?" Howell asked.

"Oh yes," the stranger replied. "Let me tell you everything about myself that you need to know."

"You are not an Englishman, nor a Welshman, sir."

"Correct. I am Canadian."

The man sat on the bed next to Howell.

The following morning at eight o'clock it was discovered that John Howell had made his escape during the night. There was uproar and a search was immediately instigated. It was never established how he had escaped, as the door to his cell was open, unlocked. There were no other clues.

A search also started for the mystery visitor. He had announced himself as a lawyer, retained by the Howell family. He had been searched before being allowed into the cell, but found to have nothing suspicious about his person. But he could not be found, and Mari Howell's father insisted that he'd hired no lawyers.

There was much speculation and accusation in the newspapers. Questions were asked in Parliament about the containment of prisoners, following this easy escape by a notorious criminal. Two guards attested that the cell had been locked, and checked during the night.

John Howell's whereabouts were never discovered.

49

Maggie looked again at petty crimes in and around Liverpool in mid-December 1875. But her mind was only half on the subject. An idea had occurred to her, gathering pace as the day went on, until it had become an action plan, something that she had to talk to Zelah and Nick about as soon as possible.

The thing was: why were they waiting for Morgan Sturridge to make his move? They had to find a way to flush him out. They should turn the game against him. She thought their best option was go to his hotel and wait for him in the foyer, or even go to his room and search it. She was a little vague on the details of *how* they would get into the room, but was sure they could figure something out. Maybe she could persuade Bob to give her some crafty tips of how to break into a hotel room. As she was thinking about this her mobile rang; it was Bob.

"Got some information for you," he began without preamble. "Your man, Sturridge, odd. No record of him in or out of the country in the past two months."

"I think it's what we expected. We've got the answer to one question now, though."

"Who he is?" Bob asked.

"No, *what* he is." There were a few seconds silence before Bob's voice blasted the phone away from her ear. "You mean he's one of *them*? Shit! Don't you go anywhere near him. Keep away from him, OK? If he tries to contact you, get hold of me."

"OK, OK," she replied. "Yes, I now believe he is one of *them*. But I don't have any plans to go near him." She thought this probably wasn't the best time to ask him for tips on breaking and entering. "I don't think he's like Eira Probert, but I suppose I don't really know, so he could be. But we honestly don't know where he is."

"If he turns up, you phone me, you hear?"

"Yes, Bob, I will." She wasn't sure if she was irritated by his usual domineering attitude, or touched by his concern.

"How's your case, or cases, going?"

"Alright, I suppose. The kid's been found. But the body turned out to be his mother. Beaten up by her boyfriend. Died falling over. The kid's being brought back from London. Just saved from disaster himself. Paedophile gang." He spat the last words out. Maggie didn't comment, but resolved to tell a sanitised version of the story to Alice.

"I presume no word from Joan yet?"

"Nothing, dammit."

"Well, let me know as soon as."

He ended the call and Maggie went back to her computer, but was interrupted by a text before she got going again. It was from Zelah, saying that she was on her way back, should be there around eight-ish, and to 'hold the front page!' She'd found something.

Maggie went back to the newspaper archive and the Liverpool newspapers, of which there were three possibilities, the *Post*, the *Mail* and the *Mercury*. She began a search in mid-December, 1875 and continued through to January 1876, trying each paper in turn. After an hour of searching her eyes were tiring. She decided to give it five more minutes, and swore out loud.

In the edition of Saturday, 29th December, 1875, there it was. A story so bland that she almost missed it. It was the report of a young labourer who had been robbed of his money and clothes after getting drunk in a pub in the Everton district of Liverpool the previous Wednesday. He had been beaten, tied up, and left in a coalhouse. When he regained consciousness his shouts and yells had roused the occupants of the house, who had untied him and called the local constabulary. He had been in the coalhouse for three days. He had been robbed of all his possessions and wept bitterly, because he'd lost all his money to buy a ticket for his passage to America on a steamship leaving the following day. He had worked for years to save the money and now had to return home with nothing. He was unable to give a description of the thief, as he had been hit from behind. He remembered talking in the pub, but they had all seemed friendly. The police spoke to regulars of the pub, but no one could remember anything out of the ordinary. It was Christmas and there was a great deal of drinking being done. At the time of going to print no progress had been made in apprehending the thief.

There then followed a dire warning about the evils of drink for young men of a susceptible nature. The victim's name was Jonathan Hammill. The story had been on page ten, and was similar to stories appearing each week in a port town where violence and robbery were everyday occurrences. So, it was a passage to America, and here was the connection to his new name. Maggie felt a thrill of excitement at the find.

Maggie tried various sites to see if she could find the names of ships leaving Liverpool. She didn't know if John Howell, now Jonathan Hammill, would have worked his passage across the Atlantic or bought a passage in steerage, where he could blend into the crowd of working class men and women of all nationalities and denominations on their way to America to start a new life. She already knew that there were no passenger lists at that time for emigrants.

Hadn't she read something about the registration of entrants into the United States? Yes! Castle Garden, America's first official immigration centre, at the tip of Manhatten. She found the site and an email address, and requested what records were available between 18th to 25th January 1876. This should be a wide enough period, given that she had a name and approximate age to quote.

290

The email was sent. All she could do now was sit and wait for a reply. Which was unlikely to come before the following day, at the earliest.

And what then? It was another ten years before John Hammill's name appeared in Canada, in Shelburne. There was nothing she could do about that and it wasn't that important, anyway. They wanted the link between John Howell and Jonathan Hammill and it looked like Maggie had found it.

A hammering of footsteps on the stairs told her that one of her children was about to appear. Jack put his head round the door. "You ready?"

"Ready for what?"

He rolled his eyes. "My careers evening at school. My appointment's at eight. Remember?"

She had forgotten. She was in two minds as to whether to tell him that she couldn't go. She would have asked Zelah and or Nick to be there to stay with Alice, but there wasn't time to find out where they were. She tried Nick, but his phone went to voicemail, so she left him a message to ask what time he would be getting back. Then she tried Zelah. Same thing, Zelah had said she would be back by eight and it was now five minutes to. She called upstairs to Alice. She'd have to go with them.

"I'm not coming. I'm fine here." Alice stood at her bedroom door, refusing to come down. "I don't want to go out. It's late."

"Alice, you're in no position to refuse. Now go and get ready!" Maggie was shouting and Alice was on the verge of tears, when a text arrived. It was from Zelah. She was on her way and would be there in five minutes.

"OK," Maggie shouted to Jack. "Get your coat on. I'll just wait until I see her coming, then we'll set off. Alice, Zelah is going to be here as soon as I arrive."

She and Jack ran out and jumped in the car, engine revving.

"I see her," Jack said, pointing to a gap in the trees.

"Right, let's go." They drove out to the main road,

where they saw Zelah's car coming towards them. Maggie flashed her lights and Zelah flashed back.

Maggie drove at speed to the school, telling herself that it was only a couple of minutes and deciding that nothing serious could happen in that time. They arrived about fifteen minutes late and the teacher sitting behind the desk was drumming her fingers at the two empty chairs in front of her. Jack slid into one, Maggie into the other. Maggie did not to apologise. Not in this school.

It was supposed to be a discussion about what Jack might like to do with the rest of his life. But the first five minutes was a monologue, about the value of education and not wasting your life on what the woman called 'other stuff'. Maggie's feet were drumming on the floor, and she held her fists tightly in her lap with a fixed look of interest on her face.

When Jack finally got to speak, he talked about how he enjoyed history, especially since his mother had become involved in historical research. He turned to her, smiled, and nodded. The teacher's face didn't move. But when Jack said that he wasn't sure if he wanted to go to university, because of the debts and the doubtful use of a history degree, the woman became animated. There followed another lecture on how education was never wasted, and that his family should encourage him to not take such a short-sighted view.

Maggie was prevented from interrupting, which she had promised Jack she wouldn't do, by a text. Making it as obvious as possible she reached into her bag, found the phone, held it up and saw that it was from Zelah. Smiling at the teacher she said, "Other stuff," and swiped it open. What she saw froze her. She quickly put the phone in front of Jack who read it. They jumped up out of their chairs and ran from the room.

He has been to your house. Come home now.

50

Maggie drove across the town in less than ten minutes and arrived to find Zelah on the doorstep, with an expression that Maggie couldn't decide was anger, fear, or both. Behind Zelah was Alice, clinging to Zelah's waist, sobbing and unable to control her breath.

"What's happened?"

"Let's sit down," Zelah said. "Alice needs to explain."

Alice moved out from behind Zelah and pointed a shaking finger at Maggie. "You let one of *them* come to our house!"

"I didn't let anyone come to our house. Now tell me what happened." Maggie was shouting, out of fear, and Alice jerked backwards. Before Allice could speak Maggie said, "And I told you not to answer the door. To anyone." Her intense look caused Alice to put her finger down, but she also put her head down and folded her hands together.

"When you've finished," Zelah said. "She has something very important to tell you, so just shut up accusing, Maggie, and listen, OK?"

Maggie turned to shout back at Zelah, but saw the fear in her face.

"OK," she said. Then to Alice, "You, come with me."

They all trooped in to the sitting room and sat down.

Maggie took a couple of breaths, then she said, "Alice, please just tell me what has happened. How long after we left did he arrive? Zelah should have been here within seconds."

"The road was blocked," Zelah said, "for a few minutes. Whatever it was, and I thought it was a small animal, just disappeared."

"But I saw your car turn into the road. I flashed at you and you flashed back."

293

"That's right." Zelah shook her head. "I was here seconds after you left."

Alice didn't look up. "It seemed like it was just after Mum left. I went down to the kitchen to get a drink. I could see someone at the door. The bell rang. I thought it was Zelah. Then a voice called me. It said 'Alice, I'm a friend of Nick's and I have some very important information and a message for him. Could you please take it from me?' I walked to the hall door. He said again that he had something for Nick. I thought it would be OK. So, I opened the hall door and I stood in front of the front door. Then he put a card through the letterbox."

"Do you still have it?" Maggie asked. Zelah handed it to her. It was a simple business card, printed on one side *Morgan Sturridge, V&R Services*.

"What does that mean?" said Maggie, turning to Zelah.

"Keep listening," Zelah replied.

"As much detail as you can manage," Maggie prompted Alice.

"So, I opened the door. He said 'Hello Alice. You are just as an associate of mine described you.' Then he asked if he could come in. I said no. He smiled. So then he said 'Tell Nick Howell that Morgan said it's time. He knows where. I will meet him there.' I shut the door in his face but he just stood there. I shouted 'What's V and R anyway?' He said it's for 'vengeance and retribution'. I didn't really understand, but I bolted the door and ran in here. Then I heard someone trying to open the door with a key. I went back out. I could see it was Nick. So, I unbolted the door. I told him what the man had said. And I told him what I'd seen. He nodded and went back out. He told me not to answer the door. A couple of minutes later, Zelah arrived. That's it."

"Did you show the card to Nick?" Maggie asked.

"Yes. He didn't say anything, though."

"And what else you saw," Zelah prodded.

"What?" asked Alice, confused.

"Why you thought he was one of *them*?" Zelah said

294

slowly, trying not to show her impatience.

"Oh, yeah. Well, obvious really. He had no colour. Just like Miss Bigbutt. And the same as her, he didn't breathe."

"What the hell?" Maggie said.

"I never identified it," Zelah said, "but I always felt that something was, what shall I say… enigmatic about him. So, did the staff at the hotel. Probably why he always walked slowly and crept up on you. It wasn't obvious."

"Hang on a minute," Maggie said. "When did you speak to Nick?"

"He arrived just after the thing left."

"This is bizarre," Maggie said. "It wasn't just me. Jack, you saw Zelah coming too, didn't you?"

Jack nodded.

"So, he came here, followed by Nick, in the thirty seconds between me leaving and Zelah arriving?"

"Looks that way," Zelah replied. "It must have have taken at least ten minutes, but that's not important right now." She turned to Alice. "*Where* did Nick go, did he say?"

"No, but I think he's going to meet that thing." Alice look repulsed.

"Zelah, could you please stay here with Jack and Alice. I'm going…" she looked around, "…out."

"Bugger that," Zelah replied. "You're going to the manor after Nick and Morgan Sturridge. I'm coming. They'll have to come too," she added.

"Is Nick in trouble?" Jack asked.

"I think so," Maggie replied. "Look I really need someone to stay here," she pleaded. "In case anything else turns up."

"I'll stay," Jack said. "Just let me know what's going on. Take Alice, though. I don't want to be responsible for her. And not in a bad way."

"I don't want to be looked after by you. And I know things about this this stuff, so I'm coming with you." Alice had that stubborn look that Maggie didn't feel like fighting right now and she was desperate to get out of the house and find Nick. "OK," she said, but don't you dare answer the door, Jack, to anyone, you hear?"

"Yes, Mum, now go," said Jack.

"If you come with us, Alice, you stay with me. You do *nothing* that I don't tell you to do and if I say you leave, then you leave. Understood?"

"OK."

"This is not good," Maggie snapped at Zelah as they ran from the house.

"We work together," Zelah snapped back. "Alice is vulnerable, and she's better off with us than here with only Jack."

Maggie drove dangerously fast to get to the manor. She parked the car haphazardly in the car park; they got out and ran up the path towards the front door.

"How are we going to get in?" Alice asked.

"That will have been taken care of," Zelah replied.

There were no lights on. Its whitewashed façade was lit by the full moon. As Zelah predicted, the front door was slightly open. The darkness inside gave no clues as to what might be happening.

Maggie pushed the door, which duly creaked. They stepped into the foyer. "Here we go," she whispered, taking a step into the entrance hall. The area was lit just enough by the moonlight to make out the closed door to the café on their left, the bottom of the stairs ahead, and the open entrance to the museum on their right. All was silent. Then she caught something elusive, caught on a breeze that was coming in from the front door.

"There's no one here," Zelah said. "Maybe we've got it wrong. Maybe we should be at the hotel."

"It's wherever Uncle Will is," Alice said, matter-of-factly.

"Who the hell is Uncle Will?" Zelah asked, not bothering to whisper now.

"Oh, did I forget that bit?"

"Obviously, as we have no idea what you mean," Zelah said.

"Well," said Alice, missing the acerbity, "the thing said, 'Time to go meet with Uncle Will' or, he said 'Will'."

"I think he said Gwyll," said Maggie, "short for Gwyllim."

"And where do we find him?" Zelah asked.

"Follow me," Maggie replied and set off up the stairs. She still had hold of Alice's hand, and she dragged her, followed by Zelah, up the stairs, into the Great Chamber, around and past the bedroom at the front of the house, along the corridor, left up the shorter flight of stairs and left again, until they were at the start of the short walkway with the uneven floor, facing the oldest door, which was closed. Maggie paused. They could hear the murmur of voices behind it. Then, a loud shriek. She ran, almost pulling Alice off her feet, seized hold of the door ring with her free hand and threw it back so hard that it bounced off the wall.

In front of them, barely lit by two candles, Morgan Sturridge stood in front of Nick, hands held out in supplication. In a raised hand, Sturridge was holding a heavy onyx vase in line with Nick's head.

As they stood on the step he paused, then slowly lowered his hand. "Well, here you all are," he said in his quiet Canadian accent. "Not unexpected, I supposed. Welcome. I was just about to kill your friend and colleague."

Maggie let go of Alice's hand, pushing her gently backwards, and stepped forward over the threshold. She was hit by the stinking sulphurous smell. The thing that had been eluding her slotted into place.

"Of course! Eira Probert," she said. "You were always here."

Morgan Sturridge put down the object he had been holding onto the table and looked at her with a smug expression. "I believe you know my mentor," he said. He turned to look over his shoulder. "Let's all have a cosy chat."

He waited, Maggie felt the excitement of anticipation exuding from him. She put her hand back and took Alice's hand in hers. Zelah took Alice's other hand. Nick moved away from Morgan and placed himself on Maggie's other side. Morgan looked less content, less sure of himself.

"Teacher?" he called. "Show yourself."

"She can't," Maggie said. "She can't put herself in front of me, or of Alice. She can't get past us. We aren't afraid of her, Morgan. Nor of you."

"Why do you want to hurt Nick?" Alice piped up. "That's not nice."

Morgan didn't reply. He was still looking at the corner from which expected Eira Probert to appear.

"It's because of him," Nick said, pointing at the chair in the corner.

"That's the one Mum touched, when that lady said not to," Alice said. "I knew she's done it. Who's there?"

It was Nick who answered. "The person who's in that chair is the cause of my family's curse. He's Gwyllim Hywel. He killed his brother and his brother's son, and he thought he'd killed his niece, Morgana Hywel. But she didn't die. Did you, Morgana?" Maggie and Zelah turned to look at Nick who was staring directly at Morgan Sturridge; who nodded and slowly applauded.

"You worked it out. Well done, you."

Where does Eira Probert come into this?" Maggie asked.

"She saved me, Maggie Gilbert. Pulled me out of the river where he had thrown me. After breaking every bone in my face and arms with a rock. I was dying. I might even have been dead, and she pulled me out. She offered me a deal. I could have eternal revenge on him. It was *my* manor, *my* inheritance. He was the second son, but he wanted to be first. So, he killed everyone in his way. Then he turned out my mother and sisters and they died paupers while he had all of this. I had to watch that. Ever since, thanks to my teacher, I've been able to make sure that every second son did not survive. I had their fathers kill them." His face lit up with a smile of gratification.

"Not very successful then, were you?" Zelah said

boldly. "You got Gwyllim to kill his son. But Peter was an accident. John Howell was a psychopath and would have done something terrible anyway. And Nick's father died in a plane crash before he was born. If you're the Angel of Death, well, your wings need a service."

He looked at her with cold contempt. "Mrs Trevear. Let me show you what he did to me." He put his hands over his face. When he took them down again Maggie and Zelah recoiled and Alice screamed. One eyeball hung out of its socket. The face was a mass of blood and tissue, both cheeks were smashed with bones protruding, the jaw broken at an angle across the face, blood running out of the mouth where teeth had been.

"And this is just my face. My arms and legs were broken and smashed, too. Now, here's an interesting question," he spat at them out of his bleeding mouth. "What would a parent do to save their child?"

"That's how you did it," Nick said. "You showed them this and told them you'd do the same to them if they didn't kill their second son. Right?"

"Quite right," said Morgan Sturridge. "I just showed this face and raised a rock above their stupid head. Gwyllim killed a son he loved. Not just for the child, you understand. But for the manor. He died of fear, you know. After my visit he spent his nights sat in that chair, waiting for me to come back. And still he does."

"And Peter's father?" Nick asked.

Morgan sighed "An accident, as you rightly say." He stopped to wipe blood from his mouth. "The boy fell into the ditch. But the father didn't go in after him, he just watched. So, I think I can claim that one. Beat his wife, too. But I persuaded him to hang himself.

"John Howell, now where do I start with him?" He glanced back over his shoulder, before carrying on. "He was a joy. He was a born serial killer. Got out of prison, with my help of course. I wasn't going to let him stay there, what a waste. He got to the USA and murdered his way to Canada. And that poor woman he married, oh dear."

"Sorry to interrupt, but she did OK for herself," Zelah said. "And the Hammills didn't do too badly, after all."

He sneered at her.

"You lost out with my father," Nick said.

"Yes, shame that. I've got you, haven't I? And you can hardly say you've had a *happy* life, now can you, Nick?"

"No, but I have one now. There's nothing you can do to stop that."

"Oh, but I can, people. My teacher will be here soon." He checked over his shoulder again. "You won't escape this time, Maggie Gilbert."

"I already have, and she's really not coming," Maggie replied. She looked at a spot behind his head. "Ready for round two, Eira? Come on, we're waiting," this last in a sing-song voice.

There was a stirring of the air, followed by a smell of rotten eggs. She looked at Morgan. "If you think you'll finish us off between you, you couldn't be more wrong. I will say it for the third time. SHE'S NOT COMING."

His air of smugness disappeared, replaced by concern, then a flash of fear, as he realised that Maggie might be right.

"We're going. You can do what you like, Sturridge, or Morgana, or whatever… whoever you are. I really don't care," Zelah said. "Come on, let's get out of here."

"Hold on a minute," Maggie said. "Morgan, you're on your own, now. Will you, could you, let this go? Redemption is always possible."

He snarled at her, "There's no salvation for me, and maybe I don't want to let it go. I lost everything."

"Not everything," Alice said.

He looked directly at her. "Stupid girl."

"Wait a minute." Alice turned and ran out of the room. Her footsteps skittered down the stairs. They were all so shocked that no one spoke. The footsteps came back up the stairs again. Alice entered the room, holding the hand of a small, delicate looking boy. He walked on stockinged feet and was wearing breeches and a shirt with a frill at the neck. His hair was shoulder-length.

Morgan reeled, grabbing the edge of the table. "Twm," he said, in a girl's voice.

"Morgana," the boy said. "I waited for you."

Maggie frowned at Alice and whispered, "Who is he?"

"He's Morgana's brother. I met him a couple of weeks ago, when we came here for lunch. I told you. He's Tom. He was waiting for his sister."

"Can you take me away, now?" the boy asked in a trembling voice.

"I… I did not know thee was here, Twm. Why didst thou not speak?"

"I had none to tell I was waiting, Morgana," and he walked forward and put his arms around her. For a moment, she hugged him tightly. But then she pushed him away. "Too late, Twm, too late. No forgiveness for me. Go away now."

He stumbled backwards and almost into Maggie, but Alice pulled her away. "Don't touch him," she said. "It's hard for him to show himself like this." Maggie bent down to look closely at the boy. He had looked human when he entered room, but close up Maggie could see that his surface was like an old oil painting, covered by tiny cracks and worn patches.

He turned and walked out of the room. "You bitch," Alice shouted at Morgana, "He's been waiting for you, for centuries. He'll be back in his room, crying and lonely."

"That is not my concern," said Morgana. "Go, all of you. My teacher and I will decide what to do with you."

Maggie sighed "You don't get it, he *is* your concern. I pity you Morgana. That was your chance."

She looked uncertain, but didn't reply.

"Let's go. OK with you all?"

Morgana took a step toward them, snarling, but as she spoke a door slammed below, followed by footsteps running upstairs. Heavy footsteps, and more than one person. Bob Pugh came running in, and almost knocked Maggie over. Behind him was Jack.

"Do you ever listen to anyone?" he yelled at her.

"Of course, I do," she replied. "Doing what they say is another thing."

"I should have known, you—" he stopped, mouth agape, staring at Morgana. "What the fuck is that?"

"Let me introduce you, Inspector Bob Pugh, this is Morgana Hywel, born around 1715, missing ever since, lately masquerading as Morgan Sturridge, our conman."

He looked at her, expecting her to explain the joke, but her expression was serious.

"And have you noticed anything else unpleasant?" she asked.

He looked around, taking everything in. "Bad smell."

"Can you guess?"

It took a few seconds for the puzzled look to disappear from his face. "You're fucking kidding me!" he said.

"No, I am not. Eira Probert, this is the great-grandson of your unfortunate minister, Robert Pugh."

Again, there was a rippling of the air.

"See what you mean about the smell, Maggie. Sulphur, with a hint of dead cat?"

He had remembered what she had said about the fear.

"Yes," she replied. "Now, are we all ready to leave?"

"Your show," Zelah said.

"Nick's actually."

"I don't give a fuck whose show it is. We all need to get out of here, now." Bob turned towards the door, pushing Jack in front of him and the others followed. Nick paused in the doorway, turning back to look at Morgana. "I'm sorry," he said.

On their way down the stairs, Zelah, who was walking in front of Maggie, asked, "How did you know she was there?"

"I noticed the smell as soon as we walked in the door. Didn't you?"

"No," Zelah replied. "Not a sniff."

"It was Eira Probert's scent. Eau de smelly hair oil and rotting flesh. I wasn't entirely convinced, but it came back to me. You remember I said that there was something that Stella told me, that I couldn't remember, that was bothering me? Well, she told me there was a yellow stain on the floor in the attic rooms that came and went. Eira has been there a long time."

"Hurry up, you two," Bob shouted from the entrance hall as they turned the corner to face the final staircase to the ground floor. Jack, Alice, and Nick were already down.

Halfway down Maggie thought she heard something behind them, turned for a second, but there was nothing. Then, a great screeching and a gust of wind hit her full in the face, pushing her down. Zelah turned back, eyes panicky.

"Go!" Maggie shouted at Zelah. "Just go."

A cloud passed over the moon extinguishing the light inside the manor, and for a second Maggie couldn't see. She felt a rush behind her. The noise was deafening. A hand scraped her back, as something hit her hard, knocking her breath away. There was single, flat, crunching sound.

The moon came out again. It illuminated Zelah, lying on the floor, lifeless, blood pouring from of a wound on the back of her head. On the floor beside her lay the onyx vase Morgan Sturridge had in his hand.

* * *

The next minutes were chaos. Whatever had come down the stairs disappeared. Bob took charge, using his mobile to call an ambulance and the police. He took off his jacket and covered Zelah with it. He checked her pulse. "It's weak," he said to Maggie who was standing above Zelah. "But she is alive."

Behind Maggie, Nick had an arm each around Jack and Alice. Jack was trying to take off out of the front door. "We have to see who that was, and where he went," he said, struggling with Nick. "Let go of me." But Nick held him tight, until he stopped struggling.

Bob was on the phone with the paramedics, who were giving him instructions. Blood was flowing from Zelah's head across the flagstones. Maggie bent down and took hold of Zelah's hand, rubbing it gently. "This is my fault. I'm so sorry."

51

Immediately following the attack Bob had taken over, checking Zelah's airway and pulse, checking she was breathing. When the ambulance arrived, he gave the paramedics a brief account of what had happened and they took over. He and Maggie had followed in the car to hospital and Nick had taken a reluctant and complaining Jack and Alice home.

Zelah spent hours in A&E being monitored and diagnosed. Maggie's memory was confused, eventually having to calm herself to answer what questions she could for the trauma team. They had swung into action the minute the ambulance had arrived and taken Zelah to the resuscitation unit. Within minutes, they had attached a mass of wires and tubes, working quietly and calmly whilst Maggie's heart beat like a jackhammer. The consultant had decided to intubate Zelah, explaining to Maggie that as Zelah was still unconscious she would be at risk of not being able to control her breathing and swallowing, and also that they needed her to keep her head still so that a CT scan could be carried out. At that moment Zelah had moaned and muttered something. But she wasn't making any sense, nor responding to her name being called, so the intubation carried on and she was whisked away for the scan.

Bob had stayed around, waiting to see what was happening. "I don't think it's fatal," he said. "I've seen a few of these. If there's no big bleed inside her head, she's got every chance."

304

Maggie took a couple of deep breaths. "How long will it take to get the result of the scan?"

"About half an hour, probably. Shall we get a cup of tea?"

She was going to object, but instead nodded. She wanted to get angry, shout at someone, anyone. Because she knew it was all her fault. She had been so stupid, so arrogant.

"You coming then?" He was at the door. She followed.

She couldn't settle in the coffee shop. Bob was talking at her, going into detail about a plan of what they should say, how to deal with the enquiry that would follow and to leave most of it to him. But she couldn't take any of it in. Halfway through her drink she put the cup down, stood up and walked out.

After around forty minutes, by which time Maggie was pacing up and down the corridor of the resuscitation unit, Zelah was brought back. Maggie went to sit beside her. It was another ten minutes before the consultant arrived to speak to her. She braced herself.

"It could have been worse," she said, at which point Maggie let out a great cry of relief.

"It's going to be OK," the consultant carried on. "There is a skull fracture, but it's linear, not depressed. The bleed was mainly outside the brain, minimal internal bleeding. We're going to take her to theatre to clean and close the wound. Then she'll spend the night in the ITU. We've also scanned her neck and spine; I gather Zelah fell down some stairs when she was hit." Maggie nodded. "It all seems clear. No neck injury. All in all, she's been lucky. We'll keep her ventilated overnight, then see how she is tomorrow. We'll probably start to wake her up during the day. Are you OK? Do you have any questions?"

Maggie nodded, then shook her head. She felt as if her tongue was stuck to the roof of her mouth. Bob, who had been standing behind her, took her hand, and Maggie found her voice.

"Is there any brain damage?"

"Unlikely, I think. I can tell you more after the surgeon has closed up the wound. But, in my experience ,the outlook is good. Of course, she's going to have the mother and father of all headaches. And she may have lost some memory. But, we'll see."

"Can I go with her?"

"Better not, Mrs Gilbert. Why don't you go home? Come back in the morning. She'll need to be settled down in the ITU, which takes time. And if she's going to wake tomorrow, you'll be better able to support her if you have some sleep."

Maggie was reluctant, but Bob persuaded her to go. "They'll call if anything changes," he said.

* * *

Back at the house Alice had succumbed to sleep, but Jack and Nick were still up. They both jumped up and peered around the door as soon as they heard the key.

"What news?" Nick asked, holding a hand cupped under his chin.

"I think she's going to be OK," was all Maggie could say.

The following day Maggie spent at the hospital, in the ITU waiting room, occasionally being allowed in to see Zelah. The unit was not what she expected; bright and cheery. It was the most sophisticated place in the hospital, so there was a constant range of beeps, rings, alarming whoops, and the constant suck and pull of the machines that breathed for the patients. Every bed was taken. Maggie fell asleep in the waiting room a couple of times, unable to fight the weariness that was now hitting her in repeating tidal waves.

Bob had returned a few times, checked on Zelah's progress, but had not stayed, telling Maggie that he would talk to her in more detail once Zelah was conscious. Throughout the day, Maggie hoped that something would change. It wasn't until late afternoon that a clutch of doctors arrived to begin the process of waking Zelah up.

At first, she was drowsy, agitated, unknowing of where she was, speaking nonsense. The nurse reassured Maggie that this was normal. Slowly, as the evening wore on, she reached a higher level of consciousness, sufficient to ask Maggie, "What the hell is going on?"

"You got hit on the head," Maggie replied quietly.

"Who hit me?"

"We aren't sure. It was either Morgan Sturridge, or Eira Probert."

"What were they doing in my house?"

"They weren't in your house, they were at the manor. Don't you remember?"

Zelah's face contorted with the effort of thinking. She shook her head, and moaned.

"Don't worry about it," Maggie said. "You're OK but you're going to be sleepy for a couple of days. When you wake up properly I'll tell you all about it."

Zelah lay on the pillow looking puzzled but resigned to the fact that moving was not a good idea, and she closed her eyes. Her hair, which Maggie had never seen any other way than piled elaborately on top of her head, had been taken down and was hanging loosely at her neck. In the ITU bed she looked smaller than Maggie was used to.

The following day Zelah was transferred to a side ward in another part of the hospital. When Maggie arrived at ten she appeared to be sleeping peacefully.

A registrar arrived and checked the paperwork at the bottom of Zelah's bed.

"How is she doing?" Maggie asked.

"Quite well," he replied. "She had a slight temperature overnight and we did think about taking her back to the ITU, but after a few hours it went down again. She's breathing well and waking enough to say a few words. So, on the whole, we're pleased with her progress."

"Any idea how long she'll be here?"

"A few more days. Four or five, I'd say," he replied. Then he left.

Maggie sat for a few minutes, then took her phone out

of her bag. She had promised Nick news. She was just typing a text when there was a movement from the bed.

"Has he gone?" said Zelah, drowsily.

"Yes, he's gone," Maggie replied.

"Good. They keep waking me up."

"Just checking, I guess."

"When can I go home?"

"Couple of days yet. You had a big blow to the head."

"What happened?"

"I explained last night."

"I can't bloody remember."

As Zelah lay with her eyes closed Maggie went through the whole story from the time they left the house. Zelah remembered driving back from Kew, but after that it was a blur. "I was at your house. Then I was here." She slurred.

Maggie was concerned at the slurring. She was going to find a nurse to question, but a consultant arrived to do a ward round. He pronounced himself pleased with Zelah, adding that it would take some days. "You are having some post head-injury symptoms, Mrs Trevear," he said slowly. "Give it a few days."

"I am neither deaf nor stupid," came the response from the bed.

"Improving already," Maggie commented.

"Is there news of Mrs Trevear's assailant?"

"No news, I'm afraid," Maggie said. He gave her a questioning look and she turned away, as Bob arrived. He was in uniform. He acknowledged the consultant, who said, "It's too early to question Mrs Trevear, Inspector. She's going to be drowsy for a while yet."

"Not a problem," Bob said. "I'm here to see Mrs Gilbert. We won't be needing a statement."

"I thought you were a detective?" Maggie said. "Why the uniform?"

"Oh. Funeral. Old colleague. We need to talk about Tuesday night."

308

She knew that there were whispers about what they had been doing at the manor late at night, why there was no forensic evidence at all, and the way in which the investigating officer was being evasive about detail. There was one particularly ugly rumour that the perpetrator was one of them. Maggie had to steel herself and ignore it all. She knew that it would seem suspicious if she didn't give any details, but they had agreed a story and she was doggedly sticking to it.

One of Bob's first calls, and subsequent meetings, had been with his senior superintendent. The same person who had warned him off the Eira Probert story the previous year.

"He understood, knew it wasn't anyone we've got any chance of catching. He's going to take the heat."

"How much did you tell him?" Maggie asked.

"Everything," Bob replied. "Only way, really."

She agreed. He told her that there had been raised eyebrows in the force, but they had gone along with his story. They knew when there was something they weren't meant to question and kept away from it. Uncomfortable for him, the talking behind his back, but he just had to suck it up, he explained. Anyway, he had enough to go on with, having arrested the man who had murdered his girlfriend. Paperwork to be done, about three trees' worth.

"And the other thing I wanted to tell you. I heard from Joan last night. He thinks he's got a lead."

"Really?" Maggie sat up, and realised that she had shouted, well not quite, but too loud for a hospital ward. "Let's go and get a coffee," she whispered.

"I'm not asleep," came from the bed. "You can talk in front of me. Unless you're keeping secrets."

"No secrets. We'll stay here." Maggie said and turned to Bob, who had taken a spare chair. "You two haven't met properly yet. But, proof, if proof were needed, that she's getting back to normal. So, what's the news?"

He leaned towards her. "Joan found a couple of dozen

men with the same name, and all roughly the right age. He's been going through them, seeing what they know about their background. This prospect is from Segovia. Lives in the city with his wife."

"I don't know… where did you say?" Maggie said.

"Segovia," said the slurred voice. "North of Madrid. Roman aqueduct running through the centre."

"Right," Bob said. "Anyway, this Hugo Vilaro was a bit hesitant at first. But he warmed up and told Joan that his mother had told him before she died that he was adopted. Said it explained some things, like why he had blonde hair when both parents were dark. Anyway the mother told him when he was a kid that the hair had come from grandparents. But he was never sure. She didn't give him any details, said it didn't matter."

"Of course, it matters," Zelah chipped in.

"Agreed. Anyway, guy agreed to meet Joan. He's going there today. Going to call me tonight."

"How will we know if he's our man?" Maggie asked.

"Let's hope Joan can get him to do a DNA test." He hesitated for a moment. "It's going to be a lot for him to take in." He pulled at his ear. "He's an old man. Don't want to cause him too much bother."

"Not that old," Zelah mumbled. Bob frowned at Maggie, who raised her eyebrows and chuckled under her breath.

"Anyway, got to go. Have to be at the Civic Centre for eleven. I'll call you later." He reached across and squeezed her hand, then walked off the ward.

"PC Plod gone?" Zelah asked after a couple of minutes' silence.

"Don't call him that," Maggie retorted. "He's a good bloke. Bossy, but good."

"He likes you. But he won't get far doing bossy with you."

"Go back to sleep."

Zelah grinned.

An hour later a member of the family history society turned up as promised and Maggie went off to get some lunch. News of Zelah's injury had spread across the genealogy community in South Wales and there had been phone calls and visits. The local family history society had arranged for someone to come in to relieve Maggie so she could get some lunch each day.

Maggie spent the hour in the canteen eating and writing notes. She had expected to cancel her weekly radio slot, but the station was keen to have her keep to it. The story of Zelah's assault had been in the news for the past twenty-four hours. The producer thought it would be great to hear from Maggie, to get the 'inside story'. She had decided to say it was a conman, who they had caught out and who had made a run for it. With a bit of luck, she could go on telling the story for weeks, and it would give her a chance to square her story with Zelah when she was well enough, and with Nick.

Back on the ward Zelah had awoken to eat a little, but then gone back to sleep. Nick turned up early.

"I couldn't concentrate," he said. "Thought I'd rather be here, with you two."

They talked over again what had happened, each time hoping that something might come back to them that they had missed, but nothing did. They came to the conclusion that they were never going to find out who, or what, had come down the stairs behind them and hit Zelah. They also had to accept that they would never know if Zelah was the intended target.

"I had just been knocked down," Maggie said, "so it could have been meant for me."

"Or it could have been meant to hurt your friend, or it could have been random. We're not going to know, Maggie. Don't torture yourself with it."

"I feel so–" But that was as far as she got.

"If you're going to try to blame yourself, I strongly

advise you not to. And don't argue with me, I'm a sick woman," said Zelah.

"Anyway, what about the dimension we came across?"

"You mean, the time range?" Maggie asked.

"Of course that's what I mean. Did Morgan Sturridge make thirty seconds stretch to ten minutes?"

"I think so," said Nick with a deep sigh. "Something else we didn't know about – these anomalies. But let's not try to understand. We aren't like them and we can't understand."

Maggie and Zelah nodded in agreement.

* * *

The following day another society member, a lady called Susan, arrived at lunchtime to sit with Zelah while Maggie went to get lunch. Zelah was sitting up for short periods and wasn't sleeping so much. She was still being regularly monitored, including through the night, which was making her snappy. Susan said that they had been chatting, but Maggie thought that Zelah looked drawn.

"I can stop people coming, if you're not up to it."

"I'm up to it. I've known Susan for twenty years. She's a good woman. Wouldn't like to hurt her feelings."

"OK. Rest now."

Zelah sunk back onto her pillows. She was asleep within a minute.

When Nick arrived at three, he sat down and started to talk immediately. "I went to the Celtic Manor before I came here. He's gone, checked out that night. Paid his bill in cash, and left. Receptionist said he didn't leave with any luggage, but when they went to clean the room, there was nothing there."

"Do you think he'll… she'll… ever try again?" Maggie wondered.

"No reason, except spite. And revenge. Maybe she can't get past it. It's what Eira Probert made her, poor girl."

"So, that's a real possibility then. You'll have to keep vigilant, Nick."

"I suppose so. How's Zelah?"

"Improving. Awake more today. She doesn't say, but I think her head hurts a lot." She glanced at the bed, but there was no comment forthcoming.

"How long will she be here?"

"They aren't saying. A couple more days, I guess," Maggie said. "I've been thinking. When she's ready to get out I'd like her to come back to my house to stay. Just for a few days until she's ready to look after herself. What do you think?"

"Good idea," he said. "Probably won't want to stay long. But if you can persuade her, a couple of days will do her good. Sell her on your cooking."

Maggie smiled. "I'll do my best. I'll go now, if that's OK. I have to complete my notes for tomorrow. Oh, and by the way, I got a response from Castle Gardens in the USA. John Howell entered the US there. We knew he went there from Morgana, this confirmed it."

* * *

After she had collected the children, who asked about Zelah, and were pleased to hear that she might be coming to stay with them, Maggie cooked a meal then sat down to write her notes. She had remembered, albeit distractedly that she hadn't heard back from Bob. He would, no doubt, phone when he had something to say. She picked up her pen, but her attention was caught by her mobile ringing: it was Bob.

"We've got him," he said.

52

Maggie's mind had been so focussed on Morgan Sturridge and how she was going to spin the story that, for a moment, she had to think what he was talking about. Then she realised, and she screamed and jumped up.

"Are you sure? How do you know? What–"

"Calm down," he interjected. "Joan went to see him today. His mother told him he was adopted, we already knew that. He told Joan that he guessed it was something to do with the war because of the date. But, he didn't know what to do. And he hasn't been sure if he wanted to know, so, he left it to fate, which came in the form of a phone call from Joan. Anyway, he knew that he had been born in Falset. His mother told him that his birth mother died when he was born. His date of birth is the same as the information we got from Amalia Balaguer and LLuis: late April, 1939. Amalia said the baby had been baptised in the town. It'll be in the register."

Maggie thought for a few seconds, then asked, "How far is he prepared to go now, to find out?"

"All the way," Bob replied. "He's done a DNA test. Joan is sending it off for an analysis. Jeremy put his DNA in the missing children database. We have to wait now to see if it's a match."

"How long?" Maggie asked.

"A few days. Ordinarily, it would take a few weeks, but thank God Joan had a favour to call in, and he decided this was the one."

"Where does that leave us with the probate court?"

"I'll inform them that the DNA test result is coming soon. They will postpone, I'm sure. So, we wait."

It was hard to concentrate on her notes, but in the end Maggie forced herself to do it. After a two hours she thought she'd made a reasonable job, for the first telling.

The following morning Maggie delivered her piece on radio. People started to call in immediately, asking for more of the story, but were told to wait until the following week. She also hinted that she had more information to come on the Spanish case of the missing child, which also stimulated great interest. She told listeners to watch the Maze website for more details.

From the radio station, she went straight to the hospital, where she found Zelah sitting up, complaining that her tea was cold. A nurse, who was biting her lip, said she would make another cup as soon as she had a moment free. Maggie's offer to do it was accepted unanimously.

Returning with the tea, Maggie decided this was a good time to speak to Zelah about leaving the hospital.

"They said they want me in over the weekend for monitoring, but I said I wanted to go home. They don't want me to do that, because I live alone. Not yet."

It was the perfect opening. "How about coming to stay with us for a couple of days? We'll let you sleep as much as you want. You'll have an en suite room. And the tea is always hot."

Zelah looked like she might protest, but stopped. "OK," she said. "If you can get me out of here today."

It took a couple of hours, but eventually, a registrar came and examined Zelah. He agreed that, provided Maggie would be staying with her, Zelah could go. He gave Maggie a list of instructions, which Maggie summarised to Zelah as, "If you start to feel worse, tell me and we come straight back."

With Zelah's agreement to anything that would release her from the ward, they arrived back early in the evening. Zelah reluctantly had to admit that she was exhausted. And with that revelation she retired to bed and slept for fifteen hours.

Over the weekend everyone decided to catch up on sleep, to be ready for a get-together on Monday morning. Zelah said she would be ready, although Maggie suspected that the headaches were worse than she was admitting. But, she had to take Zelah at her word.

On Sunday morning, Maggie drove over to Zelah's flat to get her some clean clothes and pick up her post. She was intrigued to see that there was a letter postmarked Cornwall. But Zelah dismissed it without opening it. "Advertising. I'll bin it later."

Zelah also said, by Sunday evening, that she was ready to go home. Maggie got her to agree to Tuesday, but thought she wasn't going to be able to persuade her beyond that, and she understood her need to get home. To be alone and have some space.

Maggie had invited Bob to join them for the meeting on Monday morning. She had asked Nick and Zelah if they were OK with this, and they had both agreed. She had looked for a sign of reluctance from Zelah, but there was none. Just a hint of sarcasm.

"OK, I'd like to meet the plod properly."

"Good idea," replied Maggie. "Chance to thank him for saving your life."

As it turned out, he texted to say that he was going to be late. They decided to get on with other business. A number of cases had fallen behind because of the concentration on Morgan Sturridge and the manor. "We have to catch up," Zelah said. "Can't afford bad feedback, whatever the reason."

They organised an order of attack for each case. They didn't mention Morgan. Maggie suspected that each of them was avoiding starting that conversation. She certainly was. She offered to make tea but as she stood up, Nick said, "About the elephant…" They both looked puzzled. "… in the room," he went on. "Anyone want to say anything?"

"Me," Zelah jumped in, banging her hands on the table. Maggie and Nick sat still, unsure what could be coming. "I have a few things to say. One, it's a first for me, working with someone with serial-killer DNA. Two, you

316

weren't that good on TV. Three, the bastard never actually paid us."

There was a pause, then the three of them burst out laughing.

"Ouch," Zelah put her hand to her head. "Too much fun. Not good for my brain."

Maggie made it to the door but here was a furious knocking and door bell ringing. "What the hell?" Zelah said. "Be careful, Maggie."

Nick got up to join her, but Maggie had already reached the door, and recognised the outline. As she opened it, Bob pushed the door open, burst into the hall, picked her up and gave her a great smacking kiss.

"The results are in," he shouted. "The results are fucking in. Hugo Vilaro is Jeremy's son."

"Put me down, you idiot," Maggie shouted at him. Then she gave him a return hug. "That's wonderful news, Bob."

He was sporting a crazed grin, smacking one fist in the other hand.

"Come in here, meet my colleagues."

He enthusiastically shook hands with both.

Zelah said "I'm supposed to thank you for what you did for me last week," she smiled warmly.

Nick said nothing, just looked at the glances passing between Maggie and Bob, which Zelah also didn't miss.

"Does he know?" Maggie asked.

"Joan is going back today, to tell him. I've got to get to the probate court, and I thought you might like to join me? Appointment is at half-two."

Maggie hesitated.

"Go," Zelah said. "Nick and I can pick up the kids. We'll wait here for you."

"Excellent, thanks," said Maggie.

Then Bob said to Maggie, "This is going to be interesting."

317

"Can't wait to meet the American again. Hard hats and body armour?"

"Best police issue. Plus, a stab vest."

Maggie laughed. "Shall I meet you there?"

"No, let's go together. In fact, why don't we go now? Pick up some lunch in Cardiff."

"Good idea," Zelah said, standing up and herding Maggie towards the door. "Leave everything here to us."

"I'm supposed to stay with you," Maggie said.

"I've got Nick. He has strong blood in his veins. What else could a girl need? Now, get your face on and get going."

Maggie turned to Bob. "Ten minutes," and she ran upstairs.

They left shortly afterwards, chatting and planning.

Zelah smirked at Nick. "Might as well give them as much time together as possible, don't you think?"

Nick shrugged.

"Oh, well, it may not come to anything," said Zelah.

He shrugged again.

* * *

Just before two-thirty Maggie and Bob were in the hallway outside the court, waiting to be called in.

There was a commotion at the entrance, and Mason Haussmann strode in with his lawyer. He was shouting at someone over his shoulder. Maggie could see a red-faced security guard being calmed down by a colleague.

"He's on form," Bob said. "This is going to be fascinating. Looking forward to seeing how he's going to get out of this."

"Can't wait," Maggie replied.

A clerk came from behind an ornate door and called for parties in the case of J Allen.

Bob took a deep breath, and he and Maggie walked into the courtroom.

Even though they suspected that Mason Haussman had known all along that Jeremy's baby had survived, it still came as a shock to discover the evidence he had been relying on to claim the inheritance.

He had presented an annotated copy of the register from the convent close to Falset. The priest had given over a copy the diocesan record books, as Maggie and Bob suspected. Despite the terrible things that had gone on in the convent, the nuns took care to record each death. What they saw was the record of Lola's death. The cause of death was 'childbirth' and just below it, but clearly in another hand and added later, was 'and child, name unknown, stillborn'. Someone wanted to make sure their misdeeds were well covered up.

* * *

"But he knew it wasn't true," Maggie explained to Zelah, Nick, Jack, and Alice when they met in the pub for a celebratory meal later that evening. "He'd picked up enough titbits of information from the people he spoke to, to know that the child had survived. He didn't know how or where, but he must have thought it was a godsend when he met the priest and got his hands on that register. He was arrogant enough to think that we couldn't find out anything further. But, he must have been worried, enough to send that private investigator after us, to check on what we were doing. I guess that when he heard the last place we visited was the church, he thought he was home and dry. But he just couldn't argue with the evidence we provided, to show that the baby survived. Especially the DNA evidence."

"How did he take it?" Nick asked.

"It was priceless. Absolutely beside himself. I've seen some angry people in my time, but never seen anyone so close to spontaneously combusting," Bob replied. "He screamed at everyone. Threatened me, told me he'd get me 'dealt with'. Accused me of wanting the inheritance for myself. Threatened Maze too, so you'd better watch out. God knows what he'll do next. I think he really needed the money."

"Nothing for him to hang around for, but I'll find out if he leaves the country, don't worry. The threats give me the opportunity to treat him as a violent suspect."

"Thanks," Zelah replied. "What happens now?"

"I've already called Joan. He's going to let Hugo know. I'm going to invite him and his family to come over and stay with me. See what they've inherited and think about what they want to do with it."

"There's a lot of paperwork involved," Maggie explained, "before they can say it's truly theirs. Probably going to take months."

"But no reason why they couldn't come over in the meantime," Bob said. "I'd like to meet them."

"Me, too," Maggie added.

A waitress arrived with six glasses and a champagne bucket. "My treat," Zelah said.

Maggie poured and Bob helped hand the glasses round. There was orange juice for the children.

Zelah made a toast: "To Maze Investigations… and Bob… and… surviving a blow to head."

They all raised their glasses.

"And to not doing any more probate work," Maggie said.

"That I will toast to," Zelah replied. "The response to the story about Morgan Sturridge and my head slap is quite something. And we've a few more enquiries. I think we'll have enough to do for some time."

53

On March 15th, Maggie, Bob, and Zelah stood quietly in front of a memorial stone in Alexandra Gardens behind the City Hall and University of Cardiff. They were with a group of over fifty people supporting the International Brigade Cymru Branch. The assembly was observing a minute's silence for the Welshmen who had gone to Spain from 1936 to 1938 and not returned. Some of their descendants were present.

It was a small memorial, but, Maggie thought, poignant. It had a carving of a dove of peace and a quotation from La Pasionaria's speech to the International Brigaders. From where she stood Maggie could only see the first few words, but it seemed to her that they were sufficient. *You are history. You are legend...*

The previous year had been the eightieth anniversary of the journey of the first group of men from Wales to Spain and there had been commemoration events throughout the year, she'd really not noticed at the time. They attended today's commemoration on Jeremy's behalf.

Maggie promised Hugo that she would take photographs for him and send him details of the ceremony. She had not yet discovered a record of Jeremy's service, as he had never told anyone where he was going nor spoken about what he had done when he came back, for fear of imprisonment. But a member of the International Brigades Association had given her a lead to a commemorative museum in London that she was going to follow up.

They had finally met Hugo and his family at the end of February when he accepted Bob's invitation and travelled to Wales. His wife had died some years previously. He was accompanied by his son, his daughter and two grown-up grandchildren. One of the grandchildren had just completed her training as a vet so she was particularly interested in Jeremy's animal sanctuary. She was a fierce young woman, whose name was Lola.

No one had commented, except for Nick. "Yes, it's a common name, but there's no such thing as coincidence."

"She's been a handful; she needed a cause," Hugo explained to Maggie in good English. "Here, I think we have found it. You will be seeing a lot more of her in the future."

Although Hugo was now silver-haired he explained that he had been blond. Bob showed him the photograph of Jeremy as a young man, with Lola and their friend Lidia in 1938. The resemblance was remarkable. But Hugo couldn't think of Jeremy as his father. He told them that his parents had been wonderful people, had loved him unreservedly. Hence, he had never suspected that he wasn't their natural son. Now that he finally learned what they had done he loved them even more.

"I didn't like that we had to move around so much when I was a child," he said, "but I put it down to the war in Europe and the fascist regime. Now I know that they must have been worried about the authorities finding out what they did. They were such quiet people. I never suspected that they were heroes."

"I think a lot of heroes are quiet people," Maggie replied. "Real heroes don't always proclaim their heroism."

He already knew the story of Lola, his birth mother. He had tried to find out where she had been buried, but had found nothing. The convent had been destroyed. He suspected that bodies had been moved. Nothing had been found at the site.

Bob gave Hugo the photograph he inherited from Jeremy, of him and Lola with their friend, that he had used to such good effect in Spain. He already had made copies for Roser Sivils and LLuis Portell. This had been a poignant moment, as Hugo looked at his natural parents for the first time.

322

After staring at it for a while, he said to Bob, "This is a great gift, thank you. So many sacrifices, all in vain. The world does not learn from its mistakes."

"Sadly not," Bob agreed.

"There were so many in Spain taken from their parents at that time. All old now, probably many dead. Not enough justice."

"Will you talk about what's happened to you?" Maggie asked.

"Yes, of course," Hugo had replied. "Human stories are the only way to keep humanity alive."

Maggie told him about the Welsh arm of the International Brigade and the upcoming event. She had already decided to join the organisation. Hugo had given her permission to tell the story of Jeremy and Lola. He was pessimistic about any change that it might bring about, but Maggie had been more upbeat.

"I agree, Hugo. Human stories are what matters. It's what we relate to. If you only manage to touch a few people, it's a few more who know. The knowledge will spread, albeit slowly."

* * *

The minute's silence was over. A Welsh women's choir sang songs of the civil war in English and Spanish. Then, the event was over.

There was going to be tea and coffee and speeches in the Temple of Peace across from the park, but they decided to skip it. Maggie thought that Zelah looked tired. She had recovered well. On a follow-up appointment at the hospital a young doctor had said that she was recovering well for her age, for which he got an earful. He had backed off swiftly.

They found a café across from one of the university buildings, ordered sandwiches and hot drinks and sat down.

"I was wondering," Maggie began, "now that Jeremy's legacy has survived, if we could put up a small memorial at the sanctuary. You know, to him and Lola. I don't think young Lola would mind. He was her great-grandfather."

"I like the sound of that," Bob said. "I'll look into it."

"I can put something together about the civil war," Nick added. "Might be educational for people who visit, once there's a vet there again."

Maggie noticed that Zelah wasn't joining in, seemingly distant from the conversation. "Looks warmer than it actually is," Maggie said to her, shivering.

"Still a bit chilly," Bob remarked, although outside the sun was shining and Maggie's car recorder had told her that the temperature was twenty degrees. He too had seen what he thought was Zelah's fragility.

"If you're all thinking that I've turned into a snowflake, damn well think again," she said. They went to protest but she held up a hand to stop them. "I've got something on my mind. Before my head slap," (she continued to refer to her accident in this way, despite encouragement to take it more seriously), "I would probably have put this in the bin." She reached into her bag and took out the letter postmarked Cornwall, which Maggie had retrieved from her flat. "But, I have taken it seriously, just not in the way that you all think."

"Tell us more. This is starting to remind me of the night you told Nick and me about what you'd done with Maze."

"Not quite. It's a letter from a solicitor in Cornwall. My sister died and left me a legacy."

"Good God," Maggie spluttered. "I told the hospital that you didn't have a family. That I was as close as it got to next of kin!"

"Quite right," Zelah replied. "I hated the bitch. She wasn't my real sister, I was adopted. Actually, by people who really didn't want me. What she left me was, it turns out, the only thing I ever truly owned."

She reached into her bag and brought out a small box.

324

She opened it to reveal an engraved silver ring, of rather an odd shape.

"It turns out that when I was found as a child this was all I had on me, together with a note. It said it belonged to 'the child' but 'she must never put it on', and I never knew about it. They kept it from me, until *she* died."

They all stared at the ring in the box on the table.

"And, apparently, there's more. Jewellery, rings, that is. So, I have to go down there and meet this solicitor."

"Does this mean that you're going to find out about your real family?" Maggie asked.

"Absolutely not," Zelah replied. "Whoever they were, they didn't want me, and that's been fine with me. I know who I am. Just because I'm a genealogist, doesn't mean I have to find out about my own story."

"Do you really not want to know?" Nick asked. "Really?"

"Absolutely, positively not. But I want to know what more there is to do with these rings. I do like a mystery. Look." She closed the box and looked up at them, regarding their puzzled faces with amusement. "I know who I am. I know as much as I need to know. Why poke a stick into something that doesn't need to be disturbed?"

"Up to you," Maggie said.

"Good," Zelah replied. "That's settled. But, I would like it if at least one of you came with me.

"Because, I'd like to introduce my colleagues to the real Zelah Trevear. What do you say?"

Acknowledgements

Many people have given me encouragement, support and constructive criticism in the writing of this second book in the Maze Investigations series.

At Wordcatcher Publishing, David Norrington and Peter Norrington for superior editing and polishing.

I am indebted to my friends Cheryl Coppell and Joy Croome, who read and improve my drafts and call out my many errors, and Pauline Cutting whose medical expertise ensured that my description of A&E procedures was rigorous and authentic.

This is a work of fiction and the characters are all my inventions, and I have of course used licence with the supernatural elements of the book. But some of the events are motivated by history.

For guidance and help with the places, times and history of the Spanish Civil War I would like to thank Alan Warren of the Porta de la Historia, in Catalonia. Alan is a leading expert on the 15th International Brigade and the role played by the British battalion in that conflict.

My sister-in-law Sally Cutting accompanied me as excellent travelling companion, interpreter and driver in and around Catalonia for a research trip that turned out to be deeply moving. We visited many of the museums and memorials from the Civil War and learned much about the role of the British, and in particular the Welsh fighters, many of whom did not make it back home. And to Nano Gruber, for checking and confirming all things Spanish.

For anyone who has an interest in the history of the Welsh in Spain there are books written by the men who did come back.* The aftermath of the war was horrific for the Spanish people, especially the women. *Prison of Women* by Tomasa Cuevas details true accounts of their suffering under the Fascist regime. But also of their bravery in the face of incarceration and torture. There are also many testimonies and accounts of the fate of the *Lost Children of Franco*. These stories are, again, all true, much to my horror.

For ensuring that I have suitably represented the town of Shelburne, Nova Scotia, I wish to thank Louise Lindsay of the Shelburne Historical Society. This is a beautiful town and Zelah will be visiting again.

LLanyrafon Manor is a handsome historical building in Cwmbran. I grew up watching it from afar, as did Maggie. The Llanyrafon Manor Members gave me some fascinating information about its history, including the ghost stories. I hope that any readers who can will visit. The boy's bedroom is there, over the entrance porch. But I did invent the chair.

Finally, my children, Stewart and Alice, are a continuing source of inspiration. Every day.

*Bibliography

Britons in Spain John Rust
XV International Brigade – Records of British, American, Canadian and Irish Volunteer in Spain 1936-1938 - Frank Graham and Warren & Pell Publishing
From Aberdare to Albecete Edwin Greening
From the Rhondda to the Ebro Alun Menai Williams

Lightning Source UK Ltd.
Milton Keynes UK
UKHW021136200120
357272UK00013B/1458